FIGHTING FOR SOMEDAY

THE SOMEDAY SERIES #1

M. M. KOENIG

Emma —

Love is always worth fighting for!! I hope you enjoy Bri's — Trey's story!

M. M. K.

FIGHTING FOR SOMEDAY

THE SOMEDAY SERIES #1

By M. M. Koenig
PUBLISHED BY M. M. KOENIG PUBLISHING LLC
COPYRIGHT © 2018 M. M. KOENIG
All rights reserved. Except as permitted under the U.S. Copyright Act of 1976, no part of this publication may be reproduced, distributed, or transmitted in any other form or by any means, including photocopying, recording, or other electronic or mechanical methods, without the prior written permission of the author.
This is a work of fiction. Names, characters, places, and incidents either are products of the author's imagination or are used fictitiously. Any resemblance to actual events or locales or persons, living or dead, is entirely coincidental.
This novel is not a standalone. You've been warned.
The Someday series is a prequel to the Secrets and Lies series.
This book has strong language and sexual content. It is intended for readers that are 18 years and up.
Cover Design © L.J. Anderson, Mayhem Cover Creations

DEDICATION

This book is for Isaac, Jakob, Kade, and Kali. Thank you for letting me be a part of your life. You've changed mine more than you'll ever know and I'm so grateful for every memory you've given me.

ALSO BY M. M. KOENIG

SECRETS AND LIES SERIES
Conflicted
Complicated
Concealed

THE SOMEDAY SERIES
Fighting for Someday
Waiting for Someday
Finding Our Someday

THE HIGH SOCIETY SERIES
Taming J

VISIT http://www.mmkoenig.com for purchase links and upcoming projects!

CHAPTER 1

TREY

The walls in my room rattled as a stampede of kids ran through the hallway. A soft knock sounded on my door. I didn't need to look at my alarm clock to know it was a quarter after six. Keeping to a solid routine was a way of life I'd gotten used to long ago. My door was my mom's first stop before she got the rest of my siblings up.

Mom moved around our cream-colored, two-story, Victorian house like a ninja at all hours of the day. It was a pain having her practically undetectable, roaming around at night, but having a deck and a railing outside my bedroom that was easy to shimmy down made sneaking out a breeze. Being the oldest of five kids made escaping the chaos vital. I was lucky my mom was cool as hell, so she didn't bust my ass too much when I did slip out.

After rubbing my sleepy eyes, I tossed the covers off my head and sat up. Seeing the posters of all of Chicago's sports greats and my favorite rock bands on my tan walls made me wish even more I was at the end of my senior year rather than being stuck at the beginning of my junior year. I groaned after scanning over all the clothes and other crap covering my dark-brown hardwood floor. Football started a few weeks ago and shit was piling up in my room, which wasn't all that helpful to my mom.

She opened my door, walked over to my closet, and hung my Chamberlain uniform on the doorknob. Her long blonde hair was in a pristine bun. Most people would say I looked exactly like my dad. My six-foot-two frame, broad shoulders, and light brown hair were all him, but I got my gray eyes from her. I was the only child she passed them on to and loved sharing that trait with her.

Mom opened the shades before sitting on the edge of my bed and patting my legs, a warm smile on her face. "Treahbar, up and at-um. The bathroom should be free in ten and breakfast will be on the table in thirty. While collecting dirty clothes last night, I noticed the collar of your white, button-down shirt had a dark red spot on it, so I washed it for you. I *assume* it's ketchup and not blood."

She was the only person who could call me by my real name and not get the shit kicked out of them. Since I could talk, I made it known I preferred Trey, but that didn't matter to her. My dad and I came to an understanding years ago. My brothers and sisters didn't dare use it—not if they wanted to live to see tomorrow.

I flashed a lopsided smile. "You worry too much. Mia and I stopped for a quick bite at That's-A-Burger on our way home yesterday."

The drumline in my head pounded even harder, but it wasn't nearly as bad as last night. I couldn't tell her Sebastian and Miles jumped me after practice—at least my fists ended our latest scuffle.

Mom gave me a pointed look. I rolled my shoulders and said, "You know how sloppy I can be with their double cheeseburger and loaded fries."

As she inspected every inch of my body to confirm what she already suspected, her eyes seared into me. Dad worked long hours, so she ran the household and didn't need any extra stress. Keeping my ten and eight-year-old brothers and my seven-year-old twin sisters in line kept her more than busy, so I did my best to handle my problems on my own.

"They must be working you pretty hard at practice because when you got home last night, you had three helpings of corned beef, mashed potatoes, and carrots before you devoured half of the chocolate cake I made for dessert. That's a lot of food—even for you."

"I'm a growing boy. What can I say?"

Mom sighed. "You're my son, and I love you with all my heart, so I won't press you for the details on what *actually* happened. Just remember I always know when you're lying, so it better be worth it if you're going to try and slip something by me."

Fuck! I don't know why I even try. She's better than a lie detector.

My face flushed as I mumbled, "I'm sorry, Mom. I didn't want to upset you."

She brushed my hair up, saw the fresh gash, and shook her head. "It doesn't need stitches. Put some Neosporin on it with a butterfly bandage so it heals faster. If this is happening at school, you need to tell me."

"I was playing basketball at lunch and it got a little escalated. It was a well-nailed elbow to the head. I'm fine," I promised.

"I know things are different for you at Chamberlain. Your dad and I are always here for you, so please tell us when it gets to be too much. It's an amazing opportunity, but we can always find another school that's a better fit. And just so we're clear, I'm not a fan of this fighter mentality you've had going on lately. You're better than that, Treahbar," Mom chastised.

The bruises on my ribs ached even more. Sharp pains settled in my chest and left a large knot that blocked my airway. I hated letting her down. She stepped into the hallway and picked up the pajamas that had been tossed near my door as the little ones made their way to the bathroom.

I hopped out of bed and took the few articles she had in her hands. The hellions would be downstairs soon, demanding breakfast, and they were never quiet about it. Mom squeezed my cheek and headed downstairs.

After picking up the mess in the hall and making sure everyone had on the outfits laid out for them, I shuffled into the bathroom, washed up, and patched up the cut on my head. Once the bandage was secure, I put on some deodorant and cologne before going back to my room to change into my uniform.

Jeans, shorts, T-shirts, and jerseys sat in neatly folded piles on my desk. They added insult to injury while I changed into the boring black pants, white button-down, and navy sports coat we were required to wear at Chamberlain. Once my royal blue and white tie was in place, I put my clean clothes away, shoved my homework into my messenger bag, and trotted downstairs.

Tara and Tawney were singing and running in circles around the island in our kitchen, making it hard for anyone to walk around—let alone cook breakfast. I grabbed them by their sides and held them upside down on my way into the dining room.

Scrambled eggs, bacon, and toast, along with pitchers of milk and orange juice, were on the table. I made up their plates and poured them each a glass of juice. After hearing Thomas and Tory shouting at each other, I kissed the girls' heads and went to check on them.

On my way into the living room, I snatched a few toys strewn across the threshold and tossed them on the couch. Tory had their shared handheld gaming system behind his back. With his fists curled tightly together, Thomas' swing grew more aggressive as he moved closer to Tory.

"Give it to me, you moron!" Thomas hollered, shoving Tory so hard he flew back several steps and landed on his arm.

I jumped over the ottoman, grabbed Thomas, and plopped his butt on the brown recliner behind me. "Don't move," I growled, shaking my head in disapproval.

He leaned back and crossed his arms, a lot like I did when I was pissed off. I bit the insides of my cheek so I didn't smile. Both boys were little mini-versions of me whereas the girls looked like our mom, but all of us shared the same hotheaded, Irish temper. If he hadn't almost hurt Tory, I would've laughed the whole thing off, but

Tory landed dangerously close to the coffee table, and I knew firsthand hitting it led to stitches.

I knelt in front of Tory. He held his arm tenderly, so I surveyed it for any broken bones, but didn't see any. His chin trembled as a few tears trickled down his cheeks. I wiped his eyes and hugged him. "You're going to be okay. Give me the game and go get some breakfast before Mom takes you to the bus stop."

"Why can't you drop us off at school like you used to?" Tory asked in between sniffles.

A ragged breath escaped as I picked up both boys' backpacks, verified their homework was there, and set them by the door with their jackets. I squeezed Tory's shoulders. "Because I started at my new school, remember? I'd take you, bud, but then I'd be late for my own."

"I miss our car rides to school. The kids on the bus are mean. They shove us out of our seats and try to take our lunches," Tory whined.

I glanced at Thomas to see if Tory was telling the truth and he nodded before wiping away the tears welling in his eyes. Knowing I should be there to protect them from bullies made the anger surging through my blood vessels potent. The decision to attend Chamberlain wasn't supposed to have adverse effects on their lives and I wanted to rip the heads off anyone giving them trouble.

My eyes drifted between the two of them. "We'll figure something out, guys. I'll talk to Mom about it, okay?"

Tory smiled and ran into the dining room. Thomas jumped up, but I gripped his collar and turned him around. He kept his eyes on the floor, his face full of shame.

I tilted his chin up. "You know why I'm pissed, right?"

Thomas nodded. "He just gets so annoying sometimes. It really is my turn to have the DS on the bus and he was being a brat by not giving it to me."

"It's in the Little Brother Handbook to press the buttons of their older siblings. If I recall correctly, you're *very* familiar with those tactics," I pointed out, chuckling.

His mouth spread into a tiny grin before he tugged at my tie and scrunched up his nose. "I might be. You look like Dad on Sunday morning before we go to church when you wear these clothes. I don't like them."

"Trust me, little man, I hate them too," I replied while readjusting my tie on our way into the dining room.

After Thomas took a seat and I filled up his plate, I scooped up some eggs and bacon, added some ketchup, and dumped it all between two slices of wheat toast. Mom strode into the room and picked up the empty dishes from the table. I kissed her on the cheek and murmured, "I love you, Mom. I'll be late if I don't leave now. The boys are ready to go, but I didn't have a chance to check the girls' bags."

"Don't worry, dear, you've done more than enough. Mia's waiting for you on the porch. If you can try to convince Micah to go to school today, Lyla would appreciate it."

I snorted. "I'll try, but I doubt he'll listen to me. It *is* Friday, after all."

She frowned and motioned for me to leave. I devoured my sandwich on my way out the front door. Using extra force to slam it shut probably wasn't necessary, but I didn't want to see Mia and Micah making out on the porch *again*.

They were my best friends and had been since we were five years old. I'd seen them fight, poke fun at one another, and nearly everything in between, but seeing them put their tongues down each other's throats was new. It was a long time coming, but they didn't have any shame anymore.

Since the day Mia moved to our neighborhood, the three of us had been a package deal. She was at our houses more than her uncle's loft above his bar. By the time we were six, she had closet space at both places. My mom and Micah's doted on her like she was their own. Frankly, she could've passed as my sister. Mia shared the same average height, long blonde hair, and slim features as my mom. The only difference was her dark brown eyes.

Mia drove me up the wall most days, but she was like another sister to me and our personalities were a lot alike. We were competitive in everything we did and had been pushing each other in school and sports since kindergarten. She didn't know it, but I needed her way more than I'd ever admit. Mia kept me on the path I wanted to be on to ensure I did something with my life.

Micah was my bro, but he was on a one-way path to be like every other delinquent in our neighborhood. Going to class didn't matter to him. He was more interested in making a quick buck than focusing on what he should be doing to give him a future that didn't land him in prison.

I banged my fist on the side of the house to get their attention, but they didn't even acknowledge my presence. Mia was across Micah's lap with her arms draped around him as they swayed on the porch swing. He pressed kisses to the side of her neck while fiddling with the white collar peeking out from under her navy sweater vest.

"I'm leaving in five seconds, so you better wrap that shit up or you're taking the bus to school, Mia," I snapped, rattling my keys for emphasis.

Micah rolled his eyes. "I'd never make you walk, babe. I told you I'd drop you off, but you keep insisting it isn't necessary."

She jabbed a few fingers in his burly chest. "It's not. Trey doesn't mind taking me. Besides, you need to get to school yourself."

"Yeah, you should try going a full week at least once this year," I added, striding across the freshly-cut grass.

I hopped into my dark blue Acura, started it up, and revved the engine so Mia would hurry up. Micah swept in for a parting kiss before opening her door. Once she was inside, I peeled out and headed toward the highway to hell.

CHAPTER 2

TREY

"They really are letting in any piece of trash into Chamberlain these days, aren't they?" Sebastian remarked, ramming his shoulder into my back.

"The standards around here have really dropped. We should probably take it upon ourselves to improve them," Miles snickered, shoving at the back of my head.

I clutched the cool metal of my blue locker in a futile attempt to control my temper and not beat their asses. This had been their daily routine in between classes for the past week. The only thing going for me was it was two o'clock and I only had one more class left.

God help me, this is only the first fucking week of school. How am I going to make it eight more months without killing these rich pricks?

After they realized I refused to turn around, they gave me a parting shot and strode down the hall. My heart walloped against my chest as dark red streaks crept up my arms. If it weren't for my parents, I wouldn't have tried to get into this school.

Once I started high school, my folks reassured me they'd find a way to put all of us through college, but as a working-class family, I had a hard time believing it. My dad already worked nonstop to keep his construction company solvent. On top of that, he took on second shifts as a security guard. It was a rarity for him to be home for dinner during the week, but necessary to make ends meet. After my siblings came along, my mom gave up teaching to save on daycare. Even with the private tutoring and substitute teaching gigs she picked up, it would never be enough to give us all a shot at higher education.

Over the summer, Mia mentioned Chamberlain had a financial aid program and urged me to apply for it. If I wouldn't have filled out the paperwork, she would've gone behind my back and did it anyway. She was just as stubborn as me. I easily qualified for the financial aid, but in the end, I was positive my athletic superiority sealed the deal.

Technically, the high school didn't award sports scholarships, but a prospective student exhibiting exceptional skills in the classroom and on the field was a shoo-in. I didn't have to try out for the football team here—Coach Barry knew firsthand what I could do with a football without throwing it. I ran for just as many touchdowns last year as I threw and planned on doubling those stats this year.

When another self-righteous asshat from the JV team rammed his shoulder into mine, the small sense of peace I obtained while thinking about the benefits to being here vanished. I punched the back of my locker and the loud sound of it made the punk scurry down the hallway. My nostrils flared and I took deep breaths to keep myself from going after him.

Part of me wished they'd try to fuck with me on my turf. They wouldn't last a minute in Bridgeport. If Micah and I didn't give them a beatdown, any of the gangs on the south side would make them regret being born. Micah was as built as me and his chiseled face and large frame were enough to scare anyone. What really made people fear us was our tattoos.

Most sixteen-year-olds wouldn't be able to find a place to ink them, but there were more than a few around our neighborhood willing to add to our growing collection. As much as our parents hated them, it didn't stop us. I was more than fine with adding to the bad boy label everyone loved to give me.

Bells rang throughout the school, warning all students there was two minutes to get to class. As people hustled in the direction of their classes, a few more assholes from the team made sure their fists connected with me. I clutched my Calculus book so hard a few pages tore from the seam and snatched a notebook before slamming my locker shut.

I stuffed my book into my backpack, slung it over my shoulder, and loosened my tie. No wonder my lungs felt so deprived for air. The damn thing was like a noose around my neck. As the late bell rang, I cursed under my breath on my way down the long corridor.

The black-and-white checkered floors and the white walls plastered with framed pictures of prior headmasters reminded me how much this place resembled an insane asylum. I shoved open the large, wooden doors and strode along the red stone path in the enclosed courtyard at a leisurely pace.

A couple of groundskeepers kept a cautious eye on me while they trimmed the bushes. The judgmental stares around here knew no bounds and I fought off the urge to flip them off. After seeing one of them pick up a walkie-talkie, I started jogging. Ending up in the headmaster's office the first week of school would put me in hot water at home.

I reached my building and ran down the empty hallway to my classroom. Doing my best to be as quiet as possible, I opened the door and kept my head down while walking to the back. I slid into the ancient wood desk, retrieved my book from my bag, and opened it. I tried to focus on the fine print, but listening to all the snickers around me made my ears burn. It was like they were on their Superman setting. I heard every disparaging word spouted about me.

"Didn't your white trash parents teach you how to tell time, Donovan?" Sebastian sneered before running a hand through his spiked, jet-black hair.

"Doubtful. They're probably too busy rearranging all the lawn ornaments in front of the double-wide they call home," Miles goaded.

My head shot up about as fast as my hands curled into fists—more than ready to knock Sebastian out of his seat. His average frame didn't stand a chance against me in a fight. I'd gladly beat the life right out of his soulless, light blue eyes.

Mr. White strode to my desk with his arms crossed and pinned a lethal glare on me. The muscles in his neck throbbed as he tossed a tardy slip down. I kept my gaze from him and put it in my notebook. He huffed and banged his fists on my desk and my head jerked up so fast I was positive my neck had a pretty good case of whiplash.

The contempt on his face spoke volumes as he snapped, "If you're done interrupting my class, Mr. Donovan, maybe you can actually contribute today? We expect all our students to participate. I'm sure your last school didn't care about such things, but we have high expectations around here. This attitude of yours might have been acceptable at Robertson, but it's not at Chamberlain. If you don't change your ways, you won't just find yourself kicked out of my class, but out of school. The waiting list here is miles long and we can easily dismiss the riffraff taking up precious space."

He walked to the front of the classroom and scribbled a series of equations on his tablet that appeared on the whiteboard behind him.

"You know, he really does remind me of that worthless punk from *Aladdin*. Disney got that movie all wrong. There's no way a pathetic piece of shit would ever outwit a sorcerer and marry the princess. At least in the real world, we can rectify those things. I doubt it's going to take very long to get the garbage out of here and that will make plenty of people happy," Sebastian quipped with a snakelike smile.

Miles ran a hand through his sandy blond hair. "Trey is as dumb as he looks. We probably won't have to do a damn thing to get him out of here. He'll fuck it all up on his own. That's pretty much a guarantee when you're dealing with lowlifes from the south side."

Sebastian high-fived him. "You got a point there, bro, but that doesn't mean I'm not going to have my fun before it happens."

My pen snapped under the pressure I'd been applying while trying to solve the problem on the board. I rummaged around in my bag for another one that I'd probably end up breaking.

"Would you assholes shut up and pay attention? Lord knows you need every bit of help you can get. In case you didn't know, a silent man reflects confidence. The only thing your little insults are proving is just how insecure you are, so do yourself a favor and shut up," a soft, angelic voice hissed.

I glanced around and saw Sebastian glaring daggers at someone off to the left, but whoever the chick was didn't acknowledge him. My eyes darted around the room a few times, but I couldn't pinpoint who spoke up. Mia was a few rows ahead of me and glimpsed over her shoulder. For as tight as her jaw was, she'd been clenching it for a while. She opened her mouth to snap at a few guys sitting next to her who were still snickering, but I gave her a sharp look to shut it. She sighed and focused on the equation.

My heart twitched. I shouldn't have been such a dick to her, but she knew better. I made it clear when we were in grade school that I didn't want her sticking up for me. It was one thing to have your boys do it, but when a girl did, best friend or not, it wasn't helpful at all—no matter how well-intentioned. After seeing Mr. White glaring at me, I went back to my calculations.

After the hour slowly passed by, the bell finally rang and I slammed my book shut before putting it in my bag. I stormed into the hallway but didn't get very far. Mia blocked my path. With a fierce glare, I motioned to get out of the way. She moved to the side but kept pace with me on my way to my locker.

"Trey, please talk to me. If you won't let me stick up for you, the least you can do is vent about it," Mia pleaded.

"There's nothing to say. As I've told you many times, guys don't need to sit around and chitchat about things for the world to keep on spinning. I've got practice and so do you. Waiting for me is going to get you into trouble. I've seen your coach in action and he's going to have your ass for being late," I shot back.

I reached my locker, tossed my backpack into it, and headed for the doors leading to the sports pavilion. The dejected look on Mia's face made it clear she didn't care for my fast dismissal. Once we were outside, she veered off toward her locker room and I shuffled over to mine.

As I got dressed for practice, I couldn't help but wonder if Miles and Sebastian, along with most of the faculty, had some sort of agenda to get me expelled from Chamberlain. Considering how the past week had gone, it sure seemed like it. I shook off those thoughts, laced up my cleats, grabbed my pads and helmet, and jogged out to the field. I wasn't about to waste another second thinking about all the jackasses gunning for me. If I did, it wouldn't end well.

It was probably going to be one of the hardest things I ever did, but there was no way I'd let these privileged pricks get the best of me. I owed it to my parents and myself to suck it up for the next seven hundred and some days until graduation. With each step I took, those words ran on repeat in my head, fueling the fire inside me to push myself even harder. No one was messing up my chances at getting out of the south side—not today, not ever.

CHAPTER 3

TREY

Coach Barry tapped at his military-style Timex before signaling for me to take a few laps. I set my helmet down on the sidelines, snagged a football, and ran around the track. With each stride, I savored the rush of adrenaline surging through my muscles. The anger circulated through my pores, but it was no match for the dominance I felt when I held the pigskin in my hands.

After sprinting the last lap, my legs burned. Coach Barry motioned for me to stop, so I hustled over to him. He patted me on the back. "Son, you keep running like that, they're going to steal you from us and put you on the cross-country team. Do you know how fast you ran that mile?"

"No, sir," I answered, stretching out my arms before putting my helmet on.

"In under six minutes. Do us all a favor and save it for the field. We got the Wildcats for the season-opener and they've got one of the most aggressive teams in the conference. Are you ready to get out there and command this team?" Coach Barry asked, clutching my facemask.

I nodded and took the field. We started practice off in typical fashion with up-downs until a few of the weaker guys puked their guts out. Blades sliced away at the muscles in my legs and arms, making every movement ache even more, but I refused to stop.

Even though it was the first week of September, the humidity was still unbearable. The heat radiated from the ground, leaving a hazy fog for us to deal with, on top of trying to act like a team for the next three hours.

Coach Barry shouted at us to run some laps around the track. After a few more guys threw up and Coach Murray mentioned he was flirting with insanity, he told us to get some water. I blinked a couple of times on my way over to the coolers, doing my best to get my vision to focus in this muggy weather. In between chugging water, I stretched out my sore muscles.

After my bottle was empty, I tossed it to the sidelines and jogged over to Coach Barry to see what playset he wanted me to use. He was next to a guy I hadn't seen on the field in the past three weeks in what seemed to be a relaxed conversation.

"Don't worry about being gone, Shane. Your defensive slot is still yours," Coach Barry reassured, patting number sixty-nine on the back.

I shook my head in disbelief and waited for today's game plan. Coach Murray eyed me with disdain, but that wasn't out of the ordinary.

"Trey, I want you to make the calls out there. Next Friday, I don't want you looking to the sidelines for direction. I want to push the ball as much as we can with no huddles, run the score up before halftime, and then spend the second half shaving time off the clock. You're a dual threat and we haven't even explored all the options I want to do with your rushing capabilities. For now, we'll stick with your steel left arm. Do you think you can rule this team like a leader, or are you going to continue letting that chip on your shoulder get bigger by the day?" Coach Barry asked, hitting the sides of my helmet.

"I'm your man, Coach."

The grin on his face grew before he gestured to sixty-nine. "I want you to meet your co-captain, Shane West."

Shane was the same height as me, packed with a lot of muscle, so he probably weighed a bit more than me. His dark brown hair matched his eyes. Shane extended a hand and I shook it. Before I released his hand, I tightened my grip. He grunted and pulled his arm away.

Coach shook his head, not thrilled with our tense exchange, but I didn't give a fuck. He focused on me. "He's a two-time All-American defensive lineman for this team and a hell of a go-to receiver when we're in a pinch on offense. You two will be my eyes and ears on the offensive and defensive lines. With your exceptional talents, I expect perfection on both sides of the ball. Do you gentlemen understand?"

We nodded and he signaled for us to take the field. As we walked to the fifty-yard line, Shane's lips moved, but I didn't bother to listen. He crossed over the line of scrimmage and settled into his slot on the strong side while I motioned for the offense to huddle up. After picking an option run, I marched up to the line and stood behind our center.

"Ready, set, go!" I shouted, catching the football and pitching it to my left.

Miles let the defensive guy across from him run through the line. Our running back got leveled about seven yards behind me and the ball flew out of his hands. I chased it down and fell on top of it before five guys jumped on top of me. The extra weight threatened to crush me, but I clutched the ball to my chest until the whistle blew.

"I swear to God, you boys will run nonstop if you don't come together as a team soon," Coach Barry bellowed, a fierce glare in his eyes.

Shane head-butted Miles hard with a muttered warning not to fuck up again. He took his spot and motioned for me to call the next play. Picking another pitch play, we lined up and I shouted for the football, but another missed block led to more of the same.

I high-fived the few guys holding the line and gestured for Shane to have at it with the pricks still grappling with me being their quarterback. Coach Barry crossed his arms, a curious look on his face as he watched us.

Shane grabbed a few of my linemen by the shoulders and shouted, "Get your fucking shit together *now*. If you blow one more play, I won't have a problem sending every one of you to the emergency room."

He gave their shoulders a parting shove, crossed over the line, and crouched down. Even with their helmets on, it was clear from their anxious expressions that Shane wasn't a guy you fucked with. I gave him an appreciative nod before signaling for the guys to huddle up.

Lucas, one of the few sophomores on our team, followed Shane's lead and got in the space of the guy next to him. He shoved at his shoulders and shouted, "If you let him through one more time, you'll wish you'd never been born. I'll hit you so hard, you'll still be feeling it next year. On the ball, boys! Let's get this shit right this time!"

I walked up to the line of scrimmage to run the same play. After rattling off my count, our center hiked the ball to me. I pitched the ball to my left and stood back, expecting the same result, but the line held and our running back sprinted for a touchdown.

Shane and a few of the other juniors on our defensive side clapped their hands before huddling together to go over their next play. After settling on a passing play to a slot route, we ran up to the line. Right after the ball reached my hands, Sebastian nailed Lucas in the ribs and swept out his feet so he fell hard on his back.

A few guys helped Lucas up and he gasped to catch his breath. I rested a hand on his shoulder. "Are you okay?"

He nodded, but it was obvious he was in a lot of pain as he struggled to breathe, so I waved for the trainer to help him off the field. I brought our side together and narrowed my eyes at Mason. He ran out to replace Lucas on the line.

"Let Sebastian through," I snapped.

"What? Whether we let him through or not, he's just going to keep taking shots like that until we're all carted off the field. Sebastian is *always* a jackass. It doesn't matter if it is on the field or off it," Mason hissed, tossing his hands in the air in frustration.

"Exactly. So, let me take a shot at him. He hasn't received a hard hit from me yet." He gave me a skeptical look, along with a few of my other linemen, so I pounded on their shoulder pads until they lightened up.

"Just trust me, it'll be a moment none of you will forget," I reassured with a cocky smirk.

We hustled up to the line. I repeated the play and shouted for the ball. After it was in my hands, I moved to my left before coming back to my right. Mason let Sebastian through and I dropped back a few steps. Once he was a foot away, I tossed the football downfield to my open receiver and hunched over, sending Sebastian head over ass behind me.

"You fucking asshole!" Sebastian shouted, landing hard on his shoulder and back.

I crouched down next to him as he rolled around, like the pansy he was, and grabbed his facemask. "I bet that does sting a little. It isn't the first time I've done it to someone and it sure as hell won't be the last. Now, I don't give a flying fuck what your problem is, but if you ever injure another one of your teammates, I'll make it hurt twice as bad next time."

"You're a fucking piece of shit. No one wants you here. Just give up already and go back to your double-wide on the south side," Sebastian spewed, his eyes as black as coal.

I gave his helmet a hard shake. "I don't care if you like me or how much you despise me being on this team, you're going to learn to deal with it or you're going to find yourself in a world of hurt. You can do whatever you want to me during school, but when we're on this field, you'll play the game with the respect it, and your team, deserves. Believe me, you rich son of a bitch, what I can do to you off the field is far more frightening than on it, so consider this your last warning."

Sebastian shoved my hands off his helmet and spit on my cleats. He cussed under his breath on his way to the sideline to get checked by the trainer. With his arms crossed, Coach Murray watched the trainer appraise Sebastian and shot a murderous look my way.

He probably thought his expression would intimidate me, but it didn't. I was positive he was one of the many around here who wanted me gone and was more than likely just waiting for the right time to come at me with some sort of threat. Seeing as he was our assistant coach, I knew there wasn't all that much he could do to me and shot a smirk his way to reinforce it—just to piss him off even more.

I turned around to face the guys. "The same goes for the rest of you. I could give a shit less if you like me. You better come to play, boys. I play to win and you better too!"

"That's fucking right, men! When you're out here, you better bring everything you got and leave the petty shit at home. I hate losing just about as much as I despise drama, so you can take this as my first and last warning. If you disrespect anyone on this team while we're on the field, I'll beat your ass so hard, you're going to pray for death," Shane shouted, jumping side-to-side and keeping his gaze on the defensive men who'd blown their assignments.

The rest of the practice was more productive than any of the two-a-days we'd had in the past several weeks. Shane's commanding presence was sorely needed on our defensive side. I wasn't signing up to be his best friend, but he at least earned my respect.

I SPENT a little extra time in the shower, to try and ease all the points of pain on my body, but it was a futile attempt. After wrapping a large white towel around my waist, I headed back to my locker and changed into a pair of black mesh shorts and white T-shirt before sliding on my socks and sneakers.

Every limb in my body was about ready to fall off. The bruises on parts of my legs and arms were already on their way to a nice dark purple. As I leaned over to lace up my shoes, sharp pains shot up my back. I crisscrossed my arms to loosen the tightness in my muscles until I got home and could give them their usual ice down.

Once the pain faded to a dismal ache, I grabbed my bag from under my feet and inspected it to see if the immature punks on the team left me any surprises. While I sifted, Shane came out from the showers. He dried off before throwing on a pair of cream cargo shorts and a maroon polo shirt. After running a towel through his brown hair a few times, he tossed it in one of the huge laundry buckets off to the side and sat down next to me on the dark blue steel bench.

"So, did the hazing already happen, or are the pathetic attempts they're making on the field to level you all they've tried?"

I shrugged and zipped up my duffle bag. "It's nothing I can't handle. They can ruin my clothes, try to shove me around in the hallways, and spout off in class, but it's not going to make me quit. They're fucking idiots for even thinking it'll make a difference. I grew up on the south side, for Christ's sake. Nothing breaks us."

My harsh tone didn't faze him. He chuckled, slipped on his brown flip flops, and stuffed the dirty clothes into his bag. After shoving his pads into his locker, he set the combination, slung his duffle over his shoulder, and leaned against the gray lockers behind him.

"If I would've been here the last three weeks, that shit wouldn't have happened. *Period.* Their immature behavior may not bug you, but it has always bothered me. It won't happen anymore. You've got my word."

I jumped up. "I don't need you to fight my battles. I can handle my own. And since you brought it up, where the fuck *were* you the last three weeks? It isn't fair to any of us to have you waltz in here the week before our first game and get a guaranteed starting spot. Your parents must donate a ton of money to this school for that shit to slide."

Shane stepped away from me, but kept a hand raised in the air with his head cocked to the side. His face hardened as he said, "You're new around here and I really don't know you yet, so I'll let you getting into my airspace go, but it better not happen again. Not that it's any of your business, but my dad is an ambassador and we weren't able to return to the States until the area we were in was secure. We were supposed to return two months ago, but a militant uprising blew that to hell."

Icy waves of guilt spread through my body and I rubbed the Celtic wraparound tattoo on my right arm to calm my nerves. Shane crossed his arms and waited for the apology I more than owed him. "Listen, man, I'm sorry. I don't know what else to say other than I'm glad you guys made it back okay."

Shane sighed. "It's cool. I'm sure the bullshit going on around here has you ready to blow any day now, so I can see why you jumped to that conclusion. I may have grown up with half of the pricks around here, who think they're hot shit because of their parents' bank accounts, but that doesn't mean I share the same mindset. Just try to remember that and we'll call it even."

I released an overdue breath, snatched my duffle bag, and settled it on my shoulder. "Yeah, I can definitely do that."

He slapped a hand on my back. "Now that the girly shit is out of the way, it might help the morale on the team if we kept a united front. I have a few thoughts on how to do that."

My face was wary as I asked, "What do you have in mind?"

As we headed out of the locker room and toward the stairs to get to the courtyard, Shane glanced at his watch and swore under his breath. He raised his hand for a fist bump. "I have to run, but let's hit the weight room on Monday before school to go over a game plan."

I pounded his hand. "Okay, I'll meet you at six."

He disappeared through a set of doors that allowed him to cut across the junior hallway and out to the parking lot. While making my way through the courtyard, I couldn't shake the guilt swarming through me for passing judgment on Shane. Regardless, I wasn't ready to drop my guard or trust him. Those two conflicting emotions whipped through me like a sixty-mile-an-hour windstorm and my overexerted body became heavier with each step. By the time I reached my hallway, I was ready to go home and pass out.

I had to do whatever it took to win on the field, and if that meant having him as an ally, then that was what I'd do. Football was the only upside to this place, so I had to do my part to keep it that way. That wouldn't happen if we had a losing season. After I reached my locker, the few kids lingering in the hallway ran off with their heads down. My eyes bugged out as I read the words painted on my locker.

Go home, gutter punk. Your trashy ass isn't welcome here.

The anger I'd tapped into at practice burned hotter than it had all day and ripped away at my insides, begging for me to just release the pissed-off beast deep within me. All I saw was a growing canvas of red taking over everything around me. I arched my arm back but couldn't follow through. Wiggling to get my arm free only tightened the person's grip, so I whipped around, ready to attack with my other fist.

Coach Barry held my shoulders. "Take a deep breath, Trey. If you lose your head now, it'll feed into the reaction these kids are trying to get out of you."

"You're telling me to let this go. Are you fucking kidding me?" I shouted, yanking my arms free.

He crinkled his eyebrows while shaking his head. "Watch your mouth, son. You've got more integrity than most of the kids here, so just calm down. There's an easy fix to this situation without vandalizing more school property."

I pounded the locker next to mine, sank to the checkered floor, and rested my head on my knees. As my blood boiled over, the only thing I heard was the incoherent humming in my head and the sharp breaths I sucked in as I tried to maintain my wits.

When Coach rested his hand on my shoulder, I about jumped out of my skin. I didn't see him take a seat next to me. I glanced his way, waiting for some sort of words of wisdom adults were supposed to have in times like these.

"Trey, do you know why we chose you out of the thousands of applicants for a full-ride here?"

I snorted. "I think the answer to that is pretty obvious. I proved that much on the football field this afternoon after I sent Sebastian off to the trainer's office."

He smirked before his brown eyes became serious. "As gifted as you are in sports, it wasn't even in the top ten reasons why we thought *you* were the best fit for a spot here."

I scoffed. "I'm not sure I believe you."

"Well, it's true. High school isn't easy for anyone. It doesn't matter what side of the city you grow up on. A lot of people deal with their issues and pain by lashing out at others."

"I know *that*, but it shouldn't end up being a free pass for people to be complete dicks all the time. There has to be a line somewhere—even for the rich and privileged."

"I agree, but that's not really how the world works, and I think you know that." My face flushed fire engine red. Coach tugged at the collar of his white polo before squeezing my arm. "I don't agree with it, but what you need to remember is high school is just a small stepping stone to the goals we have for ourselves. Losing your head every time someone picks apart a superficial aspect of your life is going to land you on the fast track to nowhere."

"I don't understand how so many people, namely the teachers, can turn such a blind eye to things happening right under their noses. What's worse is that some of them have no problem airing out their own opinions of me being here and that only allows the bigger douchebags to keep getting away with anything under the sun," I snapped through gritted teeth.

Judging by the hard look in his eyes, he knew what I was saying. Coach smoothed out his tense face and pointed out, "We're drifting off topic. Did you know your pre-SAT scores were the highest this school has seen in almost ten years?" I gazed at him, slack-jawed and wide-eyed, before shaking my head. "Your standardized test scores throughout the years are the highest the state has seen. When we reviewed your academic record, we were more than impressed, but that's not entirely why we chose you either."

If my perfect GPA, good scores, and athletic abilities weren't it, I was at a loss as to why I was here. At this point, it was looking like they selected me so the rich kids had someone to torment and I flung my hands in the air for an actual explanation.

"Trey, we picked you because of the young man you are *outside* of these grounds. In our home interview with you, it was obvious how much of a centerpiece you are to your family—not to mention the important values your parents have already taught you that years of academia never will. It's the code of honor you have for yourself and your loved ones that solidified our choice."

I opened my mouth but couldn't find the right words. Aside from my parents, no one had ever really saw that much in me. His mouth settled into a warm smile. "We need more young people like you going out into the world. Graduating with a diploma from here can open a lot of doors for you, but you have to get control over your temper or it'll never happen. There's only so much I can do to help you with that on the field. The rest is up to you. There's always battles to be fought, but just be smart when it comes to the ones you choose for yourself."

Coach patted me on the back. "There's a bright future for you here. You need to give things more time to settle, and I hope you do, because five colleges from around the state have already approached me about you. I've read your application essays and know Eckman is at the top of your list. If you work hard, I have no doubt they'll offer you a full-ride. I'll do my part to help you get it, but you need to put in a bigger effort as well."

Without another word, he headed toward the janitor's office. I blinked a few times, not fully grasping what he just laid out there. The jackhammer pounding away at the inside of my skull made it difficult to focus. I sifted through my bag, popped four aspirins, and shuffled to the stairs that led to Mia's hallway.

Coach better be right about my shot at getting a scholarship to Eckman. If he isn't, I don't stand a chance in hell at making it through the next two years here. I'll end up murdering someone if things continue the way they are now or end up getting taken out myself. The latter is more than likely going to happen first. There are more than a few people around here that would love to see me six feet under and they're rich enough to pull off a hit like that without anyone being the wiser.

CHAPTER 4

TREY

I forced my lead-filled feet down the stairs and through the long corridor. Sweat trickled down my neck from the fire still sweltering inside me. I ran my hands through my shaggy hair and massaged my temples to ease the building pressure in my head.

As I got closer to Mia, it looked like soccer practice had worn her out. Her face was blotchy and her blonde hair was in a messy ponytail. For once, there weren't any jocks lingering around her locker. Over this past week, it was like the line for the hottest ride at the county fair with the number of guys who lined up to chat with her in between classes and after lunch. The way they gawked and pawed at her made me want to knock a few of them to the ground.

I loved Mia to death, but she attracted a lot of attention and couldn't really be held responsible for how it fed into the ever-present rage within me. I'd always see her as an annoying sister, but I wasn't blind either. Her flawless skin and exceptional curves were enough to make any Neanderthal around here drool.

Mia ignored me as she stuffed books and notebooks in her messenger bag. Between her appearance and irritated attitude, the soccer team must've ran the entire time. A few guys from our Calculus class sized her up and whistled on their way down the hall. I shot them a lethal glare, crossed my arms, and took a protective stance in front of her.

After the guys ogling her disappeared through the door, I unfolded my arms, leaned against the locker next to hers, and picked away at the scabs on my knuckles. I was so caught up in removing any evidence of a fight from my hands I didn't see who tapped my shoulder. A riled breath escaped as I curled my fists together.

Mia peered at me, then to her right, and giggled. I turned around and saw a beautiful brunette with the most stunning green eyes staring at me. Her perfect complexion and killer bod weren't what captivated me the most. I didn't need to know a damn thing about her to know I'd follow her mesmerizing eyes anywhere. There was a kindness to them I rarely saw in people around here, or anywhere, for that matter.

In a pair of skimpy black shorts and a tight blue tank top that left nothing to the imagination, she squeezed in between Mia and me, flashing a smile that showed off her perfect white teeth. She didn't seem nearly as wiped out from soccer practice as Mia. Some water droplets trickled down her neck and I almost licked my lips while watching them fall into the curves of her shoulder.

I wonder what it would be like to have my tongue travel along that line. How have our paths not crossed until today? Where the hell has this goddess been all my life?

My mind ran away with itself. I didn't know a thing about this chick and she'd only end up in heartbreak for me. She was one of *them*, so letting my guard down was out of the question—no matter how smoking hot she was. Try as I might on that front, the blood surging through my body settled in my dick.

A wily grin fell from her succulent lips. I wasn't about to let her think she was winning in whatever unspoken chat we were having, so I gave her a panty-dropping smile. She probably thought I'd ask for her number when I finally did speak, but I wanted to make sure she knew I had the upper hand. With her amazing rack, guys more than likely dropped to their knees at the bat of an eye, but I wasn't about to give in to that impulse.

Well, princess, I'm not one of those guys. You'll have to work a lot harder and I can tell you're going to enjoy trying. Let the games begin, sweetheart!

Her eyes shifted from playful to intense. I raised an eyebrow and ran my tongue across my lips—just to mess with her some more. After she spotted my tongue ring, her knees wobbled and it was clear she was trying damn hard not to clench her thighs together.

I focused on Mia. "Are you ready to go? I want to get the hell out of here."

My voice was a little deeper than most guys, but the edginess to it took her friend by surprise. Mia's eyes flickered between us. "I see you're in another one of your *moods*. Just give me a second." I glared daggers at her. She gave me her stink eye. "Since you're set on being an ass, I'll do the introduction for you. Bri, this is Trey. I'd apologize in advance for his jackass ways, but then that's all I'd be doing, so I'll give you my blanket apology now. I'm sorry."

Bri stepped closer to me and another strong rush of blood shot straight to my dick. Shuffling back, I kept my face clear of any emotion. The smile on her face was one of the sweetest I'd ever seen and itt was becoming difficult to hide my thoughts from her. My body was practically humming because of this chick.

She extended her hand and I noted the multi-colored nail polish on her fingernails before shaking it. Bri clearly wanted to show her independence and what I suspected was a wild side any way she could, making her even more intriguing. Every cell in my body was more receptive than it had ever been as I held her delicate fingers. My heart rate skyrocketed, feeling more alive than ever. Not needing her to figure any of this out, I released her soft hand and shifted my weight so my bag kept my lower half covered up.

"It's nice to finally meet you, Trey. Mia has had nothing but good things to say about you over the years. How's the new school working out so far?" Bri asked.

I know that angelic voice. She's the one who came to my defense in Calculus. How did I not notice her before now? Not only am I fucking idiot, but I'm also blind as a bat.

"Nice to meet you. The school is a school. Nothing worth putting a second thought into," I mumbled, gazing away from her.

My body was already mutinying against me, so I needed to focus on *anything* else. Bri tilted my head back to hers and kept her hand on my cheek. "Didn't your parents tell you it's rude to look away from someone who's having a conversation with you?"

I wiggled my chin free. "I wasn't planning on a discussion. It's not really my thing. And even if I were to have one, it wouldn't be with *anyone* from this school."

She winked. "I might just have to change that for you, handsome. You look like you need to lighten up."

I scowled. "It's a bit daunting to even try to when I'm around a bunch of douchebags who have sticks so far up their asses that the light of day is nowhere in sight."

A devious smile curled at the corners of her mouth and I got lost in every aspect of her gorgeous face. She was a whole different kind of beautiful. That word wasn't enough of a descriptor and I made a mental note to look up all the ways of articulating the kind of exquisiteness she possessed. Her nose and high cheekbones were perfect and the way her neck muscles twitched as she laughed made it hard for me not to press her body against mine.

She rested a hand on my chest. "You're not wrong about the kids here, but just remember not *all* of us are like that. If you keep storming around these halls, you'll keep giving them the ammunition they need to torment you. Don't let them bother you."

I opened my mouth to argue, but she placed a finger over it. "I'd rather not see you get expelled. I hear you're an all-star quarterback. Mark my words, in a few weeks, everyone will be begging to be your friend."

Bri swayed back and glanced at Mia, who was oblivious to the two of us until Bri nudged her elbow. Mia glanced up for a moment before diving back into the black hole of her locker.

I narrowed my eyes at Bri. "I'd rather throw myself off a cliff than associate with *anyone* from this school. *No one* here is worth my time."

Mia decked me upside the head and snapped, "Stop being such a jackass. In case you missed it, Bri is being really nice to you. The least you could do is be civil."

Bri opened her locker, shoved some books into her backpack, and tossed it over her shoulder. As she did, I caught a mixture of vanilla and honeysuckle. She smelled amazing and the urge to be closer to her grew. I rubbed my arm across my forehead to check for a fever. I didn't know what was going on with me, but I wasn't a big fan of it.

My dick throbbed, wanting nothing more for me to pin her up against the lockers and kiss her until she begged me to fuck her. There was no way the pretentious pricks around here could satisfy someone as self-confident as her, but I was more than up for the challenge. Just thinking about what Bri would be like in bed made me shuffle closer to her. I curled my hands together to prevent myself from taking hers, holding them above her head, and kissing the living daylights out of her.

Don't fantasize about fucking her. You need to leave before you do something really *stupid.*

Bri slammed her locker shut and it was exactly what I needed to get my head out of the gutter. She shook her hair out and the wavy brown locks framed her face. My stomach dropped to my knees and I sucked in a ragged breath. The spark in her eyes fired even brighter as she ran her finger under my chin to close my mouth before focusing on Mia.

"I'm not sure what my folks are forcing me to do this weekend, but I'm sure it's something, so I'll plan on seeing you Monday morning for breakfast." Mia stared at her, a puzzled look on her face. Bri rolled her eyes and tapped the side of Mia's head. "Coach Nocky talked about it at practice. We're getting together in the mornings before school next week to go over our game plan and do all that team kumbaya shit, so we're ready for our first match on Friday."

Mia groaned. "I remember why I blocked it out in the first place. I hate doing that crap and despise getting up early even more. Isn't sleep more important than food and being all warm and fuzzy with one another?"

"I'm not dignifying that with an answer. Just remember we have a quiz in Advanced Bio on Monday. I'll do the assignments for Calculus and Psychology, so you need to do the ones for English Comp and Advanced Sociology. We can swap in the mornings while we pretend to listen to Coach drone on about the Panthers."

Mia's face blanked again. Even I wondered where her head was at because she was always on top of her shit.

"We're ranked number one in the state and they're dead last, so I don't know why he's even sweating the game. Usually, I zone him out when he goes on his tangents, but you've been such a space cadet lately, I've been paying attention for both of us. Seriously, what's up with that? And you need to stop giving me the same lame-ass answer you have been," Bri said, putting a hand on her hip and raising both eyebrows.

Mia shook her head as her face flushed bright red. They engaged in some unspoken conversation I stood no chance of understanding. My eyes flickered between them for a minute before I gave up. Something Bri mentioned hit me at full force. Bri was in all the same classes as Mia, so that meant she was in my Calculus and English Comp classes.

How had the last four years gone by without me knowing she was Mia's best friend? My mind went into overdrive as I tried to recall seeing her around our neighborhood, or even in school the past week, but I had nothing. A large knot tangled together in my stomach just as fast as my heart sank.

After Mia left me behind in junior high, anything school-related for talking points quickly became off-limits. I had been a complete asshole to her whenever she talked about her new friends or Chamberlain. For someone who hardly ever cried, I'd made Mia shed tears on more than one occasion for trying to share this part of her life. Even though that was behind us now, I hadn't really been approachable in the past few weeks.

As I watched the two of them, I grew more confused. They carried on without words for several more minutes. It reminded me just how useless it was to attempt to even try to figure out a chick. They'd forever be a mystery and their ever-changing minds alone was one of the many reasons every guy on earth would agree with me.

By the end of their unspoken conversation, it *seemed* like they were going to talk later tonight, with actual words and everything, but who knew at this point. Mia glanced at me and I gave her a pointed look, making it quite clear I was about two seconds away from leaving her behind.

"I like your divide-and-conquer plan. I'll need peace and quiet to study for the test and to get all the assignments done. That won't happen at the loft. Way too much noise from the bar travels upstairs. Trey, do you think your mom will care if I crash at your place for the weekend?" Mia asked with her puppy dog eyes.

My focus remained on Bri, who was watching Mia and me, her eyes inquisitive. My head spun about as fast as a top. I really wanted to know what she was thinking and it pissed me off that I even cared.

After she caught me staring with no shame *again*, I held my breath and looked at my hands. I curled them together so tightly they'd become white. The self-inflicted pain was necessary. I could only hop from side-to-side so many times before they picked up on why I was doing it.

Bri's fucking with me. I'm like a little pet project for her now. That's the only explanation. She's gone out of her way in a very short amount of time to reveal just how sexy she can be. She'll be haunting my dreams for weeks, if not months, to come.

She readjusted her backpack and leaned into me. "I'll be seeing you soon, sweets." Her hand ran from my abs up to my chin before she gave me a soft kiss on the cheek. "I know you like what you see. Trust me, the feeling is *very* mutual."

Her lips slipped into a shrewd smile before she headed down the hallway. My head fell forward while I watched her sashay away. It was like a desert had taken up residence in my mouth as I stared at her amazing ass.

Bri turned around, winked at me, and shouted, "I meant what I said, gorgeous. I'll see you around. I'm taking it upon myself to wipe that hard edge off your face and show you a good time. And *believe me*, I'm a good time."

Without another word, she made her way out the doors to the parking lot. My jaw remained ajar, completely blown back by her self-assured remark.

"Are you about done gawking?" Mia asked, smacking my forearm.

I stormed toward the doors Bri just disappeared through. "Whatever. Let's get the fuck out of here. I've had my fill of this side of the tracks."

When I remained silent, Mia shoved at my shoulder. "Yeah, I'm sure that's it. I saw how you looked at Bri. You like her. Give her a chance. She's not like the others."

I shot her a murderous glare. "Mind your business, Mia."

She narrowed her eyes for more, but I wasn't about to get into it with her. I hated how she knew me so well. It was a pain in the ass, but I also knew her and with how spacey she was with Bri, it was obvious she was hiding something.

I slowed down. "Why did you ask if you could stay over? You know my mom never cares. She misses having you around."

Mia released a nervous chuckle. "I don't think I can stay at Micah's anymore. I wasn't sure if Lyla talked to your mom, so that's why I asked. They always seem to be on the same page."

She tried to remain nonchalant but couldn't look me in the eye. I ran my hand over her red cheeks and Mia stuck out her tongue before slapping my hand away. I continued to torment her with lewd gestures and kissing sounds until she finally mumbled, "Lyla caught us in a compromising position the last time I stayed over. We aren't allowed under the same roof without a set of eyes watching our every move."

Stopping mid-stride, I hunched to my knees and laughed so hard tears dripped down my cheeks. Mia pounded her fists on my back and I laughed even harder. "She caught you guys having sex! That's fucking priceless!"

"Why don't you say it a little louder? And it's not funny, you ass.

We weren't having sex per se and thank God for that. I don't think I'd ever be able to look at Lyla again if that were the case," Mia muttered once we reached my Acura.

I opened the door, tossed my backpack and duffle bag in the backseat, and hopped inside. After shoving the key in the ignition, I adjusted my mirrors and waited for her to get in. "If you're banned from the house, it sounds like she saw more than enough."

Mia gave me a sheepish smile. "She got an *eyeful*, but I wouldn't change how the night went one bit." I raised an eyebrow. She grabbed her bags from her feet, threw them behind her, and confessed, "Micah asked me to be his girlfriend."

I cranked the ignition a few times before the car turned over. Someday, I'd have a vehicle that wasn't on its last life. Micah and I had put a lot of work into the Acura to pimp it out, but it was ten years old with over two hundred thousand miles on it. There was only so much we could do to keep it from breaking down every few months. I flipped off a few kids snickering and pointing at me, peeled out of the lot, and sped toward the interstate.

"I'm glad you guys got your shit together. It's about time. It was getting pathetic to watch."

Mia switched the radio to a pop station. I changed it back to the hard rock one it was on. The lyrics from "What I've Done" filled the car. I tapped my fingers on the wheel in time with the beat of the song, noting it had been far too long since I'd picked up my guitar and got out some of my frustrations.

As we neared the south side, I couldn't help but get wrapped up in the words. Taking the scholarship at Chamberlain was supposed to be a good thing, but so far, it'd only made me angrier than I already was most days. If I wasn't dealing with all the shit at school and on the field, I was battling with my old friends.

Except for Micah, they all had written me off—calling me a sellout. That was on the nice days. On the others, they'd just take turns trying to knock me on my ass for bailing on them. After hearing the boys admit they were having problems at school this morning, it was another thing to add to the con column for Chamberlain.

"You should really give Bri a chance. You'll never meet anyone as kind as her. She noticed you on your first day, but she's known about you for a long time. She knows how much you mean to me. I know you like her and she likes you," Mia spoke up.

Just the sound of her name sent a strange wave throughout me. It was tranquil and completely foreign. Bri shouldn't have this kind of effect on me. This constant betrayal became more aggravating by the second. I shot Mia one of my harsher glares.

Bri is way out of my league. I'll never fit in her world.

She opened her mouth—no doubt to pile on some more. I banged my hand against the dash and snapped, "Mind your fucking business, Mia. I won't say it again."

Mia frowned and crossed her arms before looking out the window. A sharp pain ran through my chest for yelling at her. "When are you going to learn how to drive so Micah and I can stop being your chauffeurs?" I asked in a playful tone.

"I guess whenever you teach me. Micah has tried a few times, but I'm not sure he's the right person for the job."

Her voice trailed off as she fiddled with the collar of her white Lions T-shirt. Mia did her best to look at anything but me. Close quarters made that next to impossible. I tugged at the part of her shirt she held on to for dear life and saw a huge hickey. She gasped and swatted at my hands.

I chuckled. "I can see why he's not the *right fit*. If you're coming over tonight, you better make sure that stays covered up. I'm sure Lyla and my mom have talked by now. If she sees that, she's going to give you a sex talk that lasts for *hours*. I've had it several times and it makes you want to claw your eyes out."

"Why do they have to talk to each other about everything? It's really annoying sometimes. I'm sure your mom is going to corner me to have *the talk* at some point soon anyway, so I might as well get it over with."

My stomach knotted up as I pulled up to an open spot behind her uncle's bar. There was something about Chase that had never sat well with me. I rested my hand on her arm. "Do you want me to come in with you or will you be okay?"

I hated seeing the way her body tensed up while she fumbled around for her keys. A half-hearted smile spread across her face as she said, "I'm going to take a quick shower here and throw a bag together for the weekend before heading over to your house. I'll be there in an hour or two, so please tell your mom not to wait to serve supper."

Before I could convince her to let me go upstairs with her, she unlocked the back door and strode inside. Mia hated every second she was there and who could blame her. Chase was unstable. You never knew when he'd go on one of his streaks and put her into lockdown. He'd go on a bender and she'd have to deal with him and his insane ways—not to mention the nonsense he spewed at her. Micah and I had never agreed with letting her stay with him, but our moms reminded us that Chase was her legal guardian and they couldn't overrule his decisions.

For as overprotective as my mom was of Mia, it blew my mind she was so adamant about not overstepping with Chase when it was obvious to all of us she was in an abusive situation. At least it was early, so he wouldn't be plastered yet. Once the light in the loft flickered on, I headed for home.

As I weaved through the alley, Bri consumed my thoughts. I hated not knowing a thing about her. What was even stranger for me was I wanted to know everything and that was not my MO. There was just something about her I couldn't resist and that scared the fucking shit out of me.

Not getting kicked out of school or beating Sebastian to a pulp already had my plate overflowing. With all the shit that happened today, there wasn't a chance in hell any of that was going away anytime soon. Getting involved with Bri would complicate my life even more. It was best for both of us if I steered clear of her altogether.

CHAPTER 5

<u>BRI</u>

I flipped to the chapter I needed in my Psychology book and regretted I took this subject and Biology for homework this week with Mia. It was my least favorite. After dealing with my parents nitpicking at me and each other all weekend at events for my dad's reelection campaign, I needed some time away from them *soon*. Their bickering grew worse by the day and it was only the third week of school. At this rate, I wouldn't make it to our first break with my wits intact.

The Psychology coursework wasn't hard to follow, but it reminded me how screwed up my family was and I tried to block that out as much as possible. I reread the paragraph, but couldn't focus on it. The words blurred together, so I stuffed my notebook into my text, eyed my Biology one, but didn't pick it up.

I gazed at the impressionist pieces on my white walls. Normally, I could get lost in the fine strokes of Monet and Van Gogh, but they weren't doing anything to calm the brewing storm inside me. Being the daughter of a senator was far from easy. I couldn't classify my life at home as abusive, but it wasn't exactly all sunshine and rainbows either. I wasn't sure why my parents decided to have a child in the first place. Neither one of them knew me. They would've been better off getting a droid.

Icy waves rippled through my body and I shivered before shoving that last thought from my mind. The weather was still relatively warm for the third week of September, but this house tended to bring out a desolation in me that was hard to shake. Our Italian palazzo-style home had three stories, including seven bedrooms, eight bathrooms, a spacious library, sunroom, and a ballroom. The decorations and furniture throughout it were stuffy and anything but homey.

My own room wasn't even truly mine, so I couldn't escape in it the way most teenagers did. It was fit for an aristocrat in Manhattan—not a Midwest girl who loved playing sports and listening to the latest indie hits. I got used to living in what was equivalent to a museum a long time ago, but never stopped longing for the normal lifestyle most kids got the luxury of having while they grew up.

I walked over to one of the massive windows in my room and pulled the ivory curtains apart. The isolated courtyard reminded me how alone I really was. The lake off in the distance was one of the few places on the property I disappeared to for solace. Varying shades of blue in the water as the sun slowly set brought a smile to my face.

My grin grew even wider as *Trey Donovan* took over my thoughts. Over the past two weeks, I'd been doing everything I could to get him to give me the time of day. There was something about his gray eyes and the way my heart fluttered whenever he was around that I couldn't resist. The way we gravitated toward one another was equally mind-boggling.

A knock sounded on my door and Kelsey poked her head inside seconds later. "Bri, dinner will be served in ten minutes. Both your parents are home, so I thought I'd give you a heads-up. You looked like you were having a rough day when you got home. Is everything with school and soccer going okay?"

Her dark brown hair was in a tight bun. Aside from her brown eyes, she looked a lot like me. She ran our household and was like a mom to me. I flopped down on my bed and forced a smile, but it wasn't enough to appease her. Kelsey sauntered over and sat down next to me.

"This school year is off to a rocky start. Since we're the reigning state champs, there's a lot of pressure to kill the competition in soccer. My classes are harder this semester, so that's an extra stressor. I'm sure I'll find my footing soon, but you know how my dad is. I really wish he'd head to D.C. for a few weeks, but he doesn't have a trip booked for a while," I whispered, sitting up and looking around the room.

She gripped my chin. "I have the utmost faith in you. Don't let what he says get to you. In two years, you'll be taking the world by storm. If you need help with your studies, all you need to do is ask."

I twisted my fingers around my cream comforter. "Trust me, you don't want to deal with my courses. They're a nightmare. Mia is in all of them with me for once, so it should be bearable with us splitting the workload, but I'll keep your offer in mind."

"It's nice to hear you two are finally in the same classes. She's such a sweet girl. Will she be spending the night on Friday?" I nodded. Her face fell as she murmured, "Your mom is hosting one of her charities here. You know I never pry into your plans, but if you're going to slip out, please let me know so I can play my part accordingly."

We had an unspoken agreement. I didn't do anything that landed me in jail or the hospital and she covered for me. It was usually easy for Mia to slip away on a moment's notice, so we'd had more than our fair share of fun tearing up the streets of Chicago over the past four years. Now that I had my license, it was *a lot* easier and Mia probably needed the breaks more than me.

After meeting her our first day of seventh grade, it was clear things at home were anything but normal. She didn't say much about her life with Chase, but her twitchiness and lack of faith in herself made it clear there was some sort of abusive lifestyle going on, so whatever happened at my house paled in comparison to hers. I was happy to do whatever I could to get her out of the loft.

Kelsey sensed something wasn't right as well, so she made sure Mia felt at home whenever she was here. With how shitty my parents were to her, it took great lengths to make that happen, but Kelsey was just as determined as me. It was a fine line to walk and not lose her job, but unlike my folks, her morality was intact.

My parents detested having Mia stay over. For the life of me, I hadn't been able to figure out what their deal was when it came to people who lived on the south side, but trying to understand the motives of a sociopath and a wino wasn't my forte either. Kelsey patted my arm, bringing me back to reality.

"After we get back from our soccer match, we're going to the football game before hitting up a party. The location is still up in the air, but I'll let you know the details by Friday night."

She squinted. "I can't help but think there's something else on your mind, and from where I'm sitting, it has nothing to do with your parents and everything to do with a boy."

I shrugged. "And why do you think that?"

"He's proving to be a challenge for you, isn't he?" Kelsey asked, her smile cunning as she drummed her fingers across her chin.

My jaw dropped. "Are you tapping my phone? I wouldn't put it past my dad to make you do something like that."

Kelsey gave me an admonishing wave of the hand. "Of course not, and even if he did, I wouldn't have followed through. I have my limits with his asinine demands."

"You and me both. The man knows no bounds, so it wouldn't have surprised me if he asked you to do something that shady. He doesn't have a moral compass."

"We could spend days talking about him. I'd rather stay on point."

"Tell me how you knew first."

"I always know when a new guy comes into your life, but this one is different than the others. You've been a lot flightier than usual. In all these years, and well, boys for that matter, I've never seen you so out of sorts."

I flopped on my back, snagged a pillow, and groaned into it. Kelsey laughed and pulled me up. Her eyes danced while she watched me squirm from her accurate analysis. It didn't help that whenever Trey was around me, I'd lose complete control over my body, but I wasn't about to admit that to Kelsey. If she knew just how much Trey turned my world upside down, the smug grin on her face would only grow wider.

With each day that passed, it was harder to keep the fiery sensations Trey ignited with a tilt of the head or lingering stare at bay. Every time I spotted his tongue ring, my body defaulted to the red-hot setting. I was more than eager to see what it felt like inside my mouth—not to mention other areas. Eventually, I'd attack him with my lips and pray he kissed me back.

"This one must really be something to have your head spinning without even taking you out on a date."

"Seriously, my parents don't pay you enough."

She giggled. "So, what's this boy's name? I need to know who's cast such a spell over you."

I blushed. "His name is Trey. He's a transfer student and one of Mia's closest childhood friends."

"I see. It's a little more understandable why you've been so off. That's a unique situation for you two. What does Mia say about your interest in him?"

"She says she's fine with it, but I don't think I'm really going to know until something happens. At this rate, that looks like it's a long way off."

She arched an eyebrow. "It sounds like he's playing hard to get. I like him already."

I stuck my tongue out at her. "You *would* like that about him."

Kelsey opened her mouth but didn't get a word out. My parents' shouting grew louder and the neighbors five miles down the road could probably hear them. Listening to them throw cheap insults at one another had been the norm since I was a toddler, but lately I longed for the quiet evenings when they avoided each other.

I hurried out the door with Kelsey behind me. We walked down the hallway and stopped at the oak, spiral staircase leading downstairs. I sat down on the top step and rested my elbows on my knees.

It sounded like it was going to turn into one of their all-out shouting matches and I preferred being out of the line of fire or I'd end up being dragged into it. When their tempers flared as high as they were now, they ended up making me feel shittier than they normally do.

"How the hell did you spend a hundred and fifty grand in one day? It looks like you went to every boutique along the Magnificent Mile and dropped several thousand at each of them. In what universe is it logical to spend fifty thousand on a handbag?" Dad shouted.

"If you had any fashion sense at all, you'd realize that Birkin bags don't come cheap and are all the rage right now. Don't snap at me for getting my fall wardrobe and accessories for your upcoming campaign tour. In all your years in office, you've insisted a senator's wife look the part. And for the record, a lot of that money was spent toward new suits and shoes for you, so don't you dare bitch at me for it now!" Mom shot back.

"I don't need a suit ensemble that costs twenty grand," Dad bellowed.

"You do if you want to save face. If you looked in the mirror every now and then, you'd see the years haven't been kind to you. Your opponents are not only younger, but a hell of a lot better-looking than you. As I recall, you'll do whatever it takes to be reelected, so trusting my fashion sense would be in your best interest," Mom snarled.

Glass shattering bounced off the walls, so she more than likely tossed a vase at him. Wood connecting hard with the surface made my nerves prickle and I heaved in a deep breath to keep my anxiety in check. The walls closed in as the weights on my chest grew. They didn't throw things at each other often, but whenever they did, it wasn't a good sign. Kelsey squeezed my hand and made me focus on her until my breathing evened out.

"Leave it to you to concentrate on the vanity aspect of being up for reelection. Then again, you barely graduated from Vanderbilt, so it's no surprise. Lord knows what would happen if you actually thought for once," Dad hollered.

"You smug son of a bitch, you seem to be forgetting that it was my family's money and legacy that bankrolled your entire campaign to get elected in the first place!" Mom screamed.

"Don't flatter yourself, Jamie. My voters appreciate and relate to me because my ancestors actually worked for their fortune."

"You keep putting yourself up on that pedestal, John. I know the truth about where all your family's money came from, along with plenty of your other dark secrets. Don't think for a minute I won't expose you. What's Sean Fitzpatrick's number again? I'm feeling a little chatty and there's a few things I'd just *love* to discuss with him."

Loud stomping filled my eardrums and I struggled to take in my next breath. Their voices faded out and the house was eerily silent. For a second, it sounded like my mom was struggling for air and it wouldn't shock me to go downstairs and see him strangling her.

I rubbed my temples and tried to make sense of their conversation. My dad and his family did business with a lot of people, so I wasn't sure what that threat meant. It was a well-known fact the Fitzpatricks controlled the mob in Chicago, along with the Fitzgeralds and Sweeneys. Considering there was a slight slur to my mom's words, it could just be her drunken, overdramatic side rearing its ugly head.

"It's six thirty and the last time I checked supper in this house was served by now. Kelsey!" Dad yelled, slamming down what I assumed was a book.

He was done with my mom and ready to scream at someone else. *Lucky me.* Kelsey extended a hand to help me up. I linked my arm with hers as we strode downstairs.

Once we reached the bottom, Kelsey whispered, "It sounds like the worst is over. I'm sure you can tell, but your mom has already had a few glasses of wine. She'll be out after dinner. Your dad has a conference call shortly after seven, so you just need to make it through the next half hour."

Her mouth curled into an uplifting smile on her way to our kitchen. I took my time walking through the foyer, ignoring the broken glass and chair, and carried on to the dining room. They were at opposite ends of the long, maple table. I took my seat in between them, wondering how they ever conceived me with the sheer hatred they had for each other.

Dad ran a hand through his black hair before loosening his navy-blue tie and picking up a paper. After winning his Senate seat, his once smooth face was more rugged and the gray to his sideburns was more prominent. Aside from the short hair, he reminded me of Aro in the *Twilight* series. He carried himself with the same superiority and his green eyes could've easily been red to match his black soul. Since green eyes were a rarity, I was grateful he passed those along to me and only that much.

Mom picked up her glass of wine and giggled at the magazine in front of her. She was already two sheets to the wind. I got her average height, brown hair with auburn tints, and voluptuous curves. I was more than happy I didn't inherit her horrid personality. Her brown eyes were glossy as she scanned the article, blinking every so often to keep the words in focus.

Dad took a sip of his brandy and read through the headlines in *The Washington Post*. After he finished that paper, he grabbed the *Chicago Tribune*, flipped to a page in the middle, and pursed his lips together. He crinkled his eyes, making the veins in his forehead more noticeable as they throbbed nonstop. He hastily tossed it aside and picked up our school newsletter.

"Well, despite your lack of contribution, it seems the team is doing well so far this year."

The entire room turned red as I snapped, "I had three out of the six goals in our last game."

Dad scoffed. "Everyone knows Brooks is the worst team in your conference, so that's not much of an accomplishment. You came out several times and were slow getting back on defense."

Every muscle in my body tightened far beyond what they should and I gripped the side of my chair to keep from blowing up. My eyes flickered over to my mom. The bottle of Merlot beside her was half gone, so I didn't bother trying to divert the conversation her way.

"We had the win. I came out so I didn't get injured. It was the best move for the team and me," I defended through gritted teeth.

"Don't kid yourself. Your conditioning is for shit. If you want to make the All-State team this year, you better start running outside of practice," Dad countered with a gleam in his eyes that made me sick to my stomach.

And today's fucked-up McAndrews' dinner is brought to you by the letter 'A' for asshole.

Kelsey walked through the swinging door and set down the platters in her hand. She took one look at me and her eyes filled with sorrow. Another one of our maids was behind her with a large Caesar salad and some side dishes. Once they were on the table, Kelsey headed back to the doorway, but waited for our other maid, who was preparing my parents' plates. God forbid they lifted a finger to do it themselves. She passed them over to them before topping off my dad's brandy and my mom's wine. She went to fill my glass, but I gave her a pointed look and she backed away.

I loaded my plate up with salmon and salad. Having the food be somewhat normal and not some foreign, expensive shit they insisted on trying because one of their stupid friends recommended it was my only comfort at the moment. I picked up the spoon to an unknown green goop to the right of me. Out of the corner of my eye, I saw Kelsey sticking out her tongue and quickly put it back. Before she returned to the kitchen, she produced another reassuring smile and I forced one for her.

There's at least another twenty minutes left of this meal and I'm not sure I'll be able to make it through it without taking a swing at the self-centered jackass to my left.

The only sound between the three of us was silverware scraping against the fine china while we ate. Mom snorted as she read a different paparazzi magazine. Dad was on the cover, so that was why she couldn't contain her amusement. It was from our first soccer game and the photographer had a prime shot of him talking on his cell instead of watching me on the field.

"It looks like the football team might make a run this year." He narrowed his eyes on me. Seeing the glare behind them made my stomach churn. "Brianna, what can you tell me about the new quarterback? Who is Trey Donovan? He's single-handedly keeping us in the running with his fine performances, but his name isn't familiar to me."

As he waited for an answer, the glower in my dad's eyes grew even harsher. He had never been a patient man. I kept my eyes on my plate and mumbled, "He's new, but very talented in the classroom and on the field. He's a friend of Mia's."

His eyes turned snakelike. I was fresh prey for the taking. My mind drifted to the one person I knew would make the next five minutes of my life bearable. Trey's glorious physique crept into my mind and my heart skipped a beat. It took everything inside me to keep my skin from flushing to the shade of pink it loved to settle on whenever he popped into my head.

"So, he's from the south side?" Dad asked, his tone full of disgust.

I stuffed a forkful of lettuce into my mouth so he wouldn't pester me for more. Judging by the enraged look on his face, he was far from finished. My chest constricted with the fear I could no longer ignore. In a matter of minutes, my palms would dampen and my airway would close.

He threw his napkin on the table and sneered, "Well, I hope he's earned his spot. We don't donate thousands of dollars to Chamberlain for them to let in these lower-class kids from the wrong side of the tracks. It was bad enough they let in that no-good friend of yours. I'll have to make an appointment with the board soon. This charity work of theirs needs to come to an end."

I tossed my fork on my plate, shoved it away, and yelled, "Mia is in the top five of our class and has led our soccer and basketball teams to state titles the last two years. Trey may have just transferred, but I've heard his academic standing is off the charts and his performance in sports is nothing short of exemplary."

Before leaving the room, I stopped next to him with my arms crossed. "In case you still have your doubts, he's already been labeled by the *Chicago Tribune* as the best left-handed quarterback the state has seen in the last two decades. You're so fixated on yourself, you probably missed that article. I'm pretty sure your money is being well spent."

"Don't forget whose house you're in, Brianna. I *will not* tolerate that kind of indignant tone from anyone, let alone my child. Lose the attitude and treat me with the respect I deserve."

Something surfaced in his soulless irises, sending shivers up my spine. I wasn't exactly sure what I stumbled on with him and didn't care to find out—not tonight anyway.

"I've lost my appetite and have plenty of homework to finish. Wouldn't want to fall short there too, now would I?"

"This is your last warning, watch your mouth. We're not finished with this discussion. Sit back down."

I stormed out of the room. "You may not be, but I am."

"Great job, John. You can't make it through one meal without being a pretentious bastard."

"No one needs your drunken two cents, Jamie. It's not like you give a damn about anything going on in that girl's life. Brianna needs a little pressure to stay on point if she's going to get into an Ivy League school on her own. It'd be nice if *someone* from your family did."

I sprinted upstairs. With each step, their shouting grew to a higher crescendo. My heart hammered ferociously against my chest and I gasped for air. The anger surging through my body was something I tried to avoid at all costs. I ran into my room, slammed the door, and cranked the surround sound. Linkin Park replaced their voices. I snatched my iPhone from the nightstand and laid on my bed. Kelsey knocked, but never came in. She always knew when I needed to be alone. I brought up my messages and moved down to Mia's last text.

Bri: Are you at Micah's or Trey's?

I expected to wait a few minutes for her answer, but my screen flashed with a response seconds later.

Mia: You know I'm not allowed to stay at Micah's. Stop being a smartass.

Bri: Raarrrr. Someone is still a little sensitive about that whole ordeal.

Mia: I'm at the loft. It's not conducive for studying, but I'll make

do. I don't want to stay at Trey's too much. His mom has enough on her hands without me being there.**

My heart palpitated, not liking that answer one bit. Not too long ago she made the mistake of staying there and her deranged uncle wouldn't let her leave for a week.

Bri: That won't do for either of our GPAs. I'll be there in an hour to pick you up.

I counted down, but barely made it to five before Mia called. I pointed the remote at my sound dock and paused my iPod. "This is cutting into the time you'll need to pack a bag."

"I'm fine with whatever you have in mind, but I'll meet you there. I'm sure we're going downtown, so it makes no sense for you to come and get me. It'll be a waste of time for you to come all this way for us to backtrack," Mia rambled.

"Well, you don't have your license yet, so someone is going to have to drive you," I pointed out.

"You're not usually this desperate to get out of your house this early in the week. Did you have a go-round with your dad?"

Her attempt at nonchalance was sweet, but her voice wavered at the end. The tightness lingering in my chest made me even more eager to leave before an anxiety attack hit me.

"Changing the subject isn't going to work. Either you tell me how you're going to get to the penthouse or I'm picking your ass up."

Mia huffed. "Fine, you win. Micah mentioned having a guys' night with Trey, but I'm sure he'd drop me off. Just let me shoot him a text to make sure that works."

"They're welcome to hang out with us."

"I'll be sure to pass the invite along, but I think they need a guys' night. It's been hard for them to find it with football practice, school, and all the time Micah's been spending with me."

"If they turn down an evening with us, it's their loss."

Mia giggled. "Micah's going to drive me, so I'll plan on being at the penthouse in an hour."

I anxiously chewed on my lip. "Is Trey coming with him?"

"He didn't say. Listen, I need to get packed and slip out of the bar unnoticed. I'll see you soon, sass."

"Sounds good, chickadee," I replied with a wide smile before hanging up.

I did a once-over in the long mirror in the corner of my room and darted into my huge walk-in closet. If Trey showed up with Micah, my navy mesh shorts and light blue, practice T-shirt weren't what I wanted to be seen in. I changed into my favorite holey jeans and slipped on a purple tank top before putting on a white, oversized Eckman sweatshirt. After tying my hair back in a messy bun, I slid on a pair of sparkly sandals.

I retrieved my duffle bag and scrambled around my closet, snatching a couple pairs of jeans, tops, tanks, dresses, and an assortment of heels and sandals. I scowled at my ugly school uniform and tossed that in as well. Once my bag was packed and I had all my makeup together, I grabbed my backpack and car keys before heading downstairs.

Classical garbage was playing on the stereo, so my mom was already down for the count and my dad wasn't anywhere in sight. Not wanting to take any chances, I tiptoed through the foyer. Just as I turned the knob on the front door, Kelsey tapped my shoulder. I jumped and almost knocked over the vintage mail table. I whipped around with my hand on my chest, gasping to catch my breath.

Kelsey raised an eyebrow. "Going somewhere? It's Tuesday. You're three days early on busting out for the night."

"I can't stay here. I'm spending the rest of the week in the city. I don't need to remind you how much of a terror he was on when he ran for Senate the first time. I don't plan on being his punching bag until Election Day. That's over a year away. If I don't escape after fights like tonight, he'll break me."

Kelsey pulled me in for a hug. "I'll do my best to keep them off your back over the next few days, but I recommend trying to make it look like you've been here. If they ask where you are, I'll go through my usual list of places. If they get too persistent, I'll let you know because I'll be checking on you every day."

"You know I wouldn't have it any other way. I'm leaving before my dad gears up for round two."

"He's on the phone. I doubt he'll notice you're gone tonight. Take care of yourself. Tell Mia I say hello. Oh, and no sleepovers with boys, or any wild parties."

I smirked. "Will do. Thanks for everything, Kelsey."

She shooed me out the door and closed it. I clicked the automatic start button on my keys and ran to my Lexus. After tossing my stuff in the backseat, I drove down our long driveway. It didn't take long at all before I was on the interstate.

I savored the lyrics of "Breakaway" as Kelly Clarkson's voice echoed through the car. The fight with my dad ran through my head. I banged the steering wheel, more than frustrated with the vicious cycle I'd been in with my parents for far too long.

Why can't they just love me for who I am? And why do I keep trying to make them proud of me? I hate admitting I want their approval, but a part of me always will. I mean, isn't that what almost every kid wants, especially from the people who brought you into this world?

The malevolent look in my dad's eyes when he found out Trey was from the south side made the knots in my stomach coil together even tighter. If we got together, I wasn't sure what he'd do, but I really didn't care either. I wanted a shot with Trey and I wasn't about to let anyone stand in my way—including my asshole of a father.

CHAPTER 6

BRI

The sun dipped below the horizon, casting beautiful rays of red and orange across the sky, just before I exited the freeway. I weaved through some lingering rush hour traffic and turned into an underground parking garage off Washington Boulevard. After I parked in the stall for our penthouse, I grabbed my bags, locked up my Lexus, and headed for the elevator.

When my dad ran for his Senate seat, he insisted a place in the city was necessary to save time on commuting. We didn't live that far out of Chicago, so it was a bit of a head-scratcher for me, but it ended up benefiting all of us. He used it for a lot of late nights with his staff and my mom hosted plenty of luncheons when she was on a Loop shopping kick. In the last year, I probably logged more hours here than at the house in Highland Park. It was my sanctuary.

Our penthouse was in a corner spot with an amazing view of the skyline. The two bedrooms and bathrooms were as modest as the kitchen and living areas. The den and sunroom were spacious, but the overall simplicity of it was what I loved the most. Its urban décor, between the art and furniture, was the exact opposite of the over-the-top extravagance of our mansion.

I let myself inside and couldn't help but smile while walking through the door. Not having to look over my shoulder for security still made me giddy. It took *a lot* of fights after I got my license last year, but I finally got my dad to allow me to come and go without a security detail on me. The guy who used to tail me was really cool and never ratted on me whenever I did sneak out of the house, but I despised having someone follow me around. I didn't know how long this small slice of freedom would last, so I savored every second of it.

After turning on the light, I tossed my bag on the wraparound black sofa in the living room and strode over to windows to open the long, white curtains. The cleaning staff that comes every month was here recently. I could practically see my reflection in the hardwood floors.

With the sun fully set, the skyscrapers stirred to life. I released a drawn-out breath, loving how downtown looked from this angle, and cherished the calm waves chasing away the angst still lingering in my heart. I flipped on the eighty-inch television above the fireplace and fell into the plush cushions behind me. My gaze drifted to my backpack at the opposite end of the couch. I'd get to my homework at some point, but my mind wasn't quite ready to focus the way I needed to in order to get the A's demanded of me.

I snagged the remote from the coffee table, slid off my sandals, scrolled through the guide, and set a few recordings for some of my favorite shows before settling on the CW to see what shenanigans Veronica Mars had gotten herself into this week. It was a rerun, but I didn't care. Seeing a young woman, who was brilliant, quick-witted, and put guys in their place, gave me hope we'd see more females rise to power—not just on TV but in the actual world. To my dismay, the scene on the screen was a bunch of bimbos on the beach.

"You know, I might be biased, but I just don't think those West Coast bikini babes hold a candle to the smoking hot chicks in the Midwest," Micah quipped.

My heart left this stratosphere as I fell onto the hard floor. The hood of my sweatshirt toppled over my head and I pulled it down before rubbing my sore ass. I peered up to see Mia snuggled into Micah's side, laughing at me. Before I could blink, I was pulled up.

Trey's steady hands fired up every nerve ending in my body. With tantalizing tingles spreading through me, I wasn't sure if my feet would keep me upright. I turned around to face him. His luscious lips quirked into a ghost of a smile. That was a rarity.

The way his gray eyes continued to dance made me flush from head to toe. I didn't need my body to rebel against me any more than it already was, especially in front of Micah and Mia, so I walked to the other side of the coffee table.

I gripped the back of my neck and scowled at Mia. "Is it too much to ask for a heads-up before scaring the shit out of me?"

Micah hunched over the back of the couch and laughed even harder. Trey bit the sides of his cheeks to remain silent. Mia tossed me her cell before holding her hands up innocently. I frowned while reading the three texts she sent me—the first letting me know they were here, the second saying they were on their way up, and her final warning that she was using her key and had both guys with her.

I stuck out my tongue and threw her phone back. "Well damn, the three of you could rob a bank for as stealthy as you enter a place."

"Getting into here would've been a breeze without a key. Mia has yet to find a lock she can't pick," Micah joked, tickling her sides.

"That's an interesting fact you haven't shared before now. Any other skills you want to share?" I asked, poking my cheek with my tongue just to mess with her.

Her face turned pink and she attempted to glare at me but couldn't pull it off. She shoved her phone in her back pocket before tugging Micah over to the floor-to-ceiling windows to check out the view. After seeing them exchange a heated kiss as they sashayed away, Trey rolled his eyes, sat at the edge of the sofa, and kicked his legs up on the coffee table.

His eyes flickered around the room, a hard edge on his face. The frostiness he exuded to pretty much everyone at Chamberlain was understandable, but when he was that way with me, it drove me crazy.

Trey remained silent and picked away at the frayed edges of the holes in his jeans. His light silver T-shirt had been worn so much you could see through the fabric. His defined eight-pack shined in all its glory underneath it. A Celtic wraparound tattoo on his upper right bicep piqued my curiosity. I wanted to know if there were any more on his divine physique. He noticed me staring and flashed that damn cocky smirk of his.

I wasn't sure what the temperature was when I arrived, but it was like a sauna now. I pulled off my sweatshirt, tossed it on the couch, and put my hands on my hips. His eyes widened for a split-second as he stared at my chest. A slight reddish color crept up the side of his neck. After taking a deep breath, he stared at the creases in his palms like they were the most fascinating thing he'd ever seen.

This is ridiculous. We're obviously attracted to one another. It's time to figure out what's going on in that head of his and I'm more than up for the challenge.

I sat down next to his feet and rested my hands on his thighs. "I think it's about time I lived up to my word. I'll do whatever it takes to wipe that sullen look off your face."

Trey's head snapped up and he ran a hand through his slightly wet hair. His fingers trailed along the edges of the tattoo on his right arm, almost as if it was his way of centering himself. "I have no idea what that means, but I'm not about to be your pet project."

His sharp tone was probably an attempt to make me back off, or at the very least remove my hands from his legs, but it just tapped into the lingering anger still festering inside me. Trey would learn one way or another I was a very stubborn person when I wanted to be. I refused to let him push me away any longer.

I gazed around for Mia and Micah. Their backs were to us as they kissed each other like they were about to be separated from one another for the next year. They stopped sucking face long enough to saunter into one of the bedrooms.

"Do you want something to drink? It looks like you might be here for a bit."

"If I'm stuck here, I'm not watching this snarky, girly crap. Either we change the channel or I'm out of here."

I arched an eyebrow. "You're not a prude, so leaving seems like an extreme reaction to your buddy disappearing to make out with his girl."

Trey snorted. "Believe me, I'm not. I probably know more about all the pleasure points on a body than you do, doll. It's just nauseating when you're watching two people you've known since you were five getting it on."

Hearing him refer to me as doll sent violent waves of rage through my body. I curled my hands together and took a deep breath to keep it from spiraling into the sheer panic that typically followed. Reliving one of the worst nights of my life was something I avoided at all costs.

"That sounds like a challenge, gorgeous, and as much as I'd love to prove you wrong on that front, I'd rather do you a solid instead," I countered.

"I swear you don't speak English half the time. Micah's my ride home. I'd take the train, but I'd rather not deal with anymore scumbags today. I hit my quota every day at Chamberlain."

I pulled him up, threw my sweatshirt over my shoulder, and towed him down the hall. He grumbled under his breath, but there was a curiosity to his eyes that made my heart flutter. We marched up the black spiral staircase to the second floor, through the large open bedroom in the loft area, and down the hallway to one of my favorite rooms.

After Trey saw the old-fashioned arcade games, seventy-inch television, pool table, darts, and hot tub, he practically foamed at the mouth. I stopped at the wet bar and grabbed a bottle of Patron, Sam Adams Utopias, Crown Royal, and twelve-pack of Miller Lite. I placed them on the tray along with three empty glasses, balanced it on my side, flipped on the outside lights, and gestured for Trey to open the sliding door to our secluded rooftop.

Once we were outside, his eyes widened in awe. The downtown

skyline from this angle was one very few people got to see. The Willis Tower stood out in the plethora of skyscrapers and I made a mental note to take a Ferris Bueller day soon. I set the tray on the patio table, picked up the Patron, and filled up two of the three glasses before joining Trey.

Lights from the skyscrapers twinkled across the city before disappearing into Lake Michigan. There was a slight breeze, but I barely even registered it. Seeing Trey at ease for once was a sight for sore eyes. His hand edged closer to mine and it was as though an electric charge had somehow ignited. My insides jumped along with the lights dancing across the skyline.

"The city is pretty amazing from up here," Trey murmured after a few minutes.

I gave him a soft smile and whispered, "There's a beauty to it you can't get from walking on the streets."

The pull to be as close to him as possible took over. I brushed my fingers along his and relished in the resulting tingles sweeping through my body. He sucked in a sharp breath, but didn't move his hand. His shoulders sagged a little, the tension in them falling away, and I hoped my touch was the reason. It took all my willpower not to kiss him. I'd made the first move plenty of times with guys, but I didn't want to risk it with him. He was in control and I'd wait for as long as it took for him to initiate that moment between us.

God, please let it be sooner rather than later!

"I'm glad you ended up coming with Micah."

My breath hitched as I stared at his chiseled face. The stringed lights we had along the railing and around the patio doors added an extra sparkle to his eyes, making me wonder even more who he was underneath all his broodiness. Trey trailed his fingers down my arm. Goosebumps coasted along every spot he touched and this time, I was the one heaving in a deep breath. He flashed a sexy smile and strolled over to the table.

Trey pointed at the full glasses. "Are you doing me a solid by getting me drunk?"

I shook my head a few times to regain my wits and sashayed over to him. "I don't know about getting wasted, but there is a way we can fill the time and have our own fun while those two make out downstairs."

He raised his eyebrows and sat down. I released my bun and slid my sweatshirt back on before bending over to shake out my hair. With the wind swirling around us, it was hard to hear, but a ragged breath definitely escaped from Trey. My mouth curled into a shrewd smile, loving how I got to him.

Once my mane was somewhat tamed, I grabbed a quarter from my pocket and sat across from him. "We're playing quarters, but with a twist."

Trey squinted. "What kind of twist? If it's some rich kid thing, I'll pass."

Hearing his condescending tone made my cheeks blaze. I glared at him and shot back, "It's a bit insulting that you keep grouping me in with the rest of the kids at Chamberlain. In the past two weeks, I think I've made it clear I'm not like them."

He waved his hands around us, a fierce glare in his eyes. "Yet, here we are, in what is clearly a second home for your family. Half the people in my neighborhood don't even have a place this big—let alone for it to be their playhouse. I'm not trying to be a prick, I'm just pointing out the obvious. You come from a wealthy family and enjoy all the perks."

"You know, you're a real hypocrite. You get so angry when people judge you, but you're ignorant to the fact you do it to *me* all the time," I pointed out, giving him my stink eye. After hearing my sharp tone, he sealed his lips. "In addition to taking a drink if the quarter goes in, you have to share something about yourself that no one else knows," I instructed, grabbing my glass and tilting it back.

"This seems like a total chick game, but I don't have a lot of options. It's either play this or watch those two try and seal the deal. I'd rather *not* bear witness to that train wreck waiting to happen, so let's get started," Trey muttered with a roll of the eyes.

I spit out the booze in my mouth and was grateful it didn't go up my nose or at him. After a minute of coughing, I rasped, "Is that what she's so bent out of shape about lately? They haven't had sex yet?"

Trey swallowed the liquor in his glass in one gulp, shook his shoulders as the tequila traveled down his windpipe, then filled it up with Miller Lite. "Nope, and they're both virgins, so their first time is going to be a disaster."

He laughed and I giggled along with him. Once my glass was full of beer, I looked for the quarter. It was here a second ago. Not seeing it on the ground or on the table, I glanced at Trey, who made it appear between his fingers like a magician.

Trey bounced it on the surface and it landed in the cup. Flashing his dimples, he gestured for me to drink. Every cell within me sparked to life. If he kept looking at me like that, the very little restraint I had left not to throw myself at him would vanish.

Fuck–fuckity–Fuck! This is starting off on the completely wrong foot. It's supposed to be me squeezing him for information, not the other way around.

I took down my beer in a few gulps, refilled the glass with whiskey, and admitted, "My parents are set on me going to one of the Ivy League colleges of their choice out east, but it's never going to happen. I'm applying for early admission to Eckman. The East Coast isn't really my scene. Neither are all the socialites they are dead set on me becoming besties with. Thanks, but no thanks."

The intensity in Trey's eyes amplified the sparks shooting in every direction inside me. He opened and closed his mouth a few times before saying, "Eckman is my first choice. It's the best private college in the state and I don't want to go too far from home."

My eyes never left his as we both leaned closer to the table. The electric charge between us kicked up another notch. I swallowed against the drought in my mouth. After a minute, he rubbed his cheeks, evidently putting his tough guy mask back in place.

One step forward, two steps back. At this rate, it's going to be years before he makes a move.

I stared at him, wondering what the hell it would take for him to trust me. He didn't even look at the cup before tossing the quarter down. After seeing it land inside, I groaned.

Trey laughed. "Now, now, doll, don't get disgruntled. If I'm feeling generous, I might let you have a turn."

My body recoiled and I downed my beer to ease the panic washing over me. With my hands curled together, I snapped, "It really pisses me off when you call me doll."

"That's a weak admission and obvious from the daggers you're giving me, but I'll take it since I'm going to kick your ass at this game anyway," Trey replied with a twinkle in his eyes.

As he picked up the quarter, I ran my foot along the inside of his leg. His face flushed and the quarter bounced off the edge of the glass and over to me. My lips quirked into a smug smile as I threw it down perfectly so it landed in the middle of the cup.

Trey sighed. "I know how to dance, and not just club dancing. I'm talking the waltz, tango, salsa, and so on and so forth." He finished his beer and shook a finger at me. "You *cannot* tell Mia."

I made the sign of the cross over my heart. "I swear. Out of curiosity, how did you end up learning ballroom dances? I learned them for debutante reasons, but you don't strike me as the type of guy who would willingly take lessons."

Trey eyed the Sam Adams Utopia. "What the hell is in this one?"

"The bottle is weird, but just give it a try. I think you'll end up liking it."

"I'll take your word for it, but if it tastes like shit, I'm tossing it and starting over. There's no way I'm downing something that tastes like ass during a drinking game."

I wanted an answer to my question, but let it go and chucked the quarter on the table. It fell into the center of the glass again and I gave him a playful grin. He rolled his eyes and took a large gulp of the high-end beer. After it was gone, he picked up the Sam Adams bottle and gave it a nod of approval before filling his glass with another round of it.

He leaned back and the proud look taking over his face was hard to miss as he said, "I can take an engine apart and put it back together without any help."

"Impressive. I don't know much about the inner workings of a car, but I'm aces at making sure I pay attention to all the warning lights."

Trey chuckled. "I'm not surprised. What kind of car do you drive?"

"2007 Lexus IS 350," I replied, tensing up.

He let out a low whistle. "That's quite the ride for a sixteen-year-old girl."

My eyes drifted to the skyline and the muscles in my shoulders tightened up. As the ache in my heart spread to my chest, my throat began to close.

"Yeah, it wasn't my idea, but that's what you get when your parents would rather throw cash at you than spend time with you. I turned seventeen at the beginning of August. As usual, they missed my birthday, among other things over the summer, so that was their fucked-up attempt at an apology."

"Happy belated birthday. What day was it?"

"Thanks. It was the first, so it's not like it's that difficult to remember, but that just goes to show you where I rate with them."

My body trembled at the rawness of my own words. It sucked more than anything to say them out loud, but it was probably one of the only ways I'd get through to him. He ran his fingers along my quivering chin before cupping my face. The softness in his eyes and the way he caressed my cheeks kept my tears from falling.

"I didn't mean to upset you. I'm sorry. Sometimes parents can suck."

"Yeah, well, if they handed out awards for it, my parents would be the unopposed winners every time."

He ran his thumbs across the corners of my eyes. Once he seemed satisfied I wouldn't have a meltdown, he released my face, sat back, and looked around the rooftop while tapping his fingers together. There was a vulnerability to him I'd never seen before as he disclosed, "My dad isn't around a lot, but my mom more than makes up for his absence."

"How come he's not at home much?"

I laced my fingers through his and we both heaved in our next breath as the electricity around us became palpable.

"He owns a construction company and works nonstop to support our family. Most days, he's up before the rest of us to get to all of his jobs and returns after everyone is in bed. It doesn't let him off the hook for missing out on most of our lives, but I get it."

"At least what he's doing is for the betterment of your family. My parents show up for things, but it doesn't mean they want to. I'm pretty much a check on their to-do list and not one they really want to deal with at any point in the day."

"It sounds like your folks bite the big one. There are a lot of people in this world who shouldn't have kids. Far too many of them do it for all the wrong reasons."

You're telling me. I definitely fall under that statistic. Wait a second. Are we having a conversation and touching for more than five seconds?

Trey seemed to sense the end of that topic, released my hand, and filled our glasses with Crown this time.

"When's your birthday?"

He smirked. "Halloween."

My jaw dropped before I sputtered, "Seriously? Doesn't it suck having a birthday on a day everyone gets candy?"

Trey shrugged. "Nah. When I was a kid, my mom always made sure my birthday came before any trick-or-treating. She throws one hell of a party."

"That's really awesome. I've never had a birthday party," I admitted, ignoring the pinpricks sweeping across my upper body.

His eyes widened in disbelief. "How's that even possible?"

I looked away. "Well, let me rephrase it. There's always been a party on or around my birthday, but it wasn't for *me*. It was always for *them*."

Trey cracked his knuckles. "That's fucking bullshit. I'm really sorry, Bri."

I didn't want the ache in my chest to grow any bigger, so I kept my mouth shut. He cleared his throat and gestured at the full glasses. I twirled the quarter on the table and tossed it down. It rattled around the edges of the glass before dropping in the middle. A squeal of delight slipped out of me and I raised my hands in victory. Trey rolled his eyes and finished off the contents of his glass.

"I have six tattoos and both ears pierced, along with my tongue . . . but I think you knew about that one already," Trey joked, a cocky smirk spreading across his face.

I blushed. "Ah, yeah, I spotted that when we met. It was hard to miss. How long have you had it?"

He stuck his tongue out and my cheeks flamed even more. My mind drifted to what it would feel like between my legs and I crossed them to cease the rampant tingles spreading through my lower body.

"A couple of months."

"Did it hurt? What made you decide to get it?"

"I try to do something new every few months," Trey answered with a mischievous grin.

"Aren't there laws about a minor getting piercings and tattoos?" I asked, crinkling my eyebrows.

Trey snorted. "Those things don't apply on the south side. It's all about who you know."

"I see. That's a lot of ink for a sixteen-year-old guy. I'm shocked your mom allowed it. I don't see any bling in your ears now," I pointed out.

"My folks weren't thrilled, we'll leave it at that. As far as the studs go, I take them out when football starts. Unlike some players, I don't need bling on during a game. It's a diss to the game. If your skills aren't enough to make a presence out there, then you shouldn't be playing in the first place."

"I totally agree with you. If you're not playing for the love and integrity of the game, then you have no business suiting up for a team."

His eyes were inquisitive. "The word around school is you're one of the best soccer players in the state. It kind of sucks that our games always fall on the same days. It'd be nice to see if all the hype is true."

A shy smile fell from my lips. "I do okay. I'm pissed I've missed your first two games. Our matches have been so far upstate we haven't made it back in enough time to see *you* in action. We've only managed to catch the last few minutes and the second string is in because we're up by forty. It's clear you're one hell of a quarterback. Our football team was horrible before you joined it."

His gaze drifted over downtown Chicago. When he focused on me, his face was emotionless. "I can't help but wonder if that's why I really got into Chamberlain. Coach says it was other things, but I'm not sure if I believe him. I guess it doesn't matter. If it gets me to where I need to go, I'll keep my mouth shut and outperform everyone on the field *and* in the classroom."

I grasped his hand. Making sure he saw the sincerity in my eyes, I kept them locked on him. "You don't have anything to prove. You're an amazing guy and anyone who can't see that doesn't deserve a second of your time. I don't know exactly what you're going through, but just keep in mind most people are battling something you know nothing about too. We all have our demons."

The glare in his eyes intensified as he snapped, "That may be true, but it's *not* an acceptable excuse for treating someone like shit. There are plenty of ways to deal with whatever is eating away at you without making someone miserable for your own sense of relief."

"Agreed, but not everyone is as you paint them, and you're just as guilty as they are when you judge people the way you do. If you take away anything from tonight, I hope it's that much and that you realize you were wrong about me."

He wiggled his hand free and pounded a shot of tequila. Seeing the way his neck muscles twitched in time with the way his nostrils flared, I'd struck a chord, but he needed to hear it. I tossed back a shot of whiskey, left my glass empty, and relished the burning sensation in my windpipe.

An uncomfortable silence descended upon us. After listening to a few car horns blast and several people shouting at whatever traffic accident happened, I picked up the quarter, but flicked it in the air rather than throwing it at the glass.

With the way my last turn went, any more questions would result in an argument and that was the last thing I wanted. Something told me our tempers would only flare even higher if we continued to drink. Neither of us seemed to have a filter when it came to certain subjects.

A loud growl erupted from my stomach. Trey barked out a laugh and my cheeks turned bright red. "It sounds like you're hungry. I don't know about you, but I could use some food to soak up the alcohol."

I gave him a sheepish smile. "Yeah, you're probably right. I'd rather not go to school tomorrow with a hangover."

Trey put the bottles and glasses on the tray and stood up. Before we headed for the first floor, he set everything on the bar and stood in the center of the room. His face had a longing to it while he stared at all the games.

Linking my arm with his, I teased, "We can come back and play later. I wouldn't miss a chance to kick your ass."

His eyebrows furrowed cutely together and he was back to biting the insides of his cheeks to keep quiet. I jabbed my fingers in his side, but rather than laugh, Trey winced. He smoothed out his face to try and cover up his pain, but it did very little to ease the iciness blasting through me. I opened my mouth to ask what happened, but he gave me a stern shake of the head.

I twisted a long strand of hair with my free hand. With each step we took, he seemed to sense my anxiety and brushed his fingers soothingly along the inside of my arm. The fiery sensations he created with each stroke helped, but I still felt guilty for causing him pain.

He stopped mid-step and took both my hands. "You didn't do it on purpose. Stop beating yourself up. I would hate for you to have a meltdown."

I released a soft laugh. "No, we wouldn't want that, now would we?"

His lopsided grin sent a warmness through me that had nothing to do with my raging hormones and everything to do with the way his grip tightened with each word he spoke. My body tingled in all the right places and it was a damn shame when we started moving again. He kept one hand interlocked with mine on our way down the last few stairs.

I'd be lying to myself if I didn't admit that whatever was happening between us was a once-in-a-lifetime kind of thing. The way my heart raced at the prospect of Trey becoming a centerpiece in my world was as exhilarating as it was terrifying.

There was so much more he needed to know about me, but I wasn't ready to tell him yet, especially with all the things he already dealt with at Chamberlain. Sebastian and his lackeys were nowhere near leaving Trey alone. With their persistence, it seemed like something more was underneath it all than just screwing with him for shits and giggles.

I shuddered at the thought, knowing *very* well the lengths some socialites would go to get what they wanted. Trey squeezed my hand, but I remained quiet. He didn't need to know about that fleeting thought. When he learned some of my secrets, there was no telling how he'd react. I wasn't about to risk having him walk away before I even had a real shot with him.

CHAPTER 7

BRI

Once we reached the landing, Trey released my arm and looked around for Micah and Mia, but they were nowhere in sight. Savage Garden was playing on the surround sound. There was a good possibility they were trying to seal the deal tonight.

With his hands grasped behind his neck, his T-shirt came up a little in the front, displaying his glorious, washboard abs underneath. After catching me in an all-out stare, his mouth curled into a knowing grin. Heat pooled in my cheeks and I darted into the kitchen. I fanned them in a vain attempt to get a fraction of control over myself or I really would end up attacking Trey with my mouth.

I wanted to toss out a sassy zinger to wipe that damn cocky smirk off his face, but words failed me. My brain was working overtime to ensure I kept my hands to myself. He sat down on a stool at the island while I sifted through the freezer. My face welcomed the cool air, along with the rest of my overheated body. Once I was positive I'd be able to turn around and not rip off his clothes, I grabbed a pepperoni pizza and closed the door.

I retrieved the Pizzaz from a cupboard below me, set the timer, and put the pizza on it. After turning on the oven, I rummaged through the cabinets until I had a large bowl and all the ingredients for chocolate chip cookies. A throwback song from ten years ago came on the radio and I sang along to the lyrics of "Name" while mixing together the batter.

After adding some extra chocolate chips, I did a taste test. It melted in my mouth. The oven beeped and I slid in two cookie sheets, grabbed what was left of the dough, sat across from Trey, and trailed my index finger along the inside of the bowl.

He rested his elbows on the island. "Well, aren't you a constant surprise? I wouldn't have pegged you as a baker or someone who listens to rock bands from the nineties."

I raised an eyebrow and licked the dough from my finger. "I told you I'm not like everyone else, but you're hell-bent on believing otherwise."

Trey tugged at his shaggy hair. "Oh, give me a break already. Most girls our age have shitty taste in music and would rather be doing anything else than cooking."

I giggled. "Why should I when you haven't done so for me?"

Seeing the scowl on his face as he mumbled how confounding girls were under his breath made me laugh even harder. I dove into the bowl again, ran my tongue along my lips as provocatively as possible, stuck my finger in my mouth, and swirled it around.

He leaned closer with a ravenous look in his eyes that made my heart pound against my chest. His face was inches from mine and I sucked in a quick breath before closing my eyes. Electric sparks surrounded us and sent my entire body into a frenzy. My heart raced as I waited for our lips to connect.

After feeling cold batter on my nose, I opened my eyes to see his face on the flushed side as he licked his finger clean. I glared at him and smeared a glob of cookie dough across his cheek.

"You don't want to start a food fight with me. I'll kick your ass," Trey boasted, aiming the spoon at me for good measure.

Before I could snatch the bowl from him, the Pizzaz timer went off. A playful grin spread across my face as I declared, "Saved by the bell, but this isn't over."

He rolled his eyes and dabbed at the batter. I slid the pizza onto a plate, sliced it up, and placed it on the island. Trey took a piece, but steam was still pouring from it. He bobbled it between his hands. I retrieved a couple of paper plates, stuck a roll of paper towels under my arm, and opened the fridge to get ranch dressing and some sodas.

"You're a smart guy, so I didn't think I needed to tell you it was hot. Looks like you've put that together," I mused, giving him a plate and a few paper towels.

Trey looked between me and his pizza. I poured some ranch on the edge of my plate, swiped the crust across it, and took a small bite. After polishing off his piece, he dove in for another. The oven timer beeped and I turned around to pull the golden-brown cookies out. Chocolate chip aroma filled the kitchen as I arranged a dozen on a plate and set them between us.

"This little morsel of heaven tastes fucking amazing," Trey murmured after devouring one of the cookies.

"I think that's the first compliment you've ever given me. I'm guessing that was pretty hard for you," I quipped, batting my eyes.

Trey tossed a slice of pizza at me. I looked at the streak of marinara on the corner of my sweatshirt. Flashing his dimples, Trey retorted, "That's what you get for that damn sassy mouth of yours."

"It's so on!" I yelled, soaking what was left of my piece in ranch and throwing it at him.

It landed in the center of his chest, leaving a huge red and white smudge, before falling onto his lap. He narrowed his eyes, picked up the bottle of ranch, and squirted it at me. I attempted to move out of the way, but wasn't fast enough, and a blob of it ended up in my hair.

We ran around the island, tossed a few more slices at one another, and drained the ranch bottle. The wide grin on his face matched my own as we took another lap around the kitchen. With ammo running low, I snatched my unopened soda, shook it, tapped the cap, and was about to open it. Trey bolted from the wall between the kitchen and dining room where he attempted to shield himself and ran into the living room.

He waved his hands in the air. "Listen, let's just talk about this before things get out of hand. I don't want you to get into any trouble for the damage we'll do if this food fight continues. I play to win at *everything*."

I raised both eyebrows and geared up to spray him. "*So do I*. I'm more than fine with whatever destruction we cause. The cleanup will be well worth it."

Just as the soda was about to leave the can, his cell rang and I swore he sighed in relief. Trey held up a hand as he retrieved it from his back pocket. His wide grin disappeared in an instant. "Hey, Mom, it's not even close to curfew, so I know that's not why you're calling. Is everything okay?"

Seeing the worry in his eyes grow made my breath catch in my throat. He gripped the back of his neck with his free hand while he paced around the living room. "It's okay, Mom. I'll get home as soon as I can and clean up the mess. Keep the girls in their room so it doesn't have a chance to spread to Thomas and Tory."

Trey hung up, shoved his cell in his front pocket, grabbed the remote on the coffee table, and turned off the surround sound. "Micah, wrap up whatever shit you got going on. We need to bounce *right now*."

He ran a hand through his hair and groaned after seeing marinara on his palm. I secured his other hand in mine, led us down the hallway, and into the bathroom. He cursed under his breath the entire way. For Micah and Mia's sake, I hoped they heeded the warning to wrap up their make out session or things were going to get ugly.

After turning on the water, I ran a washcloth under the faucet before tossing it over to Trey. He scrubbed his arms and neck clean. With each swipe, his muscles twitched nonstop. I had no doubt it was to rein in his growing frustration, but I wasn't all that focused on his mood. His arms had such definition to them. As I watched him run the thin fabric across every detailed line, it was a miracle I didn't fall in the tub. Steam swirled around us and it could've been from the hot water or me. I wasn't ruling out that possibility.

I peeled my eyes away from him, retrieved the shower head, and motioned for Trey to lean over the tub. He remained still, his eyes wary.

"I'm just trying to help. I doubt you want to deal with dried-up marinara in your hair on top of what sounds like an emergency at home," I pointed out, settling a hand on my hip.

He didn't seem all that thrilled, but pulled his shirt over his head anyway. His jeans and black boxers hugged his hips in all the right ways and the lower half of my body dampened. Spotting the dark purple bruises covering his ribs and sides made my heart sink. I wanted to lick every detailed curve of his eight-pack, but couldn't see past the amount of contusions on him.

With all the padding guys wore for football, I found it hard to believe it was from hits he took on the field. The food in my stomach mixed with the alcohol in my system and I swallowed a few times to keep everything down. My eyes circled the room before settling on his anxious gray ones. His entire body was so stiff—like he'd turned into stone.

Being as gentle as possible, I ran my fingers across one of the darker marks. His face was guarded as he took my hand and held it tightly. I wanted him to tell me why he looked like he'd been used as a punching bag. Trey squeezed my hand, almost as if it was a silent thank you for not questioning him about it, before leaning over the tub.

I ran the spout over his hair. Once it was damp, I added some shampoo and massaged his scalp before repeating the process with the conditioner. With each stroke, the tension in his body lessened, and it was a sucker punch to the stomach when I stopped to rinse the suds out.

As he stood up, his eyes remained locked on mine. I retrieved a fluffy white towel from the vanity and handed it to him. While he dried his hair, I picked up his T-shirt from the floor. It was a shame he had to put it back on. I wasn't quite done studying his tattoos.

Five out of the six he mentioned were between his chest, arms, and back. His Irish heritage was evident in a few of them while the others spoke to his love for sports. The Celtic cross on his back surprised me the most. He didn't seem all that religious. I wanted to smack myself for that assumption. Our talk from earlier ran through my mind and I needed to try just as hard as him not to jump to conclusions. We still had so much to learn about each other.

Trey snapped his fingers to get my attention. My lips curled into a sheepish smile as I handed him his shirt. After seeing the red blobs on it, he grumbled, "I can't wear this home. The stains will stress my mom out even more. Do you have some baking soda?"

My eyes fell to the floor. He tilted my chin up and arched an eyebrow for an answer. "Um, I'm sure we do. Is there anything else I can do to help? Is everything okay at home?"

He waved off my concern and added a reassuring smile, but it didn't really hit his eyes. There was a great deal of unease in them. "Things will be fine once I get there."

I narrowed mine for a better explanation. He was trying to act indifferent to whatever was going on, but I could tell there was something more to it.

He sighed. "My dad is still on a job and the twins came down with the flu going around at school. It's a pukefest and she needs help before the boys catch it. I'm sure they'll have it by the end of the week, but it's easier when it's spread out. It's a nightmare when all four of them are sick at the same time."

"Seeing as I've never really seen you look quite this pale, I'm guessing that's not all. You don't have to tell me, but I'm here if you *want* to."

His eyes flickered around the room, but eventually returned to mine. "I think my mom's pregnant again. She's been sick a lot lately and worn down more than usual. Granted, keeping track of five of us and Mia will do that to her, but it seems like more. I think she's trying to keep it under wraps until this bid my dad has on a major development in our neighborhood goes through. It's not like they don't want more kids, but I think it'll be easier for her to announce another mouth will need to be fed if he lands the job. The payout from it isn't something he's obtained before, so it's kind of a big deal."

It was hard to decipher what he was saying with the rambling way it all came out. He ran one hand through his wet hair repeatedly while the other traced the tattoo on his right arm. I'd never seen him so anxious and it warmed my heart to have him drop his guard.

My hand drifted to his cheek. "If you're worried I'll tell Mia, I won't. You need to know what you share with me in confidence will remain between us."

Trey cupped his hand over mine and gave it a gentle squeeze. Time stood still and the electric charge from earlier was stronger than ever as we moved closer together. He rested his forehead on mine and released an unsteady breath as his other hand drifted to my face. Our hearts raced together, creating a song all in its own that would forever remain imprinted in my brain. My body hummed as I placed my free hand on his waistline and leaned forward to close the gap between us. Just as our lips were about to connect, the bathroom door burst open.

We jumped away from each other. The shock on Micah's face was unmistakable as he gripped his backward baseball cap. "Whoa, my bad, bro. It sounded like we needed to roll right away, but if I'm interrupting something, I can get back to Mia and let you guys continue on with whatever you plan on doing in here."

My face flamed hotter than it had all night. I had no doubt Trey's face was a nice shade of pink. I'd been walked in on plenty of times in the past, but this time was *way* different. I clamped my teeth over my lower lip to prevent myself from saying anything stupid. There were no words for the shit-eating grin Micah pinned on us. My brain wasn't really functioning on all cylinders, so I couldn't rule out a slip of the tongue and bit my lip even harder.

Trey cleared his throat and kept his hands in front of him. "Yeah, we should get going."

My mouth curled into a shy smile before I said, "I'll make sure you get your T-shirt back stain-free."

"Right, a shirt. I need to have one of those on before I go home. Micah, give me yours," Trey demanded as they walked out the door.

My gaze drifted to the ceiling while I walked behind them, pondering just why God would put me through such hell to get a first kiss from a guy. Micah chuckled as he took off his black Bulls sweatshirt and the red Nike T-shirt he had on underneath.

I noticed he had a few tattoos, but they weren't anything like Trey's. Some of his looked like gang symbols. I saw why Mia thought he was so appealing. He wasn't nearly as sexy as Trey, but he was built in his own right. Micah handed his shirt to Trey on our way into the living room.

Mia was on the couch with a notebook on her lap and a textbook open next to her. She did a double-take after seeing Micah's bare chest. Judging by the salacious grin he gave her, he left his sweatshirt off on purpose. Mia blushed and gestured for him to put it on before flicking a finger between Trey and me. She opened her mouth, but snapped it shut just as fast. I glanced at Trey, who was glaring daggers at her.

"You ladies have a nice rest of your night. Micah, let's go," Trey said in a sharp tone.

Micah put on quite the show while tugging on his sweatshirt. Mia's cheeks blazed to a deep shade of red when Micah leaned over to give her a deep kiss. I about decked him over the head. I was one unsatisfied mess and it was his damn fault. Seeing those two have no shame while they devoured one another's mouths didn't help one bit. Trey stormed over to them, yanked Micah up by the back of his hood, and dragged him away.

Without another word, they disappeared out the door. I sat down next to Mia, grabbed the pillow next to me, and screamed into it. She took it, pointed to the stains and mess in my hair, and coyly asked, "So, how was your night?"

I scowled at her while shaking my head. Mia did nothing to hide her amusement before she motioned for me to get cleaned up. Taking a cold shower was probably the only thing to rid my body from the tingling sensations still firing through it.

Worst. Timing. Ever. Damn you, Micah! What does a girl need to do for the stars to align for that first kiss? I don't think I've ever wanted to kiss a boy as bad as I want to kiss Trey. Please, God, help a girl out!

CHAPTER 8

TREY

The Calculus equation in front of me made no sense, but that probably had more to do with not being able to focus for more than five seconds without Bri's gorgeous body popping into my head. I was on day five of having that damn vixen capture my every thought and it was getting harder to shun her from my mind.

In that purple tank top she had on Tuesday night, her breasts looked absolutely amazing. I wanted to suck on them until her nipples were nice and hard before licking my way south. That scenario ran on repeat for me. If I wasn't thinking about every different position I wanted to have sex with her in, my mind drifted to our conversation.

That damn sassy mouth of hers proved to be a force to be reckoned with, but it was nice to talk to a girl who had something *real* to say. I already knew her bluntness on some matters would be hard to swallow, but I loved that she was always genuine. Everything she relayed came from her heart. Bri was as beautiful inside as she was on the surface and I was out of reasons to stay away from her.

I know I need to keep my distance, but the struggle has become way too real. I've never wanted anyone as much as I want her.

My dick stirred to life when her scorching green eyes flashed through my mind. I cursed under my breath at the control she had over my body without even knowing it, readjusted my jeans, and thought about football plays to halt the blood charging south.

"Knock, knock," Mia said, poking her head around my door. "If it doesn't work to do a driving lesson this afternoon, we can do it some other time. I know you've had a lot on your plate. Are the kids feeling any better? I should've come with you to help."

Thinking about all the vomit I cleaned up over the past few days was all I needed for my hard-on to disappear. Once it was gone, I stuffed my notebook in my book, grabbed my keys and Cubs hat, and met Mia in the hallway.

"It made its way around the house. I'm happy my mom is finally back on her feet. And don't worry about not coming by. If you did, you would've ended up getting it. Trust me, you don't want to play in a game with a hundred and two temp while puking your guts out," I replied, picking up some clothes and toys.

She paused to straighten out one of the many pictures of us kids over the years lining our cream walls, then took the clothes from me to put in the bathroom. I put the toys I collected into the boys' and girls' rooms.

A guilty look descended upon her face. Mia fidgeted with the end of her pink Lions soccer T-shirt. "I still should've been here to help you. Between football practice, school, and everything you do around here, you're going to run yourself into the ground sooner than you think."

My health was the least of my concerns. After the boys went back to school, Thomas came home with a black eye. He claimed he was playing football, but I didn't believe him. The split lip Tory sported the same day made it clear more kids were giving them trouble, but neither of them would tell me the truth about it. Short of holding them upside down and shaking it out of them, I had gotten nowhere on figuring out why they were suddenly targets.

Having them get roughed up at school didn't sit well with me. My gut screamed it wasn't a coincidence, especially with all the shit I dealt with from Sebastian and his toadies. Until I had something to connect it all, I intended to keep it to myself. My mom had more than enough to deal with and I didn't want to stress her out even more.

I put on my baseball cap, keeping the brim of it low. I narrowed my eyes on Mia. "It was probably best for everyone that you stayed with Bri. She needed the support and it kept you from getting sick."

Mia scrunched her eyebrows together. Her frustration was evident by the crease in her forehead that loved to make an appearance when she was pissed, but she kept her mouth shut on our way downstairs. Once we reached the living room, I couldn't help but smile. My parents were snuggled together on the couch watching an old black-and-white movie.

"We'll be back in a couple of hours. Do you need anything while we're out?" I asked, giving my mom a kiss on the cheek and patting my dad on the back.

He held my mom a little tighter and replied, "No, the rest of the kids are down the street for a birthday party. I'll pick them up in a few hours before cooking dinner for everyone. If you won't be back in time, please give us a call."

It really sucked that my dad worked all the time. When he was around, he was so damn good to my mom and us. Whenever he walked into the house, he insisted my mom stay off her feet and he did everything from braid the girls' hair, helped the boys with their homework, and played the latest *Madden* game with me. It didn't happen often, but I sure as hell appreciated it when it did.

"Assuming Mia doesn't kill us once she's behind the wheel, we should be back in time for supper," I joked, chuckling.

Mia jabbed a few fingers in my side and I hissed in a breath. My ribs were a little tender from the hits I took during Friday night's game and the puking I did all day before it. Dad studied my every move. Keeping my arms crossed, my face remained indifferent. The less than pleased look on his face was all I needed to see to know he'd bring it up later. Whenever it looked like I was in any pain, he attributed it to fighting.

"Just try to stay out of trouble. You remember what I told you about women drivers, right?" Dad asked in a teasing tone.

I smirked. "Sure do. Best advice ever, old man. We'll see you in a bit."

"That advice better have been we're excellent behind the wheel and we only humor a man by letting you think you're teaching us a thing or two about cars," Mom spoke up.

She winked at us and tapped Dad's stomach. He gave her hand a loving kiss and murmured, "Yes, dear, I do believe it was something along those lines."

"That's what I thought." She gave his cheek a light peck and gestured for us to go. "You two be careful. I love you both."

Mia's wide smile matched mine on our way out of the house, across the freshly-cut grass, and over to my Acura. As I passed by the spoiler, I stopped to make sure the lightning stripes Micah and I put on earlier this week were holding up.

Seeing they hadn't peeled, I opened my door. "I'll drive us over to Englewood. You can learn the basics in one of the parking lots over there before taking on the roads around here and the interstate. We'll tackle that on your next lesson."

After she got in, Mia looked between me, the stick shift, and dashboard with a great deal of distress in her eyes. "I'm not so sure about this anymore. I doubt you'll be very forgiving if I crash your car."

"Driving a stick isn't as hard as people think. With me as a teacher, there's no way in hell you'll get in an accident. When I'm done teaching you, you'll be able to fly around these streets like a precision driver," I boasted, cranking the ignition.

Keeping the right amount of pressure on the clutch and gas before shifting into reverse, I backed out of the driveway and turned onto the side road leading to the interstate. I quickly moved into first and zipped down the road. Mia watched in awe as I seamlessly handled the gears and drifted around the corner.

"Are you sure going to Englewood is the best place for us to go?" Mia asked.

"It's the only place with plenty of abandoned buildings and parking lots, so it's the best location for you to actually get everything down so you can get your license on the first try. Besides, you know I won't let anything happen to you. If something looks sketchy, I'll get us out of there before you can blink," I reassured.

I slid between two SUVs, veered right, and exited onto the freeway. The way she fiddled with the bracelets on her wrists nonstop wasn't the best sign that my car would make it through this tutorial without getting some sort of scratch, but her anxious behavior wasn't anything new. She always doubted herself and I blamed Chase. Over the years, Micah and I had done our best to try to get her to have more faith in herself, but it wasn't all that easy with him treating her like a piece of garbage every chance he got.

My grip on the wheel tightened as I thought about how shitty Chase treated Mia. He was like Jekyll and Hyde most days, but what was worse was how he looked at her. Whenever he did, his eyes had a coldness to them that rubbed me the wrong way.

I had no doubt the guy had a dark side and secrets to him, but I wasn't entirely sure what lengths he'd stoop to when it came to making Mia miserable, so I never dug too deep into it. I shoved those thoughts out of my head and shifted into fifth gear. It wouldn't do Mia any good if I was in a pissy mood while trying to teach her how to drive.

After coasting down the freeway for a bit, I took one of the exits into the Englewood area and scanned around for the perfect lot. The more space I had to work with, the less likely I'd be repairing my car. As much as I loved my wrench time with Micah, I wasn't a fan of dropping money into a vehicle I didn't plan on having in a few years. The plan was to get my black '69 Camaro running before I left for college.

"So, what's going on with you and Bri? It looked like you guys had a great time the other night, but you haven't spoken to her since. Why are you playing this hot and cold game? You like her. Just ask her out already."

I frowned. "It's not that simple and you know it. Do you really think her parents are going to let her date a guy like me? From everything you told me about them, they hate anyone and anything to do with the south side. It's shocking they let you two be friends."

Mia sighed. "I'll admit, they're a piece of work, but it isn't about them. It's about Bri. You need to give her more credit than you do. She's not going to let anyone tell her who she can date, especially her folks. If she takes pride in anything, it's proving them wrong whenever they underestimate her, which is pretty much all the time."

I smirked. "I hear what you're saying, but it's not really any of your concern. I also won't be told what to do. If it's in the cards for us, then it'll happen. And in case you forgot, I haven't had a lot of spare time in the past few days. Not talking to Bri wasn't personal."

Mia shook her head and grumbled, "You still don't have a clue about women. Just try and be civil to her tomorrow at school."

When we rolled up to a red stoplight, I flipped on the radio. Loud bass from my speakers as "Sugar, We're Goin' Down" blared through our open windows made the punk in the red Ferrari next to us shake his head. I did a double-take. He seemed oddly familiar.

Driving around in a car like that on the south side was asking for trouble. After checking my rearview mirror and spotting Kieran Fitzpatrick in his light blue Mazda RX behind me, I cursed under my breath. I could tell by the malevolent look in his eyes that he was going to fuck up the dude next to me.

It was always best to avoid him and his brothers and not just because their dad was a major mobster. They ran the gangs around here and weren't known for showing mercy toward anyone who didn't belong. Plenty of wealthy and prominent people drifted over to our side of the city. I suspected most of them wanted an in with the mob—if anything, for protection—but it wasn't all that easy to get in with them.

The Fitzpatricks were regulars at Chase's bar and made their disdain for the rich and elite around Chicago known. I'd seen firsthand what they did to get *that point* across. I wasn't afraid of much, but those guys were a different kind of crazy. You didn't want to be on their bad side. Once the light turned green, I stepped on the gas and left them behind us.

Mia glanced over her shoulder and the color drained from her face. "Now, I'm really not sure about this whole driving thing. Why did we have to see Kieran? That's got to be like an omen or something. That kid is going to be lucky if he makes it out of the south side alive."

"Don't worry about it," I replied, doing my best to remain indifferent.

After crossing through the next intersection, I swerved into an empty parking lot across from a bunch of rundown buildings. The lot was about the size of a football field. Mia only had the large abandoned brick building off to the left of us that could really mess up my Acura and that kind of damage was at least repairable. I shut off the car, got out, and went over to Mia's side to open her door. She rubbed her sweaty hands down her holey jeans and looked at me as she got out, still as uncertain as ever.

I smirked before swapping places with her. "You'll do fine. Just take a few deep breaths. All you need to do is master five different gears. Oh, and try not to hit anything or anyone."

She rounded the car and hopped in on the driver's side. "I'm not making any promises. I barely made it ten feet before stalling Micah's Mustang."

I snorted. "That's more than likely because you two had your tongues stuck down each other's throats. It's hard to shift properly under those circumstances. Seeing the way your cheeks are turning as pink as your shirt, I'm more than right on that assessment."

Mia rolled her eyes. "Well, it's not like we have any alone time anymore, so we tend to make out when we're in his car and we barely have that these days. Your mom had *the talk* with me and she's been keeping close tabs on us."

I put on my seatbelt. "As much as I'd love to razz you some more on this subject, let's stay on point. If you fuck up anything on the Acura, you're paying for it. That might motivate you a little more."

"If anything happens, Micah will fix it, just like he always does when it breaks down. Speaking of fixing things, do I need to worry about this thing blowing up? He said you guys were tinkering with it the other day and added NOS," Mia replied, tugging on her strap to ensure it wouldn't snap free if she ended up crashing.

I gave her a dismissive wave of the hand. "We may have souped things up a little. You're not going to be learning any of those buttons anytime soon. Now, Micah taught you the gears and how the clutch works, right?"

Mia nodded, but turned a little green as she did. I patted her arm reassuringly and she forced a small smile. "Well, the first thing you need to know is that the gears in every car are different. Before we begin, I want you to get a feel for this car."

Her foot eased down on the clutch as she shifted between the various gears. After a few minutes, she seemed to have a feel for them and peered at me for her next set of instructions. The tension in her shoulders faded a little, so that was a start. If she remained as nervous as she was, she'd end up crashing for sure.

"Is it back in neutral?" I inquired. Mia grasped the shifter and nodded once she confirmed it was in place. "Alright, press the clutch down and start the car. Rev the engine a few times before shifting into first gear. The hardest part about driving a stick is finding that medium where the clutch comes up as the gas pedal goes down. Once you figure that out, you'll be good to go."

Mia squealed in delight after she started the car and got it into first gear without stalling. I narrowed my eyes for her to stay focused. She bit her lower lip while upshifting into second. She did a couple of laps around the lot in that gear before I motioned for her to speed up and shift into the next one. As she went from second to third, she lost her footing on the clutch and we came to a screeching halt.

Her face was a cross between frustration and fear as she twisted her hands together and muttered, "Fuck, I'm really sorry, Trey. I didn't mess anything up, did I?"

I shook my head. "You did just fine. Besides, it's my fault. I forgot to tell you the most important thing about driving."

She arched an eyebrow. "And what's that?"

"If you don't feel in control of the car, it will own you and that's not how it works. You need to drive like you own the road and everyone on it," I replied with an encouraging smile.

Mia rolled her shoulders, more determined than ever. Starting the engine with no issue, she had us moving in no time. For the next hour and a half, Mia circled around the parking lot like an eighty-year-old grandma in the lower gears and like she was auditioning for the *Fast and Furious* franchise in the higher ones. She had drifting down and I wasn't sure how to feel about that. Teaching her bad habits probably wasn't the best before she even had a license, but she needed to learn some of those skills to drive our streets.

I was so focused on her not hitting the building on our last turn that I didn't notice Sebastian, Miles, and Aubrey. They had to have just come from Sunday brunch. Polos and khaki cargos weren't something you saw a lot of around here. There was also way too much product in their hair and their over-the-top bling made them even more of an eyesore.

"Shit, this can't be good," I muttered under my breath. Mia lost her focus and stalled the car. She glanced in the side mirror and her face turned stark white. My face was firm as I said, "Stay in the car. I'll deal with these douchebags."

Her lower lip trembled before she hissed, "Let's get out of here. If they're down here, it's to cause trouble with you. They're not worth it."

I strode over to where they were standing in front of their Aston Martin with their arms crossed. Curling my fists together, I cracked my neck. The last thing I needed was to get into another fight, but I wasn't stupid either. The odds of this showdown ending peacefully were slim to none.

Keeping an arm's length between us, I waved my hand around in the air. "I think you guys took a wrong turn. So, if you're not down here for Positano's famous deep dish, I suggest you head back to your side of the city. You have *no idea* what you're dealing with in this neighborhood."

Sebastian shoved my shoulders. "Believe me, we're right where we want to be. I got a call from my older brother and he said he had the shit beat out of him before the dickheads stole his car. I wouldn't put it past you and your delinquent friends to be the ones who did it, especially since he described your piece of shit Acura to perfection."

"Listen, you prick, get your scrawny ass back into your car and head north. If you don't, you'll end up like your brother, but it won't be my fists dishing out the beatdown. It'll be someone far worse than me and the smell of blood is something the guys in gangs on this side of town thrive on."

"You boast about how badass you and your neighborhood are, but I haven't really seen any of it. If that bullshit you pulled on the football field a few weeks ago is all you got, then you should put your tail between your legs and head back to the double-wide."

Miles spat at my feet before taking a swing at me. I saw it from the get-go, sidestepped the attack, and added a karate chop to the back of his head. He barely had enough time to put his hands in front of him to keep from face-planting onto the pavement. Aubrey lunged at me and I extended a leg to send him flying by me.

They rolled around on the ground and groaned, but I remained focused on the asshole across from me. Sebastian crisscrossed his arms and I took several steps back. He ran at me like a bull who just saw a red flag. I held my hands out to brace for the impact as he picked me up and attempted to toss me onto the concrete, but I maneuvered out of his hold, pushed him down, and bashed my fists into his ribs.

After landing a few solid blows, leaving him gasping for air, I wheeled around to see the other two racing toward me. When Sebastian rolled over and grabbed my ankle, I gave his arm a swift kick, forcing him to let go. Each blow I gave these pricks was like downing an energy drink. I'd be able to go several rounds with this circle and not even break a sweat.

"You fucking asshole, is that all you got?" Sebastian bellowed.

"I'm just getting started," I sneered.

Just like linebackers, Miles and Aubrey squared up across from me before they barreled toward me. Their shoulders hit my upper body and I flew backward a few feet. My body connected hard with the asphalt and pain shot in every direction. Ignoring the burning sensation taking over my chest, I wheezed in my next few breaths.

They leaned over me and swung at my head. I brought my hands up to defend myself from their punches. By focusing on smashing in my face, they left their legs open and I took them out by the knees with two calculated kicks. Arching my arm back, I nailed Miles square in the jaw. As he hit the ground, I turned to my right and sucker-punched Aubrey in the gut.

I coughed to catch my breath, retrieved my hat, and wiped my eyes to clear my blurry vision. The three of them were on their feet and dumb enough to charge at me again. As they approached, I lined up to kick Aubrey before moving to my left to land a hard blow to the side of Miles' head and flipping around to land a high kick to Sebastian's shoulder.

As they scrambled to their feet, Micah tore into the parking lot and came to a stop in between my car and Sebastian's, his tires leaving a trail of smoke. He hopped out and raced at Miles, who was a few feet away from me. Micah jumped with both feet in the air to land a kick to Miles' upper body that sent him flying into the windshield of the Aston Martin and leaving several cracks in it.

Sebastian's face filled with rage and he spat out a bunch of blood before he ran at Micah. He bent over just like I did on the football field to send him up in the air and five feet behind him.

I knelt in front of him, socked him in the ribs, and yelled, "I told you, you're out of your league. We're done here."

He remained unmoving. Aubrey jumped from side-to-side before trying to throttle me. I elbowed him hard in the back and he dropped to his knees. Miles zigzagged my way, but stopped mid-stride after hearing gunshots. I didn't need to look around to know who fired those bullets. Kieran and company would be here soon enough.

I grabbed Miles by the collar of his shirt, held him above me, and warned, "If this ass-kicking wasn't enough, then maybe the gang rolling up will be. If you want to get out of here without a few bullets as souvenirs, I suggest you leave."

"Trey, we need to go *now*. It's not our fault if these pussies find themselves in a world of hurt at the hands of the Fitzpatricks." I didn't move. Micah banged the top of his Mustang and screamed, "We're jeopardizing our own safety. Let's roll!"

After hearing sirens with the gunshots, I dropped Miles and sprinted to my car. Mia crawled over to the passenger side, shaking nonstop. I started it up and peeled out of the parking lot. We took a hard left, blowing through the red stoplight, and drifting into oncoming traffic on the opposite side of the road. I cranked the wheel right and dodged through two cars to get back on my side and catch up to Micah.

Mia glanced behind her and shrieked, "Kieran just made a U-turn and nearly took out a few pedestrians on the sidewalk before nailing the back end of Sebastian's car. Why are those dumbasses following us? Do they have a death wish? I thought you told them to leave."

"I did. Sebastian is a fucking idiot. I don't give a shit if he gets smoked by the Fitzpatricks. He's taken this class warfare to a whole new level by coming down here," I shot back and peeked in my side mirror to see him gaining on me.

The cops spotted the Fitzpatricks' Mazdas in the mix and dropped out of the chase. My heart pounded harshly against my chest as I shifted into a higher gear. Micah and I maneuvered our cars between both sides of the road to lose them.

Finally hitting a stretch on the side roads that wasn't completely flooded with traffic, I floored it and contemplated whether to try out the NOS. I grabbed Mia's cell from her trembling hands, hit the speed dial for Micah, and the speakerphone button.

"I'm not a big fan of your new classmates. Not only are they following us, but they're drawing Kieran toward Bridgeport. What's our move?"

Narrowly weaving through a set of cars while dancing along the centerline, I blew through the intersection. For as fast as my heart was hammering against my chest, I knew Mia's had to be beating twice as fast, but she needed to get a handle on it or she'd end up hyperventilating.

I huffed. "We'll have to improvise."

"Alright, follow my lead," Micah instructed.

He whipped around so quickly I barely managed to hit the brakes and make the turn myself without hitting the side of a light pole. I straightened the wheel and gassed it. We coasted down the road for another twenty feet before heading toward the South Shore.

Mia glanced in her side mirror. "We have a good news-bad news situation."

"I know how you just love to tell a story, but now isn't really the time to string it out, sweetheart. What's going on behind us?" Micah asked as nicely as possible, but he didn't really pull it off with the barking way it came across.

She chewed on her lower lip. "Right, sorry. The good news is the Fitzpatricks seemed to have grown bored and stopped following us. The bad news is Sebastian gained an ally and they're going to be in our backseat soon."

My eyes darted to the rearview, and sure as shit, there was another car on our ass. "I should've known that prick was lying to me."

"What are you talking about?"

"It's the Ferrari from earlier. Sebastian said it was his brother and he had the shit kicked out of him and his car stolen. Clearly, that's not the case. I swear I'm going to pummel that jackass so badly he'll need a face transplant," I seethed, gripping the wheel until my knuckles cracked.

"That may not be necessary. We have more company and these cars are on our side," Micah spoke up.

Two Eclipses flanked my sides. The heavy weight sitting on my chest lightened as I saluted them. Logan was behind the wheel of the bright orange one to my left, and Jesse owned the road in the lime green one on my right. Micah slid between Jesse and I. Mia's eyes were wary while she glanced between me and the guys as we motioned our next moves to each other.

Sebastian and his brother tried to keep up with us, but it wasn't possible with the way we swerved in between vehicles at the last second and used the sides of the road as an extra lane. Coming back into a straight line, the boys and I hit the gas as we flew off the interstate and over to the side road running adjacent to the freeway.

Mia gripped the dashboard with one hand and kept a death grip on her seatbelt with the other. "I'd just like to go on record and say, whatever you guys are about to do, I'm one-hundred percent against. We'll end up getting killed if we keep racing around the streets like this. Oh, and the cops are back in the mix again. I assume that has to do with the fact that our average speed for the past five minutes has been a hundred."

"Baby, don't worry about the cops. They'll have their hands full with the pricks behind us. We're coming up on the warehouse that is usually empty. We need to lay low after we pull off our next move," Micah replied in an amused tone.

He sped up to take the lead and Logan followed him. I maintained my speed as Jesse dropped behind me. The adrenaline pumping through my veins was one drug I'd gladly become an addict of for life. There wasn't anything like a street race. The thrill that went with it was like no other. If I wasn't afraid of going to jail, I'd enter them on a regular basis.

Once we traveled a few more blocks and hit an open stretch, I hit the switch for the NOS. Sebastian and his brother struggled to keep up with us. Jesse whipped around at the same time I did and we drove toward them like we were playing chicken.

When we hit the intersection, we cranked our wheels to avoid hitting them head-on, but nailed their bumpers perfectly. They collided and created a traffic jam. The lights changed from yellow to red as we turned around and floored it to catch up with Micah and Logan. Frustrated drivers on all four roads hopped out to yell at them and the cops stopped to deal with the people creating a scene. Neither of us wanted them to spot our plates and activated the NOS. The side road went by in a blur. My heart raced along with the car and I loved every minute of it.

"Now, that's how we roll on the south side!"

Mia didn't share my enthusiasm but smiled nevertheless. We caught up with Micah and Logan just as they turned left into the alley leading to the abandoned warehouse. After Jesse and I pulled in, Logan and Micah shut the doors. The way Mia remained still as a statue made me wonder if she suffered some sort of shock.

I gently nudged her shoulder, flashed a cocky smirk, and teased, "And this stop concludes the Trey Donovan School of Driving. I hope you learned something."

My nonchalant attitude brought her back to earth. Mia punched the side of my arm several times, her eyes a little wild and crazed, as she screeched, "Don't you ever do that to me again! After that whole fiasco, I don't know if I'll ever get my license."

I chuckled while getting out. Micah gave me a shit-eating grin before helping Mia out. Her legs seemed a little wobbly and she leaned into him for support. He whispered in her ear and whatever he said calmed her down because she didn't look like she was about to pass out anymore. I walked over to Logan and Jesse, who were leaning against their cars with their arms crossed.

"It's been a while, Donovan. You know word travels fast on the streets. We were on our way to see you give those preppies the beatdown they deserve for rolling onto our turf, but we missed the show. We couldn't resist joining the chase to help you boys out—not that you really needed it," Logan mused.

"Yeah man, it's been too long. And your help to end that race was more than needed. Thank you," I replied, readjusting my Cubs cap.

Their blank stares caused a familiar weight to resurface in my chest. As I stepped back, they raised their eyebrows for a better explanation. Clasping my hands behind my neck, I took a quick breath. "As far as those asshats go, the only thing I can say is they're stupid fucks, who haven't listened to any of the warnings I've given them so far. Who knows? Maybe the ass-kicking they got might get the point across, but I doubt it's the last we'll see of them."

With Mia tucked into his side, Micah gave both guys an appreciative fist bump. "Trey stood up for our neighborhood and everything it represents, the way he has always done, so maybe you guys can see that the rest of the assholes around here leave him alone. I'd continue to try and do it, but that requires going to school on a regular basis, and that's just become daunting for me."

Mia shot him a disapproving look, but he ignored it. She gazed between me and the other guys warily. Logan pulled me in for a bro hug. "I'm sorry about the shit you went through this past summer. I hope you realize it wasn't anything personal when I didn't offer any support."

I stepped away. "It's all good. Dealing with the people around here who want to have a go-round with me doesn't faze me anymore. It's these rich fuckers who think they own the world that have really become the issue. They're lucky the Fitzpatricks showed up when they did."

Jesse shuffled over and gave me a high-five. "We got your back. We'll deal with anyone else giving you a hard time. They should've never turned their backs on you in the first place. If you need us at all, you know we're only a phone call away."

My cell vibrated and I groaned after seeing the time. "Hey, Dad, we lost track of time, but we're heading home now. I'm sorry I didn't call," I answered in a rush.

Dad released a heavy sigh. "Don't lie to me, Trey. We've already heard from several sources you were in a fight with some kids who have lawyers who will sue our ass before you can even blink. What the hell were you thinking, son?"

As I processed the severity of the situation, my heart dropped. "I'm sorry. I swear I wasn't looking for any trouble. They came at me. Before I knew it, one thing led to another and punches were being thrown."

"We'll talk more about this when you get home. Get your ass back here safely with Mia. Your mom and I will be waiting to talk to both of you," Dad snapped, hanging up.

I gave Mia a pained look. "We better say our goodbyes. My parents want to talk to us. They know about what just went down and to say they're pissed is an understatement. I'm sorry you got wrapped up in it."

Mia shook her head, muttered several choice words under her breath, and kissed Micah on the cheek. "You should get home too. If his parents are ready to read us the riot act, your parents are going to do the same to you. You're usually in enough hot water with them as it is."

Logan and Jesse didn't need to say a word for us to know they felt bad for the three of us. As I drove away, not looking forward to what was waiting for me one bit, I took the smallest amount of comfort in knowing I'd gotten a few allies back. After what went down today, I needed them more than ever.

CHAPTER 9

BRI

"Are you out of your freaking mind? You're going to kill us before we make it to the party. I don't know much about driving, but I'm pretty sure you're not supposed to use your knees to steer the car," Mia pointed out and tried to grab the wheel.

I rolled my eyes and swatted her hands away before putting the finishing touches on my eyeshadow. Once my eyelids were rocking my smoky, yet mysterious look, I tossed my makeup into my purse and focused on the road. My face now complemented my multi-colored sundress. Aside from her scowl, Mia looked amazing in her strapless black dress.

"You really need to relax. You've been on edge for weeks. If you're still stressing out over being walked in on with Micah, you need to let it go. It happens to all of us at one point or another. And by the way, there are *plenty* of uses for your knees. Steering a car isn't even in my top ten," I said, jabbing my tongue to the side of my cheek.

Her face flushed a deep shade of red and I poked her until she started laughing. Mia kept her gaze out the window. The color in her cheeks spread to her neck, making it evident she was recapping all the naughty things she did with Micah recently.

Every time our conversation turned to sex, she reacted like this. I wasn't sure why she got so embarrassed, but I didn't complain either. The constant pressure to be perfect on the field and in class was sucking the humor right out of our lives.

Our soccer coaches were bordering on the insane side with the amount of practices and conditioning we were doing to remain first in our conference. When we weren't trying to keep up with their high demands, we were buried under loads of homework and studying for the SATs. That was just the shit I dealt with outside of my house.

My dad had been on the warpath since our blowout. I shoved our latest argument out of my head and peered at Mia. "So, are you going to tell me what happened during your driving lesson last weekend that has left you so skittish lately?"

Mia refused to look at me as she mumbled, "I'm only jumpy in the car with you. Your lack of focus on the road and the lanes you fly between has always been a concern for me."

I snorted. "That's *such* a line of bullshit and you know it. Listen, if you don't want to share why Trey showed up with a shiner on Monday, that's fine, but don't lie. I have a strong suspicion it has to do with Sebastian, Miles, and Aubrey being out at the beginning of the week and coming back with plenty of bruises of their own."

"If you really want to know, you should talk to Trey. I'm not getting in between you two, especially with the weird state whatever you call what's going on between the two of you is in," Mia shot back.

I dismissed her attempt to change the subject and mulled over the other bizarre things that happened this week at school. A lot of girls threw themselves at Trey with no shame. He was now *the guy* to have on your arm. The green-headed monster deep within me sprang to the surface and I gripped the steering wheel a little tighter. The only thing that brought me a shred of comfort was he didn't show any interest.

"I'm not trying to put you in the middle, but come on, Mia, you have to admit things this past week have been more than interesting, especially now that everyone wants to be Trey's friend."

"Yes, I'll admit it's been strange to see how things have changed with the kids at school, especially since the faculty has upped their game to make him look like a fool during class, but I really don't know what it's all about. I doubt Trey does either. I think we can both agree it's best he doesn't dwell on it too much and neither should you."

When people spoke to him, Trey didn't say much, but that was no surprise either. He barely talked to me. I would've been deeply hurt if he dropped his guard for anyone else. What really surprised me was he didn't seem to realize he moved up the popularity scale at Chamberlain.

My stomach stirred as I thought about what game Sebastian and the faculty were playing. One way or another, I'd get to the bottom of it. I planned to talk to Trey about it, but have been waiting for the right time. When it came to talking to him about anything, timing was everything, and so was his mood. I'd never met a person who was so difficult to navigate at any given moment of the day, but I've found I rather enjoyed trying to figure him out. I wanted to grill Mia some more, but held my tongue after seeing her tightly-clenched jaw.

I glanced at the clock to see it was eight, picked up my phone, and sifted through all the incoming texts until I got to Peyton's. This week's *it* party was in Evanston. The street looked familiar, but I couldn't place it with all the other ritzy areas around here. I finished reading the rest of her message, laughed at the SOS to pick her and Kylie up at Eckman, and stayed on the side roads heading south.

My thoughts drifted back to Trey. His fine ass popped into my head and my heart raced even faster. He looked smoking hot in his football pads earlier this evening. We didn't have a soccer match during their game and I finally got to see him in action. I already knew his muscular frame was akin to a Greek God, but watching him send opposing linemen twenty feet in the opposite direction before he threw a seventy-five-yard touchdown pass was downright thigh-clenching. I really wanted him to use those gifted hands on me. For as talented as he was with them on the football field, something led me to believe he'd find ways to use them in the bedroom that would change my life.

He's sex on a stick and I'm desperate to lick every part of him.

He single-handedly got the win for our team but shied away from all the reporters who wanted to interview him after the game. Instead, he pointed out other players who were chomping at the bits for a chance in the spotlight. His modesty was just as sexy as his pure athleticism. Butterflies fluttered around in my stomach and spread throughout me. I was practically vibrating from them.

This past week, we gravitated toward one another in the halls and after practice. Subtle brushes from him were enough to tide me over for now, but I *needed* more from him—physically and emotionally. When it came to how he felt about me, his thoughts were clear, especially when I caught him in a full-on stare. He wanted me just as much as I wanted him, but continued to fight it.

The tune on the radio station switched from "Sexyback" to my new favorite song, "First Time." Every time it came on, I fantasized what it'd be like wrapped up in Trey's arms and getting lost in his lips while listening to the sweet lyrics in this song.

"You're thinking about Trey, aren't you?" Mia asked, chuckling.

"Well, since you won't share what's going on in your sex life, I can't live vicariously through you, so letting my imagination run wild with all the naughty things I want to do with him seems like the next best thing. But, out of curiosity, how did you know?" I asked, arching an eyebrow.

Her lips spread into a coy smile. "Your eyes have a deep sense of longing to them whenever he's in your sights or thoughts. What is it about him anyway? You've never acted like this with any other guy you've set out to get. I'd love to see you guys get together, but you're just acting so differently with him."

The anxiousness in her voice gave away her *actual* opinion on us getting together.

"I know what you're thinking. Trey isn't like the other guys I've dated. For the last two years, I'll admit it was a personal challenge for me to go after anyone who seemed unattainable. Trey could be classified that way, but that's not the case with him. And contrary to popular belief, I can sustain a relationship with a guy."

Mia stopped chewing away at her bottom lip. "I'm sorry, Bri. I wasn't implying anything. What you do in your relationships is your business. It's just...you're both my friends...and I don't want to see either of you get hurt."

I grabbed her hand so she'd stop twisting them together. "I appreciate your concern, but it really isn't up to you. It's up to him. I've made how I feel about him *very clear*, so the ball is in his court. I know he likes me, but he hasn't made a move, and I'm not sure he will."

She raised an eyebrow. "Does that mean you're giving up on him?"

"Of course not, but I want to make it clear, your opinion isn't a factor on whether I do or don't. I love you to death, but when it comes to him, I'm going to do what I want...whether you like it or not," I replied, my face as serious as my tone.

The stunned expression on hers and clear hurt in her eyes hollowed out my stomach. This wasn't something I wanted to fight about. We promised each other a long time ago that a guy would never come between us.

I turned down the radio. "I'm sorry, Mia. That came out harsher than I intended. If anything happens, I promise you won't lose me. I don't even need to talk to Trey to know he'll say the same thing. You just need to have a little faith. I know it's not really your thing, but I'm asking you to try."

Mia's face remained blank. I tapped my chin and mused, "This whole thing with Trey isn't what's bothering you, is it? And I doubt it has to do with whatever happened last Sunday either. The way you've been acting for the last few weeks, I'm guessing it's Micah. Please just tell me. I might be able to help."

Her eyes flickered between me and the scenery passing by, clearly debating with herself. After a minute, she murmured, "If I tell you, you promise you won't laugh at me?"

I crossed my fingers over my heart. "I swear. What's really going on in that head of yours?"

Mia kept her eyes from me. I picked up my cell from the console, dialed Micah's number, and put it on speakerphone. Her eyes bugged out and she grabbed for my phone.

"What the hell are you doing?" Mia shrieked.

I held it out of reach and gave her a pointed look to just tell me or we'd be hearing firsthand from Micah.

"Ugh! Fine, you win! I'm freaked out about having sex. We've done pretty much everything else, but we haven't crossed that bridge yet, and it's totally on me," Mia blurted out.

She lunged across the car, yanked my cell away, and ended the call. Micah called back, but she cleared it and shot him a text saying it was a butt dial, before putting it in the cup holder between us. She buried her beet-red face in her hands, making it damn hard for me not to laugh.

Once the giggles were good and repressed, I asked, "I'm guessing you've seen each other naked, right?"

"Yes, when his mom almost caught us, we were between third and home. We've been…oh, God, why is this so difficult to say?"

It took all the muscles in my face to keep my smile as earnest as possible when all I really wanted to do was give her the biggest shit-eating grin ever. "It'll be a lot easier for both of us going forward if you get it all out now. Then, I can at least tell you whether you're being crazily over-obsessive about something or if it's a legitimate concern."

"Over the last month and a half, we've perfected all the oral things and foreplay. All that's left is sex and I'm wigging out about taking that final leap," Mia admitted, her voice getting more high-pitched with each word.

I arched an eyebrow. "What are you exactly scared about? I've shared some of my experiences with you. You should have a pretty good idea of how it all works. From the sounds of it, you've mastered foreplay, which is half of what sex is all about."

My teeth clamped the insides of my cheeks as I continued to keep my promise to her, but the embarrassed look on her face didn't help the situation.

She groaned into her hands. "Yes, I've been more than enlightened by you, but it hasn't helped me. What if it's awkward for us? We're both virgins. What if I'm not good at it? What if it hurts? What if I'm so bad Micah thinks he made a mistake after we do have sex and breaks up with me?"

It took me a minute to process what the problem was because it came out in one jumbled sentence, but I got the gist of it.

I gave her an encouraging smile. "It's always awkward the first time. It's going to hurt, but don't worry about that either. The best way to look at it is practice makes perfect and it's even better when it's someone who really cares about you the way Micah does. I have no doubt he's going to make it special and that you're okay. The guy I was with for my first time was an asshole. If I were you, I'd get it out of the way so you can get a grasp on how amazing sex can be."

"You never mentioned it hurting or that the guy you were with was a jackass. Why would you not tell me those *very important* details?"

"I was thirteen and not exactly sober when it happened. I hate thinking about it. I was way too young and it didn't go exactly how you'd imagine."

Just thinking about some of the situations and people I spent time with over the years at the parties my parents forced me to attend made my stomach recoil. During junior high, I was as two-faced as they came and just getting to know Mia. We didn't see much of each other outside of school during those two years. It was before I found my voice and I tended to go with the flow.

I would've never had sex with Sebastian, but he really didn't listen to anything I had to say that night and threatened to ruin my reputation. I was on the shallow side and the prospect of losing friends scared me. I probably could have fought harder to get him off me, but I didn't. It ended up being the worst night of my life and it was my fault.

I tried to erase that horrific memory by jumping from guy to guy. I'd made out with more guys than the average teenage girl, which wasn't that big of deal, but I'd also slept with some of them. Aside from Sebastian, every guy I had sex with since cared for me and I had feelings for them. I enjoyed sex a lot but could've been a little more reserved. That number was *much* smaller than the ones I'd kissed, but it was still too high for a seventeen-year-old girl.

After finally coming to terms that kissing countless guys and sleeping with some of them wasn't going to change how horrible my first time was, I changed my dating ways. In the last six months, I'd only gone on a couple of dates and they all ended with a simple goodnight kiss.

My head spun about as fast as my stomach churned and I rolled my neck a few times to regain control over my body. I sucked in a deep breath and reminded myself I wasn't that girl anymore. Without knowing it, Mia helped me become a better person.

By the time we started high school, I changed social circles and refused to be as superficial as my parents and the people I grew up with. When it came to guys, it just took me a little bit longer to change my ways. I wasn't perfect and was always trying to be a better person than I was the day before. Now, I was a version of myself I could at least be somewhat proud of.

Sadness consumed Mia's dark brown eyes, making it clear she understood there was more to the story. "That sounds terrible, Bri. I'm really sorry."

I winked at her. "Don't be. I've figured out a lot of tricks. Now when I have sex, it's never bad."

Our night wasn't about to be ruined because of a series of stupid choices I made in the past. I rarely allowed myself to think about that night in its entirety. It was my way of coping and wasn't the healthiest, but it worked for me. Seeing the street for Eckman, I turned right and focused on the fun night ahead of us.

Mia giggled. "I definitely know that to be true from some of your stories."

I pulled up to the dorm Peyton texted me. I looked at Mia and reiterated, "Trust me, take the plunge. Get the first time out of the way, so you can get really good at sex."

She opened her mouth to debate, but ended up groaning instead. Peyton and Kylie were staggering toward my car with beers in their hands. Whenever they caught wind of a college party, they attended it. Even though they were still juniors in high school, they had already made quite the impression on more than a few campuses around Chicago.

Their long blonde hair was all over the place. I guess it was something they were still fully clothed. They had on short black skirts and V-neck shirts with contrasting colors that drew any onlooker to their chests.

Peyton struggled with the door on the passenger side. Mia reached behind her and opened it. Kylie slid in before Peyton and spilled Miller Lite all over the backseat. Peyton laughed, wobbled as she got inside, and dumped half of her beer on her feet.

"Ditch the cans, ladies. I'm not taking a hit for either of you tonight," I snapped, shooting them a glare to reinforce my point.

"Oh, come on, Bri. We're taking side roads over to the party. We won't see any cops. Even if you do get pulled over, they won't give *you* a ticket," Kylie whined, pouting.

"Yeah, lighten up. *No one* is going to touch Senator McAndrews' daughter," Peyton slurred, tossing a hand in the air.

"It's not up for debate," I bit back, fighting off the abrupt rush of anger surging through me.

They huffed and passed their cans up front. Mia took them, hopped out of the car, and strode over to the trashcan a few yards away. After she disposed of them and got back in, I opened the glovebox. She snatched the perfume stashed in there and sprayed it behind her. We rolled down our windows to get a little more air circulating in the car as I headed toward the lakeshore.

When I turned onto Edgemore, my stomach plummeted. I remembered why the street was familiar to me. It was Sebastian's house. With how sketchy Mia was this past week when it came to him, I wasn't sure how she'd handle seeing the jackass outside of school.

I knew he'd go out of his way to make a scene with me, but that wasn't anything new. For some convoluted reason, he had held on to this torch for me. I'd made it *very clear* there wasn't a snowball's chance in July we'd ever be an item, but the boy wasn't all that bright.

After weaving my way up the secluded road, I spotted the multitude of cars parked on both sides of the street near Sebastian's house. He definitely pulled some strings to keep this shindig off the cops' radar. His dad probably paid off someone. That was his usual MO when he wanted to have a party.

People bitched about my dad taking advantage of his political position and calling in favors, but Sebastian's family was far worse. With his dad being a renowned attorney for Chicago and their fortune being built on old money, he got away with pretty much everything.

As soon as I found an open spot in the private cul-de-sac, I threw my Lexus into park, but didn't get out. I needed a minute to get control over the sheer panic running through my body. Mia's forehead scrunched together as she kept a careful eye on me. I pretended to fix my makeup before grabbing my purse and hopping out.

My nerves settled some as Trey crept into my thoughts. I spotted a dark blue Acura off to my left and my heart raced for a split-second. I blinked a few times to determine if it was his, but it wasn't. It was missing the silver racing stripes he recently added. My breath hitched when I realized there wasn't a chance in hell he'd be at this party, but a girl could dream.

I know my heart wanted him, but my head still had its doubts or maybe it was my past that made me question things with him. My heart still beat a mile a minute just thinking about Trey. All I needed was a few more hours with him outside of school to convince him he wanted me as much as I wanted him.

Not seeing his Acura was probably a good thing, especially since this was Sebastian's house and I doubted things were far from over between those two. Even still, my nerves tingled with a glimmer of hope that he might just show up tonight.

CHAPTER 10

BRI

As we strolled up the brick driveway, I couldn't help but laugh at Mia. Her face was awestruck as she took in the enormity of the house. It looked more like a castle you'd see in England than the suburbs of Chicago. The stone structure and perfect landscaping fit the statuesque look people around here went for to show off their fortune.

"Hey, Bri, I heard your overhead kick led to the game-winning goal against DePaul. I can't wait to see what you do against St. Francis next week," Vance said with a charming smile.

"Thanks, but it was a team effort. Mia was the real hero. We wouldn't have won without her defense and three goals," I replied and gestured for him to give all the praise to Mia.

His eyes scanned over her for a minute, but he remained silent. Her face turned red and she nudged my shoulder for us to keep moving along, but we didn't make it very far.

"Bri, it's about time you got here! You've got to show me that trick you do with the limes," Tinsley shouted, swirling her quarter glass of tequila.

She leaned against the railing and struggled to keep her head up. Vance and Thatcher snickered when her head rolled around some more. She was lucky it was still attached.

I laughed. "Maybe later. I'm going to ease myself into the evening rather than diving into the deep end right off the bat."

"Boo, that's so lame. You used to enter a party with shots in your hands. What happened to *fun Bri?*" Poppy slurred from behind Tinsley.

"You know I'm always fun. I just intend on making it to midnight, but I can't say the same for you," I rebutted with a wink.

Poppy shook her finger at me and spilled half her beer all over Tinsley's green Gucci dress, leading to a slew of profanities and bitch-slapping. Vance took the stairs two at a time to get to the girls. Whether it was to break it up or encourage them to rip each other's clothes off was yet to be determined.

"Hey, Bri. It's been a month since I've seen you around the country club. Are you ever going to show up for Sunday brunch?" Blaine asked, wrapping an arm around my shoulders.

His eyes were a little too hopeful for my liking. We dated briefly last spring, and it was fun, but he wasn't the guy for me. There was no spark with him. I knew he wanted another shot, but I made it very clear it wasn't going to happen.

"Not this Sunday, but I'm sure I'll be at one soon enough. I promised my mom I'd start attending at least one a month. She hasn't bugged me about making an appearance at anything yet. I'm going to ride it out for as long as I can," I replied, stepping out of his embrace.

Blaine's face lit up. "That's great. I should try that with my mom. Maybe you can give me some pointers."

I forced a smile. "Sure. We're going to keep mingling. I'll catch up with you later."

Mia rolled her eyes and I couldn't really blame her. Blaine was undressing me with his eyes. I shrugged before mouthing for her to keep her comments to herself. Peyton and Kylie darted through the front door as we made our way to the backyard with our arms linked together. The turnout for the party was bigger than I'd expected. Most of the junior and senior class were here, but there were a lot of sophomores and freshmen—not to mention a bunch of kids from other schools.

A multitude of kegs were in the center of the gazebo. The fire pit off to the left of it was ablaze. Plenty of people were around it playing different drinking games. From what I heard when we walked by one group, it sounded like "I Never." That game was dangerous with most teenagers, but lethal with prep schoolers.

My eyes drifted over to the pool off to the right. A bunch of kids were already trashed, half-naked, and playing chicken. There was an audience cluttered at the edges, hooting and hollering. Mia and I paused to watch Emma put an annoying, narcissistic chick on our junior varsity soccer team in a headlock before dunking her.

"Bri's here! Now, the real party can start," Sebastian shouted.

He ripped me away from Mia, wrapped his arm around my waist, and wiggled his tongue between his index and middle finger.

"Grow up, Sebastian," I snapped as every fiber in my being recoiled in disgust.

"Now, don't be a prude. Since when do you care about lewd gestures? You used to laugh like everyone else. Besides, you know you want me," Sebastian slurred, trying to bring me closer and making my muscles clench even tighter together.

Dread and panic coursed through me in a competition to see which one would overpower me first. "I'll *never* be your anything. Leave me alone and let it go already."

All of the bruises covering parts of his face and arms had faded to an ugly yellowish color. His eyes were bloodshot and he reeked of pot. I winced at the pain shooting up my side as his grip grew stronger and attempted to grind his body against mine. Acid ran up my throat and I sunk my nails into his bicep, keeping them there until blood spilled over and he released me.

"That was a real cunt move, Bri," Courtney snarled from behind us.

She glared at me before making a fuss over the dark red scratches on Sebastian's arm. If he had half a brain, he'd go for the girl who had a crush on him since the first grade and stay the hell away from me. He gestured for her to run along. Courtney scowled at me on her way back to the circle of girls who followed her everywhere.

"Rarrrr...you know I like it rough," Sebastian purred into my ear.

He slung his arm over my shoulder and tried to kiss my cheek. I moved out of the way and literally felt the color drain from my face. My head was fuzzy and it took everything inside me to push back the memories of that night. He tried to step forward with me in tow, but stumbled over his feet and almost fell to the ground. As he tried to catch his balance, I wiggled free and made a beeline for the keg.

"Sorry, he slid in between us like the snake he is before I had a chance to blink. Your face is practically white. Are you okay?" Mia asked, her voice shaky.

I knew she was trying to comfort me, but her face was as ashen as mine. She wrinkled her eyebrows together, clearly assessing where my head was at, and handed me a full cup of beer. I rolled my shoulders a few times to cease the jitters crawling up my spine.

Mia stopped studying my every move and looked around for Sebastian. I saw him before she did. He gave me *the nod* while licking his lips. Gagging, I turned around. Vivid images from past parties ran through my mind and all my muscles constricted.

When the pressure in my head grew, I knew he was still staring at me. A huge knot settled in my back and the weight of it spread through my upper body. I glanced behind me to see him finish off the joint in his hands and holler for some tequila shots. Whatever he did next made Mia's eyes bulge out of their sockets and she bared her teeth to him.

I downed my beer in a few gulps, refilled my cup, and took down my second one in a few swigs. Mia looked like she wanted to say something about my power drinking, but remained quiet and sipped on her own. It probably wasn't in my best interest to slam two drinks in a matter of minutes, but I needed some sort of buzz, if only to numb my prickling nerves.

"A few more of these and I'll be dragging your skinny ass into the pool for a chicken challenge of our own," I teased.

"If you keep drinking like a sailor, you'll be face down in the sand in an hour and I'll be calling for the town car to come and get us," Mia retorted.

I gave her a flippant wave of the hand, replenished my cup, and navigated us toward the sandy beach. When I spotted a familiar teddy bear face, my mouth slid into a wide smile. Shane's muscular six-foot-three frame was hard to miss. Dressed in his typical cargo khakis, white tank, and sandals, he waved his hands around while he told a story.

With his dad being the U.S. ambassador for Thailand, he'd gotten to see a lot of places there and around the Pacific Rim that faced challenges we never dreamed of having to deal with here in the States. He'd seen firsthand how the world worked outside of our parents' elite circle and had a different outlook on life because of it. When things spun out of control for me, Shane was my voice of reason. He was always there to pick me up and steer me in the right direction. No matter how far I fell, he never lost faith in me. There wasn't a year that went by where I wasn't grateful for the closeness we'd held on to over the years.

Over summer break, we tried keeping in touch, but it was hard with him traveling to Thailand to be with his parents. Time zone differences were a bigger pain in the ass than people realized. I meant to catch up with him after he returned home, but we weren't in any of the same classes. Toss in our opposite sports schedules and we barely had time for small chitchat when we passed each other in the hall or coming out of the sports pavilion.

"Oh. My. God. Hell must've frozen over or I'm definitely going crazy," Mia murmured and pounded the rest of her drink before rubbing her eyes.

I glanced around, but only saw Shane chatting with a guy across from him at the shoreline. Plenty of waves rolled up to them, but neither one seemed to care. I blinked while absorbing the broad set of shoulders and very familiar backside of his friend. My jaw dropped about as quick as the butterflies in my stomach sprang to life.

Trey's ass looked amazing in his black skull-and-bone board shorts. He ran a hand through his shaggy hair and laughed at Shane as he got even more into his tale. Finally seeing a genuine smile on his face rather than the scowl that was usually there was nice. My heart warmed at the sight of it, as did everything south of me, but that had more to do with the new spots of ink I discovered on his sculpted body.

I sent a silent prayer upstairs for how well the fire pit, stringed lights, and tiki torches illuminated the backyard and shoreline. I couldn't tear my eyes away from the large tribal tattoo going up his right leg. It looked like another Celtic one, but I'd have to get a closer look to be sure. I really wanted to trace the wraparound tattoo on his shoulder leading to his back with my tongue.

If there's ever a shot at that happening, it's tonight, and about fucking time. A girl can only pray so much for the same thing before wondering if I'm being heard at all.

After weeks of avoiding parties, it seemed a little odd to have him show up now, especially here. Then again, with the new attitude a lot of kids around school had for him, maybe he had a change of heart. Mine sunk, doubting that was the case at all, and I wished even more I knew what was really at play when it came to Sebastian and Trey.

Shane spotted us and gestured to join them. Mia skipped over to them, while I made my way over at a slower pace, enjoying my view of Trey's fine ass. Mia reached Trey and wrapped him up in a tight embrace. He gave her a brief squeeze. She rolled her eyes before giving Shane a huge hug. As I approached them, Trey gave me that damn cocky smirk of his and my knees wobbled on cue.

The alcohol in my system numbed my nerves, but not quite all my senses. I caught the masculine scent of Trey's sandalwood musk and moved a little closer to him. His cologne was an unneeded aphrodisiac. The horny side of me wanted to kiss the hell out of him, but my brain still had a fraction of control.

Shane and Mia engaged in a conversation about upcoming events at school. As he sipped on his beer, Trey remained silent, but kept a close eye on them. I waited for him to say *anything*, but he gave me that thousand-yard stare he loved to use when other people were around us. I wanted to point that out, but I'd already dealt with Sebastian's jackass ways and had three beers. Jumping into mind games with Trey wasn't in my best interest.

I walked over to Shane and gave him a hug. Once I stepped away, it was impossible not to see Trey's tightly-clenched jaw and my stomach flip-flopped. I really wanted to know what was going through his mind. The "tough guy" façade was so damn hard to navigate.

It was like my heart had an open wound and no matter how hard I tried to stop the bleeding, it gushed nonstop, leaving an unfathomable ache. Deep-seated pain shot through it now, just thinking about how unpredictable his mood swings were, but I refused to let them stop me. I worked too hard to peel back the first layer of him and was set on getting through the next one.

"It's been far too long, Shane. Why is now the first time we're hanging out with one another?" I asked in a joking tone.

"Well, it's hard to get a moment with a social butterfly like you. You should get an assistant so common folk like me can make an appointment to catch up," Shane quipped.

I poked his side, but he deftly moved out of the way and finished off the rest of his drink. Mia downed hers and smiled while she watched us. Trey pinned the murderous glare he tended to use on most of the kids at school on Shane and me. Shane noticed his rigid stance and motioned for their empty cups. They passed them over and he gave me a push to start walking toward the gazebo. I frowned at him, but he narrowed his eyes for me to keep moving.

As we strode away, I slung an arm around Shane's waist. I glanced behind me to see Trey staring at us. The look on his face was a cross between clear confusion and royally pissed off. Facing forward, I fought off the pangs of guilt for screwing with his head.

"What's new with you?" I asked, almost a little too casual.

Shane glimpsed at my arm before brushing it aside. "You never did subtle very well. If you're curious about Trey and me, he's finally letting his guard down and acting like we might just be friends. If he's some sort of conquest for you, I'm asking you to be careful."

A nervous chuckle escaped from me. "Is that any way to catch up with an old friend? After being away for a few months and not seeing each other around school, most people go with the traditional 'How was your summer?' or 'How's your classes?' It's nice to see you too."

He crossed his arms. "Cut the bullshit, *Brianna*."

I jabbed at his chest until he stepped back a few feet before shooting him a no-nonsense look not to invade my space or call me Brianna. Shane waved his hand in the air for an answer. Once we reached the kegs, I took the cups in his hands and filled them with beer. On the ledge of the gazebo, there was an assortment of hard liquor and soda bottles. I grabbed the Crown and Coca-Cola, filled up half of the cup with whiskey, and topped it off with soda.

After swirling it with my finger, I took a long drink. A hint of caramel traveled across my taste buds, but the potency made it difficult to swallow. The slow-burning sensation in the center of my stomach crept into my windpipe and I forced down another gulp.

Once my acid reflux was under control, I focused on Shane and admitted, "I'll make it very clear we're just friends. It's nice to see Trey finally getting along with someone. It's been a month and I've barely scratched the surface with him, so you shouldn't be stressing out about anything happening between us anytime soon."

He raised an eyebrow. "That's a little out of character for you. Usually, you'd move on by now. I told myself a long time ago I wouldn't bother trying to figure out how a chick's mind works because it's a whole lot of batshit crazy if you ask me. If he's not making a move, it might be for the best. If Coach Murray hadn't threatened to bench him if he didn't start spending some time with his teammates, he wouldn't have come—even with the newfound popularity he seems to have acquired this past week."

I squinted. "Why would he push him to come to this party? It's no secret around school that Sebastian and Trey are enemies. It just seems odd for Murray to push him to be here. What's even more mind-boggling is that he even knows about it. Isn't he supposed to try and shut it down if he does? It's not like any coach wants their athletes drinking and smoking. And I'm glad you noticed the sudden shift with the kids at school. I'm happy to see him getting treated better, but it's so out of the blue. I'm at a loss on the *true motive*."

Shane ran a hand down his face. "Sheesh, I haven't heard you talk that fast in years. The only answer I have for you is I don't know. I've been thinking the same things all night, but it's not like I could ask him about it. Murray made it clear he better attend this party and it wasn't up for negotiation. As far as everyone at school, who the fuck knows there? Maybe most of the student body was on their period the past month."

My mind reeled about as fast my stomach stirred. "But, why—?"

He clamped my mouth shut and I bit down until he removed his fingers. "I don't have any answers for you. I'll have his back if anyone tries to start shit. I've been keeping him away from the kids who've given him the most trouble. He's made small talk with a lot of people who've talked to him this past week, but that's it. I suggest you let all your questions wait for another day. If you bring them up tonight, you're just going to stir the pot."

Forcing a smile, I clinked my cup with his half-empty one. "Fine. I want you to know I *really* like him. He's not a challenge."

Shane grabbed my cup and took a drink. He scrunched his face together and gagged a little. "This is strong, but I know you're not drunk yet. You don't appear to have lost your mind, but I'm not ruling that out. I saw your run-in with Sebastian and you handled yourself there, so it can't be him either. There's something else at play. Now, what could it possibly be?"

I slapped his arm and snatched my cup. "Stop being a jackass. And don't even get me started on the egotistical charade Sebastian carried out in front of everyone."

Shane frowned. "Maybe you *didn't* handle yourself. If you need me to step in there, you know I will. I've beaten his ass before and wouldn't mind doing it again."

I shook my head about as fast as a cartoon character. "That won't be necessary. If I need a set of fisticuffs, you'll be the first one I call."

"Sounds good. That tastes like shit by the way."

"You just can't handle hard alcohol. You never could."

Shane smirked. "Let's get back to what's going on in that pretty little head of yours. You *never* back down easily. The end of the world is clearly around the corner." He paused and tapped his chiseled chin. "Or maybe you're *in love* with Trey. That would be a first for you. Care to elaborate?"

His taunting tone had the opposite effect he was going for. My cheeks flushed as Trey's mysterious gray eyes and intense stare flitted through my mind. I didn't believe in love at first sight and that wasn't the case with us, but there was *something* drawing us together.

Between the amount of alcohol in my system and a momentary lapse of sanity on believing this magnetic pull between us was indeed love, my face flamed even hotter and I pounded the rest of my drink before refilling it with the same concoction.

"Whoa, slow down there, turbo. I don't want to have to throw you over my shoulder just to get you out of here. Trey has really gotten to you, hasn't he? Color me intrigued," Shane mused.

His deep brown eyes were full of curiosity while he waited for me to respond. The longer I remained quiet, the wider Shane's grin grew. He chuckled before taking a sip of his beer. As the weight of his words ran on repeat, the pressure in my chest intensified.

Am I in love with Trey? How the hell do you know when you are?

CHAPTER 11

BRI

I wasn't sure how long I stood there, pondering the conundrum of what love could be interpreted as in this day and age, but it must've been a while. Seeing Shane's shit-eating grin, I knew he was about to tease me some more. Before he had a chance, Sheila slithered between us. She'd been crushing on him since we were freshmen. If she wasn't such a snotty bitch, Shane probably would've given her a shot. She went out of her way to flaunt her family's fortune and put down anyone who wasn't as wealthy as them. For those reasons alone, he dismissed her.

Sheila flashed one of her flakier smiles before resting a hand on Shane's shoulder. Always the gentleman, he shot me an apologetic glance as he listened to Sheila babble about her summer on her parents' yacht. My head was a tad on the fuzzy side and the music seemed louder than ever as it blared through the backyard. I leaned against the railing to catch my bearings.

After massaging my temples for a minute, I snapped my fingers at

Shane and nodded to where Mia and Trey were waiting for us. His face was torn. He didn't have it in him to step away from someone while they told a story. Sheila rambled on some more about all the parties she attended overseas.

Her high-pitched voice didn't help the ax picks chipping at my skull. I snatched Mia's cup and made my way back to the beach. Trey would just have to wait for his refill. I blinked to get my vision to focus and regretted downing my mixed drink so fast.

With each step, my body became heavier and I needed to sit down as soon as I reached Mia and Trey. Thankfully, there were quite a few loungers on the beach and one of them was about to become my new bestie while I sobered up.

Keeping a straight line was difficult with the people bumping into me. A huge wave of relief soared through me when I finally reached the sand. The DJ switched from a hip-hop tune to a song I detested —"Crazy in Love." It wasn't Beyonce's fault either. Groaning inwardly, I walked as fast as I could without tripping. Before I made it the final few feet to Mia and Trey, Sebastian jumped in front of me. In an instant, my skin prickled and I scanned around for an escape route.

"Let's dance," Sebastian demanded, snaking an arm around my waist.

"Let's not," I shot back, holding the cups over his head.

He smirked and tightened his grip on my hip. If my balance wasn't already out of whack, I would've kneed him in the balls. Just as I was about to dump the booze over him, someone yanked him back by the collar of his light blue polo. He lost his footing and fell to the sand.

Trey stepped in between us, kept an arm extended, and growled, "She said *no*. I know you're not the sharpest tool in the shed, but no still means no. Leave her alone!"

Glaring daggers at us, he stepped closer. Trey shoved him and mouthed something I didn't quite catch. Sebastian staggered back a few steps and glanced around the beach. Once he spotted his friends, he pointed a finger at Trey before stumbling toward his lackeys. Their entire exchange confused the hell out of me and I tapped the side of my head with hope that the fuzziness overtaking my mind would subside and my brain would start working at full capacity again.

Trey cursed under his breath and took one of the cups from me, placed his free hand on the small of my back, and ushered us over to where Mia stood in awe. His fingers brushed along my backside and I savored the delightful sensations spreading through me.

My airway closed and I desperately tried to get control over the electric current Trey created with each gentle caress. A timid grin fell from his scrumptious mouth as he handed a cup to Mia, took the one I barely had a hold of, and set it in the sand.

He appraised me, his eyes full of concern. I opened my mouth to tell him I was fine, but my words failed me, so I nodded. Potent waves of desire pooled in my stomach and I inhaled a shaky breath. I'd never had anyone look at me the way Trey was right now. The usual intensity of his stare was there, but it was as if he didn't see or hear anyone around us.

Trey chuckled as he ran his finger under my chin and closed my mouth. After sucking in a gush of air, I leaned into his muscular frame to keep myself upright. My lips were desperate to touch his. It took every rational cell in my brain to stop myself from kissing him, but if he kept trailing his fingers along my body, I wouldn't be able to resist much longer.

"I'm sorry if I overstepped, but you looked like you'd rather walk through the fires of hell than be next to him for another second," Trey whispered, tucking a strand of loose hair behind my ear.

His deep voice sparked an inferno inside me. My skin tingled in a tantalizing way I'd never experienced before tonight. As I stared into his mesmerizing gray eyes, the people at the party faded away. I couldn't go another minute without showing him in even the smallest of ways how much I wanted him. I got on my tiptoes and softly kissed him on the cheek.

Picking up my drink, he scrunched his eyes together, brought it to his nose, and sniffed. His horrid expression after he smelled it made my cheeks burn with my embarrassment. He passed the cup over to Mia. She repeated his process, tasted it, and spat it out just as fast.

FIGHTING FOR SOMEDAY

"Shit, Bri, unless you plan on passing out in the next half hour, you can't finish this drink."

I feigned being outraged. Trey leaned in so close I felt heat emanating from him. He cupped my face and whispered, "She's right. I'll go and get you a water. Try to steer clear of drunk pricks while I'm gone."

Trey barely made it a few feet before Sebastian shoved him across the sand. His toadies stumbled behind him and circled around the two of them. Mia grabbed my shaky hand and we walked over to where they stood in a heated standoff.

"We're on my turf now, you son of a bitch, and we have unfinished business. You got a lot of fucking nerve showing up here, but I rolled with the request to allow it. *No more.* I don't care if I fuck up the plans people have for you. I won't let your worthless hands touch Bri. You're nothing but south side trash. Stay away from her," Sebastian yelled.

Mia's eyes were as wide as mine. My fuzzy brain scrambled to put the puzzle pieces together, but I still had no clue what Sebastian's deal was when it came to Trey. He blocked Sebastian's punch and marched over to us.

He took a defensive stance in front of me and snarled, "Your threats have fallen on deaf ears. I'm not buying into any more of your lies either. As far as our unfinished business, I think that shit was tied in a perfect little bow, but if you need a reminder, I'd be happy to do it all over again."

Sebastian pushed people out of his way until he was in front of Trey and gave him another hard shove, but he didn't move. Nailing Trey in the jaw, he shouted, "What's it going to take to get you out of my school?"

Partygoers joined us and we found ourselves in a large circle. A healthy dose of fear shot through me. Mia's grip on my hand tightened, so I knew she was freaked out too.

Trey spat out the blood in his mouth and sneered, "My seven-year-old sisters can throw a punch better than you. If that was supposed to hurt, you're going to have to try a lot harder. You don't have what it takes to beat me in a fight. You *never* will."

My eyes flickered between Trey and Sebastian. Seeing Mia's body go stiff made the cinderblock on my chest grow ten times heavier. Trey let Sebastian take another swing, but he missed by a mile. After the first blow to his chin, Trey sidestepped every punch and never raised his fists to defend himself or took a swing of his own. Sebastian's face turned dark red, his rage on the rise with his failed attempts. He continued to try to clock Trey, but Trey eluded him every time. Seeing the smirk on his face, it was almost like Trey enjoyed making Sebastian look like an ass.

A hush rolled over the crowd and the DJ cut the music. Sebastian's friends jumped to help him, but he waved them off, swung at Trey's sides, and almost fell over.

After regaining his balance, he screamed, "Fight back, you piece of trash!"

Trey's eyes darkened while he cracked his knuckles. "Say it again, I dare you."

His stone-cold expression and the warning in his tone sent chills through my body. The panic in Mia's eyes was undeniable as she begged, "Trey, *please don't*. Let's just go."

Seeing the complete terror on her face made him take a few steps toward us. Sebastian stumbled in front of him, shoved his shoulders, and shouted, "You're nothing but a worthless piece of shit. You always will be."

The next few minutes flew by in a blur. Trey kicked out Sebastian's legs and his back connected with the hard-packed sand along the waterline. He dragged him away and pushed his face into the ground. Between having the wind knocked out of him and the sand covering his face, Sebastian gasped for air. Trey rolled him over and punched him so hard we all heard the crack of his jaw.

Trey pushed his way through people, took my hand, and motioned for Mia to go. The crowd parted like the Red Sea. Trey shook nonstop with the rage he struggled to get control over.

We were almost to the gazebo when Sebastian yelled, "That's right, *gutter punk*, walk away like the piece of trash you are."

The lethalness overtaking Trey's face stopped me from moving another inch. Waves of trepidation barreled through met. Mia mouthed for him to let it go, but he shook his head, released my hand, crisscrossed his arms, and turned around to face Sebastian.

"What the fuck did you say?" Trey asked, clenching his fists.

Sebastian shoved partygoers out of the way to get over to us before he gestured for Trey to bring it on. "You heard me. The janitors can paint your locker all year. The message is just going to keep coming back until you get the point."

Trey ran at full force toward Sebastian and pummeled him to the grass. He arched his arm back and proceeded to use Sebastian's face as a punching bag. Screams rang through the crowd as Trey landed punch after punch, his eyes growing darker with each one.

Sebastian held his arms over his face to protect himself and got in a few good ones of his own, but they paled in comparison. His friends tried to pull Trey off, but he sent them flying in opposite directions. Everything blurred past me and I forced air into my body to ward off an impending anxiety attack.

"Trey, stop!" Mia shrieked.

The tears running down her cheeks matched mine. He ignored her and bashed Sebastian's ribs. "Trey, please stop!" I shouted.

For a brief second, he looked around for me. Shane pushed his way over to us, secured Trey from behind, and held him in a chokehold as he dragged him away. After they were a few feet from Sebastian, Shane released him and Trey turned around with his arms swinging. Shane deflected his punches and smacked him upside the head to get him to snap out of it.

Trey blinked a few times, glowered at the frightened crowd, and stormed away. I looked at Mia and the petrified look on her face mirrored my own. Neither of us followed him. Shane crouched down next to Sebastian.

"Get the fuck away from me, West. As far as I'm concerned, you're just as worthless as your new trailer park friend," Sebastian bellowed, clutching his sides.

Shane towered over him and landed a shot to his gut that made Sebastian curl into the fetal position. His nostrils flared and he stomped toward Mia and me. Red splotches covered his arms and face as he worked to even his breathing. On our way to the front of the house, I heard Sebastian still yelling shit, but Shane ignored him and marched to the edge of the driveway. He glanced around the yard, but Trey was nowhere in sight.

Shane punched the mailbox so hard it left a huge dent. I opened and closed my mouth several times, not knowing what I'd even be able to say to calm him down and ended up remaining silent.

He grasped the back of his neck and muttered, "I promised I'd keep him out of trouble. I was gone for ten minutes and all hell broke loose."

Shane raised his arm to hit the poor mailbox again, but I held onto his arm until the tension in his shoulders subsided. He took a few deep breaths to regain his composure, pulled me into his chest, and gestured for Mia to join us. She walked over and Shane wrapped his arm around her.

"I'm so sorry. I told both of you I had his back and I wasn't there for him. I let you two down. I should've never left him alone."

"It's not your fault. Trey came to my defense. If anyone is to blame, it's me," I choked out, desperately trying to keep my tears from spilling over.

Mia tightened her grip around me. "It's not either of your faults. Sebastian would've found a way to coerce Trey into another fight."

After Shane released us, his gaze remained on Mia, but she stared at the pebbles on the road, like there was a message in them only she could figure out. He tilted her head up to see tears trickling down her cheeks. The intensity of his stare made it clear he wanted to ask her something but didn't want to cause her any more pain.

He scanned the yard. "I doubt anyone will bother you two. I need to find Trey before anything else happens, so just stay here."

Between his stern tone and the way his arm muscles rippled, we nodded in agreement. My eyes widened while I watched him stomp off to his left, glowering at anyone who dared to get in his way. Aside from some frightened freshmen, it was just Mia and me at the curbside.

Mia ran her hands down her face. My nerve endings prickled and the cement in my legs was sure to make me topple over any second. As we sank to the grass, Mia rested her head on my shoulder.

"I've seen a lot of crazy shit go down at these parties over the years, but nothing like that. Mia, you have to tell me what happened last weekend," I whispered, taking her trembling hand in mine.

She gave it a tight squeeze. "Sebastian's older brother got beat up near our neighborhood. He ended up coming down and confronting Trey. One thing led to another and they were in an all-out throwdown."

I scrunched my eyebrows together. "Guys fight all the time, especially those two. What else happened last Sunday?"

Her face paled. "One of the gang leaders on the south side was responsible for his brother's beatdown. He must've heard about Sebastian being down there and came after him—gunshots and all."

My eyes narrowed to slits in demand for *all* the details. She bit her lower lip and admitted, "We ended up racing around the streets. Some other guys jumped in to help Micah and Trey get them off our asses by executing some precise blows to their bumpers. Sebastian and his brother crashed into each other and it created quite the traffic mess. Trey's parents were furious with him. With all the fighting over the past few months, he's pushed them to their limit."

"I can understand all the fighting to a degree, but tonight was way different. It was almost like he took pleasure in beating the shit out of Sebastian. I know guys get off on that kind of stuff, but it was like he wasn't even here anymore."

"Yeah, I can't argue with you there. He didn't always use his fists to resolve things, but it's been a tough go of it for him lately. I'm surprised he hasn't imploded yet. He's been a walking time bomb for weeks."

"I think this evening was a clear explosion on his part. I can always tell when I have a partial truth out of you. What else are you holding back?"

She buried her head in her hands. Tilting her chin upward, I raised my eyebrows for an answer. "What happened last weekend got out around school. I think that's why everyone suddenly wants to talk to him. I'm sure the girls just want Trey because he's your classic bad boy. I'm assuming the guys are lining up to be his friend so he doesn't kick the shit out of them."

My forehead creased with my growing confusion. "Why didn't you clue me in when I asked you about it? How did so many people find out about it and not me?"

"Trey didn't want you to know and made me promise not to tell you. He's noticed people are being nicer to him, but he doesn't care. He made it very clear to everyone that they better not say anything about the fight. That's probably why you didn't find out. The gossip mill was shut down before you got to school Monday morning."

I glared daggers at her. "You should've told me, Mia.. We're best friends. We promised guys weren't going to come between us. If you don't want me to become completely pissed at you, I'd suggest you share whatever else you're holding back."

Tears poured down her face. My heart twisted, knowing it was my harsh tone and punitive words that sent them over the edge, but I didn't appreciate being out of the loop.

She wiped her blurry eyes. "When Trey got into Chamberlain, he got labeled as a sellout by everyone he used to go to school with. The way he represented the south side last weekend is sort of a double-edged sword. He got the respect back from his old friends and they're leaving him alone, but that isn't going to matter if his parents send him away."

I gasped. "Do you really think it'll come to that? He seems so central to his family."

More tears rolled down her cheeks. "He is, and Micah and I would be lost without him too. His parents don't want him to get into a situation they can't get him out of. If he keeps beating up whoever says the wrong thing to him, juvie isn't out of the question. It would break his parents' hearts and devastate their kids to send Trey away, but they'll do it to keep him out of trouble."

As I thought about that possibility becoming a reality, my own tears fell. Just thinking about it brought on a dreadful ache I never wanted to experience again. Throwing my heart into a blender would be easier to handle than the agony taking over my body.

I hugged Mia. "We won't let that happen. Between the two of us, Micah, and Shane, there has to be a way to break the vicious cycle he's in now."

Mia looked at me like I was crazy. "Trey is the most bullheaded person I've ever met. His stubbornness goes way beyond mine."

I'm not willing to accept a world where Trey isn't around anymore. It's not even about how badly I want to be with him. A forced change like that would break his family in more ways than one. There are enough broken homes in America. I refuse to let his be one of them.

A wave of adrenaline surged through my body with my newfound determination. As I wiped away a few straggling tears, the fatigue overtaking me earlier dissipated. "I'm pretty damn stubborn myself. You, of all people, know that much. If it means offering my body up for sex whenever Trey wishes, I *suppose* I can make that sacrifice. You know, whatever it takes."

She snorted out a giggle. "That's true. Your tenaciousness is like no other. I'm not sure how you're going to help him get a better handle over his rage, but I'm all for you doing whatever you think will work. I'm pretty sure you're the only one that stands a shot at making him change his ways."

I stared at her warily. "You don't seem as unsure about us being an item as you were before we got here tonight. Who are you and where's my cynical best friend?"

"There's just something about you that brings out a side of him I've never seen. I think he wants to let you in, but he isn't sure how to do it without making himself vulnerable. I didn't really notice it until now because he always has his guard up, but he dropped that façade more than once around you tonight and that means something. I'm not sure how to explain it."

"Well, try, because I'm more than curious to know why you're singing a different tune."

"Trey has never really given a girl more than a passing glance. Don't get me wrong. He's been with plenty of girls, but it's never lasted long. With how he looked at you earlier, I know that's not going to happen. He isn't searching for anyone else the way he used to. All he seems to see is *you*. I know he wants to ask you out, but he doesn't think it'll work."

"How can he think something won't work if he doesn't even try to find out?"

Mia stared at her hands and mumbled, "I think you know as well as I do that he's very stuck on social statuses. I love him, but he's just as judgmental as Sebastian. I think part of him knows it, but he doesn't know how to look at the world any differently. I'm not sure what it'll take to get him to stop judging people by what's on the surface."

Several scared partygoers tiptoed past us on their way to their cars. I massaged my temples and grumbled, "He definitely needs to see people for who they are on the inside. By not letting anyone in, he's taking the easy way out. We don't get to choose where we come from or who our parents are. It pisses me off he keeps using that as an excuse for not asking me out. He knows damn well there's a lot more to me."

Another group of kids kept their heads to the ground as they scurried up the cul-de-sac. Mia looked at her watch and then around the yard. "If anyone can remove his blinders, it'll be you."

My hand drifted to her forehead to check her temperature. "I'm glad you have that kind of faith in me, but it's not like you to be so optimistic. If you're not coming down with some sort of sickness, I'm seriously questioning whether that fight caused you to lose your marbles."

She brushed away my hand while sticking out her tongue. "I'm not sick. The world can be very unkind, but it never seems to affect your faith in people. You've always had more hope in humanity than me.

That's one of the many reasons why you're the person who stands a shot at reaching Trey before it's too late."

I swallowed against the lump in my throat. "Well, now I don't know whether to feel flattered or frightened. Talk about putting pressure on a girl."

Mia squeezed my arm. "I didn't say all of that to put pressure on you. It's going to be a team effort. You asked what I saw tonight that made my opinion change and I gave you an honest answer."

A bright set of headlights blared in front of us. The black town car coasted down the road at a snail's pace. My nerve endings suddenly awoke from their dormant state and goosebumps ran up my arm as the vehicle came to a stop.

We glanced around for Shane or Trey, but only spotted a few drunk sophomores puking in the bushes at the edge of the house. The driver got out, dressed in a black-and-white uniform, and opened the back door. My heart pounded like a jackhammer against my chest and I held my breath. He gestured for us to get in, but we weren't about to leave our trusty curb without some sort of explanation.

"Hello, Ms. McAndrews and Ms. Ryan. My name is Albert and I'm here on behalf of Mr. West. He requested we collect you. If you could please pass over your car keys, my associate will follow us in your Lexus."

Albert approached us like we were wild animals, ready to run at the first sight of trouble. Obviously, we weren't doing a very good job at hiding our reservations. I looked around for his colleague and almost jumped out of my skin when I saw him standing next to me. Grasping my chest, I heaved in my next few breaths. I didn't see him get out of the car—let alone make his way over to us. The dude moved around like that butler in *Mr. Deeds*.

I rummaged around in my purse, somehow found my keys in the bottomless pit to the bag, and passed them over. Albert extended a hand to help us up, but we remained unmoving. My spidey sense tingled nonstop. For as sweaty as Mia's hand was, she was just as uncertain as me.

"We can't leave without Shane and Trey," I said, my voice cracking.

He looked to the sky, seemingly to maintain his patience. "They have already been picked up by a different car. If you'd like, I can call Mr. West so you can confirm his whereabouts before we go, but he insisted we not waste any time in collecting you."

That admission sent a whole new wave of unease through my prickly nerves. I pulled Mia up and we hastily got in the car. Albert slid into the driver's seat and sped off. I retrieved my cell, scrolled to Shane's number, and hit the call button. It rang once before going straight to voicemail. Mia went between Trey and Micah, but she didn't reach either of them.

She tossed her iPhone into her purse with force. "What the hell is the point of having a cell if the other person doesn't pick up?"

"I can't get a hold of Shane either. Of all the times to ignore our calls, now isn't really it. Where do you think they are?"

Her face fell about as quick as her tear ducts sprang to life. "I'm not sure, but I doubt Trey would go home. Sebastian got some solid punches in while they were fighting. If he shows up to his house with a face full of bruises, it's game over. I thought he'd call Micah, but it's even more unnerving not to have him pick up."

Everything inside of me twisted and turned as frigid chills ran up my back. It was like that creepy couple of minutes before a devastating tornado rips apart everything in its path. I tapped on the black window separating the front and back of the car. Once it was down, Albert looked at me in his rearview mirror. His eyes were less than pleased, but I didn't really care how much of a handful we were for him.

"We've had a really shitty night and can't reach Shane or Trey. Where did they go?" I inquired, giving him my stink eye.

"Mr. West requested two vehicles and drivers on a rush for pick up at the Du Ponts. I've been waiting for the other driver to provide us with their location, but I haven't received it yet. I apologize for the inconvenience and will try to reach my colleague and Mr. West again."

He punched a bunch of buttons on the steering wheel and the sound of a phone ringing echoed through the car. It rang for a minute then went to voicemail. He tried Shane, but didn't reach him either.

Mia anxiously twisted her necklace through her fingers as she tried reaching Trey and Micah again. All the alcohol from earlier was about to make a reappearance with a vengeance and my mouth watered because of it. I clutched my arms around myself, rested my head on the seat, and looked out the window.

Streetlights flew by in a blur and I focused on the familiar scenery until we hit a bump. The hard liquor still lingering in my stomach pressed for release and my body struggled to register every area bearing an insufferable ache from not knowing Shane and Trey's whereabouts.

Just as I was about to shut my eyes to ease the pressure in my head, Albert's phone rang. The window between the front and the back coasted up. My eyes were ready to fall out of their sockets and I gazed at Mia to see hers were just as wide as mine. I reached for the window, but didn't have a chance to knock on it before it glided down.

"Mr. West and Mr. Donovan checked into the Waldorf Astoria. We'll arrive within the next ten minutes. You'll need to stop at the front desk and request the keycard he left for you." I shook my head and opened my mouth. "Those are the only instructions I have for you. You'll have to direct anything else to Mr. West."

The enraged look on Mia's face made it very clear she was ready to strangle someone—*soon*. Feeling the abrupt rush of heat running up my neck and pooling in my cheeks was a testament to my own frustration, but there wasn't much we could do from the backseat of this car. Mia pulled up Trey's number, but I snatched her cell and stuffed it in my purse. She gaped at me in disbelief.

"If they haven't picked up yet, they're not going to. At least we know they're okay and we can throttle them in a few minutes."

Mia scowled. "Just give me my phone back, so I can—"

I pinched her lips shut. "So you can what? Get the same results? All it's doing is pissing you off. Just let it go."

Mia huffed until I released her lips. She crossed her arms and griped, "Fine, but I swear, when they're within reaching distance, I can't be held responsible for my actions."

I gave her a half-hearted smile. My gaze drifted back to the cars passing by us. Lights streaming from the skyscrapers that brought me comfort a few weeks ago only filled me with dread as we got closer to the city. Not checking into my family's penthouse or Shane's wasn't a good sign and the ache spreading through my heart reaffirmed it. As much as I needed answers to the growing amount of questions flitting through my head, the desolation seeping into my pores led me to believe I wouldn't like any of the answers when I did have them.

CHAPTER 12

TREY

My left leg shook nonstop as I stared at the cream bricks on the building across from me. Even with the thick patio glass door shut, I could still hear Shane. After we checked in, he had been on his cell, pacing around the suite. He was probably on it during our drive, but I wasn't exactly with it. The angry monster deep within me, who took pleasure going all Hulk on anyone, finally got what he wanted.

Shane's voice grew louder. Knowing his frustration was because of me made me gasp for air. I more than deserved to feel like a pillow was over my face. Shane walked past the patio and paused to look at me. His face was expressionless and I gazed away.

I ran my hands down my cheeks and winced when my fingers brushed along a few open cuts. Beads of sweat trickled from my forehead and into the gash above my eye. The sting of it wasn't punishment enough. Having large amounts of salt, vinegar, and dirt dumped into it would be a start.

It would take a goddamn miracle to keep this fight from my parents. I banged the sides of my head, hating myself for losing control, especially with someone as insignificant as Sebastian. I glanced at my phone to see if Micah called or texted, but only saw a screen full of missed calls and texts from Mia. As much as I should pick up her call, I couldn't do it.

Shane assured me he'd get all of this buried so our coaches and teachers wouldn't find out about it, but I found that hard to believe. After my parents chewed my ass out for last weekend's fight, my mom pulled me aside and confirmed she was pregnant, but hadn't told my dad yet. She begged me to do better for our family. All the shit I'd been putting her through couldn't have been good for her or my unborn sibling, especially with Thomas and Tory having their own problems with kids at school. I rested my head on my clasped hands.

Lord, if you can please help me get out of this mess and figure out what the hell is going on with my brothers, I swear I'll stay out of trouble and be the man my family needs me to be.

A soft pat on my shoulder brought me back to reality. Shane gestured for me to take a seat. After he sat down, he pulled ten mini alcohol bottles from his cargo shorts and divided them up between the two of us. He downed the tequila in his hand, scrunched up his face as it traveled down, and put the empty bottle on the table.

I couldn't look him in the eye. The punches I took to the gut were a distant memory compared to the excruciating ache attacking my stomach now. If Shane wouldn't have stepped in, I would've beaten Sebastian until he was ready to be carted off in a body bag.

Shane cleared his throat. "Did you hear from Micah yet?"

Shaking my head, I twirled the vodka bottle around in my hands. Shane took it, set it down, and swallowed some of his whiskey. "My dad is confident you won't lose your scholarship. There's going to be some repercussions, but nothing we can't handle if we deal with it together."

I gaped at him in disbelief. "How the hell can he wipe away everything that went down? Call me crazy, but that just seems impossible."

His face was unreadable. "Are you sure you want to know?"

My heart raced. "He's putting himself on the line to save my ass, so yes, I really want to know what he's doing to make everything go away. I don't know much about Sebastian's family, but I'm pretty sure they have the ability to bring down the wrath of God against anyone who crosses them."

I pounded the vodka, set the empty bottle on the table, picked up the rum, and downed the booze in one gulp. My limbs tingled and I welcomed the numbness.

Shane took a deep breath. "You're not wrong. But before I tell you, I have to ask you something."

I picked up the tequila. "You saved my ass tonight. Ask away."

His eyes narrowed to slits. "Were you swinging at Sebastian or every person you peg as a rich prick?"

I opened my mouth, but no words came out. Shane finished off his last bottle of vodka, slammed it on the table, and crossed his arms.

"I've tried to show you on numerous occasions you can trust me. I've gone out of my way tonight to prove that to you *again*. I can't pull these types of strings ever again and I'm not sure I'd want to either."

"Listen, I'm really—"

He ran a hand across his throat and I snapped my mouth shut. "The guy you were while beating on Sebastian isn't the same person I see on the football field or even around school. I don't blame you for being as angry as you've been over the past month, but you need to find a better way to manage that shit."

I swore the color in his eyes shifted from light brown to black and the intense glare behind them made it very clear he didn't want an apology.

"I'm not done. When are you going to draw the damn line? If you keep carrying on this way, you're going to put someone in the hospital. There's no coming back from that downward spiral. If you want to amount to more than what most people expect out of you, then start fucking doing it. You walk around like the world owes you something. The world doesn't owe any of us."

"I know I can't keep fucking up. I'm sorry for being such a jackass. Trust is a hard thing for me to extend, and even harder for me to show, but I do trust you. I'm beyond appreciative of the lengths you've gone to for me—not just tonight either. You've had my back on the field and I never thanked you for it."

"Either you're a really good liar or you actually just admitted something meaningful for once. I'm not entirely sure, but I'll give you the benefit of the doubt."

"I deserve your skepticism. I'll show you I'm not just blowing smoke up your ass because you helped me. As much as I hate talking in general, I know I need to do it more. Tonight is as good as any to work harder at keeping a conversation going. I'm curious about one thing," I replied, raising an eyebrow.

Shane drank another bottle of tequila. "What's got your wheels spinning?"

"Why is your dad so willing to help me?" I questioned, opening a bottle of vodka and taking it down in two swigs.

His eyes had an edge to them as he admitted, "My dad grew up in Englewood."

"Wow, I would've never guessed that in a million years."

Shane's face fell. "That's exactly my point, Trey. You see what you want to see rather than giving people a chance."

My gaze drifted to the table. "I know you're right. Mia's been saying how you and Bri are different, but I haven't wanted to hear it. I swear I'll try harder."

His expression was wary. I'd spent enough time with my dad on construction sites to know what a steel beam weighs and it was like fifty of them were on my chest now.

"My dad has some very damaging information on Sebastian's parents. I'm not sure what he has, but it's obviously enough to ruin them. He's already spoken with his dad. He's guaranteed me they won't be pressing charges."

My jaw dropped and it shocked me that it didn't hit the floor.

"He's not a fan of blackmailing people, but given the circumstances, there wasn't a way around it. The headmaster can't do much about students fighting off school grounds. We'll be questioned about drinking and drugs at the party, but without any concrete proof we indulged in either, they can't do anything to us. It takes care of the situation at hand, but I doubt Sebastian is done with you. In fact, he's probably far from it, so you better figure out how to deal with him without swinging your fists."

I grimaced. "I don't doubt that for a second."

His phone rang, but he cleared the call. I pointed at it and asked, "Do you need to call Bri back?"

He finished his last bottle of booze. "Nah, I'm sure she's pissed at me. I already spoke to their driver. They're on the way. I'd rather deal with her backlash all in one shot rather than in spurts. When she's irate enough, Bri can go on all night."

It wasn't exactly what I wanted to hear and the way my heart continued to beat at a rapid pace reaffirmed that much, but I wasn't going to push him. I opened the last bottle of whiskey and took it down in a gulp.

"How did your dad end up becoming an ambassador?"

"He worked his ass off in college and afterward on various campaigns. That's how he met our president. With my mom's background, he could've had his picking of any political career, but he chose to pave his own path. He's always wanted to do what he could to help areas around Chicago, but he has an even greater passion for assisting countries around the world. When he was asked to be an ambassador, he jumped at the chance," Shane replied with a proud smile.

My eyes widened. "He sounds like a pretty incredible person."

Shane shrugged. "He's pretty cool most of the time. I don't get to see him or my mom a lot because of his work, but what he does is important. They do their best to make up for it when they can."

"So, does that mean you're here on your own when they're overseas?"

"My grandparents moved in with us long before my dad became an ambassador. During breaks from school, I join my parents in Thailand. He's the ambassador for that country, but he helps plenty of other ones when he can. We travel around to a lot of the countries in the Pacific Rim. It's really opened my eyes to all the different cultures and impoverished areas in this world, but this summer might've been my last trip."

"How come?"

"When I couldn't return to the States because of the uprising, it scared the shit out of him. He'll never admit it, but I think it's why he's remained stateside for the past month."

The chill in the air blasted through me. "I'm guessing he was less than thrilled to hear about what went down with Sebastian."

He smirked. "He wasn't happy, but he also trusts my judgment. It doesn't hurt that both my parents detest the Du Ponts."

"Why is there bad blood between them?" I asked and about kicked myself again for being so intrusive.

I'm turning into a goddamn girl, and if that is the case, I'll have to rethink this whole approach to being more open because I won't become a gossip.

Shane laughed. "Either the alcohol has loosened your tongue or you're going out of your way to prove to me you'll be different going forward. Regardless, it's nice to hear you ask questions rather than jump to conclusions."

I gave him a sheepish smile. The grin on his face widened as he explained, "Well, you haven't asked about her, but my mom comes from a very rich family. Her parents had a good relationship with the Du Ponts back in the day, but it all changed after she fell in love with my dad. They treated her like a pariah for marrying outside of her social circle. That's why I can't stand any rich dick who goes around and flaunts their parents' money. It's also why I've always had a distaste for Sebastian. He's tried to act like my friend over the years because we come from loaded families, but we've never gotten along with one another, especially after what happened between him and Bri."

I tried in desperation to grab onto one of the fifty questions running through my mind. Dread filled my heart as I focused on the last part. The idea of Bri being hurt by him made me wish I killed the bastard. "What did he do to her?"

There was an uncertainty to his eyes, but what stood out the most was the stone-cold expression on his face. He really did hate the asshole as much as me.

"It's not my place to share. You'll have to ask her."

His definitive tone made it clear that was a closed subject. I checked the time on my cell. "Shouldn't the girls be getting here soon? I'm surprised they're not going to Bri's penthouse."

"My folks recommended we all stay here for the weekend. They worry about Bri and have never liked the idea of her staying at her family's penthouse alone. I've told them more than once Mia is usually with her, but they don't like that scenario either. They have a soft spot for both girls," Shane admitted.

"So, why this hotel? This suite has to be costing you a fortune," I pointed out.

He squirmed around in his seat. "It's sort of easy for my family to get reservations here."

I raised both eyebrows. "Care to elaborate?"

"I guess you could say my mom is sort of an owner," Shane replied with caution.

My eyes sprang open as I exclaimed, "Holy shit! Is she like some sort of heir to the Astors?"

He gave me a slow nod and I nearly fell off my chair. "Don't read too much into it. She's a *very distant* descendant. Her family built their fortune on real estate and hotel investments throughout the East Coast and eventually here in the Midwest. My mom went to Harvard, which is where she met my dad. She got a degree in management and he got his in political science. As he went down the political route, she supported him, but wanted more for herself. She went back and got a master's degree in international business."

"She sounds like a damn genius."

"She's one of the smartest people I've ever met. Playing Scattergories and Scrabble against her is a bitch. She's been quite savvy with her investing, which is how she became a shareholder to this hotel, among quite a few others throughout the United States and overseas."

Before I could grill him some more on what was a very interesting family background, there was a loud slam from inside the suite. Shane cursed under his breath and got up. I followed suit and almost needed to sit back down to get the white dots behind my eyelids to disappear. I blinked a couple of times to regain focus and followed him through the patio doors leading into the bedroom.

I glanced at Shane to see his lips moving, but no words came out. Mia could be a pain in the ass to deal with when she was pissed off, but I could handle her. Bri was a force of nature for sure, but I doubted she'd give Shane too much hell for not returning her calls. The way his face paled once we reached the entryway to the living room made me second-guess myself.

Mia was on the black leather couch with her back to us. Her fingers were literally pounding against the keypad of her iPhone. She swore like a sailor with each word she typed.

Bri was near the short wall dividing the front door and kitchen. Her gaze flickered between the two of us before she pinned a lethal glare on Shane. If she had supernatural abilities, I wouldn't be surprised if lasers shot out of her eyes and at both of us.

"Look, before you get bent out of shape, you have to know I couldn't take your calls while I was trying to sort this shit out," Shane said, his eyes pleading.

She tossed her hands in the air and shouted, "Are you fucking kidding me? You could've texted me that much and I would've understood, but you went with radio silence. For a seemingly smart guy, you sure can be a real dumbass. Do you have any idea how freaked out we've been for the past hour?"

Shane walked backward until he hit the side of the sofa. Bri stormed over to him, grabbed his nipples, and gave him a titty-twister. Shane screamed so loud the entire floor had to have heard him. The phone rang seconds later.

Great! The last thing we need is to piss off someone around here. We have more problems than we can handle at this point.

Shane massaged his chest as he walked to the fireplace and picked up the call. Bri stood with her hands on her hips, glowering at him. I backpedaled toward the suite behind me. Mia jumped up from the couch and blocked my path. She raised her fists to pound on my shoulder, but I locked them in a hold with one hand and clamped my other one over her mouth.

"Yes, I'm aware of the late hour and apologize for the disruption. No, everything is fine. I just stubbed my toe on the coffee table and didn't hold back how it felt. You won't have to worry about any other noise complaints."

Shane hung up, pointed at the girls, and grumbled, "Don't make me a liar. I'm not arguing with either of you on how I handled the situation. If I had to do it all over again, I'd do it the exact same way."

Mia bit down on my hand until I released her. I held up a finger. "I get you're beyond angry with me, but up until about twenty minutes ago, I haven't really been in the mental state to handle any sort of conversation. I'm sorry I didn't pick up either, but I knew you were going to ask me a bunch of questions and I didn't have any answers for you."

"I get your point, but it's still not okay. You scared the shit out of me tonight. And with Micah not picking up, the thoughts running through my head got really dark. I don't know how to live my life without you two. For the first time, I had to stare that reality in the face. You *know* what your parents might do if they catch wind of what happened," Mia choked out, her chin quivering.

Pulling her into my chest, I wiped away the tears trickling down her cheeks. "I'm so incredibly sorry. I wish I could turn back the clock and do the evening all over."

She hugged me with all her might. My tender ribs protested, but I kept her in my embrace until I was sure her waterworks subsided. She sniffed before giving me a small smile and heading back to the couch. I looked at Bri. The clear hurt in her eyes was a knife to the heart.

Shane wrapped his arms around her shoulders and she ran her fingers under her eyes to keep the tears from spilling down her cheeks. His cell rang and he released Bri. As he read his text, he headed into the bedroom on that side of the suite.

Mia was back to angrily texting. The terror in her eyes was something I never wanted to see again. The agony attacking my body almost made me drop to my knees. Every second she spent with

Chase was in fear. She didn't need to experience that around me. It was my job to help make that feeling go away—not add to it.

Bri tugged me with her into the room behind us. After shutting the door, she ushered me to the bathroom and gestured for me to take a seat. With how she manhandled Shane, who was bigger than me, I was a tad on the frightened side as to what she might do, plopped down on the side of the tub, and gripped the sides of it so I didn't fall backward.

Her hands trembled while she rummaged through the cabinets and drawers. The very loud silence between us shredded my insides, leaving me raw and wrung out. Not finding whatever she needed, she grabbed a few towels and washcloths from the rack above the toilet and faced me.

Kneeling between my legs, she turned on the water. The vanilla scent coming from her silky brown hair filled my nostrils and I savored it. Once the temperature of the water was what she wanted, Bri ran the washcloth beneath it before resting on her feet. She heaved in breaths while wiping away the blood spackles along my neck and shoulders. I opened my mouth to apologize, but she placed two fingers over it.

"It's my turn to talk and you're actually going to listen for once."

Her striking green eyes were barely visible with the tears pooling in them. I forced air into my deprived lungs. "Bri, I'm so—"

"You really have a hard time listening, don't you?"

My cheeks burned with my embarrassment. A tiny grin spread across her succulent mouth. "I know you're sorry, but that's just not enough. I'm sure Shane has the situation handled, but whatever he does isn't going to mean shit if you continue to swing at anyone you deem as an asshole who has wronged you in some way. I need you to promise me something."

Bri slid her hands under my tank top and pulled it over my head.

"Err, what are you doing?"

Now really didn't seem like the time for either one of us to get naked, but that didn't stop the abrupt rush of hot blood from going straight to my dick and making it shoot up. I squirmed around to readjust myself. She rolled her eyes before tossing my top behind her.

"It's not what you think. I want to see how many fresh bruises you have so I know how much ice to grab. It's going to take some work, but we can probably get them and your black eye to fade some. Your cuts aren't too bad, so they should close up by Sunday. I doubt it'll stop your parents from asking you about them, but I'm sure you can say it was from your game."

I cupped her face. "I'm *so* sorry. You'll never know how much. And I'm *really* sorry for being such an asshole the past few weeks. You deserve so much better than how I've treated you. If you give me a chance, I'll prove to you I'm not a complete jackass."

Bri wiped the cloth along my collarbone one last time and shut off the water. After seeing the amount of blood on the washcloth, her face turned strikingly white and she looked away. I ran my thumbs along her cheekbones until she focused on me again.

Her chin trembled before she said, "I accept your apology. You need to promise me you're done fighting. Watching you beat the shit out of Sebastian terrified the hell out of me. I honestly thought you were going to kill him. Promise me you're done."

I rested my forehead on hers, ran my thumbs upward to wipe away a few straggling tears, and confessed, "You have no idea how much I wish I could erase tonight and the memories you'll always have of me because of it. I can't promise you I'm never going to get into a fight again because that's just not realistic, but I can promise you I'll try harder to avoid them. It reminds me of what Coach said to me a few weeks ago. I didn't listen to him or you, for that matter, but I hear you now and will make sure any battle I take on is *worth* fighting for."

More tears streamed down her gorgeous face. "Trey, the next time you think about raising your fists, you need to consider the risks you're taking. You're swinging at your future and you have so much going for you. I'm not asking for me. I'm asking for Mia. I truly believe she can't live without you and that your family can't either. If you won't do it for yourself, do it for them."

"I promise I'll walk away from the stupid fights, but if someone jeopardizes the safety of my family, friends, or *you,* I won't be able to do it. That's just not who I am. I won't stand for anyone hurting the people I care about," I contended, resting our locked hands on my thigh.

A sultry look settled in her wide eyes. Suddenly, it was like I was the only person who could satisfy the want within her. *Holy fuck!* I couldn't stop staring at her delicate mouth, desperate to explore it. I was a goddamn idiot for not kissing her before tonight.

Bri blew a few strands of hair covering her eyes out of the way, clearly irritated I hadn't initiated anything yet. If she only knew how badly I wanted to pull her into my lap, wrap her legs around me, and kiss the daylights out of her, she probably wouldn't be so frustrated with me. She squeezed my hands and leaned toward me with her eyes closed. My heart rate skyrocketed. The intense pull to her was almost too much to resist. My entire body begged for me to kiss her, but I just couldn't do it.

After a minute, she opened her eyes. The disappointment alone about leveled me, but the clear hurt from earlier reappeared with a vengeance. She looked away, but I tilted her chin back to me and tenderly brushed my lips across her forehead.

"I've never wanted to kiss anyone more than you. *Never.* It's been torture not to give into it so far, and it's taking everything within me not to, like fucking everything, but I refuse to do it now."

Bri scrunched her eyebrows together and fought off another bout of tears. She rose to her feet and crossed her arms over her amazing breasts. I shifted around to keep my hard-on somewhat concealed, but that was becoming a losing battle.

"Are you still stuck on not giving me a chance because of my family? Nothing has hurt me more than you pushing me away for a reason as fucked-up as that one. I *know* you feel something for me. Why are you still fighting it? It's beyond stupid at this point and I'm not leaving this bathroom until you just kiss me already."

I gave her a panty-dropping smile. It was a dirty move on my part, but I knew her cheeks would fill with color and rile her up in another way. On cue, the pink taking over her face and the unsteady breath she released made me grin even wider.

"I'm telling you, sweetheart, that sassy mouth is something else and I can't wait to kiss the hell out of it. It'll be a kiss you'll *never* forget."

She narrowed her eyes in demand for more. I jumped up from the tub, hauled her into me so quickly she squealed, and kept a firm grip on her hips. "I'm not going to kiss you right now because it'll be tainted by everything else that happened tonight. I don't want Sebastian or all the ways I've screwed up with us so far to be part of it."

Her eyes widened and she opened her mouth, but I moved my hands to the small of her back and massaged it until she eased her body into mine. We remained locked together and I cherished how my heartbeat began to match hers and held her closer.

I rested my head above hers. "When we have our first kiss, I want it to be about *us* and nothing else. I know you deserve better than me and I'm going to try to be the best possible version of myself for you. I've never felt as strongly about someone as I do about you. It scares me to admit it now. I've given myself so many stupid reasons to stay away from you. Even though I don't fit into your world whatsoever, I'm willing to try and find a place in it, because you're *worth* fighting for, Bri."

Her mouth was agape as she stared at me in awe. Out of nowhere, she hastily moved a few feet away from me. I squinted and didn't bother to hide my confusion with her bizarre reaction. The red pooling in her cheeks grew even darker and she fanned them a few times. I stepped forward, but Bri held up a hand. I stopped and raised my eyebrows.

"You can't just say something like that to a girl and expect her not to jump you right then and there, especially when you're all barechested with your washboard abs practically begging to be licked. That's by far the most romantic thing anyone has ever said to me and I need a minute to cool down," Bri admitted as the redness in her cheeks traveled down her neck.

I tried damn hard to contain the laughter building in my chest, but it slipped out against my will. She glared at me and said, "I dare you to keep laughing. As much as I want to strip you down and have a first with you that neither of us would forget, I'm fighting off the urge to do it. I *want* the moment you promised me and you're chuckling at my efforts to not get naked with you right now. If you cherish your nipples, you'll stop laughing at my expense. I went easy on Shane. With the rainbow of emotions going through me, I can't be held responsible for any of my actions and any possible damage it may cause you."

My teeth dug into the sides of my cheeks. I didn't want my nipples ripped from my body, so pushing her any further wouldn't be all that bright on my part.

Before Bri walked out, she looked over her shoulder. "You need to cover up more of your body. I'm going to see if the front desk has a first aid kit, get some aspirin, and grab some ice. You might want to apologize a few more times to Mia while I'm gone because when I return, I'll tend to the cuts on your face, and then you're going to hold me until I fall asleep."

I smirked. "I can handle most of what you asked, but how do you expect me to cover up more of my body when all I have is a tank top and shorts? It's not like we stopped off for a change of clothes."

Bri looked to the ceiling. Once she was done with what seemed like a pep talk with herself, she rested her hand on the side of the doorframe with her face a cross between amused and annoyed. "For as much as you like to call me a smartass, you're about as colorful as I am with the words that come out of your mouth. Shane is pretty tight with the staff around here. He can get someone to borrow us something for the night. Whatever he can come up with will have to do until tomorrow. If you're holding off on kissing me, you need more clothes on or I'll level the playing field. We'll see how much restraint you have then."

My grin turned conniving as I teased, "I like where you're going with that notion."

That look of *pure need* took over her face and the south half of my body was ready to take her. I really wanted to goad her some more by pretending to untie my shorts, just to see how far she'd take it, but refrained. That wouldn't be very gentlemanly on my part, but fuck, it was incredible to know she wanted me as much as I wanted her.

"I'm kidding. Nothing is happening between us tonight, but this kind of foreplay is definitely a turn-on. When we do cross that bridge, it'll be perfect," I promised.

Her face softened before she headed out of the room. Staggering back a few steps, I closed the toilet seat and sat down. My body had literally gone through the wringer, but I never expected to have all the aches disappear. A liveliness I only experienced whenever Bri was around replaced them and I savored how every single cell in my body pulsated now.

Every touch from her resonated deep within me and that was just the beginning of all the ways she affected me. The way she looked at me like I was the only person in her universe when she spoke made my heart beat even faster. In the past, I would've said the hell with it and kissed her, but she warranted the best of everything. With the vast differences in our lives, I knew it would be a complicated road for us, but I was more than willing to travel it to be with her.

CHAPTER 13

TREY

While Bri ran around the hotel, I took a really cold shower. It was unfair on my part to rid my body of all its horny impulses, but after our intense exchange, I needed it. Once I felt like a giant iceberg, I turned off the water and wrapped a towel around myself. I slid my boxers back on, along with my shorts and tank top, before running the towel through my hair a few times.

I sauntered out of the room to check on Mia. She was still in the same spot on the couch, texting away. With the glare Mia pinned on her phone, it was a miracle the damn thing didn't burst into flames. I pulled out my cell to see if Micah returned my texts, but didn't have anything from him. She saw my blank screen and rested her head against my arm.

"This is *so* unlike him. He answered earlier, so it's odd for him not to now. It's not like I expect him to get back to me seconds after I call or text, but it's been *an hour*. I thought about calling his house, but I don't want to worry his parents or get him into trouble. Do you think he's okay?"

"I'm sure he's fine. It's Friday night and neither one of us were around. He's probably out on the town with the guys."

Mia sniveled and I expected another round of waterworks, but they never came. "I'm *so* sorry. I saw how scared you were earlier. I shouldn't have done that to you. Please, *please*, understand you don't have to be afraid of me."

"I'm not afraid of you. What terrifies me is you don't seem to have any control over yourself anymore. There are some pretty serious consequences you could face if you don't stop using your fists to resolve things. You could've killed Sebastian. Did you even hear us screaming at you to stop?"

My face filled with shame and I gazed away from her. Mia gripped my chin, forcing me to look her in the eyes. They pleaded for some sort of explanation.

"He tapped into this angry side of me I'm always struggling to keep under wraps. Most days, it isn't too difficult to keep it together, but hearing all the shit spewed at me just unnerves me in a way I've never had to deal with in the past. I'm not ashamed of where I live or my family, but the way the kids and the teachers at school treat me makes me feel worthless. I *hate* feeling that way. It's not a justifiable reason for beating the crap out of everyone who pisses me off, but it's the only thing I've been able to do to keep from blowing up."

"You exploded at the party. If this isn't the worst of what's to come, then I'm not sure I want to be around for your next explosion," Mia replied, her eyes wary.

I idly trailed my fingers along the Celtic ink on my right arm to ease my prickly nerves. "I won't repeat what happened tonight. I would never do that to you or Shane and Bri. I just need to figure out how to tune out all the people giving me shit. It shouldn't bother me, but it does, and I'm still figuring out how to handle it."

"Trey, it's what you have in here that matters." She rested her hand on my chest for emphasis. "Whoever can't see the incredible guy you are underneath all of your broodiness isn't worth your time. I believe the bubbly brunette, who left looking happier than I've seen her in weeks, has pointed this out to you on numerous occasions. It's about time you start listening."

Mia gave me a coy smile before wiggling her eyebrows for details. I tickled her sides until she gasped for air and squirmed away from me.

"You're such an annoying brat sometimes, but I hear you. I swear I'll get it under control. Lord knows what will happen to your sanity if I'm not around to talk you off the ledge when Micah doesn't get back to you. Speaking of, there he is now," I teased, pointing at her cell.

Micah: Are you okay? Is Trey okay? I've never had this many missed calls or texts from you two. I'm so sorry, babe. My phone died while I was playing poker with Logan and Jesse. I'm fucking freaking out. Call me.

Mia hit the speed dial for his number. I squeezed her shoulder, strode to the room Shane went into, and lightly tapped on the door.

He poked his head out, his face flushed and practically panting. I raised an eyebrow. He glanced behind him and asked, "What's up? I figured, once Bri pulled you away, I wouldn't see either of you until morning."

I grasped my neck and tried to peek over his shoulder. He gestured for me to get on with it. "Yeah, about that. It's a long story. Umm…are you hiding a spy in there or something? You're acting really weird."

Shane scowled. "You didn't make things worse with her, did you? Fuck, Trey, Bri may not look like it, but she's more fragile than you think. If you hurt her more than you already have so far, *I'll* kick your ass."

I curled my fists together, not really caring for his elusive remark about Bri, especially since his current behavior was rather sketchy. "Believe me it's not like that at all. She demanded I put on some more clothes and said you know some people who could help us out."

"Shane, I thought you were about to show me a real good time. What can possibly be more important than a naked girl in your bed?" a soft voice from behind him purred.

Bright red streaks crept up his neck before he stepped back inside and whispered something to her I didn't quite catch. I scratched my head, wondering how I missed her slipping into the suite, but then remembered the bedrooms have private entrances. A minute later, he made a call downstairs, and hung up. His lips twitched as he eyed his door.

I gave him a playful shove. "Don't let me hold you up. I can figure out the clothes situation on my own."

Shane laughed. "No, it's cool. I took care of it. They'll have everything ready in a few minutes. Just go to the front desk and ask for Manny."

"I won't keep you from your girl. I'm sorry I bothered you. I didn't know you had one," I replied, genuinely shocked.

He smirked. "She's not *my* girl. She's just a girl I spend time with on occasion. It's not serious. Don't mention it to Bri or Mia. I don't need them weighing in on my love life. You know how they like to psychoanalyze all that shit."

I gave him a fist bump and headed back to my room. Plenty of things that went down tonight remained unclear to me, especially his comment about Bri being fragile, but I didn't have the brain space to wrap my head around it. I flopped onto the bed and stared at the ceiling.

Out of nowhere, the surround sound kicked on throughout the suite. The strings of the guitar and the beat of the drums spoke to the musician in me. They reminded me I still hadn't picked up my guitar. It had always been a release for me, just like a good street race, and I needed to start doing those things again if I stood a shot at dealing with whatever was thrown at me next.

I didn't pay attention to the lyrics very often, but this song captivated me. As I listened to the last few lines, my heart rate sped up. It was like Howie Day wrote the song with Bri and me in mind. The intensity of our connection scared the shit out of me, but I refused to run away from it any longer. We collided in every way and it was the kind you'd regret the rest of your life if you didn't run head-on into it and be grateful you got the chance to be with someone who filled up a void in your life you didn't even realize was there.

A loud sound came from outside and brought me back to reality. I darted over to the door to look through the peephole. Bri was struggling to hold onto all the stuff in her hands. I opened the door in a hurry and scooped everything up, along with the bag slung across her shoulder.

The abruptness of it took her by surprise. An adorable smile spread across her face as she walked inside. Bri took the bag from me and dumped the contents on the huge king-size bed.

"I was in the lobby when Shane called and picked up the clothes." Bri paused and pointed at my wet hair. "Taking a shower was a very dirty move on your part. Put these on before I live up to my word to even the playing field."

She tossed a pair of black mesh pants and a white, long-sleeve Bulls T-shirt to me. I caught them, batted my eyelashes, and teased, "I figured you'd want me in a snowsuit."

Bri rested a hand on her hip while rolling her eyes. "It's not like we were going to get a lot of options with it being after midnight. Just go and change, smartass."

I scanned over every fine curve on her body. Her vivacious sundress was hard not to tear off when I first saw her at the party, but it was a crime to let her keep it on now. A sly grin fell from her lips, making it very clear she knew I wanted to undress her.

All the effort I put in to regain a shred of control over my dick vanished. He jumped up from his short nap and was ready to play. Closing the distance between us in two strides, I flung her over my shoulder and slapped her fine ass.

"What are you doing?" Bri shrieked.

I set her down and handed her a baggy pair of blue shorts and a Cubs T-shirt. "If you think, for a second, I'm letting you sleep in that dress, think again, darling. Put these on."

Bri shrugged, trailed a finger along her collarbone, and attempted to remove the strap. Slapping my hand over hers, I rested my head on her shoulder and did my best not to pull it down myself.

"I really do want what you promised me earlier, but seeing as you took a shower, it's only fair to mess with you, especially after making me wait *weeks* before finally admitting you want me. It's game on, sweets. You're going to suffer tonight just as much as I am."

She licked a slow teasing path along my neck and over to a spot underneath my ear. Tightening my hold around her, I tried in vain to halt the wanton desires running rampant through me.

Fuck! She's not going to make this easy at all. Goddamn, vixen, you tease of a woman! And the masochist in me loves every second of it. I may have met my match with her.

Once I was positive my dick wouldn't do all the talking for me, I loosened my grip on her hips. Bri inched closer to me, her breaths becoming heavier. She tilted her head up, a wily grin on her face, almost like it was an unspoken dare for me not to toss her on the bed and have sex with her until the sun came up.

Her eyes were ablaze as I gently blew along her neck and her earlobe before nipping on it. Goosebumps covered every inch of her neckline and made their way down her arms. Her knees wobbled as she gasped to catch her breath. Flashing my cockiest smirk yet, I stepped away from her. Bri shook her head a few times to regain her wits and shooed me toward the bathroom.

I quickly changed and poked my head through the door to ensure Bri had on clothes. The last thing I needed was a glimpse of parts of her body I hadn't seen yet. She was like a younger version of Jennifer Aniston. I had restraint, but I was also human. Seeing her in the center of the bed, in clothes that were easily two sizes too big for her and her hair in a messy ponytail, made me grin. She looked adorable, yet sexy as hell.

I hopped on the bed across from her. She placed handfuls of ice into towels. Bri retrieved some Neosporin and butterfly bandages from the first aid kit.

Before she squeezed some ointment on her finger, I took her hand in mine. "You really don't have to take care of me. I'm a pro at this stuff."

She wiggled her hand free and caressed my cheek. "I want to. You're always taking care of everyone else. Let me take care of you."

I put my hand over hers. "Okay. Just know I plan on taking care of you too. I haven't done a very good job showing you I can, but I promise you I will, Bri."

My heart rate tripled as our eyes remained locked in one of the most passionate stares we'd shared yet. She released my cheek, rubbed some salve on her index finger, and gently ran it above my right eye and below my left one. Bri added some more to her thumb before sliding it over a few of the smaller cuts along my jawline. The softness of her touch, coupled with the tenderness in her eyes, was too much for me. I *needed* to hold her.

After she put butterfly bandages over the deeper cuts, I straddled her legs around me and trailed my hands lazily along her waistline as she tossed the stuff into the kit. Her breathing became intermittent. I didn't intend on riling her up, but the way her eyes rolled to the back of her head with the last swoop of my fingers, I fired up every part of her.

Having her on top of me made my blood pump, but I fought off the urge to grind into her. She closed her eyes and tilted her head back when I blew along her neck. Her legs tightened around me and it took restraint on my part not to pin her to the bed and show her just how much I wanted her.

My fingers took on a mind of their own and fiddled with the hem of her shirt, desperate to remove it. I licked along her neck, pausing to kiss several freckles that led to her earlobe. I gently nibbled on it and retraced my path back to the base of her throat.

She gasped and rocked her body into me. My dick really wanted to be freed and it was difficult not to do just that. Sensing it, Bri grinded into me again and I reciprocated with a thrust of my own. Her body quivered as I slid my hands to her hips in a poor attempt to keep her still. When she bucked into me again, the heady sensations inside me grew even stronger.

"This feels so damn good and I can honestly say I haven't ever been this turned on so quickly. What are you doing to me, Trey?" Bri asked in a soft moan.

I removed my lips from her neck and heaved in a breath. "Your neckline is too amazing not to explore."

She gyrated into me and I gripped her hips a little tighter. I ran my nose along her jawline and over to the other side of her neck, savoring her sweet honeysuckle scent. I started to pull away before things went too far, but she slid closer and trailed her mouth along my neck.

The softness of her mouth created a frenzy inside me and I kissed every possible spot on her throat on my way over to the small diamond stud. Bri released a satisfied moan, practically a plea for more from the way it fell from her lips, and I committed it to memory.

My cock pulsated in demand for so much more than just the soft touch of her skin and lips. Clenching the sheets, I twisted my hips beneath her and nearly exploded when Bri whimpered and dug her nails into my sides. Her legs trembled, along with the rest of her body, and I really wanted to send her over the edge.

The push and pull within my body was very difficult to navigate. Our strangled breaths were the only sound in the room other than the fast beats of our hearts. She teased her lips along my neck. I closed my eyes, choked back a moan, and rocked into her.

She slid down my lap and lifted up my shirt. When she trailed her fingers along my waistline and my abs, my last shred of restraint hung on by a thread. Bri paused for a minute and my body cried out at the loss of her delicate hands. She pulled my shirt up further . . . and dumped ice on my stomach.

"Holy shit! The least you could do is give me a damn warning," I yelped, opening my eyes.

Bri flashed one of her sexier grins while rolling her shoulders. "You looked like you needed to cool off. God knows I do. Besides, I told you I want to take care of you. I never said I had the greatest bedside manner, especially when you're making it *really hard* not to continue rocking my body into yours. You have no idea how long it's been for me. If I didn't stop, I wouldn't have had any problem just letting you have your way with me without even kissing me."

I arched an eyebrow. "Maybe, instead of using our exceptional abilities to turn one another on, we should get some of those details out in the open?"

Bri rubbed her eyes in disbelief. "Did I hear you correctly? Are you actually saying you *want* to have a conversation?"

I gave her a slow nod. She pinched the inside of her arm and watched the color shift from white to red and back to white again. I crinkled my eyebrows. A timid smile curled at the corners of her mouth.

"Nope, not imagining it." I rolled my eyes. She stuck out her tongue. "I've been waiting for you to open up for weeks. It's a tad shocking to have you want to share rather than me having to use a metaphorical crowbar to get anything out of you."

I leaned back into the plethora of pillows behind us. Bri was still on my lap, but I made damn sure she was as far down on my legs as possible. "I'm not a big talker. I never have been. It's not personal. I promised Shane I'd start trying harder. I know I need to *ask* and not *assume*. You've put in the most effort to try and get me to talk and I froze you out. I owe you the most hours of conversation."

Bri looked at me with such elation, it sent my heart off to the races. The heat around us started to rise and it was time to shift gears. I put my hands above my head. She blinked herself out of a lusty daze and moved the ice pack to a new spot.

I sucked in a sharp breath from the coldness of it. As she ran it over some fresh bruises, she slid off me and rested on her side with her head propped up by her free hand. Suddenly, the towel disappeared and the wetness of the ice cube trailed down my ribs, making me shiver. Her hand ran along the droplets and sent a whole different sensation through my body. After doing it several more times before it melted entirely, Bri started over with a new cube on a different patch of bruises.

Her face turned from playful to guarded. "Since you're looking for details, we might as well get out the number and then maybe I won't feel like hurling any longer. I'm sure the guys on the football team have said plenty about me and I'd like to set the record straight."

"The number?"

"The number of people we've slept with. I know you're not a virgin and I'm positive you've heard I'm not. I'm sure people have filled your head with plenty of things about me and it's not all true, so don't believe everything you hear."

The sadness in her voice sliced through me. I set the ice pack off to the side of us, secured her hand in mine, and rolled on my side to face her. Sharp pains shot through my ribs, but I kept my eyes on Bri, who stared at the painting above the TV like it was a Monet. It wasn't anything close to that impressive.

I brushed away a few strands of hair from her eyes. "You've been spot-on with how judgmental I can be, but I'm not a gossip. Frankly, it's when I hear people talking shit, I'm trying my hardest not to punch them."

Her face tensed. "I just want you to know I'm not a slut. I know how I've been coming off tonight, but you have to understand a lot of it is out of my control. You're *very* different for me. I've never really felt this way with a guy before and everything is just so much more with you. It gets overwhelming to hold in when all I really want to do is pounce you."

I chuckled. "You want to pounce me? I've had a lot of girls want to do different things with me, but I can't say I've ever had one say they wanted to pounce on me."

Bri pouted. "Making fun of someone is not conversing, Trey."

I caressed her cheek. "You're right. I'm sorry. But just for the record, I never thought you were a slut and quite enjoy how you are around me. Please don't change that one bit. It's been harder than you'll ever understand for me not to rip off your clothes and have my way with you. I don't want to do that with you."

Her face fell. "What the hell are your intentions then?"

I grabbed her trembling chin. "That came out wrong and is one of the many reasons why I tend to keep my mouth shut. I want a lot more with you than just sex, Bri. That's all it's ever been for me with girls and it's not that way with you at all. I don't want a quick fuck to appease my hormones."

My hand drifted to her forehead and I tapped it. "I want to know everything going on in here and that's never been anything I've cared about in the past. You're a constant surprise and I can't get enough of what comes out of your mouth. I may tease you, but I love how you speak your mind without a worry in the world. You're so damn strong and I don't think you even know it."

Her eyes started to water. My fingers trailed down to the center of her chest. A small tear escaped the corner of her eye and I kissed it away. Bri shivered, grabbed the ice bucket, and dumped more ice cubes on my eight-pack.

Son of a bitch! Score another one for her. That's fucking cold. I really want to jump up, but my needs are secondary to hers. She needs to hear me. It's more than clear she has her doubts, and not just about me, but about herself.

I ignored the way my stomach recoiled against its new frozen tundra. My hand remained firmly on her chest as I confessed, "I *really* want to know what makes this tick because you're the most incredible person I've ever met—inside and out—and I'm in awe of you most days. That's just a couple of the reasons why I want to take things slower with you. You deserve to be appreciated and respected. I hate myself for how I've been around you. I need to make up for it. Things will never be right with us if I don't."

Her face was apologetic as she scooped up the ice. She put a pile back in the bucket, but kept one cube and pressed it along some bruises along my waist. Her fingers made every part of my body pulsate. Panic consumed her eyes and made my mind race as fast my heart. I slid us closer together, so our noses were inches apart. She couldn't avoid looking at me with this new position.

"I lost my virginity shortly after I turned thirteen. In the last four years, I've dated *a lot* of guys, but I sure as hell didn't sleep with all of them. Most of the kids at Chamberlain will tell you otherwise. Some of them were just a couple of dates. Some I went out with for a few weeks before realizing nothing was there. I'm not entirely proud of the six I did sleep with, but I can't really take it back either. I'm not that person anymore. It's been months since I went out on a date and even longer since I slept with a guy."

She buried her head into the pillows. I caressed her cheek until she focused on me. Her eyes remained full of fear. I gave her a lopsided smile and admitted, "I've made out with more girls than I can count, but only slept with eight of them. Plus, I lost my virginity when I was fourteen, so if anyone is a slut in this room, it's me. You have my full permission to call me a manwhore."

Bri giggled. "I'm going to remember this moment. Not that I intend on rolling that horrid nickname out down the road, but let the record show you gave me full permission to do so."

"Well, let it also show, I was never in a relationship with those girls. We never went out on dates. I always made it clear that wasn't in the cards, so I'm not a complete asshole. I don't need to ask if that was the case with the guys you've slept with. I know you're definitely not the kind of girl who would sleep with someone you didn't truly care about."

Holy fuck! The word anxiety wasn't really in my vocabulary. I never got jitters before a big ball game or test and didn't realize how lucky I'd been. The way my stomach tied itself into the tightest of all constrictor knots wasn't something I was a fan of.

I fully expected Bri to be looking at me with nothing but disgust. That wasn't exactly the case, but not comforting either. Bri was a million miles from this bedroom as she meticulously ran ice along my eight-pack in the same pattern. After doing it five times in a row without saying a word, I shook her shoulder, forcing her to drop the ice.

"I know it probably wasn't what you wanted to hear, but I just wanted to be honest with you. I've always been safe with the girls I've slept with," I rambled, taking her freezing hand in mine.

Bri blinked, clearly confused. I tilted my head to the side to try and read her, but was at a complete loss with the blank stare on her face.

She shook her head after another minute. "I'm sorry I zoned out. Um, I went on birth control years ago, but don't like leaving much up to chance, so it's been double the protection for me."

My eyebrows furrowed together. Not knowing why she spaced out like that made every muscle in my body tighten up.

Bri fished out a few more ice cubes. "Now that the big stuff is out in the open. What's your favorite color?"

I ran a hand down my face and cracked my neck. I was pretty sure I got whiplash in the last five minutes. My mouth slid into a genuine grin. "Blue. What's yours?"

"All of them. You can find a beauty in all of them, but if I had to pick one right now, I'd say gray," Bri murmured, a shy smile on her face.

I cocked an eyebrow. "You don't say? My eyes just happen to be that color."

She poked my shoulder. "Don't let it go to your head. I'll probably have a new one in an hour."

My hand caught hers and I pressed a soft kiss to her palm. She sucked in a quick breath. "That's several kisses you've snuck in so far—not to mention that whole other fiasco you pulled off with breathing and brushing of your lips along my neck. If it hadn't rendered me speechless, I would've said something. That's cheating. I get some of my own and I'll be picking where."

I wiggled my eyebrows. Flashing a wicked grin, she slid a couple of inches down the bed until her face was across from my abs. I tried to picture our football playbook but couldn't see anything other than every delectable curve on her body.

Potent waves of desire coasted through me grew with every brush of her hands. Her amazing rack, heavenly smell, and scorching green eyes warmed every part of me. Knowing her mouth was inches away from my erection, I gripped the sheets to keep myself from picking her up and rocking into her.

Bri trailed the ice through every crevice of my abs until it disappeared. She lowered her head and licked away the droplets of water. Panting, I tightened my grasp on the thin fabric in my hands. It was the only thing preventing my throbbing dick from taking on a mind of its own and burying it deep inside of her.

"Fuck, you've got one amazing mouth, Bri," I groaned.

Every area she was kind enough to caress with her gifted tongue flamed hotter than any thermometer could record. After she sucked along my belly button, I trembled and needed to think about *anything* else or I'd flip her over and make her moan my name.

I tried to think of a question to ask, but my brain couldn't process much more than her mouth roaming around on my stomach and the heady desires inside me she stirred to life with each flick of her tongue. Bri sucked and swirled along every crease before picking up her pace.

My dick became harder and I wasn't sure how that was possible. Everything about her surrounded me. It took all my willpower not to wiggle my hips to encourage her to go further south. The softness of her skin as she brushed her hands along my sides sent tantalizing waves through my body. It was right up there with her intoxicating vanilla scent. Every time I caught a whiff of it, I wanted to explore her mouth for hours.

I begged in a drawn-out moan, "You need to stop *now*, Bri."

She tugged my shirt down before sliding back up to the pillows and resting her head in her propped-up hand. "I love how you respond to my touch. I can't even begin to tell you what it does to me."

My mouth curled into a sinful grin. "As you once said to me, the feeling is *very* mutual. Why'd you pick that particular spot?"

Her elbow failed her and she crashed into the pillows. She shook her head in disapproval and whined, "You know what the look does to me. You're not playing fair, Trey."

I turned up my smile another notch so my dimples were on full display. Her blush deepened and she cursed under her breath. I lightly touched her rosy cheeks and purred, "Sometimes, I can't help myself. You make it too easy. But let's get back on point. Out of all the places to kiss me, why that one?"

Shockingly, her face became even redder. "Because you have lickable abs and I've been wanting to do that for a while."

"Let the record show you can lick them whenever you want."

The playfulness in her eyes shifted as she pulled them together. There was too much distance between us and the pull to have her as close to me as possible took over. I tucked several strands of hair that escaped her ponytail behind her ears.

Bri rested her head in the crook of my shoulder and traced

patterns along my chest. "Better get back on point before we push each other too far *again*. What's your favorite quote?"

My gaze drifted to hers. "'The truth is, everyone is going to hurt you. You just got to find the ones worth suffering for.'"

Her eyes danced, somehow making them even more mesmerizing, and the sight of it warmed every part of me.

"Bob Marley. Very nice. I've always been a fan of that one," Bri admitted.

I tapped her nose. "Constant surprise. I wouldn't have taken you for a Marley fan. What's yours?"

Bri rolled her eyes. "You've got to stop underestimating my taste in music."

I narrowed mine for an answer. She looked around the room. A shy smile fell from her lips before she whispered, "'Live as if you were to die tomorrow. Learn as if you were to live forever.'"

"That's impressive. Who said that?"

She delicately traced along the outline of the Celtic moon tattoo above my heart. "Gandhi. It's pretty solid advice if you think about it."

"I completely agree. As stubborn as I am, I do try to learn something from every situation," I confessed, tightening my hold around her.

Her fingers trailed down to my stomach and she caressed along all the creases of it. If this was how we fell asleep tonight and I didn't wake up tomorrow, I'd die a very happy man. Even with a shirt on, her hands awakened every part of me in more ways than one. As much as I loved the headier desires, I cherished the serene waves she created too. It was all still very new to me, but I'd gladly welcome these feelings for the rest of my life.

"What's your favorite restaurant?"

"I like pretty much any cuisine and have a willingness to try anything. If you're asking for one, I'd say Pippins Tavern. I know it's a pub, but their burgers are the best around and the fried mac and cheese bites are to die for," Bri answered around a yawn.

"One of my all-time favorites is Murphy's Bleachers. I can't wait to get back to Wrigley for a game and the awesome food at Murphy's," I chimed in.

Genuine surprise spread across her face. "I would've taken you for a Sox man. The Cubs are my team too. I haven't been to a game this year, which is unheard of for me."

I tickled her sides until she moved closer to me. Slinging an arm over my chest, she tried to tickle my other side, but I grabbed it and tenderly kissed her wrist.

"Who's assuming now?" I teased.

She scowled, jabbed my chest, and rebutted, "One time! If we were keeping score, I'd be kicking your ass by a large margin. Don't let your ego inflate too much."

"I'll do my best. You know the Cubbies are going to make it to the postseason. It's the best time to go."

"Unlike most girls, I actually like a date at the ballpark. You better start planning." She paused to wink at me. "It's not like I don't enjoy a good fashion show, though."

"Now the second one sounds more like you."

"I'm serious. If I had to pick one over the other, I'd pick baseball every time, so don't toy with me. Your nipples will pay for it if you do."

I gave her a mock salute. "Duly noted, darling. What's your favorite song right now? I'm sure I'll study your iPod soon, but I'm curious what your favorite song is at this very moment."

Bri chewed nervously on her lip. "The song I've been digging lately is 'First Time.' It's got a catchy beat to it. What's yours?"

"There are so many to pick from, but if it's this very second, then I'd have to say 'Chasing Cars,'" I replied, nonchalant.

Her face was skeptical. "I'm not sure I believe you. That song was just playing five minutes ago."

I squeezed her side and reiterated, "Yes, and I forgot how much I really love it, especially with you in my arms, so just lay here with me and believe it."

"You know, Trey Donovan, you can be a real sweetheart when you want to be," Bri murmured, snuggling into me.

I patted my chest and declared, "You haven't seen anything yet, my lady. I have weeks' worth of gentlemanly things to do to make up for the wasted time."

She gave me a tender kiss on the cheek. My body hummed in response as I rested my forehead on hers. Her eyes were as serious as ever as she said, "I'm looking forward to it. *Please* don't fuck this up."

"I won't, Bri. I've wanted this just as much as you, but didn't feel very deserving of you," I murmured, kissing the top of her head.

Her eyes drooped, making it clear I needed to get my next couple of questions out fast.

"What's your favorite flower?"

"Lilies, but daisies are a close second."

My heart skipped a beat and she tapped my chest for an explanation. "My mom's name is Lillian, but my dad's nickname for her is Lily and her favorite flowers are lilies. It took me by surprise for them to be yours too."

"I'm not even going to bother asking you the same question. I don't think guys have favorite flowers."

I feigned being offended. "Yes, you're absolutely right. Last question. What's your favorite kind of gift to get?" Her body tensed up and I rubbed her shoulders until she relaxed. "I know you get tons of things thrown at you from your parents. I'm asking what *you* like. Something you treasure—not something you receive because someone is trying to make up for not being there for you."

"As cliché as it sounds, I like getting jewelry, but not the expensive stuff. I love bracelets and necklaces that speak to who I am. What about you?"

My heart swelled with her answer. She loved the simple things in life—just like me. "I love receiving gifts that have something to do with a part of my life I'm passionate about—like tickets to concerts or ball games."

"Good to know," Bri whispered, closing her eyes.

I pulled the comforter over us. Her breaths became heavier as she fell into a deep sleep. I looked forward to repeating this with her every chance I got. My mind raced with all the places and things I wanted to do with her. I could've watched her for hours, but my tired eyes demanded sleep.

The immensity of the night crept back into my thoughts. As much as I wanted to believe I'd have more control over my temper, I wasn't an idiot either. There was no way Sebastian was done with me and far too much sat in the unknown category when it came to him.

I tightened my hold around Bri. Having her asleep in my arms was probably more than I deserved, but I tried not to dwell on it. I would do everything in my power to be who she needed me to be and more. Whether she realized it or not, she stole a small piece of my heart tonight. I was nowhere near ready to give her all of it, but I was sure as hell ready to try and worm my way into her whole heart and make it *mine*.

CHAPTER 14

TREY

Heat radiated from my body and awoke me from a deep sleep. Ignoring the sweat trickling down my temple, I held Bri closer. I didn't know if it was morning or afternoon when I woke up. With the blinds drawn, there was next to no light in our room.

She was still sound asleep with her head on my chest and her legs intertwined with mine. We fit together as perfect as any puzzle. The steady beat of her heart as it thumped against my chest exhilarated every cell within me. Tranquil waves coasted through my body and I knew sleeping alone in my bed was never going to be the same.

I'll just have to sneak her into my room. That's going to be a hell of a lot easier than sneaking into hers. Something leads me to believe her dad is going to be just as much of a problem for me as Sebastian.

Every thought I shoved aside last night pressed to the forefront of my mind and my stomach sank. I hadn't considered how things would be for us once her folks caught wind of it. Before I could dwell on it, a soft knock echoed from the door, but I didn't bother getting up. I wasn't ready to face anything outside of this suite or let go of Bri. After a minute, the banging grew louder and she stirred. As I started to untangle myself from her, Shane walked into the room.

"Sorry, man. I wouldn't have woken you up if it wasn't important. There's someone here to see you."

After I successfully slid out, Bri shifted so she was on her stomach. I rested my elbows on my knees and ran a hand through my hair. Shane motioned for us to go. I changed into my shorts and tank top, patted my pockets to confirm my wallet was still there, and followed him.

I paused in the doorway, stretched out my back and shoulders, and asked, "What time is it? Who's here?"

He whipped around with a finger up to his mouth. He eyed Bri carefully. She rolled around, hugged a pillow to her chest, but remained asleep. He shoved me out the door and closed it as quietly as possible.

Before we took another step, I stopped him. "What the hell, dude?"

"You never want to wake a sleeping bear. Bri is *not* a morning person. Fuck, I'm not sure she's even an afternoon person. It's only eight and it's the weekend. She *never* gets up before eleven when she doesn't have to. I didn't want to risk her even batting an eyelash. She can be unbearable when she doesn't wake up on her own," Shane replied with a shit-eating grin.

I chuckled. "I'm not surprised to hear that, but in all fairness, I kept her up pretty late last night. When she does get up, she might be grumpy anyway."

Shane arched an eyebrow. "Moving a little fast, don't you think?"

I glared daggers at him. "We *talked*. I haven't even kissed her yet."

His eyes widened to saucers. "Seriously? I figured that at least happened."

Jabbing a few fingers into his burly chest, I said, "No, I'm taking a different approach with her, so she knows just how much I care. I doubt Mia and Micah would seal the deal here when they've already been walked in on once before. I'm pretty sure you were the only one who got laid last night."

"Listen, my dad is here to see you. If we could ixnay on any of that kind of conversation while we eat breakfast with him, it'd be great."

My heart rate hit supersonic mode. "Fuck, other than apologizing repeatedly, what the hell do I say to the man? I'm sure this isn't a shocking revelation, but I don't do well with parents."

Shane snorted. "You don't do conversing well in general, so stop freaking out. Just answer whatever he asks you. Most importantly, don't lie to him and you'll be fine."

"Easy for you to say. You're not the one he bailed out," I muttered, pinching the bridge of my nose.

"Were you serious about Mia and Micah? With how all over each other they were at the end of last year, I figured that ship sailed over the summer."

"Yeah, I'm not sure what the hold-up is, but I'm sure I'll find out soon enough. If it doesn't come from Micah, I'm sure Bri will tell me."

He raised both eyebrows. "So, Bri's your girlfriend and you haven't kissed her? Well, fuck me. You'll have to show me that magic trick."

I quickly shook my head. "I don't do labels, especially that one. It's as bad as when someone throws out 'I love you' after one date. It should always mean something when you do and not be something tossed out for the hell out of it."

His eyes were wary. "Well, just be clear with her about all that. Don't put thoughts in her head. She deserves better than that, especially from you."

"I've been more upfront with her than any other girl I've laid eyes on. I respect her more than you'll ever know. I didn't say that to be an ass. I said it because it's the truth. I mean I haven't even taken her on a date yet."

As we strode into the living room, Shane ran a hand down his face. We eyed Mia and Micah, who were snuggled together on the couch and still out cold, and tiptoed past them out of the suite. We were whisked down to the lobby faster than I preferred. When the doors opened, I forced my feet to move forward. On our way into the restaurant, I took a deep breath to ease the pressure in my chest. Shane picked up his pace, but I maintained my tortoise one. He grabbed the newspaper out of his dad's hands and pulled him up for a hug.

Shane was the spitting image of his dad. They shared the same chiseled face, solid body frame, brawny shoulders, brown eyes, and messy brown hair.

"Pop, this is Trey Donovan. When he's not a brooding bastard, he's a pretty decent guy. I'm glad you got to meet him before heading back to Thailand. Is Mom with you?"

My heart pounded a mile a minute by the time I got to his secluded table in the corner. Sweat trickled down my forehead and I wiped it away—not that it did any good. My palms were just as damp. I slid them down my shorts and extended one to his dad.

He clasped my hand in an ironclad grip. By the time he let go, my fingers tingled. He motioned for us to take a seat, sat back down, and picked up his Bloody Mary. "Yes, your mother is here. She's having a few words with the staff."

I wrung my shaky hands together to keep from fidgeting under this man's intense stare. Out of nowhere, a male waiter dressed in all black appeared. "I see the rest of your party has arrived. May I take your drink order?"

"I'll take a mimosa," Shane spoke up.

His dad decked him upside the head. "You'll have an orange juice."

Shane rolled his eyes while rubbing the spot his dad smacked. The waiter arched an expectant eyebrow at me. I forced out, "I'll have water, thank you."

With all the knots in my stomach, I wasn't sure I'd even get that down. Before the guy left to put our drink order in, his dad motioned for a refill on his Bloody Mary and passed over the menus that were at the edge of the marble tabletop.

"We'll take three orders of the American Breakfast. If you can put a rush on it, I'd appreciate it."

The waiter hustled off in what I assumed was the direction of the kitchen. It was hard to tell since the place had more of a bar décor to it than an actual restaurant. There was a row of booths directly across from the bar, but the rest of the space had tables like ours. The old-fashioned red chairs had a floral pattern to them and no arms, making it damn difficult for me to keep my hands in check. At least with something to grip, I could try to control my overly anxious nerves.

His dad cleared his throat to get my attention. Releasing a shaky breath, I opened my mouth, but he held up a hand. "I'm sure you're very sorry and you can save that for the end of our meal. I have a few things to get out first."

I gulped against the golf ball in my throat. His face was impassive as he admitted, "I've been watching you a lot longer than you think, Trey."

My eyes widened in shock. Shane looked at him, his forehead scrunched together. The corners of his dad's mouth twitched, seemingly amused with us. "I may be gone for a good portion of my son's school year, but I'm still a member on a few boards, including the admissions one. I saw your application come in over the summer and was one of the members who voted for you."

"Wow, sir. Thank you so much. I mean it. This school is opening up opportunities for my future I would've never had otherwise," I blurted out.

He took a sip of his drink. "My name is Aiden. Anyway, you were the one that was most deserving of the scholarship. I'm sure you think otherwise, but that's not the case. You're a very intelligent person, so I was rather disappointed when Shane told me what happened last night."

I opened my mouth to slip in one of the thousand apologies and thanks I owed him, but I snapped it shut just as fast with the harsh glare he pinned on me. An apologetic look filled Shane's face before he sauntered away. He stopped in front of a petite brown-haired woman and kissed each cheek. Shane pulled out a chair at the bar, took her black leather jacket, and sat next to her.

Mr. West smiled at the two of them as he set his empty glass down. He clasped his hands together, his face pensive. "It's on the unethical side for me to step in the way I have, but I know firsthand what these kids are putting you through. Just so we're clear, this is the one and only time I'll be doing it. Since it took *a lot* of phone calls to keep this quiet, I need to understand this situation with Sebastian a little bit better. I have my suspicions based on what I've gathered from Shane and see on the football field, but I'd like to hear it from you."

"It's more than Sebastian giving me a hard time at Chamberlain. He's just been the most aggressive about trying to get me expelled," I stammered.

Mr. West arched an eyebrow. "Is the faculty also part of the problem?"

I nodded, my face grim. He drummed his fingers across the table. "I see. That's rather unsettling to hear and makes me feel better about helping you. Why haven't you spoken to the headmaster about it or your parents?"

My gaze fell to the table. "My folks have a lot on their plate right now and our family really needs this school to work out. Coach Barry does what he can to help me, but I'm sure it's rather daunting when you're going up against most of the staff. I don't know a lot about the headmaster, but he doesn't seem all that approachable. I'm also not a big talker in general."

Giving me a partial smile, he said, "Yes, Shane mentioned that much. That's not an excuse, Trey. You need to use your head and realize when to keep quiet and when to speak up, especially if tensions are running high. Throughout your life, there are always going to be situations that are difficult to deal with and you need to do the *right thing*, rather than taking the easy way out."

I hung my head in shame. "Regardless of how bad I'm being treated, I should've never resorted to violence. I know that and I'm really sorry for how poorly I've been handling things so far. Whatever punishment comes my way, I more than deserve it."

"I'd like to get a few more details about this party at Sebastian's. Shane mentioned Coach Murray was rather pushy when it came to attending it. Do you have any idea why that may be?"

"I can tell he's not a fan of me being at Chamberlain, but that's not shocking, considering how many other people fall in that group. His demand for me to go to the party was just as strange as some of the stuff Sebastian spewed while we were fighting."

Aiden motioned for me to elaborate. I ran my hand across the abrasions on my knuckles. "Sebastian made it seem like me being at the party was a setup. He didn't care if he blew up someone's plans by picking a fight with me. He said I'd get what was coming to me anyway. I'm not sure what that means, but I haven't thought about it a lot either. I've been more concerned on whether I'll be sent away or thrown in juvie."

Our drinks and food arrived and he took a long drink of his Bloody Mary, then dove into his plate and gestured for me to do the same. Despite the ball of nerves in my stomach, I scarfed down my eggs, bacon, and potatoes rather quickly. He finished off his plate just as fast and shoved it to the side, his eyes deep in thought.

"In light of that information, I'll be looking into matters a little deeper. It doesn't sit well with me that you were coerced into going to that particular party. You don't want to get involved with those types of people. I don't want you to think about it. Do you understand?"

I exhaled. "Yes, sir, I mean, Mr. West."

"As far as punishment is concerned, the school is aware of the party and a good deal of the students who were there. The four of you will be called into the office on Monday. There isn't any solid evidence to prove you were drinking or fighting. My suggestion is to let my son do all the talking. He's very good at debating. I'm sure some penance will be extended, but it won't be suspension or expulsion."

"Is there any way I can deal with it on my own without involving the other three? I don't want them to be dragged into this any more than they already are."

"No, I've already set the ball rolling for the four of you to be questioned together. Like I said, let Shane handle the headmaster. It's not his first rodeo with him."

"What about the cops? Are the Du Ponts really not pressing charges?"

A smug smile teased his face. "Don't worry about them. If they heeded my warning at all, they won't be going to the authorities and will be keeping a better eye on their jackass of a son."

My jaw dropped at his bluntness and he chuckled. "I had my own Sebastian when I was your age. It's part of the reason why I was willing to help. I know exactly what you're going through, Trey. Your repayment to me isn't going to come all that easy for you."

"I'll do whatever you ask," I answered straightaway.

He slid over a business card. "Obviously, stop using your fists to resolve things. Use your head and keep your goals in mind. You have a lot of ambitions and can achieve them if you channel your anger. I expect you to call me once a week. I realize how important it is to have someone you can talk to outside of your parents and friends. Someone who relates to your situation. I know my son is a good kid and trying to be there for you, but he doesn't understand what living on the south side is like and all the obstacles that come with it. You can consider our chats a therapy session to get out your frustrations."

I shoved his card into my shorts. He finished his Bloody Mary, buttoned up his black suit jacket, and adjusted his red tie. "Shane is in Tai Chi. You *will* enroll in his class."

"With all due respect, my parents had me in karate for years and it didn't help the anger issue very much," I rambled and slapped my head for being so damn rude.

"Tai Chi is different. Martial arts are incorporated in it, but what I expect it will do for you is help you find your center and ways to channel your anger in a non-violent way."

His stern tone wasn't to be argued with and I quickly nodded my agreement to his request.

"Good. That covers it. If I find out about any more fights or trouble at school, you'll regret it. Now, I hate to eat and run, but I need to settle the bill, collect my wife, and say goodbye to my son."

I jumped up with him and held out my hand. "I won't let you down. I'm so sorry for the position I've put you in, but more grateful than you'll ever know for helping me out of this mess. I promise to do all the things you requested. Thank you again."

His grip on my hand was a lot easier to handle this time around. He patted me on the back and headed over to Shane and his mom.

Mr. West gave Shane a hug. "We'll be back in a month. Behave yourself while we're gone. I love you."

Holding Shane in a tight embrace, his mom kissed his cheeks. There were tears in her eyes when she released him. "I love you, my boy. You need to call us every day. There's no exception to that rule."

I walked over to the entryway to give them some more privacy. As I waited, all the crap Sebastian yelled at me ran through my head, along with all teachers who went out of their way to embarrass me at Chamberlain, and the little punks giving my brothers trouble. I couldn't help but wonder if it was all connected. As the pressure in my head grew, I tapped the side of it to redirect my thoughts so it didn't implode.

Several minutes later, Shane joined me and we headed for the elevator. My insides were a bloody mess and it was hard for me to remain upright. Even though I should feel reassured things were going to get better, I couldn't shake the pesky feeling in my gut. My fingers gravitated toward my wraparound tattoo, desperate to trace the ink to calm myself. I circled them around it several times in a vain attempt to appease my jittery nerves, but it did very little to settle them.

Shane nudged my shoulder. "Earth to Trey. Did you hear a thing I said in the past five minutes?"

"Sorry, man. That was just an intense breakfast. My mind drifted to some of the things that remain unknown, but I don't want to dwell on it. What were you saying?"

"Did you get Mia anything for her birthday? Bri shot me a text while we were at breakfast to let me know they slipped out to do some shopping. She mentioned Micah told them to get their girl time in now because he's planned the rest of Mia's birthday weekend. I feel like a dick for forgetting it was today."

I slapped my forehead, utterly disgusted with myself. "Shit, I forgot too. I'm on a real fucking roll for being an asshole these days."

Micah paced around as he talked to someone on the phone. He

ended the call as soon as he saw us enter the suite and charged over to me. Shane stepped in between us with an arm extended to Micah's chest, but he swatted it away and shook a finger at me.

"Mia filled me in on what happened. What the fuck were you thinking, Trey? You know the consequences and need to stop putting Mia in danger. You may not care what happens to her, but I sure as hell do. One of these times, it's not going to end in your favor. How do you not get that?" Micah shouted.

"I do, Micah. More than you think. I'm really sorry about everything. I swear it'll never happen again."

As he stepped back, all the muscles in his neck stopped twitching, but his eyes demanded more of an explanation. A lightbulb flicked on in my head and I glanced at the clock to confirm the time. *Ten thirty.* After fishing my wallet out of my pocket, I handed Shane the credit card my parents had given me for emergencies. This technically wasn't, but I had to do something to start making things right with Mia or Micah really was going to beat me to a pulp.

"I know what I'm getting her for her birthday." Shane's face was inquisitive as he glanced between me and the card. I looked at Micah. "I'm sure you have the whole day planned, but can you sacrifice this afternoon for a game at the ballpark?"

Micah debated with himself for a moment before nodding.

"Call the Cubs' box office and get us tickets," I instructed with a wide grin.

Shane bumped my fist. "You got it. I know a couple of people down there. I might be able to get us a good deal."

He walked into his room. Micah's hands were grasped tightly on his baseball cap while he stared at the ceiling. Once he finished mumbling to himself, he glared at me and snapped, "It's taking everything in me not to punch you. I know you and Mia don't always get along the greatest, but she's like your damn sister. You'd never put the rest of your siblings in danger, so forgive me if it's blowing my fucking mind that you keep doing it with her. She's got enough on her plate with Chase."

The pain attacking my heart was well-deserved and I couldn't bear to look at him. He cleared his throat, demanding I give him my attention. My gaze centered on him as I reiterated, "I'm sorry. I really am. I've apologized to Mia and will continue to do so. You have every right to take a swing at me. I more than deserve it."

Releasing a disgruntled huff, Micah unclenched his fists. "You're my boy, so I'll let this one go. But, so help me God, if you ever scare Mia like that again, I'll give you the beating of your life. I love her and can't live without her."

I stared in disbelief, slack-jawed in all, and finally sputtered, "I didn't know you were in love with her. I had no idea it was that serious already."

His face softened. "I've never loved anything or anyone as much as I love her. I want to give her everything she's always deserved and more. I also want to keep her safe. You better swear to me you'll think about that the next time you're inclined to raise your fists around people who could ruin your life and hers."

I rested my hands on his shoulders. "I swear, Micah. She *is* a sister to me, an annoying one at times, but I do care for her. I won't do anything to jeopardize her safety or future."

"You know I always have your back. I'm sorry you got suckered into another fight with that rich prick. This whole social warfare thing seems to have gone a tad far. Do you think there's another reason behind it all?"

"Part of me thinks there might be more to it, but who the fuck knows. Understanding the mindset of the rich and privileged isn't really my forte. Right now, there is only one person who I want to spend my time thinking about."

His lips quirked into a shit-eating grin. "So, you're finally going for it with Bri? Way to jump right into the deep end by sharing a hotel room with her. She seems pretty classy. You might want to take it slow."

I shook my head on my way over to the couch, picked up the remote, and changed the channel to ESPN. "I haven't even kissed her, smartass."

He feigned rubbing his eyes and playfully swatted my arm as he sat down next to me. "Maybe you *are* turning over a new leaf in all areas of your life because the Trey Donovan I know usually seals the deal right away."

I scowled. "Bri's different. I've never met anyone like her. I want to do it right with her."

Shane joined us, a smug smile on his face as he handed over my credit card. "We're sitting in the first row along the third baseline. Prime spots for catching foul balls."

As the possible price flitted through my head, the color in my face drained. Shane plopped down on the other side of me. "Don't sweat it, Trey. My guy in the box office gave us a really good deal. I don't mind chipping in."

"No, it's my treat," I rebutted.

Shane focused on Micah. "How long ago did they leave? The game starts at noon."

"It was shortly after you two did. I'll give Mia a call to see where they're at."

Micah dialed her number. Once she picked up, the grin on his face grew even wider while he paced around listening to her. He was happier than I'd ever seen him. I was a real shitty friend for not seeing it sooner.

"Hey, babe. Where are you girls at?"

Shane and I remained engrossed in the scores to try to give him some privacy.

"Sounds like you ladies had a great breakfast and have already hit quite a few stores, but I need you to swing by another one before getting back here."

Whatever her response was made Micah roll his eyes. "Yes, I know it *is* out of the ordinary for me to ask you to keep shopping, but you need to stop at one of the sports shops and pick up some Cubs gear for all of us."

Micah barked out a laugh and handed the phone to me. "I'll let you fill her in on the rest."

"Hey, Mia. First, I wanted to say happy birthday."

"Um, thanks, Trey. Why are we picking up sports stuff?" Mia

asked, confused.

"Well, I thought a great gift for you would be a Cubs game. I know it's been a while since you've been to one."

Mia shrieked with delight and I held the phone back to keep my eardrum from blowing up. Once her and Bri finished rejoicing, she came back on the line and exclaimed, "Thank you so much, Trey. You didn't have to do that. We'll pick up everything and get back there so we can make it to the game on time. Thank you again!"

"You're welcome, Mia. We'll see you ladies soon," I replied, hanging up.

I tossed Micah's cell back to him, returned to the couch, and focused on the TV. The three of us spent the next half hour catching up on the pro scores and discussing the Cubbies' chances at a real run for the World Series. As the topic turned a little more heated, the girls burst through the door, giggling as they did, and we broke from our debate.

Mia walked over to Micah, pulled him up, and gave him a quick kiss. Her eyes were anxious as they flitted between me and him. I mouthed everything was fine and Micah reinforced it by whispering in her ear. She snuggled into his side with a wide smile on her face.

Shane grinned. "Happy Birthday, Mia. I meant to have a gift for you before today, but didn't get around to it. I'll make it up to you."

She gave him an admonishing wave of the hand. "I don't need anything, Shane. Just hanging out with all of you is more than enough for me."

My gaze drifted over to Bri, who dropped a couple of the shopping bags next to Mia, and strode over to Shane to hand a bag over to him. She gestured to go change and he disappeared into his room. On her way over to me, she clutched the remaining shopping bag and locked her free hand with mine.

After closing the bedroom door, I turned to face Bri. She dumped the items in the bag on the bed and I sauntered over to stand right behind her, taking in her sweet scent. It no longer felt like my insides were being ground up like hamburger. Wanton waves traveled in every direction that made me want to spend the entire day appreciating every aspect of her. I brushed her hair to the side and placed a gentle kiss below her ear. Bri shivered as she picked up a jersey and hat. She put them in my hands, snatched the remaining clothes, and disappeared into the bathroom.

I quickly changed into the snug faded jeans and white Wood jersey she gave me, then played with the bill of the baseball cap to get it adjusted to my liking. As I put it on, Bri returned and I almost dropped to my knees. The light blue raglan T-shirt had a V-cut to it that made it difficult not to look at her amazing cleavage, but what got me was her shorts.

Her tanned legs were on glorious display and to say they were short was an understatement. The pockets came out of the bottom, so it wouldn't be all that hard to slip a hand up them and reach her hot spot. My dick sprang to life just thinking about it. She tied her hair back into a ponytail and put on a Cubs hat that matched her shirt.

Bri cocked an eyebrow. "Since you're staring at me with no shame, I assume you like what I picked out for myself."

I hauled her into me. "You always look beautiful, but seeing you in these clothes does things to me."

A mischievous grin curled from her mouth. "Good things or bad things?"

I rocked my body roughly into hers. "Good things. *Very good things.* You look sexy as hell and I'm having a really hard time keeping my hands and mouth to myself."

Her face flushed to a dark shade of red as she whispered, "So, don't keep them to yourself."

"Don't tempt me. We have places to be and it's still not the right time," I growled.

She frowned. "My patience is growing thin with your insistence on the *right time*. If it doesn't happen soon, I might just combust."

Her tone was close to a whine and I couldn't help but chuckle. Her eyebrows furrowed deeper, her frustration evident. I kissed her cheek and motioned for her to take the lead on our way out of the bedroom. She released a disgruntled sigh while opening the door. For how hard I already was, it would be a long afternoon trying to resist her sassy mouth and even hotter body, but I was determined to make it a few more hours before making her lips mine.

* * *

THE FIRST COUPLE of innings of the game met all my expectations and more, especially since the Cubs were killing the Pirates. I loved watching Bri's face light up with each run we scored and hearing her cheer. She scarfed down more food than I did. Seeing a girl eat something rather than pick away at it because they were counting their calories was refreshing.

On numerous occasions, I wanted to tip her back and kiss the hell out of her, but I managed to keep my tongue in my mouth. That didn't stop my fingers from brushing along her thighs when my hand wasn't locked with hers. Our motions were in sync, right down to sharing food with one another, and it made my pulse quicken each time she slipped me a bite or drink of something.

As the bottom of the fifth inning began, I trailed my hand across her tight stomach and groaned into her shoulder after my fingers grazed her belly button ring. The prospect of kissing along that particular piercing ran through my head and the sinful desires that followed that train of thought should be downright illegal.

"You're fucking killing me, Bri. A belly button ring. Really?" I asked in a heated whisper.

Her lips were a mere inch away and I wanted to devour them.

She tilted my chin up, a devious smile on her face. "I can tell you approve of it. Now just imagine the cool metal of it between your teeth."

My pulse quickened and the pull to kiss her was too hard to resist. Just as I leaned in to capture her mouth, the crack of the bat and the roar of the crowd caught my attention. I turned in enough time to snag the foul ball coming right at us.

Bri shook her head and muttered, "I swear timing is not on our side at all. Nice catch, slick."

I chuckled at the annoyed look on her face. "I've got cat-like reflexes. Besides, it's probably better we focus on the game. We'll have our moment soon enough."

Crossing her arms, her eyes narrowed into a playful glare. "You're enjoying stringing out our first kiss way too much. I'm beginning to think you were put on this planet just to torture me."

I flashed my dimples. "That might be true, but you've been doing the same thing to me."

Bri pouted and tossed in a set of sappy eyes. "You do it to me way more than I do it to you. In fact, I think you should make it up to me by giving me the ball."

I teased her with it a few times before handing it over. "Your wish is my command, darling."

Her megawatt smile fired all my synapses. It was another moment where it took all my willpower not to kiss her and the little vixen knew it. She ran her hand along my thigh and paused near my very hard erection. Bri gave me a *come and get it* look and I gripped the sides of my seat to prevent myself from doing just that.

I narrowed my eyes. "I know what you're doing and it's not going to work."

Bri rolled her shoulders, a naughty grin on her face. "Can't blame a girl for trying."

I looked away. If I focused on her delectable body any longer, I'd drag her off to the bathrooms. My dick throbbed, loving that scenario, but my brain was still somewhat in control. When the girls got up to head to the concessions, I was more than grateful.

Once they were gone, Micah scrolled through his texts. His body went rigid in an instant. He had been acting so strange lately. I didn't have the heart to tell Mia he lied about his whereabouts last night. Word of the fight reached our side of town. Logan and Jesse texted me this morning to let me know they did damage control to make sure my parents didn't hear about it. I asked if Micah was with them, but the last time they saw him was when they helped us out last Sunday.

Shane nudged my shoulder and pointed at the ball below Bri's seat. "You're seriously letting her have it?"

I shrugged. "Did you see the look on her face? I'd give her anything she wanted just to see that smile again."

He dropped his jaw in disbelief. I was about to tell him it wasn't that big of a deal, but his shock vanished and he looked behind us several times.

"What's up? You look like you saw a ghost," I pointed out, ignoring the jitters creeping to the surface.

"It's nothing. I thought I spotted a couple of guys who work security for the McAndrews, but it wasn't them," Shane replied, his tone unconvincing.

"Do they follow Bri around? Why would they need to shadow her?"

"They don't tail her like they used to, but on occasion they show up. I was seeing things. It wasn't them. Don't stress on it."

He tried damn hard to act nonchalant, but his body language betrayed him. As he clutched the armrests, his shoulders were rigid. The idea of anyone watching us heightened my senses and killed all the potent desires inside me. I scanned the crowd to see if anyone was staring at us, but didn't see anything.

I had no clue who would watch us. Aside from people at Chamberlain, there wasn't anyone I could think of who'd show up and cause trouble. I didn't rule out the possibility of it, but I doubted Shane would be so tense if that were the case. His unease had nothing to do with me and everything to do with whoever might show up to keep an eye on Bri.

When the girls returned a few minutes later, Bri sensed the shift in me. She didn't hide her concern as she sat down. I flashed my dimples while taking the soda and nachos from her. I distracted her, and myself, by trailing my hands along her thighs and stomach, loving when a soft moan slipped from her luscious lips.

She got creative with her own hands. By the time the last inning was over, I really needed a cold shower. Every naughty slip of her hands and mine prevented me from looking over my shoulder, but on more than one occasion, it felt like a set of eyes were on us. I slid my hand into Bri's every time my nerves kicked up a notch and savored the blissful waves that came from her touch.

Micah and Mia ended up taking off in the seventh inning so they could make it to their dinner reservation on time, but they didn't miss much. After a one-two-three ninth, we made our way out of the stadium and over to the train. After we hit our stop, we walked the few blocks back to the hotel in silence. From the pensive looks on their faces, Bri and Shane had more than enough on their minds. On our way into the hotel, Shane stopped to tip the bellboys, but Bri and I headed to the elevator bank.

I leaned against the wall. A few strands of hair had come loose from Bri's ponytail as she chipped away at her nail polish. I tucked them behind her ear and cupped her cheek. "I hope you had a good time today. We'll go on a date without our friends tagging along eventually."

Bri arched her perfectly-manicured eyebrow. "I figured you brought them along so you could torture me some more. Don't think for a second I wasn't on to your antics at the game. I'll figure out a way to get back at you. Consider this your warning."

I couldn't resist rolling my eyes. "Aside from my mom, I don't think anyone has ever busted my chops as much as you. I wasn't trying to push your buttons, but you make it really hard for me not to touch you."

"So, you're blaming me for you running your hands all over my body whenever you feel like it?" Bri asked, her face flushed.

"Yup. You're sexy as fuck all the time. And the more time I spend with you, the harder you make it for me to behave," I growled, pinning my hands at the sides of her head.

Bri feigned being outraged before giving into her giggles. "It's okay, Trey. I'm sort of getting into this whole delayed gratification thing. It's never been my thing in the past, but I'm becoming more open to it, especially with how magical your fingers have proven to be so far."

Shane joined us as the elevator arrived and we were whisked to our floor. Before he opened our door, Shane turned to us with a sheepish smile. "I snagged the number of the smoking hot blonde behind the front desk. Her shift is up. I'm grabbing my things and meeting up with her at theWit. I doubt I'll be back before tomorrow. Just make sure you check out at a reasonable time."

He walked into the suite without another word and we followed him inside at least a foot apart from one another. I thought getting butterflies was a chick thing, but with the way my stomach was bouncing around now, I wasn't so sure anymore.

Bri gave Shane a quick hug. "I'm going to grab a quick shower. Have a great night with your new flavor of the week. Try not to impregnate her."

After Shane gave her subtle shove, she giggled on her way out of the room. I ignored the way my pulse quickened at the sound of her laugh and focused on him. "Are you sure it's okay for us to stay another night? I don't want to take advantage of your family's generosity any more than I already have."

Shane stared at me, his eyes curious, yet serious at the same time. "It's really fine. My family is more than okay with you two staying here. They know how much Bri needs breaks from her house. They don't know you two are in the beginning stages of whatever you want to call it. Regardless, I'm sure the staff around here will be checking up on you. My advice is not to sleep with her tonight. It'll end in disaster."

My rapidly beating heart came to an abrupt stop. "Why does she need breaks? What's going on at home? It feels like you're not telling me a lot, especially with how you behaved at the game."

"It's not my place to tell you. Just don't make her life any more complicated than it already is or I'll kick your ass," Shane warned, his face firm.

I crossed my arms and shot back, "The last thing I want to do is hurt her."

He walked away. I stared at his closed door for a moment before sitting down on the couch. It felt like I'd rode the Tilt-a-Whirl one too many times as I thought about what Shane tried telling me without saying it. There was a hell of a lot more that went on behind closed doors at the McAndrews' house. I needed to know more about what was going on before I wreaked any unnecessary havoc in her life.

CHAPTER 15

BRI

I lingered in the hallway to listen to them. When Shane nearly blabbed about how things were at home for me, it took all my willpower to stay put. If Trey found out about even half of it, he'd run for the hills or lose his temper and do something stupid.

Their voices dwindled off. Not wanting to get caught eavesdropping, I darted into the bedroom and straight for the bathroom. My twitchy nerves and raging hormones were in competition with each other. Needing to get some control over both of them, I got rid of my clothes, flipped on the water, and stepped in. The frigid temp made me want to hop out immediately, but I jumped around until my body could handle it.

After taking one of the coldest showers ever, I quickly dried off. My mind drifted to the next twenty-four hours I'd have with Trey. Heady desires chased away the lingering coldness in my body. All of the sparks flickering inside me now would spread through me in no time.

Last night, I nearly had an orgasm with very minimal effort on his part, so I wasn't sure how I'd keep it from happening when he really made a move. I lightly slapped my face a few times and reminded myself that we were taking it slow. My brain understood that much but my libido wasn't even close to being on the same page.

I poked my head into the bedroom to make sure it was empty and retrieved the long-sleeve gray and black dress with irregular stitching from the bed. Aside from the neutral colors, its unique pattern was totally my style. I sifted through my shopping bag to find the red thong and lacy matching bra and changed, grabbed my purse, and returned to the bathroom.

After my eyes complemented the darker colors in my outfit, I applied some foundation and pink lipstick. Just as I finished curling my hair, "The Reason" streamed throughout the suite. As I listened to the lyrics and sprayed on some perfume, the corners of my mouth curled into a soft smile and headed back to the bedroom. Trey was in the middle of it, engrossed with his cell. I cleared my throat to get his attention.

He did a double-take. After regaining his composure, he hauled me into his chest and whispered, "You look and smell divine. How'd I get so damn lucky?"

I wrapped my arms around his neck and teased, "Well, you know, luck always runs out."

He tried to seem put off, tossing in a pout for good measure, but it didn't last very long. His lips spread into a drool-worthy smile as he asked, "Ms. McAndrews, would you do me a great honor and go out on a date with me tonight?"

My grip tightened. "I'd go anywhere with you, Mr. Donovan."

Trey kissed my forehead. "Excellent. Hand over whatever you want me to wear."

I passed over a pair of faded indigo jeans and the sky blue jacquard button-down shirt. Trey gave my cheek a soft peck and trailed his tongue to my earlobe. My body yearned for more than his lips. Before I threw myself at him, I swatted his ass and pushed him toward the bathroom. As he strode away, Trey howled with laughter. I flopped on the bed and picked up my phone.

Kelsey: Just checking in with you. Everything is the status quo around here. They're off to a charity event for the night and have brunch at the country club tomorrow. You're going to have to explain why you're not staying at the penthouse at some point. You *better* be behaving yourself. No parties or pregnancies, young lady!

I gave her the abbreviated version of what went down last night, but I should've known that wouldn't be enough for her.

Bri: I promise to fill in the blanks. If they pester you, just reiterate I've been working on a project that's due and will be home tomorrow before curfew. And I'm always on my best behavior!

My nerves prickled at the prospect of dealing with my dad if he found out I wasn't at the penthouse.

Kelsey: Tell me another one, Pinocchio. Love you!

Bri: I love you too! Thank you for covering for me!

I shoved my cell back in my purse as Trey came out of the bathroom. As I soaked him in while he dried his hair with a towel, my mouth went dry. Once satisfied, he tossed it over his shoulder and shook out his head, resulting in an amazing bedhead look. Fiery sensations trekked through the lower half of my body, making me forget why we even needed to leave. I rested my hands on his chest and inhaled his intoxicating musky scent. His fingers drifted above my ass and I bit my lower lip to keep from moaning.

"I'm sure it's no surprise, but I don't wear these shirts very often. School and church, but that's about it. If it gets you to bite your lip in the seductive way you're doing right now, I might wear them all the time," Trey murmured, tightening his grip.

As we stared at each other, I got lost in the passion behind his eyes. His fingers slid below my naval and lingered there for a minute to play with my piercing before he locked our hands together.

"We should get going. The sun is about to set. We need to arrive at our destination before it does," Trey said, his voice husky.

The rational side of my brain was curious about what he planned, but the horny side screamed out in frustration. The sensual torture over the past twenty-four hours was difficult to fight.

I squeezed his hand. "Lead the way, handsome. It sounds like you put some thought into this evening and I can't wait to see what you have in store for us."

He pinched my ass on our way out of the suite. "You have no idea. A beautiful girl like you deserves to be dazzled. I intend to do just that and more."

We strode hand in hand to the elevators. Trey punched the call button and towed me into him. He ran his nose down mine, his lips a mere inch away for the taking. A ragged breath slipped out and I willed my trembling knees to keep me upright. With the wanton desires swarming through me, it took *a lot* of effort.

The elevator arrived and was empty when we stepped inside. We leaned against the back wall with our hands still intertwined. His eyes centered on mine before they ran over my body. The electricity in the air charged through us and we inched closer together.

He palmed my cheek and whispered, "In case I haven't said it, you look incredible."

I rested my hand over his and loved how his eyes blazed brighter after I touched him. Our breaths became sporadic as we remained lost in each other's gaze. My body pleaded for me to tangle his tongue with mine. His cologne surrounded us. It was an aphrodisiac I didn't need, seeping into my pores. I pressed a tender kiss to the base of his throat. He groaned, secured both my hands behind my back, and sucked along my neck until a soft moan escaped me.

When the elevator stopped, I whimpered and he pulled away with a wicked grin on his face. On our way through the lobby and out the doors, my rapid breaths evened out, but my body still yearned for him.

His lips curled into a shy smile as he pointed at the black car parked at the curb. "I really couldn't resist hiring a driver for the night. I hope you don't mind."

Being driven around in town cars and limos was second nature to me, but this was different. Seeing the thoughtful look on his face made me feel like a princess off to the ball. The driver opened the back door and Trey helped me inside before sliding in next to me. Plenty of buildings flew past us until we arrived at The John Hancock Building ten minutes later, but I barely noticed them. Trey caressed the inside of my hand the entire ride and I couldn't get past how delightful every swoop of his fingers resonated deep within me.

After we stepped out of the car, the enormity of the skyscraper captivated me. It had always been breathtaking, but it seemed larger than life as I gazed at it now. Tranquil waves floated through my body and pinned me to my spot. It mesmerized me now more than ever before and it was because of Trey. His dimples made an appearance as he watched me. On cue, what felt like hundreds of butterflies fluttered in every direction.

Trey wrapped his arm around my waist on our way inside, led us over to the admissions booth, and purchased two tickets. After following a short line of people in front of us into the elevator, we made our way up to the ninety-fourth floor. Once we stepped out and walked over to the large windows of the observation deck, an inadvertent gasp slipped from me. The last hint of the sun's rays hit the horizon, casting red, orange, and pink hues across the sky that would make anyone lose their breath.

His eyes sparkled as he squeezed my side and confessed, "When I was six, my mom brought Micah, Mia, and me downtown. As touristy as it sounds, we took one of those bus tours where you can hop on and off wherever you like. We saw so much that day, but what I loved the most was this building and the Willis Tower. Being that high up, with the whole city around me, made me feel like I could take on the world. When I'm with you, I always feel that way."

There was a vulnerability to that admission that warmed my body in a very different way than how he'd been firing it up so far. My next breath caught in my throat as I whispered, "You make me feel that way too."

Trey kissed my cheek. "Like you, the view is exquisite. I'm glad we made it in time. I've always enjoyed a good sunset, but having you by my side gives it a new meaning."

I arched an eyebrow. "Care to elaborate?"

His face was serene as he explained, "Well, most people believe it marks the end of the day, but I don't really see it that way anymore. It's more like the beginning of something new. My mom always said God gave us this beautiful masterpiece before wiping the slate clean for a brighter and better tomorrow. The way you see the world and the kindness in your heart makes me actually believe that now."

My pulse quickened and I leaned closer to him. "For someone who doesn't talk that much, you sure know all the right things to say when you want to."

Trey chuckled. "I have my moments."

We walked around the observatory, pointing out various places downtown that were our favorites. Lights from the skyscrapers illuminated the city and danced along the rippling waves off in the distance. My insides jumped with them, relishing how his fingers slid from the middle of my back and even lower..

His lips spread into a sexy grin. "Let's go grab a bite to eat. With what I have planned, you're going to need the sustenance to keep up."

The way his magical fingers glided across my body for the past half hour already had it red-hot, but hearing that brought on scorching waves of heat that would make the devil jealous.

As soon as we stepped inside the elevator, he rested against the back wall and produced that cocky smirk of his, knowing what it'd do to me and not giving a damn we were in a full elevator. I placed my hands on his hips and ran my tongue enticingly along my lips. Trey groaned and his eyes fell to the floor. I no longer cared we weren't alone and leaned in to kiss a spot on his throat that would really make him moan, but he gripped my sides and swayed back.

I swept my lips across his neck until I got the reaction I wanted out of him. Several people shot us wary looks, but I didn't care. Hearing him moan made my toes curl and stomach flutter. It was probably in my best interest to step away from him, but I'd already become a huge fan of the way his every move shot straight to my core.

After he caught his breath, Trey caressed my cheek. "What I

wouldn't give to know what's going through that pretty head of yours."

I blushed. "It's not really an appropriate conversation topic while in the presence of others."

He pinched my ass. "Remind me to ask you about it later. Unless you want to show me instead. I wouldn't be opposed to that."

Trey ran his hands lazily along my backside and I clenched my thighs together to cease the wildfire inside me. Feeling his erection against my hip didn't help the potent sensations coasting through me one bit.

I grasped his neck and muttered, "You know, you're one mercurial man."

"Mercurial. What does that mean?" Trey asked, amused.

"You're moody and broody all the time. And on top of that, you give off a lot of mixed signals. It's hard to keep up," I answered, annoyed.

Trey nipped at my ear and growled, "I'm doing my best to take this slow, but it's hard to contain myself when I'm around you. From the second I saw you, I wanted nothing more than to pin you against your locker and make every part of you *mine*."

My retort was cut short when the elevator doors dinged open. His hand slid into mine on our way to the town car sitting curbside. A gust of wind blew strands of my hair across my face. As annoying as it was, I welcomed the cool breeze across my overly turned on body.

Our drive over to the Riverwalk was short. We stopped at the London House—one of the few hotels in Chicago I hadn't been to. Trey ushered me inside and up to the rooftop. We weaved our way through tables until we found an open one along the railing.

He slid out a chair for me to take and sat down across from me. A candle sat in the middle of the table, flickering with the light breeze. Once we were settled, I knew exactly why Trey selected this place. The skyscrapers glowed, giving way to a remarkable view of the river, and the stringed lights above us bopped along the ripples of the water before disappearing into Lake Michigan.

A waiter in black slacks and white button-up walked past us with a couple of plates. A variety of different spices lingered in the air and my mouth watered from the delicious aroma. I licked my lips while scanning over the menu.

"Please stop teasing me with your tongue," Trey spoke up, his voice hoarse.

I couldn't resist giving him a devilish smirk. "Why would I do that when you refuse to kiss me? Until that happens, you're just going to have to deal with it."

Seriousness settled upon his face as he asked, "How am I doing so far?"

I arched an eyebrow. "What do you mean?"

His gaze flickered around the roof. "I've never taken anyone out on a date before. I'm not sure if I'm doing it right."

My eyes grew wide. "You were serious last night?"

His cheeks turned bright red as he nodded and I couldn't help but laugh. The look on his face shifted from embarrassed to ashamed.

Grasping his hand, I confessed, "You're doing perfect. It's the best date I've ever been on and it's only started. You have nothing to worry about."

"I'll always worry. This is uncharted territory for me, in more ways than one." I scrunched my eyebrows together, unsure where he was going with that comment. A vulnerable look he only seemed to share with me crept up on his face before he clarified, "I didn't mean that in a bad way. I want to do this right and that means I need to be honest with you. From our conversation last night, I know you've been out on plenty of dates. I just wanted to be sure everything measured up so far."

"The dates I've been on in the past don't hold a candle to this one. And if we're being frank on the matter, I'd rather you not compare yourself to anyone else. I've never connected with anyone the way I have with you," I declared with a sincere smile.

A server stopped by our table. Trey gestured for me to go while he glimpsed at the menu. I handed mine over. "I'll take the American classic burger with fries and a water, please."

The waiter jotted down my order and ran his eyes over my body in a very demeaning way. Trey cleared his throat to get him to stop staring at me. The lethal glare he held on the guy made me shudder. Trey brought my hand to his lips and placed a tender kiss on my wrist.

"I'll have the lobster roll with chips and water. Bring our check with the food and keep your eyes to the ground when you do," Trey ordered, his tone menacing.

Our server darted to the kitchen. It didn't surprise me in the least to see Trey jealous, but he took it a bit too far by threatening the poor kid. He leaned back in his chair and I raised both eyebrows at him.

"I didn't like the way he was looking at you and wanted to make it clear I'd beat the living shit out of him if he did it again."

"You promised me you wouldn't get into pointless fights anymore. Why do I have a feeling keeping your fists in check is going to be *impossible*?"

Trey glowered. "It's *never* pointless when it comes to you. You're a very bright girl. You can't be that oblivious to how many guys check you out. If I were keeping track tonight, I'd say at least fifty, but I'm trying to control my temper, so I haven't been."

I scoffed. "You're exaggerating, Trey."

He waved a hand in the air. "Look around, Bri. I already see five guys ogling you."

I cursed under my breath after seeing a few men staring at me with no shame. When I focused on Trey again, I scowled at the 'I told you so' look on his face and grumbled, "Let's talk about something else. If we stay on this topic, it's going to make us both angrier and I'd rather not fight with you."

His face softened. "I love the sound of your laugh. It's become one of my favorite sounds."

The butterflies fluttering around in my stomach went wild. "I really love when your dimples make an appearance."

Trey flashed them to appease me and I rewarded him with a giggle. His face suddenly became very serious and I stopped laughing.

"Will you tell me more about your life at home?"

The warmth I'd felt all evening with him at my side dissipated in a heartbeat. My eyes remained on the table as I mumbled, "Tonight is going so amazing, I'd rather not think or talk about my parents."

He scrunched his eyes together. The crease between them that tended to make an appearance when he tried to figure something out was prominent. My eyes pleaded with him to let it be. Thankfully, the waiter returned with our food, waters, and the check a few minutes later. Heeding Trey's warning, he kept his eyes on the tiled stones below us while placing everything on the table. Trey handed over his credit card and the guy almost knocked over a few patrons while scampering away.

I brought the large burger to my mouth and the sauce on it made my taste buds dance. I grabbed the ketchup bottle, poured some on the corner of my plate, and swiped a few French fries through it. The seasoning on them was just as tasty as the burger.

After a couple more bites, I gazed at Trey. "What's your favorite movie right now?"

He set his sandwich on his plate and popped a few chips in his mouth. "It brought to life my favorite toy and cartoon as a child, so hands down, *Transformers*. How about you?"

"That's one of my favorites from this year too, but if I have to pick one, I'd go with *Pirates of the Caribbean: At World's End.*"

Trey groaned into his napkin. "Please tell me you're not obsessed with Johnny Depp. Mia is like in love with him and Orlando Bloom."

I smirked and took a bite of my burger. After swallowing every delectable morsel, I replied, "Guilty as charged. There's just something incredibly hot about pirates. If it makes you feel any better, *Disturbia* is a close second."

He raised his eyebrows. "I wouldn't have pegged you as a thriller kind of gal, but I'm not surprised either. If I've learned anything about you, it's that I should *never* assume what you like or dislike because I'm wrong ninety percent of the time. You're one big conundrum for me."

After I took a sip of my water, I said, "Yes, you usually are off base. The feeling is mutual by the way. What's your biggest pet peeve?"

"People who cut in lines drive me bonkers. Unless you have the fast pass at an amusement park, it's not kosher. What about you?" Trey asked around a bite of his sandwich.

"I can't stand people who don't cover their mouths when they cough. I'm all for sharing and everything, but I draw the line at germs," I answered, scrunching up my nose.

"Where do you stand on swapping spit? Does that count as germs?" Trey asked with a wily grin.

A sensual ache settled between my stomach and my thighs. *Damn traitorous body.* I crossed my legs and smiled sweetly at him. "I know what you're doing. I'm sidelining that topic. What's your favorite roller coaster?"

"That's easy. Goliath at Six Flags. *Best. Ride. Ever.*"

"Raging Bull is way better than Goliath."

"Agree to disagree."

I brushed my foot along his leg and he heaved in his next breath. My mouth spread into a shrewd grin. "Fair enough."

"What's your favorite ice cream?"

"To eat?"

He wrinkled his eyebrows. "Uh, yeah, to eat. What else do you do with it?"

I gave him a drool-worthy smile. "Maybe I'll show you later."

"I thought you sidelined that sort of chitchat. You know, you can be a real tease sometimes."

"So can you, but to answer your question, it's vanilla. What's yours?"

He arched an eyebrow. "Just plain old vanilla?"

I smirked. "Nothing plain about it."

His eyes had a playful glare to them as he muttered, "Why do I get the feeling you're talking about something else entirely?"

Flashing one of my naughtier grins, I said, "That's a possibility. You didn't answer me."

He closed his eyes for a minute and released a ragged breath. "Chocolate."

"What's your middle name?"

"Garrett. It's my grandpa's name. What's yours?"

"Maureen. It was my grandma's name."

"Did you know Trey isn't my legal name?"

A deep blush spread across my face. "Um, yes, I do know that."

He cocked an eyebrow. "Care to elaborate, missy?"

My face somehow became even redder. "I saw your file in the office and peeked at it."

He feigned being outraged. "You sly little devil. For the record, if you ever call me Treahbar, I *will* stop speaking to you."

I saluted him. "The record has been noted. What's your favorite book?"

"Outside of *Sports Illustrated* or a good car magazine, I'm not much of a reader, so I'll go with my childhood favorite, which is *Green Eggs and Ham*. What's yours?"

"Dr. Seuss is the best. There's so much you can learn from those books. I still read them on occasion. Do you want my childhood favorite or what I'm currently reading?"

"Both."

"*Oh, The Places You'll Go* as a kid. As for now, I'd have to go with *Eclipse*."

His gaze drifted upwards as he mumbled, "Lord, you and Mia are so much alike. She jumped on the vampire/werewolf bandwagon. It figures you'd be on it too."

I giggled. "Guilty again. I'm Team Edward. She's Team Jacob."

He saluted me this time. "Duly noted."

"They're making *Twilight* into a movie. It's supposed to come out sometime next year."

"If you want me to take you, I'm going to demand something in return. And I have a colorful imagination."

I snorted. "I'm sure you do, but as per usual, you're wrong again. Mia and I are going on opening night. What's your favorite candy?"

Trey shrugged. "Depends on my mood."

I rolled my eyes. "That's not all that shocking, since it swings back and forth so much."

"Snickers or Starbursts. What's yours, smartass?"

"Starbursts are on my list too, along with Sour Patch Kids and Jelly

Beans. If I'm in a chocolate kind of mood, I'd have to say Kit Kats, Twix, or M&M's."

"That's a lot of favorites," Trey pointed out, brushing some crumbs off the table.

"I didn't get candy as a child. I'm still trying to narrow it down," I responded, cringing as my brain-to-mouth malfunction set in.

He peered at me, his eyes curious. I wanted to kick myself for letting that detail slip. Fortunately, the waiter returned, collected our empty plates, and gave Trey his credit card. He signed the check and passed it over to the guy. Trey rounded the table and extended a hand. I held it tightly on our way through the hotel. When we walked past our driver and toward the river, I arched an eyebrow at Trey.

"I thought it'd be fun to take a water taxi to our next spot. It's something I've always wanted to do. I couldn't think of a better person to experience that first with," Trey murmured as we strode up the dock.

My breath hitched at his sweet words. While we waited for the next taxi to come along, I rested my head against his chest and listened to his heart. It was in tune with mine, both frantically racing. He ran his fingers through my hair before kissing the top of my head.

I patted his chest. "I knew underneath your tough exterior there was a kind and gentle soul."

"I'm not sure I'd go that far. The softness to your voice, coupled with the serene look on your face, makes it sound like I'm a saint. That's *definitely* not the case."

Some of the lewder comments and gestures the girls at Chamberlain made this past week ran through my mind and the green monster clawed its way to the surface. Doing my best to be indifferent, I said, "Yeah, saint-like is a tad off base. The word around school is you're nothing but a *bad boy*."

He rolled his eyes. "And you say *I'm* mercurial."

I smacked his arm. "There's no way I'm as moody as you are."

Trey chuckled. "Maybe not quite as bad as me, but your emotions flip rather quickly too. It's hard to keep up, but you say a lot with your expressions, so I usually have a good idea."

I put a hand on my hip. "Is that so? Alright, hotshot, what's going through my mind?"

"Well, going back to your bad boy comment, your sarcastic tone, and the scowl on your face, the girls around school have gotten under your skin," Trey replied, tickled.

"Yeah, you could say that. I've never been a jealous person. This past week, I've had to deal with that emotion on more than one occasion. I don't like it," I muttered, embarrassed.

He tilted my chin up and kissed my forehead. "Don't be. I only have eyes for you."

The wildfire he created south of me returned with a vengeance. I wasn't sure how much longer I'd be able to tolerate him saying such sweet things and kissing everything but my mouth. Just as I was about to take matters into my own hands, the next available taxi pulled up. Trey helped me into it before hopping inside with more grace than I'd ever have.

"Please drop us off at the Michigan Avenue dock," Trey instructed.

Our driver nodded and steered the boat to the middle of the river. With an arm wrapped around me, Trey pointed out various places he enjoyed stopping at when he was downtown. I snuggled closer to him and closed my eyes.

Trey nibbled on my earlobe. "Don't fall asleep now. The best part of the night is coming up."

I gazed at him warily. He gave me a lopsided grin as we pulled up to our destination. Trey handed over the fare and held my hand as I got out. We walked along Michigan Avenue with our hands intertwined. My stomach fluttered in anticipation of what came next.

We crossed the street near the Art Institute and made our way over to Buckingham Fountain. Blue and purple lights skipped along the water as it sprayed into the surrounding pool. The illuminated skyscrapers provided the perfect backdrop to the colors in the fountain, easily making it one of my favorite sights in the city.

Trey led us over to a secluded spot as he caressed patterns along my back. His gifted hands amplified the sweltering ache between my thighs. The chill in the air disappeared as my body grew warmer with each swoop of his fingers. I leaned against the railing, praying my legs would keep me upright. The passion in his eyes seared right into my soul and I shuffled closer to him.

Our chests were against each other, but it was still far too much space as far as I was concerned. I'd never really had the urge to mount anyone in public, but that really wasn't the case right now. Trey cupped my face and crashed his lips into mine. Our tongues intertwined roughly together. The cool metal stuck through the middle of his as it tangled with mine was better than I could've imagined.

Every sensual feeling thus far was nothing compared to what coasted through my body right now. He licked and swooped around my mouth none too gently and it still wasn't enough to fill the unadulterated need I had for him.

I kissed him back with just as much as zest as he did when he started it. Tingling sensations trekked through my body and I tugged on his hair, making him groan and deepen our kiss. Of all the boys I'd made out with over the years, not one of them kissed me like this was their last chance at any sort of intimacy for the foreseeable future. Trey sucked my tongue even further into his mouth. I twisted my tongue vigorously with his and damn near trembled every time it slid over his piercing.

After his teeth grazed my bottom lip, I lost all coherency and released a loud moan. Trey sucked in a quick breath and trailed his lips along my jaw, but I gripped his chin and claimed his mouth again. He rocked his body into mine and I damn near convulsed. Every swipe of his tongue became hungrier. It was already difficult not to unbutton his shirt, but it was close to impossible now. Public fornication was the least of my concerns. I *needed* him to satisfy the potent desires whipping through me like a category five hurricane.

We panted heavily, neither one of us willing to break off the kiss yet, but judging by the fuzziness in my head, the lack of air was an issue. Trey pulled away, heaving in a few breaths, and I whimpered at the loss of his lips. Breathing wasn't really a priority for me. I leaned forward to pick up where we left off, but he swayed back.

"Why did you stop?" I whined.

He smirked. "Because people are starting to stare. Let's head back to the hotel. We can continue our make out session there."

I wiggled my eyebrows. "I like that plan *a lot*."

Trey had a tight grip on my hand on our way to the town car waiting for us at the Hilton. When there was a break in traffic, we crossed the street and were whisked away. I cursed the damn stoplights that slowed us down. All I really wanted to do was climb into his lap and kiss him until breathing became problematic again.

My mind drifted to his tongue ring. Lord, it felt so damn good inside my mouth. The slickness between my thighs led me to believe it was going to feel *amazing* down there.

Trey ran his hands down my flushed face. "What are you thinking?"

I gazed away, utterly embarrassed. "Is it true what they say about tongue rings and…"

He sucked along my neck. "I'm not sure. You're the first girl to test it out. I can take it out if you don't like it."

I balked. "Don't you dare. I love it."

"I saw how much you enjoyed yourself at the game today. Care to play a different baseball game when we get back?" Trey asked, trailing his lips across my collarbone.

I bit my bottom lip to prevent another humiliating moan from slipping out and nodded. All I could think about was his damn tongue ring and how badly I wanted to test it out on other body parts. Trey ran his fingers along my stomach, pausing to play with my belly button ring and sending fiery sensations straight to my core. I rested my hand on his upper thigh and he allowed my fingers to brush along his erection for a minute before he stopped me.

Color crept up his neck as he said in a heated whisper, "Don't get the wrong idea. I don't plan on hitting anything more than doubles, but I do plan on kissing you until you're ready to go to sleep."

I kissed along the trail of red leading up to his jaw. My teeth grazed his earlobe and he released a low groan. "Just for the record, I can function quite well with next to no sleep, so you have my permission to kiss me until the sun comes up. If it's anywhere near as good as that first one, I can live without sleep for the rest of my life."

His hands ran suggestively along my arms and under my breasts. "I'm very pleased to hear our first kiss was just as good for you as it was for me."

My body craved his touch so much as I whimpered, "It was *thigh-clenchingly* good."

He gave my cheek a brisk kiss and admitted, "That wasn't even my best work."

Everything south of my naval flamed hotter than it had all night. It was like the boy had a direct line to my groin. He knew all the right things to say and do to excite it. I was just about to point that out when our driver pulled up in front of the hotel.

I flew out of the car and almost stamped my foot at Trey's sudden pokiness. He flashed that damn cocky smirk of his and slipped the driver a wad of cash. A bellboy held the door open for us and it took everything I had not to slide off my heels, grab his hand, and sprint through the lobby.

By the time we reached the elevator bank, my insides were molten lava. Thank God it was empty when we got inside. Trey sauntered to the back of it, pinned my hands above my head, and kissed the living daylights out of me.

I melded my body into his and got lost in all the intoxicating desires his lips gave me. He licked and nipped along my bottom lip before giving the upper one just as much attention. After he thrust his body into mine, I released a loud moan. When we reached our floor, I sucked in an overdue breath and Trey did the same as we made our way down the hallway.

He opened the door and picked me up. His lips traveled across the base of my throat before he sucked on the freckles below my chin he was apparently fond of. I tilted my head to give him better access and grabbed fistfuls of his hair. The growing ache between my stomach and thighs neared its explosion point. After kicking the door shut, he didn't make it any further than the island before setting me down. I wrapped my legs around him and licked along his Adam's apple.

Even through his jeans, Trey was clearly ready. I was dripping and desperate for so much more than his mouth and hands. My lips crashed against his with an urgency for him to rock into me again. He gripped my ass and grinded roughly into me, and I matched his thrusts, tangling my tongue with his.

Every twirl of his tongue made my insides throw a damn block party and I was far too close to the edge. My legs quivered and I devoured his mouth like the end of the world was near. He rocked into me with force and attacked my mouth with just as much vigor.

Trey twisted his hips into me and it was game over. My self-control went right out the window as a volcanic eruption went off inside me. I bit down on his shoulder, encouraging him to grind into me again. He obliged with several rough thrusts and euphoria spread throughout my body in a way I'd never experienced. My eyes rolled to the back of my head as I rode out the ecstasy. After I floated back to earth, I gasped to catch my next breath and opened my eyes.

Holy shit! I can't believe that just happened! That's a first!

Trey's mouth was ajar as he sputtered, "Did I just make you come?"

I gave him a slow nod as my cheeks turned bright red. His lips were on mine in a heartbeat and our mouths consumed one another until breathing became a problem.

He rested his forehead on mine. "That's another first for me. As always, you're a constant surprise."

I inhaled deeply. "Don't get a big head over it. With the build-up over the past few weeks, I'm surprised it didn't happen the second our lips touched. It doesn't help that I have next to no control over my body's reactions when you're around. It's like you have the owner's manual to it and just love pressing as many buttons as you can."

I clasped a hand over my mouth, utterly mortified I had that brain-to-mouth glitch. His lips spread into a smug grin as he said, "I can assure you I have no such book and could say the same thing about you when it comes to my body. I *will* say, I do quite enjoy pressing all your buttons."

I scowled. "I know you do. You enjoy it *way* too much."

He smirked. "That I do. The island is kind of awkward. Can we move this over to the couch?"

I nodded, not trusting my brain to send the right words to my mouth any longer. After carrying me over to the sofa, he kicked off his shoes and I did the same with my heels. Trey looked around for the remote. Spotting it on top of the fireplace, he strode over to it and turned on the surround sound. "Let's Get It On" filled the suite. *How apt.* I rested my head on the arm of the couch.

Today was by far one of the best of my life and what I needed to face what lies ahead for us. I didn't have the courage to tell him that I spotted several familiar faces. Granted, it was just kids from around school, but they happened to be tight with Sebastian. I couldn't shove his stupid threats from my head for too long.

I really wanted to know what the hell was going on and wasn't sure if his friends springing up at the game was a coincidence or if there was something more to it. The nagging feeling in my gut screamed something was up, but I wasn't ready to face it yet, especially since I wasn't sure how my dad would factor into this new development with Trey.

He made it quite clear that Trey was off-limits. If I let him think he had the upper hand in any way, he'd just make my life even worse than he already did. I refused to let him take away the one person who truly made me happy. I'd never experienced the blissfulness that only Trey gave me and would fight like hell to keep it.

Trey settled next to me and brushed his lips along mine. It brought me out of the reverie my mind had taken me. The flames flickering inside me sprang to life and my body readied itself for round two. Darker days and subject matters were in our future. Our problems could wait until tomorrow. The only thing I wanted to do right now was get lost in his delectable mouth for the remainder of the night. Maybe, if I was lucky, I'd have another mind-blowing orgasm.

CHAPTER 16

BRI

We made out for the rest of the night and then spent another amazing day together. Every detail ran through my head on my way home. It was the best distraction I could ask for as I drove to one of the places I liked least in this world. My fairytale was about to end and I wasn't ready for it.

When I turned onto our road, my heart jumped out of my chest. I killed the headlights, coasted down our long brick driveway, and parked in my usual spot near the huge tiered fountain. I grabbed my things and scanned across all the windows in front of the house on my way to the door. For seven thirty at night, it was eerily dark and unwanted weights descended upon me.

I'm freaking out for no reason. They haven't caught me yet. Deep breaths, Bri. You got this.

I couldn't shake the feeling that this time was different. As I put my key in the lock, the knob turned and I was face-to-face with my dad.

His soulless eyes were livid as I strode past him and toward the staircase.

"Get your ass in the living room, Brianna."

The ire in his tone sent chills up my spine. I dropped my stuff at the bottom of the stairs, walked into the living room, and plopped down on what was probably the most uncomfortable and ugliest brown couch in the world. As he paced in front of me, his eyes were wild with rage. My nerve endings prickled nonstop, almost like someone flipped the switch on a high-voltage current on them.

Dad cleared his throat. Fiddling with the charm bracelet Trey gave me this morning to stop my hands from shaking, I looked up. His face was usually set in an angry expression of some sort, but the way the vein in his forehead throbbed at a relentless rate made it clear he was about to flip out on me. I didn't wish for my mom's presence often, but I really wanted her around now.

"Where have you been? Kelsey told us you had a big project in your English class that was due and would be holed up at the penthouse to work on it. I don't buy it, especially since security informed me you weren't there most of the weekend. If I were you, I'd tell the truth. I *really* don't appreciate being lied to and can fire Kelsey's ass before you take your next breath. I can also prevent you from leaving this house until you graduate."

His acidic tone, coupled with the threats, brought on a bout of dread that sucked all the air out of my lungs. He hovered above me, demanding an answer. The tight grip he had on his glass of brandy made his knuckles turn white. My body slipped into a state of panic I wasn't sure I'd be able to handle without passing out.

I must remain strong. I can't show an ounce of fear or it's game over. I'll need to put on an Oscar-worthy performance to get out of this one. Here goes nothing...

"She's not lying and neither am I. The plan was to be at the penthouse to work on the project, but it's a group effort and the others couldn't get downtown with their schedules, so we rotated houses. I didn't think it was that big of a deal since it was for school. You and mom had events all weekend, so I didn't want to bother you."

My voice came out as smooth as silk. His eyebrows furrowed even deeper while he appraised me. It took every ounce of my strength not to squirm under his scrutinizing gaze. Resting my hands on my knees, I kept my face blank.

He pounded the contents of his glass and slammed it on the mahogany coffee table behind him. "You're seventeen years old and living under my roof. If your plans change, you report them to us. Do you understand?"

I dug deep to plaster on a somewhat apologetic look versus the scowl I really wanted to give him, along with the middle finger. "Yes, I understand. I'm sorry. It won't happen again. I still have homework to finish before tomorrow. May I be excused?"

"No, I'm not finished with you just yet. I want to see this project with my own eyes. Get your backpack."

Fuck! I'm beginning to have a new appreciation for Walter Scott's comment on deception. What a tangled web we weave indeed. I'm beyond entangled and have no clue how to get out of it. Dammit, Bri, think!

My brain scrambled for a minute before a light bulb flickered on. I walked over to my messenger bag. We really did have a project coming up. There wasn't a due date on the reference packet, so he couldn't question it. As much as I kept telling myself that, my heart pounded harshly against my chest as my panic climbed to a new high. Heaving in my next breath, I pulled the papers out of my folder and handed them over.

"This is the logistics of what needs to be done. I want tangible proof. Stop playing games, Brianna!" Dad shouted, tossing it on the couch.

All my blood boiled over. "It says in bold letters that it's a group project. My laptop was here. It's on Kylie's. I can call her to come over with it, but I doubt you want to interrupt her family's evening. What would her parents say about that? Not trusting your daughter's word on a simple homework assignment wouldn't be something you'd want thrown in your face during your very important reelection campaign. The paparazzi have already had a field day with the photos they've gotten of you not paying attention at my soccer games."

His eyes bugged out as he warned, "Don't get smart with me. In the blink of an eye, I can have you transferred to a boarding school overseas and don't think I haven't thought about it. You're still in Chicago because it benefits me."

I swallowed against the lump in my throat. "You wouldn't dare send me away."

He gave me an egotistical smile. "Oh, but I would. I won't let your unruly and disrespectful behavior screw things up now. You *will* start acting your part for this campaign."

A shocked gasp slipped through me and my hands flew to my face to hide my horror. The air caught in my throat was close to suffocating me. His eyes danced, daring me to goad him, but I had no words. The absolute terror taking over my body scattered my wits across the floor and I could barely think, let alone speak.

Once he realized I wasn't going to say anything, his face scrunched up in disgust before he sneered, "I can't even look at you. Get out of my sight."

Hearing the spite in his voice shattered the wall I desperately tried to keep from falling whenever he demeaned me. It was one thing to act strong, but it was next to impossible to maintain it when it felt like you were being ripped to shreds on the inside. If I didn't get out of here, he'd change his mind and continue to make me feel worthless. Tears welled in my eyes before I grabbed my packet from the couch, picked up my backpack, and bolted from the room.

As I ran upstairs, Dad shouted, "The very thin layer of ice beneath you is about to crack, Brianna. If I were you, I'd be on my best behavior for the foreseeable future. As you now know, there are plenty of things I can do to turn your world upside down and if you keep pushing me the way you have been lately, I'll have no problem putting those plans into motion."

I nearly tripped over my feet with that threat and forced myself to remain upright, but it was one hell of a challenge with the terror crushing all the bones in my body. My heart thrashed against my chest as sweat trickled down my temples. Against my will, tears cascaded down my cheeks while I sprinted to my room. I flicked on the light and the surround sound, needing to hear anything else than the echo of his villainous voice in my head, and curled into a ball in the center of my bed.

My body shook nonstop with the panic I couldn't control. I sobbed into the pillows and pounded the mattress. The past few weeks had already been akin to a walk through hell, but it was about to get much worse. There was no telling what he'd do or say to me.

The imaginary hands that lived to make an appearance when I was in this mental state were around my neck and squeezing tightly. The walls crumbled around me. My heart rate spiked even higher as I tried to catch my breath. The bed dipped and I didn't have to look behind me to know it was Kelsey. She gently trailed her fingers along my arm to calm me.

"I'm so sorry, Bri. He showed no signs of distrust all weekend. It's a little unsettling that he went thermonuclear on you. If I thought that was going to happen, I would've warned you."

Her voice was shaky, but full of apology. She blamed herself and the tears dripping on my forearm confirmed it. Needing the comfort only she could give me when I was in this house, I threw my arms around her. Holding me close, she ran her fingers through my hair.

I hated taking the medication to prevent my anxiety attacks. Over the years, she'd found a way to bring me out of it by doing exactly what she was doing now. We cried together for a few minutes until my body stopped shaking and my breathing steadied.

"Kelsey, please don't apologize. I'm so sorry for putting you in that position and for doing it time and time again. I know you do it to keep my sanity intact, but I'm not sure you should any longer. I'd never forgive myself if you lost your job and I wouldn't be able to survive living here without you," I whispered, wiping away my tears.

She gripped my chin, a stern look in her eyes. "I know what I'm doing. My concern has and always will be your well-being. I know what my part is in ensuring you hold onto your bright spirit. I refuse to let that atrocious man take that from you. I'll do whatever it takes to get you the breaks you need."

My dad screamed he needed another brandy and she rolled her eyes. Before Kelsey got up, she squeezed my side, studying me carefully. I nodded to let her know I was okay. On her way out of my room, she gave me a parting smile. I hopped up, closed my door, and grabbed my iPod to find something more comforting than Linkin Park's "In the End." Listening to upbeat pop tunes would keep my frayed nerves somewhat stable.

I sifted through my purse to get my cell. There were a few texts from Kylie and Peyton, but I ignored them. They wanted more details on the fight Friday night and as far as I was concerned, all that had been shoved into Pandora's box. There were a couple more from girls on the soccer team and I blew past them. I clicked on the one from Shane checking in to see if I was okay. I shot him a quick response to say I was fine before opening Mia's text.

Mia: I wanted to make sure you weren't in any trouble when you got home. I know how your dad can be. Even though you've reassured me a thousand times you can get away with anything, I worry. Please let me know you're okay. If you need to talk, call me.

Bri: I'm fine. I'll fill you in tomorrow.

Mia: That doesn't sound good. What happened? What did your dad do?

Bri: Seriously, I'll be okay. I have a ton of homework to catch up on. Let's plan on getting to school an hour early. We can talk and swap assignments. I'm dying to know how the rest of your weekend turned out. ;)

Mia: Sounds like a plan. :) I want all the details of yours too. Love you, sass!

My heart warmed and I smiled at the last part. It was really hard for her to express that sentiment, probably because she didn't hear those words very often. I didn't either, so we made it a point a while back to say them to one another.

Bri: Love you too, Mia!

I scrolled down to the remaining text. It was from an unknown number, but after I read it, I grinned from ear to ear. I added Trey to my contact list and reread his message, loving how my heart melted all over again.

Trey: I can't believe I had to ask Mia for your number. Forgive me. I'm still getting used to wanting to have a girl's number so I can text her all hours of the day. Since I didn't ask you for it, I promise to make it up to you. I just wanted to thank you for an amazing weekend. I'm really looking forward to our next date. x T

Bri: I'm sure I can think of some way for you to repay me. I have a very creative imagination and wouldn't mind exploring the fantasies I've already had about you.

Trey: Damn, girl! Keep throwing out sweet promises like that and I'll be crawling through your window. I've gotten incredibly lucky with the turn of events this weekend. I don't want to jinx it. Behave yourself or I'll make you tomorrow!

I squeezed my thighs together to halt the tingles spreading south of me.

Bri: Did I mention throwing out good one-liners isn't the only thing I can do with my mouth? :o

Trey: Grrr!!! Yes, I'm actually growling. You have no idea how much I want that mouth right now. BEHAVE!

I heard his growl in my head and laughed. I quite enjoyed enticing that reaction out of him.

Bri: Why would I play fair when you never do?

Trey: You must have me confused with another guy because I always play fair. But if you need a reason to be good, just do it so I can reward you. How's that sound? I have more than a few ideas for us.

Holy shit! I don't even need a hint of what he has in mind. Sign me up for it! I have no doubt it'll be incredible. He can already make my body explode with a simple brush of his lips on the right spot. God only knows what kind of ecstasy I'll reach when we get really physical.

Bri: Sounds salacious. I'll be good. How'd things go at home? I assume a lot better than expected.

Trey: That's an understatement. They bought that the lingering bruises and cuts were from Friday's game. I'm lucky it was one of

our more brutal games. I'm a little nervous about what will be waiting for me at school tomorrow but trying not to dwell on it. Shane assured me we can handle it together.

Bri: He's right. We'll deal with it together. I'm glad everything went well. I need to finish my homework so I can have deliciously naughty dreams of you.

Trey: I'm looking forward to doing a lot of wicked things with you. Think about that when you lay your gorgeous face on your pillow tonight. Until tomorrow, darling. x T

Bri: Dream of me, handsome. x B

I set my alarm, plugged in my phone to charge, and put it on the nightstand. As much as I'd rather take matters into my own hands to rid myself of the dull ache between my thighs, I wanted Trey to be the one to do it. I hopped up to grab my Calculus and Psychology books. They'd squash all my hot and bothered feelings.

* * *

AFTER NEXT TO NO SLEEP, I grudgingly got up and took a long shower. Knowing I'd be seeing Trey at school was my only motivator. My brain struggled with the basics this morning. I nearly poked my eye out while applying my eyeliner and mascara. If that wasn't enough, I put my plaid skirt on backwards the first time and just noticed a few of the buttons on my light blue shirt were off. I fixed that snafu and gave myself a onceover to make sure I hadn't missed anything else.

The drive to school was a blur. My mind kept drifting to the more memorable moments of the weekend. Mostly, it dwelled on how amazing our first kiss was on Saturday night. Before I knew it, I was at Chamberlain. There were hardly any students here, but that was no surprise since it was barely seven.

I parked my Lexus and looked around for his Acura, but didn't see it. I grabbed my stuff and made my way to my locker. After opening it up and setting my duffle at the bottom, I hung up my purse and sifted through my backpack to find my Psychology book.

A soft breath across the back of my neck sent a strong wave of a heat throughout my body. Trey turned me around, planted a very brief kiss on my lips, and dragged me over to an empty classroom. He kept the lights off and pinned me up against the wall next to the door. His gray eyes were aglow as he secured my hands above my head and pressed his lips against mine with force, claiming every part of my mouth.

His tongue tangled with mine and I wiggled my hands to free them. His grip loosened and I tutted his hair when he somehow managed to deepen our kiss. After I rocked my body into his, a low moan rumbled from his chest. He bit down on my lip and I groaned rather loudly. When he twisted his hips into mine, the fiery sensations between my legs burned even hotter. I grabbed his tie as he hitched my leg around his backside and continued our erotic tongue dance.

"Ahem, I'd tell you two to get a room, but you're already in one. The teacher is coming down the hall. You might want to get out of here," Mia spoke up, giggling.

Trey jumped away from me, panting, and my body cried out in frustration as I worked to catch my breath. I scowled at Mia and she laughed even harder as she held the door open for us. On our way down the hallway, the teacher eyed us carefully before he strode into his classroom, but didn't say anything.

Mia held her hands up innocently. "I was just trying to help."

I returned to my locker, grabbed the book I abandoned, and slid to the ground, crossing my legs. "Noted, but you don't have to take so much pleasure in ruining a *really* good moment."

Rolling her eyes, she joined me on the floor. "I'm sure you'll have plenty more. Besides, we need to swap assignments and you don't want to get detention this early in the day. Last time I checked, the administration isn't a big fan of making out and dry humping on school grounds."

Trey reached across me and smacked her upside the head. "That's a bit of an exaggeration, don't you think?"

She rubbed the spot he struck. "No, it isn't. Bri knows firsthand—"

Slapping my hand over her mouth, I narrowed my eyes for her to shut the hell up. Trey raised an eyebrow and there was very little I could do to prevent the color filling my face.

He ran his finger down my pink cheek. "When I'm with you, I don't want an audience. I'll give you ladies some girl time and wander around this place to find some secluded areas."

Trey squeezed my side before sauntering away. My eyes centered on his fine ass and I drooled a little. He turned around to catch me staring. Trey winked as his lips curled into that damn cocky smirk of his and that was all it took to reignite all the sparks in my body. I was ready to chase after him and finish what he started.

Mia gripped my chin and pointed at our books. I stuck out my tongue and passed over our Psychology assignment as she handed me our English Comp homework. The argument from last night flashed through my head and my hand trembled when I took it from her.

She nudged my shoulder, her face full of concern. "Hey, what's wrong?"

"We can talk about it later. Why don't you fill me in on the rest of your birthday? Where did Micah take you? What did he get you? Did you finally have sex?"

Her eyebrows furrowed as she hissed, "Keep your voice down. You never know who's lingering around the corner. I'd rather not be this week's gossip."

I rolled my eyes. "Trust me, you'd survive. The sharks around here always have a new rumor to share by lunchtime. Let's get back on point."

She tilted her head, her eyes wide with worry. "Fine, but only if you promise to tell me what happened at home later today. Your rosy cheeks went stark white when I handed you that paper. I *know* your dad said something to you."

I wrapped her pinky with mine. "Promise. Now, spill the beans, lady. Don't leave *anything* out."

Her mouth curled at the corners. "He took me to Catch35. The food was to die for, but I really wished he wouldn't have spent so much. We didn't need a three-course meal."

My jaw dropped before I sputtered, "That's incredible, Mia. That place is exquisite. Micah's got good taste. What else? Don't you dare hold out on me!"

The huge grin on her face was so wonderful to see. I'd never seen her so happy. "He really does, Bri. What touched me the most was how much of a gentleman he was. He held every door open for me. He even opened my car door at every place we stopped at and helped me out. His hand was either in mine or around my waist. To say he was doting, doesn't really cover it. It was exactly how you see it in the movies."

I could hardly contain my excitement and motioned for her to keep going. Her eyes were starstruck as she said, "After dinner, we went over to the Art Institute. Micah has zero interest in the arts, but he didn't complain at all while we walked around the place for over an hour."

She pulled out a diamond sapphire heart necklace. The cut was amazing and it was easily a carat. "He gave me this and a photo album of pictures of us over the years. It was *so* thoughtful and I'll treasure it forever. I would've been happy with just the photos, and tried to give back the necklace, but he wouldn't have it. My mind is still reeling over all of his extravagant gestures for something as mundane as my birthday."

My eyes widened. "That boy went all out for you. I mean, we're talking thousands of dollars. Your necklace alone is fifteen hundred."

Her face fell. "Yeah, I'm more than curious on how he got the money and not at all comfortable that he spent so much on me. I know he's in between jobs now. I have my suspicions on what he might be doing to make that kind of cash and I really hope I'm wrong."

I wrapped my arm around her shoulders. "I'm sorry I blurted that out. Don't stress about it. You said he worked really hard all summer at several jobs. Try not to overthink it, okay? Besides, when a guy wants to spend money on you, fighting with him isn't worth it. Guys always dig their heels in with stuff like that. Well, the good ones anyway. Micah is one of them."

Doubt lingered in her eyes. Her gaze dropped to her Psychology worksheet as she filled in the next circle. I finished mine and ran my thumb across the various shades of blue on my fingernails, noting I needed to touch them up soon while I waited for her to catch up.

Mia set her pen down, a dreamy look on her face. "We ended the night at The W along the lakeshore. The view of Lake Michigan was unbelievable. He went all out there with my favorite flowers and candy. Like I said, it was like a fairytale and it sucked to go home Sunday morning. Before we left, we ate breakfast at a swanky restaurant in the Loop. It was the perfect ending to what could've been a really shitty weekend."

I scrunched my eyes together. "Oh, come on, Mia. I'm dying over here. Did you guys have sex?"

Her face turned bright red as she nodded. I grabbed her hands and exclaimed, "How was it? I'm guessing by the more than pleased look on your face, it was amazing. Don't hold back now!"

Motioning at our very cluttered hallway, she hissed, "I'll tell you the rest in private. Besides, I've hogged most of our conversation this morning. The bell is going to ring in fifteen minutes. It's your turn. I want to know all about your weekend. You better start with Friday night after you two holed up in that bedroom and don't leave one damn thing out."

A warmness overtook my heart as all the incredibly sweet things Trey said and did for me over the past few days filled my mind. An even hotter streak ran rampant south of me when I recalled all the ways that boy turned me on without barely lifting a finger. Before I had a chance to say anything, Headmaster Carlton walked by us, glowering as he did, and my next breath got caught in my throat. Mia's shoulders slumped about as quick as the grin on her face vanished.

It was an unwanted reminder that we still weren't done dealing with what happened Friday night, but having a nervous breakdown over it wouldn't help either of us. Plastering on a smile, I began to share what was easily one of the best weekends of my life.

* * *

We walked on eggshells all day, just waiting to be called into the office. By the time Calculus rolled around, I was a giant ball of nerves. The blue nail polish on all my fingernails was gone, and I almost broke my long silver necklace on several occasions for how hard I'd been tugging on it in an attempt to contain my anxiety.

On our way to class, Trey placed a gentle kiss on my temple. It eased my jitters a little, but not much. I really needed a break and so did he. His back was rigid as he looked over his shoulder. When we strode past an empty janitor's closet, it took great effort on my part not to drag him over to it and make out with him for the next hour. My eyes lingered on a few other vacant rooms and a naughty smirk fell from his lips, but he shook his head.

Mia caught up with us on our way into our classroom. Her face was red as she took measured breaths to rein in her obvious panic. I kept my eyes on her until she took her seat. I nodded toward the door, but Mia mouthed she was fine. I reluctantly sat down and pulled out my textbook.

Trey slid in behind me—not caring it wasn't even his seat. The guy who had been sitting there bolted past us to Trey's spot. Rather than lay into Trey, Mr. White leaned back in his chair, grasped his neck, and gave us a smug smile. My heart dropped well below this plane of existence. I glanced over at Mia and her eyes were wide with fright.

"Would the following students please report to the headmaster's office immediately: Trey Donovan, Brianna McAndrews, Mia Ryan, and Shane West."

A hush fell over the class and Mr. White gestured for us to go, his grin somehow growing even more superior. My stomach turned nonstop and I fought against the strong urge to puke. Snickers around the classroom grew louder and I really wanted to flip them off, especially Sebastian and Miles. Enough was about to be thrown at us without them tapping into Trey's rage. Those fuckers tried to set him off before we even left the room.

Once we were in the hallway, Trey slid an arm around me. Mia fiddled with her watch and necklace on our way down the hall. We walked at a snail's pace over to the headmaster's office. Shane was outside of it, his face ashen. Trey stepped in front of all of us and opened the door.

My soccer coaches were along one wall with the sports director and football coaches standing unnervingly still against the other. Carlton was in his huge black leather chair behind his oak desk and he signaled for us to take the four seats in front of him. I glanced at Coach Nocky and his answering glare made it hard to keep my stomach contents in check.

"It's been brought to our attention that a party happened this weekend where drinking and drugs were present. It has been reported that the four of you were at this party and that you were drinking and fighting. This is your one and only shot to set the record straight," Headmaster Carlton spoke up, his tone furious.

Mia squirmed in her seat and I reached between our chairs to slap her leg. The coaches and sports director watched us like hawks. If she continued to fidget, she'd give us away.

"We were at the party, but drank soda and water. Drinks were passed in our direction and we dumped them out every time. When the peer pressure became too much, we left early and spent the evening at my mom's hotel playing cards and video games. There's a record of us checking in and I'd be happy to get that information over to you," Shane spoke up, his tone as confident as the look on his face.

Carlton drummed his fingers across his chin in a calculating way that made my skin crawl. He glared at us like he wanted to incinerate us. My coaches were still clearly pissed, but they seemed satisfied with that explanation. Coach Barry stared at Trey and Shane with his arms crossed and his eyes wary. Coach Murray stood statuesque, a nasty gleam in his eyes. He knew *exactly* what he did. I gripped the sides of my chair to prevent myself from slapping the ever-loving shit out of him.

The sports director leaned over and whispered in Carlton's ear. After a minute, Carlton huffed and mouthed something back. Mr. Wood held up his hands in defeat.

"As I'm sure you heard, Mr. Wood has pointed out we don't have any evidence to contradict Mr. West's recollection of Friday evening. Regardless, we will be keeping a very close eye on all of you."

Shane stood up, but Carlton motioned for him to sit down. "I'm not quite finished. Just because we don't have any video to prove the situation otherwise doesn't mean you're off the hook. You'll be serving Saturday detention for the rest of your respective seasons."

If my dad finds out, who knows what he'll end up doing to me. After last night, I'm not ruling out anything. This can't happen. They don't even have any damn proof!

I gave him an innocent smile. "Why are we getting detention? You just said you don't have anything against us. We didn't do anything wrong. Why are we being punished?"

Mia pinched me really hard. Without a doubt, I'd have a nice black bruise on my thigh. Coach Nocky indicated for me to zip it. I rubbed my leg and kept my gaze locked on Carlton. Trey looked at me out of the corner of his eye, begging for me to take whatever punishment they saw fit, but this was complete bullshit.

"See, that's where you're wrong, Ms. McAndrews. And if you question my authority again, I'll extend your Saturdays here through the foreseeable future. You have two years left with me."

Shane shifted in his chair and actually raised his hand to speak. Carlton nodded at him. "Sir, could you please explain why we're receiving detention? It seems a tad on the unfair side, especially since there isn't anything to contradict what I've told you. Like I said, I'd be happy to supply the supporting evidence."

Glaring at Shane, Coach Barry ran his hand across his throat. He snapped his mouth shut. Trey remained as still as a statue. Mia and I couldn't have moved if we wanted to. With the way our coaches glowered at us, the slightest movement would probably cause us to burst into flames.

"Keep in mind what you do outside this school never really remains a secret. We may not have what we need *this time*, but that won't always be the case. Let's just call your Saturdays here strategy sessions. You can work on different ways to keep your teams in line.

You're all very talented individuals, but your leadership is severely lacking and you'll use that time to improve upon it," Carlton responded, clasping his hands together with a smug smile.

I opened my mouth to dispute, but Trey slapped his hand over it. Carlton had the audacity to laugh at me. "Something more to say, Ms. McAndrews? If you'd like, I can just suspend you, but I'd rather not do that with both teams being undefeated. You should be happy with detention. Not that you deserve it after questioning me, but I'm feeling generous and won't be putting this on your academic record either. You should be thanking me, not arguing with me."

My head whipped back and forth with cartoon character-like speed.

Coach Barry ran a hand through his hair and snapped, "I think that about covers what we needed to discuss. Get back to class and don't even think about showing up late for practice."

We scrambled out the door. Once we were a safe distance from his office, I sank to the ground and rested my head on my knees. My lead-filled legs didn't have the capability of going another step and the weight in my chest didn't allow for air to reach my lungs. I blinked my eyes several times to get my blurry vision to focus.

Trey crouched in front of me and tried to lift my head, but I kept it down. Mia wrapped an arm around me. "It's going to be okay. We only have a few more weeks of regular season games and the playoffs. Having detention sucks, but it won't be that bad."

I looked at her with tears streaming down my cheeks. "I don't know how to get this past my dad. I don't know what threats he'll send my way if he finds out about this."

Mia gasped as tears pooled in her eyes. Shane's mouth was agape. Seeing the sorrow etched across Trey's face and was painful to see. He held my face and kissed away some of my tears. "I'm so sorry, Bri. This is all my fault. I'll tell the truth. I'll admit to drinking and fighting, but leave you guys out of it. None of you deserve to be punished because of my stupid choices."

My heart quivered, knowing exactly what would happen. He rose to his feet, but I grabbed his hand and gave it a tight squeeze. "I can't let you do that. I'll figure something out. I promise."

Where there was a will, there was always a way. I was as strong-willed as they came. I *would* get out of this without my dad finding out and shattering my spirit once and for all.

CHAPTER 17

BRI

By the grace of God, I'd managed to hide my Saturday detentions from my dad so far. Almost a month and a half had passed and he was still none the wiser. Having soccer practice before reporting to the library was probably the only reason I pulled it off, but I didn't dwell on it. Most days, he was preoccupied with his reelection crap. He kept close tabs on my whereabouts in the evening, but didn't seem to care as much about anything school-related.

Shrugging off those thoughts, I hopped out of the shower, strode over to the bench, and toweled off. I tossed my royal blue Lions sweatshirt over my head, slid on my black shorts, and laced up my sneakers. With my duffle bag slung over my shoulder, I headed over to my hallway to get my backpack and purse.

After grabbing all my books, I headed over to Trey's hallway. Once I spotted him, my body went into an instant state of arousal. His wet hair was all over the place as he bent over to get a book. The white muscle shirt he had on made the outline of his eight-pack visible and the sensational tingles trekking through me amplified.

"If you keep swaying this in my face, I won't be able to wait until later this evening to kiss you. Stop teasing me," I spoke up, pinching his ass.

Trey chuckled. "You think everything I do is a tease, Bri. It doesn't look like practice was as brutal for you as it was for me."

"Most of the time, everything you do is to torture me in some way, Trey. Appearances can be deceiving. We ran for two hours before getting into our offensive and defensive sets. My legs are killing me," I replied, sifting through my purse to grab the cookies I made him last night.

His mouth curled at the corners to produce a contrite smile. "You'd think both our teams finishing the regular season undefeated and keeping the partiers on both squads in check would be enough to get them to lighten up, but apparently it's not. I promise to massage the pain right out of them after we study. Are those what I think they are?"

I set my stuff on the floor and swept my lips across his. "Yes, and they're your favorites. Happy Birthday, babe."

"I told you not to do anything for me. It's just another day."

"No, it's not, and this is only the beginning. But if you really don't want them, I'm sure Mia will take them," I answered, holding the bag of snickerdoodles out of his reach.

Trey tickled my sides until I released the cookies. "Don't you dare give away my precious baked goods."

He pressed me against the lockers and the electric current he tended to cause with just the bat of an eye pulsated through my body. After ensuring the hallway was still empty, Trey blew along my neck, making the sensitive spots along it flicker to life, and opened his mouth wide enough for me to see his damn tongue ring.

Bastard. He knows exactly what he's doing to me. That piercing has been tormenting me for the past month in a variety of ways.

I subtly brushed my fingers across the front of his red mesh shorts. "I know your stance on PDA, but if you keep it up, I'll have no problem making this become painfully hard," I breathed, stroking his dick to reinforce my point.

Trey growled and I squeezed my legs together. "Stop making that sound. You know what it does to me."

He winked. "Yes, I do, but it's your fault I make it, not mine. Even with your hoodie on and your hair tied back, you're sexy as hell. It's only fair I rile you up, so you know how I'm feeling."

I rolled my eyes. "If you'd let me give you the blowjob you've more than earned, you'd experience it yourself. I have no clue how you haven't combusted at this point."

Trey smirked. "Believe me, I've taken matters into my own hands on more than one occasion. We'll get there soon enough. Just be patient."

The sexy tone he deliberately used resonated deep within my belly, creating an ache that needed to be satisfied and I leaned into him. His eyes danced as he trailed his hands along my sides. I closed mine and thanked my lucky stars for his gifted fingers. Suddenly, he stopped and my body cried out in frustration. My eyes sprang open and my skin prickled in an instant. Coach Murray gave us a murderous glare on his way down the hallway.

Once he was out of sight, I released a ragged breath. "I really hate that jackass. I still think he's in cahoots with Sebastian to make your life a living hell."

Trey pinched my lips shut. "Don't, Bri. I'm not letting that jerk ruin our night. After we get done studying for the SATs, I plan on kissing you for as long you'll let me. We don't get very many school nights to be together and I want to make the most of it."

My confused body wasn't sure what emotion to run with. Since the first orgasm he gave me, he made sure it happened every time we were remotely intimate.

I hoped he'd finally take things to third base. The hot and bothered side of me loved that plan more than anything, but my nerves still quivered. The faculty and our coaches went out of their way to keep a close eye on us. We still had no clue what Sebastian's threats meant.

It was always in my best interest to pick my battles with him so his temper didn't climb to a level that was hard for him to control. He refused to discuss what the real deal was when it came to Sebastian and everyone else still giving him trouble and I skirted talking about my situation at home every time he brought it up.

Trey snapped his fingers. "Did you even hear what I said, Bri?"

I blinked while shaking my head. His eyebrows pulled together. "Are you sure you can get out of the house?"

"It won't be a problem. My dad is in D.C. this week," I replied, waving off his concern.

Tilting his head to the side, he pointed out, "You're chipping away at your orange and black nail polish like it's a toxic material. That's not very convincing."

I quickly closed my hands. "Seriously, don't worry about it. I've gone to Halloween parties for the last several years. It won't be an issue."

"I should get going. I need to get a few things done around the house before heading out for the night. I'll see you in a couple of hours, babe."

"See you later, sweets."

Trey sauntered toward the doors to the parking lot and disappeared through them. I retrieved my bags from the floor and headed for my car. After tossing my stuff behind me, I checked the mirrors more than necessary, but couldn't help myself. I didn't have the heart to tell Trey my dad's security detail had sprung up on a few occasions in the past few weeks.

Even though he acted like he was only concerned with what I did outside of school and sports, I didn't buy it. He was probably tapping my phone and I didn't give a fuck. I refused to let him come between Trey and me. I wasn't sure what cat-and-mouse game my dad was playing, but the pit in my stomach led me to believe I'd know soon enough.

* * *

I POPPED out of my closet and held up my short black skirt with a low-cut red tank top to Kelsey. "What do you think of this combination?"

She shook her head, a smile teasing her face. "It's very revealing, Bri. You do realize it's fall, right?"

I shrugged. "Yes, and I can live with the chill in the air. Trey is always going out of his way to fire up my body. It's only fair to torment him with an outfit like this one."

Kelsey rolled her eyes. "I'm not sure which one of you enjoys torturing the other more. I will say I do really like this boy. I can't remember seeing you happier than you've been lately. When do I get to meet him?"

I changed into my ensemble, slid on a pair of black heels, strode over to the mirror, and flicked on the curling iron. "You know I can't bring him here when they're around. I thought for sure they'd go to D.C. together at some point, but they haven't. That's a separate issue in itself."

She released a heavy sigh. "Yes, that's been on my mind, especially since he's making sure his presence is felt when he's not here."

I curled my long brown locks and framed them around my face. "Exactly. I've thought about bringing Trey over to your place for dinner, but I don't want to take any unnecessary risks."

Kelsey rested a hand on her hip. "Every time you sneak out, you're taking a risk."

"You know what I mean. I'm just not quite ready to take that leap. Once I do, Trey's going to grill me even more about things around here and I'm not ready to tell him," I replied, applying my dark gray eyeshadow and mascara.

"You're going to have to cross that bridge eventually. If he's dating you, he deserves to have some idea of what you're dealing with."

It was the kick in the gut I didn't need and the ache spread throughout me. I grabbed my overnight bag, my backpack and purse, and headed out of my room with Kelsey right behind me.

Once we reached the top of the stairs, Kelsey murmured, "Your mom is out cold and won't even notice you're gone. Just make sure you're on time for school."

"I know you're not going to like this next part, but I'm staying at the Waldorf." She opened her mouth to argue, but I shook my head. "He's got people lurking around the penthouse all the time now."

"Yes, I suppose you're right. I have a lot of friends at that hotel and I'll make sure they check on you. I'm all for you getting out of this house as much as you can, but that doesn't mean you're allowed to have endless amounts of premarital sex."

Raising an eyebrow, I joked, "Who said anything about sex?"

"Bri, I know you *very* well. You pined over this boy all of September and have been sneaking out to see him whenever you can for this past month. If you haven't had sex with him yet, you're definitely trying to, especially with that outfit on," Kelsey pointed out with a shake of her head.

I winked. "Just so you know, we haven't, but that doesn't mean I don't want to."

She pinched the bridge of her nose. "I know you're always careful, but that's beside the point. *Try* to behave yourself. When you don't rush things, it makes them even better in the long run. Keep that in mind."

"I will. If anything seems off in the slightest around here, please let me know and I'll come home," I replied, my face as somber as my tone.

Kelsey gave me a hug before I made my way outside. I opened my car door, tossed my things in the back, and headed for the interstate. Traffic going into the city moved excruciatingly slow and I was about ready to pull my hair out by the time I parked on the service ramp at the Waldorf. The only thing I enjoyed during the ride was the ever-changing colors of the leaves on the trees as I passed by them. Fall was in full force. Even though I hated playing soccer in colder weather, I really loved this time of year.

With Shane's help, I reserved the same suite under a false name. As I made my way through the parking garage, I couldn't shake the feeling someone was watching me and paused more than once to glance behind me. Coach Murray's menacing gaze flitted through my mind, along with Sebastian's threats that the worst was yet to come.

A chill ran through my body and I shoved all those thoughts aside. They were for another day. Following Shane's instructions, I entered through the service entrance and headed up to the room. Once I reached the presidential suite, I swiped the keycard Shane gave me earlier today and opened the door.

Shane had the staff purchase and deliver the decorations and ingredients I needed to cook Trey's birthday dinner. An arrangement of his favorite candies, along with some blue and gray balloons, were in the middle of the island.

Lights from the skyscrapers flickered on as the sun made its final descent for the day. Seeing the rustic red and orange shades on the horizon made my heart flutter as Trey's sweet words from our first date ran through my mind. All of the ways that boy affected me without even being around was still a head-scratcher for me.

After setting the pre-heat on the oven, I surveyed the groceries on the counter and retrieved all the spices on the island, along with the chicken broth and avocado oil, to create my special sauce. Once that was in the saucepan simmering, I dug through the fridge to grab the half-pound of hamburger and two chicken breasts, seasoned them, and got them going in separate pans. *Gossip Girl* wouldn't be on for another two hours and the news just brought up my dad. I muted it and turned on the surround sound.

Usher's sexy voice replaced the news anchors as I diced up the chicken before peeling and pitting the avocados. After dicing up a few tomatoes, I added the remaining ingredients and spices to complete my killer guacamole and salsa recipes. Once I greased a pan for the oven, I scattered tortilla shells on it, and put hamburger on half of them before dicing up the chicken and tossing it into a bowl.

I turned around to grab the chicken to fill the rest and nearly dropped the glass bowl it was in. Trey was against the partial wall dividing the kitchen from the entryway, his dimples on full freaking display like a damn billboard. I sucked in a breath to jumpstart my heart before giving him my *come and get it* smile.

He sauntered toward me, took the bowl, and walked until my back was pressed against the stainless-steel fridge. I grasped his neck and savored my new favorite smell, a musky toxic aroma that only came from him.

"You never disappoint, Bri. I thought we'd just get some room service, but here you are cooking for us, shocking me once again. I haven't even tasted it, but if it is half as good as it smells, I might just drag you off to Vegas tonight," Trey murmured, sweeping his scrumptious lips across mine.

His hands slid under my shirt, but remained at my waist where he caressed patterns along it. My fingers sifted through his hair as I slid my tongue along his. Every time it went past his piercing, the urge to unbutton his belt and drop to my knees grew stronger. Tingling sensations overtook my body and it was difficult to remain upright. We sucked in quick breaths before our lips connected again. He licked along my throat until he reached my earlobe and gave it a gentle bite that sent potent waves of desire rushing through me.

Gripping his sides, I kissed his neck until he released a drawn-out moan. His erection was against my belly and I wanted nothing more than to have it inside me. He made the journey back to the base of my throat and pressed his lips softly there. Trey took a step back, a cocky smirk on his face, and I almost slid to the floor, panting harder now than earlier at practice.

"If I let go, will you be able to stand? Your legs are still on the wobbly side," Trey whispered, kissing my forehead.

I poked his chest and stepped around him. "Way to ruin the mood with your smartass remarks. I swear you're worse than me sometimes."

He handed me the bowl of chicken and gestured to the arrangement on the island. "I hope you remember why we're here before we jump into the R-rated part of the evening."

I paused from filling the remainder of the pan with chicken and gave him a wily smile. "Yes, you reminded me several times today and our conversation after practice is still fresh in my mind. We'll study, but I'm going to spoil you throughout the evening too."

He opened his mouth to dispute, but shut it after I shot him a playful glare. My lips curled into a mischievous grin. "What are your thoughts on a NC-17 night?"

Closing his eyes for a moment, Trey took several deliberate breaths. "Now, you've got my mind running away with itself. I swear you're going to be the death of me. My thoughts are the same. It's still not the right time."

I stuck my tongue out at him. "Killjoy."

He laughed, snatched the bag of tortilla chips from the counter, and took a seat at the island. "I'd love to make out with you until the sun comes up. Birthday or not, I really need to get some studying in. This past month has been a whirlwind and it's been hard to stay on top of everything. I need to do good on the SATs and it's just as important for you to ace that test."

"I hate when you're right. Just promise to make a little time for making out. Aside from that wonderful welcome kiss, my lips have barely touched yours this week. I feel deprived."

"Believe me, darling, so do I."

"We could give sneaking around at school a shot."

He meticulously traced his fingers across the ink on his right arm. "Until football and soccer are over, I don't think it's a good idea. We've made it this far without any trouble. Once our basketball seasons start, we can revisit it. For now, I'd rather not press our luck, especially with how things are for you at home. Any improvement there?"

I busied myself with the bowls in front of me. "They're fine."

The veins in his forehead began to throb. My eyes pleaded for him to accept my short answer. To my surprise, he sealed his lips and I released a sigh of relief. I fished out an envelope from my purse and handed it to him. Trey turned it over in his hands before opening it and chuckling at the naughty birthday card. When he spotted the tickets, his jaw nearly hit the floor.

"Are you freaking kidding me, Bri? Are these seriously courtside seats to the Bulls?"

I twisted my hands together. "Yes, they are. We don't have any playoff games that Saturday night. I know you didn't want me to get you anything, but I had to get you something. Are you mad I got them or excited to take me to another ball game?"

"I can't wait to take you, but this is *way* too much. Thank you so much, Bri," Trey gushed, his face still fixated in the same blown-back expression.

I waved off his shock. "It's no big deal, Trey. I want today to be great for you."

The corners of his mouth curled into a shy smile as he admitted, "It's been the best birthday I've had yet. My mom spoiled me this morning and my dad called me a couple of times to tell me how proud of me he is. Now, I have all evening with you. By the way, what are you doing December fourteenth?"

I arched an eyebrow. "That's a pretty specific date. Why do you ask?"

Seeing the boyish grin on his face made my heart flutter. I'd never had it beat like it was right now and there wasn't a doubt in my mind it'd ever beat like this for anyone else.

"Micah and Mia got the four of us tickets to see Fall Out Boy."

My jaw dropped before I stammered, "I thought they were done touring around here."

Trey chuckled. "The concert is in New York City. By some amazing twist of fate, our basketball teams don't have a game that Friday night. I was wondering if you wanted to jet off to The Big Apple with me for the weekend."

I almost dropped the bowl in my hands, but managed to nod. He jumped up from his stool and planted another sizzling kiss on my lips. My knees nearly buckled, but I threw myself into it with just as much gusto. Our tongues wildly intertwined until I was ready to pass out and it killed me to pull away to heave in a breath.

"The tickets and hotel won't be too pricey—not that you need to worry about that. I'll be taking care of everything and don't even try to argue with me about it."

I smirked. "When your voice hits that low octave, it's not worth fighting over."

"I love that band and I know you do too. Plus, I've never been there. I hear it's amazing."

"It's pretty awesome. You'll love seeing it decorated for the holidays. There's nothing like it."

His face suddenly became very serious. "Will you be able to get away for the weekend without getting into any trouble?"

I exhaled. "I'll figure something out. Don't worry about it. When's your playoff game this week?"

His lips were in a thin line as he stared me down. I gave him a stern look to answer my question. I really didn't want to fight with him on his birthday and we were nearing that point.

Trey sighed. "It's on Friday. When's your soccer match?"

I sulked. "It's on Friday too. Dammit, I really wanted to get to one of your playoff games. It's so frustrating that our matches have landed on the same day as yours."

Trey took my hand and held it over his heart. "You're always with me at my games."

My heart raced as a shy smile fell from my lips. I slid the bowls of guacamole and salsa over for him to sample. He dipped a few chips between the two. His eyes widened and he licked his lips before diving in for more. After taking down several handfuls, he released a satisfied moan. I giggled at the ravenous look on his face before adding the black beans, peppers, chilies, shredded cheese, and sauce to the tortillas.

"Damn, girl, when I walked in, this spread looked mouth-watering, but that word doesn't do it justice."

"What word does?"

The only thing I wanted to do was devour him. He was smoking hot in his faded jeans and the royal blue shirt from our first date. The sleeves were rolled up to his elbows and several of the buttons were undone with some chest hair peeking out. His chin sported the five o'clock shadow I'd grown to love over the past few weeks. Just thinking of the prickly sensation on various spots on my face and neck brought on a sensual ache between my thighs. I blinked to get out of my lusty daze and arched an eyebrow at Trey for an answer.

Trey batted his long lashes, a timid grin gracing his chiseled face. "I'd have to say heavenly—just like you."

"Why thank you, Mr. Donovan. I do enjoy your compliments when you're gracious enough to give them," I teased.

"Ms. McAndrews, in the past month you've gotten more compliments out of me than I've ever given anyone. If you don't believe me, I suggest you revisit your text messages and emails," Trey retorted.

My lips spread into a coy smile. I added a touch of cilantro and some more spices to the pan, wrapped the tortillas up, and put them in the oven. After washing my hands, I sat next to him and dipped a chip into the guacamole. As Trey watched me, the passion behind his gaze made it clear I wasn't the only one who was willing to forego food and just devour each other.

"If we're going to get anything done, stop giving me that look. The enchiladas will be ready in forty-five minutes. I suggest we get some studying in or I'll give you another birthday gift," I said, my voice throaty.

Trey rested a hand on my upper thigh. "Your wish is my command, doll. Do you want to study in here or in the living room?"

"What? The bedrooms aren't options?" I asked, ignoring the way my skin crawled with unease.

"Behave!" Trey growled.

I forced out a giggle. "If you stop calling me doll, I'll think about it."

His face became pensive. "You really hate that nickname, don't you?"

The very horrible reason I hated that name flashed through my mind and I shook my head to get rid of that terrible memory. I gave Trey a shrewd grin, but the concerned look on his face didn't fade away the way it usually did.

I fiddled with my bracelets. "Yes, I do. Any of the other pet names you've been using are fine, but that one just irks me."

He released a disgruntled huff. "Duly noted. I'll strike doll from the list, but you're going to have to give me a better answer on why you despise it so much."

I smirked. "I'll think about it. I'm glad to hear you won't use it again. Because if you would've said it one more time, I was going for your man bits."

We strode into the living room to grab our backpacks. I retrieved my prep books, flashcards, and practice tests. After he pulled out his own study materials, Trey sat next to me on the couch and trailed his fingers down my bare arm. Goosebumps sprang up on each spot he touched and I shivered. Leaning closer, he planted a deep kiss on my lips until I panted for air.

"Hello, Mr. Moody. You're sending mixed signals *again*. At this rate, we won't get any studying in. Pick one or the other because you know damn well we can't kiss and study at the same time," I rasped, scooting away.

Trey held up his hands. "I'm sorry. You look sexy as hell and it's hard to keep my hands and tongue in check, especially when we're alone."

"Ugh. You're *so* frustrating sometimes," I snapped, moving even further away.

"Are we back to taking things slow again?"

"As a matter of fact, we are. When you actually mean it, I don't mind." He gave me a sharp look. I tossed my hands in the air. "Fine, I do, but you're just so damn confusing sometimes."

He squinted. "What's confusing you?"

I massaged my temples. "Jesus, you want the list? Never mind. I'll make it simple. It's pretty damn clear you're ready to move forward, but for whatever reason, you keep holding back. Does it have something to do with me or you?"

Trey chewed on his bottom lip. "Yes and no."

I glared. "That's not an answer."

"I want to get to know more about you, but every time I ask about things going on at home, you give me a short answer or change the subject. I know something is off there and that there's more to your past with guys that you're not telling me. I've never cared about that stuff before, but with you, it's different. I *want* to know so I don't do anything to screw this up. Right now, I still don't trust myself not to. Shane threatened to kick my ass if I made your life any more complicated than it already is. That's the last thing I want to do, but it's really fucking hard with you being so closed off with some pretty damn important things."

I crossed my arms. "It's none of Shane's business."

Trey caressed my side. "Hey, don't be mad at him. He was looking out for you. Given my track record, his threat was warranted."

Every wanton desire from earlier was gone. Trey tilted my chin toward him and tenderly kissed the corners of my mouth until I became less rigid.

"His heart is in the right place, but it really is none of his business. He shouldn't have said anything to you."

"You're right. He shouldn't have. *You* should've, Bri. You should still."

"I've shared enough, Trey. You have a general idea. Until I can trust your temper is under control, I'm not sharing anything else. For the record, you haven't been all that forthcoming with things at home—not to mention around your neighborhood. You and Mia get so weird when the conversation even remotely turns in that direction. You don't think that isn't frustrating for me?"

He cracked his neck and snapped, "You've skimmed over things at home. That's not sharing. I've told you more about my family and myself than I've shared with anyone. If you want to know something we haven't covered yet, you need to ask. I can't read your mind."

My temper got the better of me as I bit back, "That's the problem! I never know what to ask because it's so hard to navigate what will and won't set you off. It's a big reason why I stick to the light topics and all things physical. At least in those two areas, I haven't pissed you off or disappointed you. My biggest concern is keeping your anger in check and there are just some things I'd rather not talk about until you have more control over it."

We stared at each other in a heated standoff. After a few minutes passed, Trey took deep breaths until his angry face smoothed out. I ran a hand down my own and did my best to simmer the blood boiling in my veins. Sparring with him wasn't something to take lightly.

"I don't want to fight. We obviously have some deeper stuff to share, but clearly aren't ready. Let's table this conversation for now," Trey murmured, squeezing my hand.

I cupped his cheek and whispered, "You've been doing so good lately. I don't want to say or do anything that will upset you. Even though things are better at school, I know there's still a lot on your plate and plenty of douchebags giving you a hard time. You're always so worried about taking this slow and doing everything right, but what you fail to realize is you're doing everything *perfect*."

He wiggled his eyebrows in a seductive fashion. "Perfect, eh?"

My other hand drifted to his face and I tangled his tongue with mine. Our mouths frantically consumed one another. Grabbing fistfuls of his shirt, I crawled into his lap and gyrated my hips into him. He groaned before bucking into me. My head became fuzzy and it pained me to break our kiss.

I tapped his chest. "Don't let your ego inflate."

Trey scoffed. "That'll never happen. You build it up and bring it back down just as fast with one of your legendary zingers."

I giggled. "You love my sassy mouth."

"Yes, I do. And if we're keeping the record up to date, it should be noted that I feel the same way as you," Trey replied, stealing a kiss.

"I've told you numerous times that everything with you is already so much more than I've ever experienced. I push for more because my body craves yours in such a way it's difficult to ignore. You set it off with a simple tilt of the head or that damn cocky smirk of yours. It's hard for me to control it all, especially when you take me over the edge, but won't go with me. I want to experience that together *badly*. God, that really makes me sound like such a whore," I muttered, putting my head in my hands.

"Hearing you refer to yourself in such a demeaning way makes me mad. Don't do it again. If you do, I'll spank your ass," Trey replied, lightly patting my bottom for emphasis.

I gaped at him. "You can be so domineering sometimes."

He gave me a sexy grin. "Darling, you have no idea."

The timer on the oven went off, startling both of us. I swept my lips briefly across his and said, "Saved by the bell again. Why don't you get everything in order for us to dive into studying after we eat while I take care of the food?"

I hopped up, grabbed some potholders, and pulled the pan out. After setting it on the island, I gathered plates, cups, and silverware. Trey licked his lips while he sat down. He eagerly filled his plate up with a couple of enchiladas before adding some chips and salsa. I joined him and put a much smaller portion on my plate.

"This is fucking amazing, Bri," Trey murmured, diving back in for more.

"I'm glad you like it. I don't get to cook it very often. I'm happy I nailed all the spices," I admitted, filling our glasses with soda.

He gobbled down the rest of his enchilada and slid another one on his plate. After devouring half of that one, he asked, "Who taught you how to cook?"

My heart twitched and I stuffed another bite into my mouth to buy myself some more time. I wanted to tell him about Kelsey, but it would open the door for him to bug me about things going on at home.

"One of our maids. I'm sure you'll have some offhanded remark about us having a staff, but be careful with your words," I replied, my tone sharp.

It was really dirty on my part to give him a partial truth and be a bitch about it, but it was the only way to keep him from interrogating me. His eyebrows pulled together. After a minute, he released a frustrated huff and went back to his food.

I wasn't ready for him to see the dark parts of my life. Once he knew, I had no doubt he'd lose control over his temper. On top of that, we hadn't really discussed what we were to one another. Was he my boyfriend? All I knew for sure was what we had together was intense. I was fine with not pushing for a label on our relationship. Something led me to believe that would wig Trey out. That was the last thing I wanted.

CHAPTER 18

BRI

After we were done eating and cleaned everything up, we settled in to study. My legs were across his lap and I had a hell of time paying attention. Trey chewed on the end of a pen while we quizzed each other and I never wanted to be an inanimate object more than I did right now.

"Did you even hear the last question, Bri?" Trey asked, chuckling.

"You're making it difficult for me to focus, Trey," I replied, snatching the pen from him.

Flashing his dimples, he caressed my thighs. "I asked what the definition for pulchritudinous was before you shamelessly started undressing me with your eyes. I'm still waiting for an answer."

"Oh please, you've been doing the same thing to me since we sat down," I pointed out.

Trey smirked. "That may be true, but let's get back to it. Answer the question."

I rolled my eyes. "There's that bossy side of yours again. I can barely pronounce the word, forget having a clue what it means."

Turning over the card, Trey put it in front of us and trailed his fingers down my cheek. "A person of breathtaking beauty. So, *you*. They should really have your picture on the card. It'd be the perfect visual."

My heart flip-flopped as I stared into his eyes. There was a twinkle to them. I leaned over and gave him a tender kiss. "Keep saying things like that and we won't get much more studying done."

Trey kissed my nose and handed me the flashcards. "One more question. Then let's break for some solo studying. I think if we study together any longer, it's not going to lead to any learning."

After looking at the next card, I snorted out a giggle. Trey cocked an eyebrow.

"What is the definition of concupiscent?"

He barked out a laugh while tickling my sides. "That's another good card for your picture to be on. It means lustful or filled with carnal, sexual desires."

I giggled while he continued his attack. My back hit the couch and I gasped to catch my breath after he pulled away. He stole a quick kiss, making my body tingle everywhere. I shoved at his chest and whined, "Don't start something you're not ready to finish, Trey. And as far as the card goes, I think you're a better fit for it."

Trey picked up a practice test from the coffee table. "Sorry, Bri. Your lips were taunting me. I'm taking this and then I promise I'll pick up where I left off."

I released a disgruntled huff and snatched my prep book. Somehow, an hour and a half passed and my vision was close to the cross-eyed point. I tried to work out my Calculus equation, but it made no fucking sense. When the numbers blurred together on the page, I placed my pencil into the book, slammed it shut, and tossed it on the floor. I kept my legs on Trey's lap, but laid on my back, closed my eyes, and massaged my temples until the lingering pain between them faded.

Trey caressed the tops of my thighs before moving to below my naval. I peeked at him and he eyed me like I was his favorite dessert. All the delectable tingles from earlier shot through every part of me. He straddled my legs around him and intertwined his tongue with mine. I gave way to it for a moment before giving his bottom lip a gentle bite and leaning back.

I raised an eyebrow. "I thought you wanted to study, mister."

Trey kissed along my neck and I rocked into him after he sucked below my earlobe. He nibbled on it and kissed along my jaw. Once he reached my lips again, he devoured my mouth until neither of us could breathe.

He gave my nose a delicate kiss and rasped, "I *am* studying, baby."

I panted. "What exactly are you learning, babe?"

Trey ran his hands up my sides and across my ribcage. "I can't get those last two flashcards out of my head. I'm taking note of every curve on your body. I'm sure it'll be relevant if any anatomy questions pop up on the test."

I placed soft kisses along his jawline, loving how his stubble made me quiver. He brought my lips to his and picked up on our vigorous tongue dance. Our hands wandered all over as our mouths consumed one another. After we took a moment to get some much-needed air, I was on my back, staring at him as he hovered above me.

Trey slid his hands underneath my shirt and gently squeezed my breasts. His attention drifted to my belly button as he feverishly sucked along it. Inching my top up even further, he outlined my bra with his hands and I panted while he tortured me with his fingers and tongue. His musky cologne intoxicated me and I was pretty sure I'd kill him if he didn't take it to the next level.

He grazed his teeth along his lower lip. "I think it's high time I appreciate this particular part of your body."

"Are you joking or being serious?"

"We have so much to learn about one another yet—emotionally and physically. We both know it, but let's move forward with one of them tonight."

I propped up on my elbows, a scowl on my face. "Why hello, Mr. Inconsistent. I figured you weren't gone for the night. You better not be fucking with me. We nearly had a blowout about this a few hours ago."

Trey tossed his shirt aside, leaving his fabulous abs on full display. I bit my bottom lip and went to discard my own top, but he stopped me. I flopped back and hit the side of the couch in frustration. Keeping up with Trey's thought process was damn near impossible.

He bit down hard on my shoulder and I tilted my neck upward to give him better access. His lips sucked along my collarbone ravenously. I moaned after he suckled on my diamond stud and opened my eyes. The hunger in his was indisputable. He grabbed the hem of my shirt and had it over my head in one swoop. With a skilled flick of the finger, my bra quickly followed. I gaped at him in disbelief. He winked and dove in for a sultry kiss.

"I'm not fucking with you. I'm going to have some fun with my new canvas. I haven't had the chance to kiss you from your naval to your mouth and plan on savoring it. Maybe if you're lucky, I'll go even further south," Trey growled.

"God, I love when you make that sound," I moaned.

He growled again while tracing patterns above and below my naval. Resting his elbows on the sides of my hips, he ran his tongue over the shapes he made moments ago. With the way his mouth skirted along my waistline, it was obvious he wanted to go further down. I wiggled my hips to encourage that course of action, but he gripped them tightly.

"Don't move or I'll stop," Trey commanded before he sucked my belly button ring into his mouth.

"My patience is growing thin," I whimpered, bucking my body into his.

The inferno between my legs spread throughout me, like those wildfires you see happening out West all the time. It was an uncontainable flame, showing no signs of slowing down. Trey pressed tender kisses along my belly on his way upward. He gently bit on each nipple, making them hard in an instant, and scooted up so we were more aligned with one another.

I kissed his chest and sucked along his collarbone. After he spent a few minutes licking and nipping my breasts, I tugged on his hair to bring his mouth back to mine. He hissed and rocked into me. A strangled moan escaped from me and he repeated the process several times before eagerly taking my tongue into his mouth.

Wrapping an arm underneath me, Trey brought us back into a sitting position. His erection was prominent and I couldn't resist rolling my hips into him. Meeting my thrust, he delved his tongue even deeper into my mouth.

My fingers appreciated every detailed curve of his chest and I gyrated into him again. His lips traveled to my breasts and he circled his tongue around my nipple before biting it. I didn't stand a chance at holding back my drawn-out moan. It became even louder when his fingers twisted and kneaded along my other breast.

Nearing my explosion point, I heaved in a gush of air before sucking hard along his shoulder and down his chest. Trey became even more vigorous in his suckling and rubbing. My legs started to tremble and it took everything I had to tear my lips away from him and sway back.

"If you send me over the edge on my own again, I'm returning the favor. That's the deal," I panted, giving his dick a gentle squeeze.

Before he had a chance to answer, a knock sounded on the door. Trey set me to the side of him, jumped up and grabbed his shirt, then handed me my bra and tank top. We hastily put our clothes back on and Trey bolted from the room to do some damage control with his erection.

I retrieved my purse and pulled out a mirror to do what I could with my hair. Fortunately, it didn't have a "just fucked" look to it and I ran a brush through it a few times. My face was on the flushed side, but there wasn't much I could do about that, especially since my body was wound up so tight I could probably do enough damage as an F3 tornado if I was spinning around. I picked up my phone to check the time, but didn't even register it after seeing several missed calls and three texts from Kelsey. *Fuck!*

My stomach dropped to my knees on my way to the door. Panic overtook every other feeling in my body and I struggled to get my feet to move. I looked through the peephole and released an overdue breath after seeing a blonde woman I recognized from the front desk. I opened the door and gestured for her to come in. She ran her hands down her black pinstriped skirt suit and adjusted her nametag, *Ann*.

"Good evening, Ms. McAndrews. I apologize for the intrusion, but your phone is set to Do Not Disturb. We have a message for you."

Dread consumed my body before I whispered, "Who called?"

Her face was pained as she said, "Kelsey did, a few minutes ago, to inform you that your father has returned from D.C. early. She's recommended you come home before curfew."

I glanced at the clock in the middle of the fireplace and cursed under my breath. It was ten thirty. I had a half hour to get my ass home before World War III ensued. Trey emerged from the bedroom, his face alarmed, and my stomach swan dived into a different dimension. Trey wrapped his arms around me so I'd stop shuddering.

"Thank you for letting me know. Please run the card on file for the reservation. If you could keep the room open tomorrow, I'll come back and clean everything up," I choked out against the lump in my throat.

"That won't be necessary. Manny has already volunteered to take care of it."

I stepped out of Trey's embrace and grabbed my purse. My hands were shaking so bad. I barely got out a couple of twenties for him and handed them to her. Ann clasped her hands together and disappeared down the hall.

Trey's face was full of concern. "Bri, what's going on? You look like you're going to pass out. Considering what we were just doing, that's one hell of a three-sixty. You're so pale right now. Please tell me what's wrong."

I forced my body out of the frozen state my anxiety had me in, snatched my phone from the counter, and tried Kelsey, but she didn't pick up. I scrolled to the text message she sent at eight.

Kelsey: Your dad came home early. I've informed him you're at the Waldorf for a study session. I've called the front desk to let

them know he might call and to cover for you. For now, he doesn't seem to suspect anything. I'll keep you posted if that changes.

The next one was about an hour later.

Kelsey: He's had a few brandy's and is agitated. He's pestered me for more details. I've reiterated your whereabouts and that you're studying for the SATs. He called the Waldorf and they repeated what I said and that you're studying with Peyton, Kylie, and Shane. He called Kylie and Peyton. They did their best to cover for you, but I don't think he's buying it. I think it's best you return home.

An anvil was on my chest as I opened the message sent fifteen minutes ago. As the walls closed in on me, I took several deep breaths in a vain attempt to halt my rising anxiety.

Kelsey: He's sending security over to the hotel. I'm calling the front desk and sending them up. You must leave *now*!

I hustled around the suite to get my things. Trey stood stock-still, his face growing more worried by the minute. Once my books were in my backpack, I grabbed my duffle bag, got keys out of my purse, and headed for the door.

Trey jumped in front of it and shook my shoulders. "Bri, you're scaring the shit out of me. I can't let you leave when you're like this. It's obvious you're terrified, but I need to know why before I let you go. You can't drive in this condition. You'll crash."

I tried to get my hands to stop shaking, but couldn't and forced a smile. "My dad's back. I need to go. I'll be fine as long as I get home before my curfew. I'm so sorry to end your birthday on this note."

He narrowed his eyes. "I don't give a fuck about it being my birthday. I care about *you*. I really want to believe you, but your body language is saying otherwise. It's telling me that even if you do get home on time, it's still going to be really bad."

"It's going to be really ugly if you don't let me leave. I need to go. I promise to text you when I get home."

"Will he hurt you?"

Tears welled in my eyes. "If he sends me to boarding school, it'll break my heart not to see you again. I'm begging you. *Please* let me go now."

Trey opened the door and strode down the hallway with me. Chills crawled up my spine, like we were being watched by someone, and I prayed his security detail wasn't already here. Against my will, tears fell down my cheeks. Trey wiped them away and cupped my face. His eyes were pained as he brushed his lips tenderly across mine. It was the briefest, yet sweetest kiss, and I cried even harder.

He towed me into his chest. "God, I wish I could go with you, but I can tell you don't want me to. Bri, you must contact me when you can or I'll take matters into my own hands to ensure you're okay."

The elevator arrived and I gave him a parting squeeze before getting into it. "Trey, I'll be fine. Please don't worry or do anything stupid."

His face was dismayed as he let the door slide shut. I hated being the reason for that look. The elevator moved slower than ever on its way down to the lobby. My heart pounded and my palms were covered in sweat. It felt like a set of hands were around my neck. I sank to the floor, held my knees, and forced air into my lungs. It took several deep breaths for me to get a fraction of control over my nervous system before I stood up and dialed Shane's number.

"Hey, Bri. I thought you and Trey were spending the night together. Why are you calling me?"

Shane's wary tone was all I needed to hear for the tears to fall freely again. I wiped them away and whispered, "I need a favor."

"What's wrong? Did Trey hurt you? I warned him what would happen if he did."

"We're fine," I rasped.

"Dammit, Bri! Tell me what's going on. You're scaring the hell out of me," Shane replied, downright exasperated.

"My dad came back from D.C. early."

"Shit!"

"Yeah, shit is right."

"What can I do?"

"Can you come to the hotel and go to the suite we were in? Kelsey told my dad I was studying there with you, Kylie, and Peyton. He's already called those two and they tried to cover for me, but he's on the rampage and sending security to check. I doubt you'll get here in time. You might need to get Manny and the rest of the staff in on it. I'm sure Trey's left by now, but if you can call him and make sure, I'd appreciate it. I don't think things would end well if he ran into security. He's already riled up because of the state I was in when I left."

"No problem. I'm leaving right now. I'll call Manny and Trey as soon as I hang up with you. Do you want me to call your dad?"

"Don't call him. He'll get even more suspicious if you do. Just try and get there as fast as you can and get everyone on the same page so no one cracks when security interrogates them."

"Will do. Why do you think he came home early?"

"I don't know. Even though things have been going good for Trey and me, it's felt like a set of eyes have been on me since our first weekend together. I don't know if it's whoever is trying to mess up his life or if it's my dad's people."

"Do you think someone tipped him off and that's why he came back? So he could catch you with him and make you pay for it?"

"I'm not sure what to think. He doesn't want me with him, but I'm pretty sure he knows we're seeing each other. There are still so many unanswered questions from Trey's fight with Sebastian that make me wonder what's going on behind the scenes. I know someone is out there, just waiting to sabotage him—*us*. It's never sat well with me that we didn't get any answers on that front," I replied while hastily walking through the parking ramp.

"Me either, but my dad warned me not to dig into it and that he'd know if I did. I'll give him a call to see if he has anything new to report. You know how he feels about you and he won't be happy to hear your dad is making your life a living hell again. Is there anything else I can do?"

I glanced around to verify no one was following me and wiped away a few straggling tears. "No, you're doing more than enough. Thank you."

"You don't have to thank me. You know I'm always here. I wish I could do more. You need to text me later to let me know how things go."

"I will. Thank you again. Bye, Shane," I whispered.

"Your dad's an asshat. Forget whatever he spews at you. You're a strong girl. Don't ever forget that, Bri." Shane replied, hanging up.

I reached my Lexus, tossed my duffle bag in the trunk, hopped inside, and put my backpack and purse on the passenger's seat. My phone vibrated as I cranked the ignition, bolted out of the ramp, and weaved my way through traffic. Once I had an opening, I floored it. Knowing I had about ten minutes to get home, I really hit the gas once I was on the freeway. Thank God, there was hardly anyone on the road. I retrieved my phone to see who texted me.

Mia: Trey called and demanded I tell him more about your dad and how things are at home. I told him your dad pressures you a lot but didn't go into details. I don't know what's going on, but I know it's bad. I've never heard Trey sound so angry and scared at the same time. I'm freaking out. I need to know you're okay. Please call when you can.

My tears threatened to fall once more, but I took a huge breath to keep them at bay. I grabbed some makeup and did what I could to make it look like I hadn't been crying. If I walked into my house with a blotchy face, it'd be a red flag for my dad.

After taking my exit, I sped down the road and pulled into our driveway with three minutes to spare. I killed the engine and sprinted to the front door. A déjà vu moment hit me when it opened up. Dad's face was flushed, his eyes bugging out.

"Where the hell have you been, Brianna?"

I dug deep down to keep my body from shaking. "I was studying for the SATs with some friends at the Waldorf. The test is coming up in November and we've been having study sessions."

The veins in his forearms throbbed at a disturbing rate. "What friends were with you?"

My face remained indifferent. "Shane, Peyton, and Kylie this evening. It's an ever-changing group. Whoever can make it attends."

His eyes were glossy as he sneered, "Don't get smart with me. I've warned you what will happen. I have security checking into matters now. I'm well aware how devious you can be and know *a lot* more than you think. Was the Donovan boy with you tonight?"

His acidic tone sent icy waves throughout my body. I kept my face steadfast and replied, "No, Trey wasn't at this session. He doesn't really mingle with anyone from Chamberlain."

Dad gripped my chin tightly and snapped, "You're lying. I know you've been spending time with that boy. He's a punk from the south side. I haven't been able to intervene over the past several weeks, but I don't have another trip to D.C. planned for a while. I don't want you associating with him any longer. If I hear otherwise, you'll regret it."

My temper went into high gear. "You don't know anything about him. You're just projecting your asinine opinion of that side of the city on him."

His hold tightened. I tried to wiggle my jaw free, but he dug his fingers in even deeper. "Watch your mouth, Brianna. I know enough about him. He's a brawler. Don't you forget I can dig into every aspect of a person's life. I have people *everywhere*. If I were you, I'd be forthcoming with anything else you're trying to hide because I'll know it all very soon. If I hear something I don't like, there *will be* repercussions."

The pain was difficult to bear and my eyes watered. Before I had a chance to respond, Mom stumbled into the foyer, rubbing her eyes. After she got them to focus, they were wide and livid. "John, what are you doing? You're obviously hurting her. Let go!"

I'd never been more grateful for her presence than I was right then. Her nap sobered her up. She wouldn't have stepped in if she was still buzzed. Dad gazed impassively at her, his eyes darkening. If I had to put money on it, he had a hard time not backhanding her.

He released his hold. "You're damn lucky your mom intervened, Brianna. This isn't over. Not by a long shot. I can't look at you for another second. You're such a disappointment. Get your ass to your room. You're grounded until I say otherwise."

My eyes widened as I opened my mouth. He ran a hand across his throat. Between the enraged look on his face and that gesture, I snapped it shut.

He stepped into my space. "Don't push me. I will take you out of sports and every other activity you're involved in at school. You're not very good anyway. Your teams can easily replace you. I can put security on you twenty-four-seven so that all you see are the walls around here and at Chamberlain."

Mom shouted, "That's enough, John! You're not grounding her, pulling her from sports, or sticking security on her. You're drunk and being a complete asshole to build up your own ego because something didn't go your way in D.C. *Leave. Her. Alone.*"

"Brianna, go to bed," Mom instructed, boring a hole into the back of Dad's head.

His eyes were wide with shock and so were mine. She never stood up to him. I skirted past the two of them. Once I reached the top of the stairs, the tears I somehow managed to keep in check poured down my face as fast as a waterfall. As I sprinted to my room, their voices roared through the house.

I didn't bother turning on the light or surround sound. There wasn't a song in the world that would drown them out or bring me any solace. My chest weighed a million pounds. I curled up in the center of my bed and tried to breathe, but it was really difficult.

Kelsey slid in behind me, but didn't say a word. There weren't really words for any of his tongue-lashings. I wasn't sure I had the strength to handle his threats for another year. My lungs burned for air and I struggled to catch my breath. Kelsey rubbed my back and urged me to breathe, but it felt like I'd been buried alive. I gasped in spurts of air as the tears cascaded down my face. My body could no longer keep up with the lack of oxygen and darkness overcame me.

CHAPTER 19

TREY

I stared at my phone, willing it to produce a message from Bri, but the screen remained blank. She hadn't responded to any of my texts or calls and it was almost twelve thirty. I tried to keep telling myself she was asleep, but just couldn't shake the nagging feeling in my gut that something bad happened.

Shane assured me Bri could handle herself when it came to her dad, but he didn't see her before she left. I'd never seen someone so terrified to go home. She was so pale and fragile. I should've followed her. She could barely hold onto her keys and was in no condition to drive.

As I paced around my room, I ran a hand through my hair every five seconds before tugging at it in frustration. I would much rather have someone pound the crap out of me than deal with the heavy weights crushing my body. I tried to wrap my head around how our evening went from the steaminess in *Cruel Intentions* to the mind-boggling end in *The Departed*. A loud crash on the deck broke my thoughts. Mia opened the door leading out to it moments later.

"Keep it down. My mom isn't feeling the greatest and finally fell asleep," I hissed.

Her face was apologetic as she shut the door. "I'm sorry. Chase is drunk and I haven't heard from Bri. My coordination is out of whack. You know I can barely walk a straight line when I'm freaking out in the smallest of ways. Right now, I'm at DEFCON One. It's a miracle I made it up here without falling off the side of the house."

I wrapped her in my arms. "It's okay. He was laying into you pretty bad, wasn't he?"

She looked at my ceiling and counted to five, a nervous tick of hers to keep from crying. Whenever she showed up in the middle of the night, it was never a good sign. She always came to my room on the nights Chase was at his worst. Mia didn't trust Micah not to take matters into his own hands and strangle Chase to death.

Once she was more composed, Mia forced a smile. "Nothing I'm not used to. Did you hear from Bri?"

I released her, sat on my bed, and curled my fists together. "No. What if something happened to her?"

Mia plopped down next to me and fidgeted with her bracelets. "She might've fallen asleep after dealing with her dad. That happens sometimes. She'll lay down without the intention of dozing off, but she does. It's hard on those nights when she doesn't get in touch with me, but I can't fault her for crashing once she's done listening to whatever diatribe he has for her."

"I don't know how much longer I can handle your vague comments about her life at home, Mia. You say he doesn't abuse her, but I can tell by the pained look on your face that's not exactly true," I snapped with a glare in my eyes.

"Trey, she's my best friend. I can't share her secrets. She needs to tell you those things herself, and in her own time. I've already said more than I should. The only reason I've told you this much is to ensure you don't do anything irrational," Mia replied with a fierce glare of her own.

"I keep trying to get her to tell me more, but she clams up every time. What's it going to take for her to trust me? She gets so closed off whenever the conversation even remotely turns toward her family. She's said enough for me to know things aren't right at home and that makes me want to beat both of her parents bloody."

"And that last part is exactly why I won't say anymore on it. Your fists of fury are never too far away and you're still way too willing to use them. Maybe you should call Mr. West or Shane. If they tell you, I'm not breaking the 'hos before bros' code."

"If I call now, he'll know it's late here and suspect the worst. I've already tried asking Shane and he won't tell me anything. I can't sit here any longer. I *need* to know she's okay. I'm going to her house," I replied, getting up.

Mia grabbed my hand to keep me from moving forward. "Trey, I don't think that's a good idea. It sounds like the situation is bad already. If you show up and get caught, you'll just make matters worse for her."

I wiggled my hand free. "It's not your call, Mia. I'm going. You can either come with or stay here."

She jumped in front of me. "At least let me call Kelsey first."

"Who's Kelsey?"

"Their maid. She runs the house but is like a mom to Bri. She'll tell me what's going on."

"What the fuck? Why didn't you call her earlier?"

Mia narrowed her eyes. "I've been trying her. She hasn't picked up. In case you forgot, it's nearly one in the morning."

Tsunami waves of anger washed over my body. I looked to the heavens above and prayed for patience. "Make the call or I'm leaving."

She pulled her iPhone out of her black fleece and grimaced when Kelsey didn't answer. I snatched my car keys off my desk and strode over to the door leading to the deck, but she grabbed the back of my Nike T-shirt before I walked out.

"I can't believe I'm saying this, but I'm going with you. If you stand a chance in hell on pulling this off, you'll need my help. Where are your binoculars?"

"Why do you need them?"

Her face was strained. "Because there's usually security roaming around her house. You didn't think you'd just be able to pull into their driveway and scurry up the ivy-covered fence leading to her room, did you?"

I marched over to my closet, rummaged around on the top shelf until I found them, and gave her a pointed look to move her ass. Mia muttered how bad of an idea this was as she headed out the door and shimmied down the railing on the side of the porch. I followed suit and jumped when there was five feet between me and the ground.

We hustled across the lawn and hopped into my car. I started it up and kept an eye on all the windows of the house. When no lights flickered on, I backed out of the driveway and sped toward the interstate.

"Where does Bri live?" I asked, tightening my grip on the wheel.

"Sheesh. You really didn't think this through if you don't even know where she lives," Mia grumbled, pinching the bridge of her nose.

"I'm not in the mood for your sarcasm. Tell me where she fucking lives," I snapped.

"Take a deep breath so you don't lose your shit and I'll tell you," Mia shot back.

I sucked in a gush of air to appease her. She stared at me, still skeptical by the look on her face, so I added a genuine smile for good measure.

"Their property is in Highland Park. If you know where Michael Jordan's house is, you'll have no problem finding it."

I gaped at her. "Yeah, I know where he lives. Is he their neighbor?"

Mia rolled her eyes. "It's not like he lives around here anymore."

"That's one of the flashier suburbs. Her house must be huge."

"It's pretty big, which is why I had to join you on this idiotic adventure. You'll never be able to navigate the place without me."

"You've made your point that this isn't a great idea, but now you can shut up about it."

She crossed her arms over her chest before looking out the window. We drove the remainder of the way in silence. Both of our tempers were at their peak and that didn't fare well for us. When we were two miles away from Bri's house, Mia motioned to pull over. I parked and we got out in a hurry. She climbed on top of the large stone ledge off to the side of the road. After surveying the place for a minute, Mia jumped down, her face cynical.

"Security isn't walking the grounds anymore. There's a lake about a mile up the road. Follow it until you reach a secluded beach. You're on the McAndrews' property then. Bri's room is on the right side of the house. It's the third window from the left on the second floor. There's a fence leading up to her room that you can climb. You better pray her window is open and their security alarm is off. Kelsey usually opens it on a night like this and turns off the alarm. You *should* be fine. If it isn't, you're shit out of luck and need to abandon ship."

I scowled. "If it isn't open or the alarm goes off, I'll figure something out. I'm not leaving until I see with my own eyes that she's fine."

"Good luck. I'll keep watch here. Make sure you pay attention to your cell. And for the love of God, don't dawdle. I don't want to press our luck or sleep in your car," Mia replied and returned to the ledge to keep vigil.

"I'll take as long as I like. You can't tell me what to do, especially when it comes to Bri," I retorted, annoyed.

"Stubborn as ever. Just go already. If you keep standing here and exchanging quips with me, the sun will rise before you even get there," Mia snapped, exasperated.

I sprinted down the road and along the lake. My eyes scanned every square inch around me to ensure no one saw me. I wasn't sure if it was the fast pace or the thought of Bri being hurt that had my lungs burning. Once I reached the beach, I paused to catch my breath.

After I wasn't panting like a dog on an eighty-degree day, I ran across the driveway. Another sharp right and I was on the side of the house that her room was on. I climbed up the ivy-covered fence. Someone upstairs was looking out for me because the window was open. I tentatively reached for the edge of the screen to jimmy it off. Not hearing any alarms, I pulled it away from the frame, kept tight hold of it with one hand, hopped inside, and set the screen down.

Her room was pitch-black, but I managed to navigate my way around it with the dim light from my phone. Bri looked so small curled up in the middle of her king-size bed. I could barely see the fluffy pillow propped under her head with her hair splayed all over it. Suddenly, Bri rolled over so she was facing me. It was hard to see, but her eyes were puffy. She'd been crying—*a lot*. The sides of her jaw were red. An unfriendly fire burned within me. I took measured breaths to keep the beast at bay, tiptoed across her hardwood floor, and crawled in next to her.

The pillow was really wet, making it clear she cried long after she fell asleep. After seeing her jawline up close, my blood boiled even more. Dark red handprints were on it and on their way to becoming full-blown bruises. My body shook with the rage I struggled to get hold of.

I did a couple of techniques I learned at Tai Chi to rein in my temper. Once the urge to rip someone's head off was manageable and I convinced myself not to beat the living shit out of her dad, I scooted closer to Bri and carefully moved some errant strands of hair from her sweaty forehead. I really wanted to kiss it, but didn't want to risk her waking up.

For the next half hour, I wished I could be inside her head. I didn't know what was going through her mind, but it wasn't good. She rolled back and forth every few minutes and the tortured look on her face damn near sliced my heart in two. When she started to cry, I rested my hand on her cheek, hoping that would chase away her pain.

Bolting up, Bri opened her mouth to scream, but I clapped my hand over it before a sound came out. She held a hand over her heart while taking deep breaths.

Once she was breathing steadily, Bri focused on me. "What the hell are you doing here?"

I tucked her silky brown hair behind her ears and put my palm on her cheek. "You didn't call. I had to know you were okay. I haven't been here long. I didn't mean to scare you or wake you up. I hate when you cry and had to touch you. Why were you crying?"

She rested her head on my chest. "I'd rather talk about how the hell you got in here unnoticed. I swear you're a ninja in another life."

"I wouldn't go that far. Mia helped get me in here undetected. I'd really like to know what made you cry in your sleep and why you have marks on your jaw. Please tell me, Bri."

She looked up with tears in her eyes. "Trey, please let it go."

"You told me he didn't hit you. It's pretty clear he's hurt you in more ways than one," I persisted.

"I'll be fine," Bri insisted.

"You're lying. If you don't want to talk, that's fine, but don't lie to me," I snapped.

"*Please*, Trey. If I talk about it now, I'll have an anxiety attack and I already had a really bad one tonight," Bri pleaded as a tear trickled down her cheek.

I wiped it away and intertwined my legs with hers. "I don't want to trigger anything. You always seem so sure of yourself. I would've never guessed you have panic attacks. Do you get them a lot?"

Bri nodded. "Sometimes they're short and I can get through them with measured breathing. The one I had earlier made me pass out. Kelsey does her best to prevent that from happening, but it doesn't always work. I have medication for it, but don't like the side effects of taking the pills. I try to rein it in with other tactics."

Her heart beat at a rapid rate. I caressed her sides until she stopped shaking and snuggled even closer to me.

"Is me being here freaking you out to the point you're going to have another one?"

"I'm scared, but I'm not ready for you to leave. Please don't go yet."

"What are the methods to prevent them? I'd like to know so I can help. I can't stand seeing you so broken up and terrified."

"You already are. Just being in your arms helps tremendously."

"What else?"

"Exercise, fresh air, massages, acupuncture, aromatherapy, yoga, sex."

I rolled my eyes. "Leave it to you to slip having sex into a serious conversation."

She smacked my chest. "It's true. If you want proof, I can bring it up on *WebMD*."

"No, that's not necessary. So, is that why the window is open and you have all that oil and candle shit on your desk? Although, I'm not sure it's a desk. There's too much stuff on it for me to be sure," I teased.

"Yes, that's why I have that stuff and keep the window open. I bet you a hundred dollars your room is just as messy as mine," Bri retorted.

"Nope," I replied, popping my lips.

She snorted. "I call bullshit. Every teenage boy's room is like a hazard zone."

I put my hands behind my neck. "Not mine. I keep it nice and tidy. I even help clean around the house and cook dinner sometimes. You're welcome to come over and see me in action."

Holy shit! Did I just invite her over? My mom is going to freak out on her. If that doesn't send her packing, the little shits will annoy her so much, she'll run for the hills.

Bri rested her hand on my chest. "I think it's only fair I get to see your room now that you've been in mine, but I can tell by how fast your heart is beating that you didn't mean to ask me. I struggle with brain-to-mouth malfunctions around you all the time. If you want to take it back, you can."

I wrapped her up in a tight embrace. Her green eyes seared right into my soul, leaving a mark that would be there for eternity. "I don't want to. I'd love for you to meet my family."

She trailed featherlight kisses along my neck. "I'd like that too."

I brushed my lips across hers. "It's settled then. Another first for me, Ms. McAndrews."

Bri gave me one of her shier smiles. "I've had plenty of firsts with you as well, Mr. Donovan."

"Tell me one of them."

"Well, you're the first boy who's been in my bed. That's a pretty big one."

I kissed her nose. "I'm just laying with you in it. None of your sexual fantasies are coming true tonight."

She stuck out her tongue. "Whose mind is in the gutter now?"

"Bri, I'm always thinking about having sex with you. I *am* a guy."

"Well, let the record show, I'm all for it, Trey."

I laughed. "It already reflects that detail. Let's get back on point. How about you come over for dinner this Saturday after we serve our stupid detention sentence?"

She flinched. "I'll let you know on Saturday. I'm not sure how the next couple of days around here will go. I don't want to say yes and then back out. That would be rude."

I frowned. "I really wish you'd tell me more about what goes on behind these walls."

Her body started to tremble. "I know you want to know. I can't right now. You can't be here when I tell you."

"Why can't I be here?"

"Because I don't trust you not to lose your temper and do something you'll regret."

I really wanted to grill her some more, but it would only make her freak out even more than she already was. I repeated my earlier maneuvers to help her calm down. Once she stopped breathing like a marathon participant, I glanced at my cell and saw it was quarter to three. I looked back at Bri to see her eyelids drooping. I held her close to me until she fell sound asleep.

Bri wasn't nearly as restless as she was when I got here. It ripped my chest apart to slide out from under her to leave, but I'd have my own set of problems if I didn't get home soon. I kissed her on the forehead before shimmying down the ivy-covered fence and running back to my car.

I think I'm falling in love with you, Brianna Maureen McAndrews. Please trust me with your secrets and your heart so I can do the same.

* * *

The angry beast had been pushing his way to the surface the past two days. The unknown with Bri and her home life, along with the douchebags around Chamberlain still giving me a hard time, was catching up to me. I couldn't shake the feeling that someone always had a set of eyes on me—just waiting to take me out. I needed to call Mr. West soon. If I didn't, I'd end up doing something stupid.

Coach Barry sensed my growing agitation before the game tonight and asked if everything was okay. I reassured him things were fine and I'd get us the win, but the dubious look he gave me made it clear he didn't buy it.

We killed the Renegades and the girls annihilated the Bulldogs. A bunch of the guys on the team were heading to a party to celebrate the win and encouraged me to join them. I *should* be out partying like most teenagers on a Friday night, but I didn't have it in me to fake having a good time. The only thing I was happy about with our win tonight was in two weeks I'd finally get a chance to see Bri in action on the field. Our games weren't on the same day for once and that realization made me grin. After flopping down on my bed, I reached for my cell.

Trey: Congrats on your win! I heard you had the winning goal. I wish you would've ridden the bus home. I wanted to give you a kiss that would make you forget your own name. I'm so proud of you. ;)

My heart rate kicked up a notch while I waited for her response. Over the past couple of days, it took her a while to respond. Part of me wondered if her dad monitored her cell. Every time I asked Bri about it, she skirted the question and that led me to believe she suspected he was doing just that. If that was the case, she didn't seem to care because she always replied with *exactly* what was on her mind.

Bri: Thanks, sweets. My goal wasn't a big deal. It was strategic passing on Mia's part. I was in the right place at the right time. A big congrats to you! I heard you threw three touchdowns and ran one in. I'm so freaking proud of you! I wanted to ride the bus home, but I didn't really have a say in it. Don't torment me with

the promise of thigh-clenching kisses when I'm not in your arms. That's mean. And you call me a tease. :/

I'd never admit it to her, but I enjoyed stringing out how far we went. Her reactions to whatever I did to her body were priceless. My dick wasn't as thrilled with the delayed gratification route. I'd never masturbated as much as I had in the past month and a half. I doubted that would change even after our first time together. Being around her left me in a constant state of arousal and I really wished she believed me when I told her.

Trey: Stubborn girl! Learn to take a compliment. Did your parents force you to ride home with them?

When we made out in my car this morning, I gripped the sides of her face and rather than lean into me the way she usually did, she winced and nearly leapt out of my lap. Bri assured me that it was fine and distracted me with her salacious lips, but knowing she got hurt made me want to crawl through her window every night to ensure she was safe.

Bri: Something like that.

What do I have to do to break down that wall of hers? With this topic, it's like trying to break the barriers in a maximum-security prison.

Trey: Why won't you just tell me what's going on already?

Bri: As you enjoy saying to me, it's still not the right time.

Dammit! That's my line. Stubborn, maddening, sexy vixen of a woman!

Trey: Grrr!!!

Bri: You're really fucking hot when you growl. Do it some more! I'll lick my lips before biting my bottom one. I know what that does to you. ;)

Trey: Gasp. Ms. McAndrews, are you trying to proposition me into sexting?

Bri: Mr. Donovan, that's exactly what I'm trying to do. You up for the challenge?

Trey: Oh, something is up indeed. As you fully know, I rise to every challenge. Bring it on, baby.

Bri: I like you're already up. That does things to me. As you also know so do I, babe!

Trey: I didn't get to touch your lips or skin enough this morning. What does it do to you?

I hopped up, tugged my gray T-shirt over my head, and locked my door. The muscles in my upper body ached from the hits I took during the game, but I barely registered it. After slipping off my black mesh shorts, I sat down on my bed and pictured her gorgeous body. Whenever we were together, she was always ready and receptive.

Bri: You know exactly what it does to me and I concur on not enough touching. When I'm with you, it's never enough. If I were with you, I'd show you how gifted my tongue is on other areas of your body.

Trey: I have no doubt, darling. However, I want to test out my tongue ring between your legs before you go between mine.

That was the understatement of the year. I hadn't slipped a finger inside her yet, but I was desperate to do that and then take her over the edge with my tongue. Running it along her clit ran through my mind far too much on any given day. I deserved a fucking medal for my restraint.

Bri: SO. AM. I. But, I DEMAND to pleasure you first.

My cock jerked, loving that idea way too much. Her delectable mouth popped into my head and I imagined Bri licking her way around my base and tip. I wanted that so badly the other day, but wasn't quite ready to relinquish control over to her.

Trey: I'll consider it. As you very well know, I will continue to retain all control.

Bri: There's that domineering side of yours rearing its ugly head and ruining the mood. Killjoy!

Trey: I don't try to kill it. I wasn't aware you were already in the mood.

Bri: When I'm around you, I'm always in the mood. Just the thought of your tongue down there has me wet and ready. That happens more times a day than I'm willing to admit. I've had to take matters into my own hands a lot since our paths crossed.

My dick was rock-hard and more than ready to slide inside her. I was an idiot for playing into this game. It would take a lot of handiwork to get to my release.

Trey: Why do you do this to me? I swear you were put on this earth to torture me with your amazing curves and sassy mouth.

Bri: Mr. Donovan, if you scroll up, you'll note my mouth and everything inside it is gifted, not sassy. And let's just say I have PLENTY of tricks I have yet to show you.

Trey: Oh, it's sassy alright, but I'll agree it's definitely gifted. Take your shirt off and shorts. Imagine my hands caressing and kissing your beautiful breasts.

They were absolutely amazing. I was still kicking myself for not discovering that fact sooner. Her skin was so smooth and the way her body arched into mine when I ran my hands and fingers across her nipples nearly made me come. I tossed my boxers on the floor and pictured her naked body next to mine.

Bri: Done. Now, you strip down. Imagine my lips drifting down your washboard abs to that delectable V of yours.

Trey: They're already gone. My lips are on their way down to your naval so I can suck on that belly button ring of yours. What's next, baby? Make me see it in my head.

Bri: My hands are just getting done rubbing you down. My mouth is about to swallow you whole and not stop until I feel your hot release traveling down the back of my throat.

Trey: Sweet Jesus! You swallow?

That is so fucking hot. I've never been with a girl who was willing to or admitted to touching herself. My tip is practically dripping. She's always finding new ways to shock me. She's so goddamn sexy. I wish she was here right now. She so owns me.

Bri: Normally, no, but for you, I definitely will.

Trey: Reading that nearly made me explode all over my sheets.

Bri: Stroke yourself and I will too. Maybe we'll make it happen together for once.

I couldn't handle it any longer. I dialed her number and waited for her to pick up.

"Please don't tell me you're calling to stop," Bri panted.

"No, I'd rather hear your voice when you come than imagine it," I breathed.

"Let's get back to stroking ourselves then. I love and I hate how you can turn my body on so quickly. No one has ever made me come like you," Bri moaned.

A low, yet seductive, growl rumbled from my chest as I wrapped a hand around my painfully hard cock. "God, your voice is so husky right now, baby. I got harder just hearing it."

She groaned, "Babe, you know what it does to me when you growl. I'm already dripping like a leaky faucet, but I want to try and make this last longer than it usually does for me. You send me over the brink way too fast."

"And you know what it does to me when you lick your lips provocatively. Stop it, so we can string this out. I'm quite enjoying it."

"I'm not even going to ask how you knew I was doing that. What I will tell you is I want you *badly*."

"How bad?" I asked in a pant.

"Like-so-fucking-bad-it's-going-to-kill-me-pretty-soon-bad," Bri rasped.

My hand sped up as I imagined her on my lap. She had a way with gyrating her hips that deserved the highest of accommodations. Her breathing increased and I moaned.

"Me too, Bri. My hand just doesn't compare to having you rock your body into mine. I fucking love how that feels so much. Having it pressed into me so I can feel your heart beating with mine and making sweet poetry as they do."

"My hands don't hold a candle compared to yours, Trey. Your magical fingers will forever be a treasure to me."

"Fuck, I wish I was inside you. I can always feel your heat when I run my hands down there and I can only imagine what it will be like when I take you."

She whimpered. "My body is clenching in all the right places. God, I want you so bad."

Hearing that her voice was even huskier made me stroke myself even faster. She was really fucking close and my own release was right around the corner.

"Slide your fingers deep inside you. I want to make you come," I demanded. Bri released a drawn-out moan and I nearly blew my load. "That's it. Twist and thrust until your back is arching off your mattress."

"I'm going to come, Trey. Please go with me," Bri begged, her moans growing louder.

That was all I needed to hear. My body started to quake and I rubbed even harder. "I'm right there with you. Come for me, baby."

"Oh. My. God," Bri moaned as she hit her climax.

"Fuck, the things your moans do to me," I hissed, stroking myself until I hit my own release.

We exchanged heated breaths until the aftershocks passed. Once I could function on all cylinders again, I cleaned myself up with a towel and slid my boxers back on.

"That's another first, Mr. Donovan."

"For me too, Ms. McAndrews. I hope it was just as pleasurable for you as it was for me."

"Pleasurable isn't the right word. Downright mind-blowing is more toward the mark. I wish I could've seen your face," Bri replied in a wistful tone.

I ran my hand through my hair a few times to give it that "just fucked" look, took a selfie, and sent it her way.

"Holy shit, you look really fucking hot after phone sex. It makes me want to go for round two, but it's almost one in the morning. We should probably go to bed so we can function tomorrow at practice and detention."

"Yeah, I suppose you're right. Even though I hate detention, I'm really looking forward to seeing you, but that's nothing new. Have deliciously naughty dreams and I will of you. We'll make them happen soon enough."

"You're such a tease. Thank you for tonight. It was certainly memorable. Bye, Trey," Bri said, lingering on the line.

"Memorable isn't quite the right word for it. Extraordinary, maybe. Bye, Bri," I replied, hanging up.

I plugged in my cell, set it on my nightstand, and made my way to the bathroom to brush my teeth. After putting my toothbrush back in the holder, I splashed some cold water on my face, headed back to my bedroom, flicked the light off, and crawled under the covers.

All I wanted to do was make Bri happy and keep her safe. Her stunning emerald eyes, beautiful face, and magnificent body ran on repeat in my head. I wasn't sure what would happen tomorrow, but I was determined to hold onto the one person I needed to survive it all.

CHAPTER 20

TREY

A loud knock brought me out of the one of hottest dreams I'd had of Bri yet. She was on top of me and riding me hard with her head arched back as she approached her climax. *Fuck!* I wanted to finish the rest of it, but opened my eyes. It was a goddamn miracle I wasn't a sticky mess. That had happened *a lot* in the past two months. I glanced at my clock to see it was six in the morning.

I cursed my rock-hard erection, threw on a pair of athletic shorts and T-shirt before pulling my favorite Jordan sweatshirt over my head. After sliding on my sneakers, I grabbed my duffle bag and hustled into the hallway. Mia leaned against the wall, rubbing her eyes with her bag slung over her shoulder. Judging by the grumpy look on her face, Micah kept her up late last night.

"It's about time. We're going to be late," Mia grumbled, following me downstairs.

"I figured getting laid on the regular would improve your crankiness in the morning, but it hasn't. I'll have to give Micah some more sex tips so your mood before the sun comes up improves," I muttered, heading into the kitchen.

I snatched the sack lunches Mom made for us, along with some energy bars and Gatorades, and stuffed them into my duffle. Mia tripped over her feet and nearly knocked over a stool at the island while trying to keep up with me. Her mouth was still agape on our way out the front door, across the dew on the freshly-cut grass, and over to my car.

As we hopped into my Acura, the sun hit the horizon. The red and orange hues were a mighty fine sight. I cranked the ignition and sped toward the interstate so we could make it to practice on time. Knowing I'd see Bri made me despise this ride a lot less than I used to. Mia ripped the wrapper off her Lärabar and took a small bite.

"Did Bri tell you we were having sex or was it Micah?" Mia asked, her face still mortified.

"Guys may not talk about things the way you girls do, but we tend to share the bigger things that happen in our lives. Of course Micah told me when he turned in his V-card," I replied, shaking my head.

Mia bit her lip before she mumbled, "Did he mention if it was good for him?"

I gaped at her. "Micah's my best friend. We have our own code of silence—just like you and Bri. Do you really think I'll tell you?"

She shrugged. "It was worth a shot."

I rolled my eyes. "I think you already have an answer to that question, especially since you have sex every day. You don't need confirmation."

"It's not every day!"

"Pretty damn close. Turn on the radio and finish your breakfast."

Flicking it on, Mia took another bite of her energy bar. Her cheeks were still slightly pink so I left it on the pop station she selected. "Ignition" filled the car and I smiled while thinking about the lyrics. It was the weekend and even if Bri couldn't come over for dinner, I'd find a way to see her. After last night, I *needed* to explore more parts of her body. Self-restraint be damned.

Before I knew it, we pulled into Chamberlain's parking lot. I gazed around, but didn't see Bri's Lexus. Seeing as practice started in twenty minutes, I hoped she made it on time. I parked at a spot near the front and retrieved my stuff from the backseat. We made our way to the sports pavilion in silence. Mia veered into the girls' locker room and I headed for the guys'.

After I changed into my practice clothes and pads, I grabbed my helmet, strode out the door, and ran right into Bri kneeling in the middle of the hall, tying the laces on her black cleats. Even in a pair of navy mesh shorts with a blue long-sleeve T-shirt on, she looked incredibly sexy. Her soccer jacket and sweatpants hung off her shoulder. When she looked up, her eyes had a burning need to them that demanded to be satisfied. My dick hardened in an instant, ready to fulfil every single one of her needs. Intertwining my hand with hers, I dragged her into their locker room.

"Trey, I thought you were against messing around at school," Bri said in a breathy whisper.

"I am, but I'm over fighting your *come and get it* look," I replied in a huff.

She smirked. "If that was the case, I would've used it more often."

My dick pitched a tent at the sultry look in her eyes. "Believe me, you use it all the time. I've just shown restraint while we're here. I can't do it anymore."

Once we were inside, I pressed her up against the first blue locker in sight and crashed my lips into hers. I claimed her mouth like a man who'd been traveling the desert in search of water and finally found an oasis. Her lips quickly parted and I tangled my tongue around hers. She eagerly caressed my tongue ring. I pinned her hands above her head, wrapped one of her legs around me, and slid my other hand up her shorts and across her panties.

"Holy shit, Bri! You're so ready. Is it from now or last night?" I asked, panting.

Her green eyes were ablaze as she groaned, "Probably a combination of both."

That look begged for me to plunge a finger deep inside her. I slowly slid one in and out while sucking along her neck. She nuzzled her head into mine and licked my jaw before gently biting my lower lip. My mouth drifted under her chin and I sucked on my favorite freckles while swirling my finger inside her. Her nails dug into my biceps so deep the skin punctured. Even with my long-sleeve T-shirt on, I felt the blood trickle to my elbows.

My teeth grazed her shoulder and I sank another finger inside her hot core, shifting from the slow pace I was going at to an unrelenting one. The warmth of her mouth as her sucking became more frantic created a frenzy inside me. She cried out when I really got my fingers moving.

It took everything I had not to strip us down and hit the homerun she'd been pleading for since our first weekend together. Her legs began to tremble and her breathing became sporadic. She closed her eyes as the quakes started to roll over her body. I twirled my fingers deep within her, desperate to take her all the way over the edge.

Just as Bri was about to hit her full climax, Mia burst into the room and immediately covered her eyes. "Shit! I'm sorry, you guys!"

Bri hunched to her knees with her face flushed. I licked my fingers, savoring the taste of Bri. A smug smile spread across my face while I gazed at her. As she tried to catch her breath, Bri gave me a shrewd grin. I glanced at Mia, who stared at the ceiling like it was the most fascinating thing in the room, her cheeks beet-red.

"I'm really sorry. I didn't expect...well, I didn't know..." Mia rambled.

Bri grabbed her jacket and sweatpants from the floor. "*Worst. Timing. Ever.* I swear to God, you and Micah have a gift for it. Spit out whatever you're here to say, Mia."

Her gaze remained on anything but us. "Peyton and Kylie showed up hungover. Coach Nocky is out for blood. I didn't know if you overslept or were stuck in traffic and came back to see if you were here. We should get going so we don't end up running the entire practice."

Bri mumbled a few obscenities under her breath and kissed my cheek. "I'd much rather continue what we were doing here, but I should go."

I nipped at her earlobe. "Maybe we'll sneak off together. The librarian has grown bored of us, so I doubt she'll notice if we're gone."

"Well, if I wasn't hot and bothered before, I sure as hell am now. Practice better go fast," Bri griped, following Mia out of the room.

I chuckled at the flustered look on her face and readjusted myself on my way out. Before heading up to the field, I stopped to grab my abandoned helmet. Once I reached the sidelines, Coach Barry stared me down while pointing at his watch. I gave him an apologetic smile and joined the guys on the track to run a few laps. As my legs fell into autopilot mode, my mind ticked off the minutes until I'd have Bri back in my arms.

* * *

Practice moved slower than molasses. After drying off from my lukewarm shower, I changed into a pair of holey jeans and my Bulls sweatshirt before lacing up my sneakers. Once my stinky practice clothes were in my duffle, I slung it over my shoulder and headed for the door to meet Shane and the girls. Coach Barry leaned against the doorframe with his arms crossed, a stern look on his face.

"You were late today, Trey. It's very unlike you."

"I'm sorry. You have my word it won't happen again. I want that title as much as you do."

He gave me a half-smile. "I know you do. As much as that is important to me, the well-being of my players is just as important. You haven't been very forthcoming when I've asked you how things have been going recently. Your attitude has improved, but I still sense there are some people giving you a hard time. If that's the case, you need to tell someone."

I shrugged. "It's nothing I can't handle." He narrowed his eyes. I crossed my fingers, doing my best to be playful with the situation. "I swear, Coach, if things get out of hand, you'll be my first call."

He sighed. "I'm always watching, Trey. Please keep that in mind. Even after the season is over, I want you to know you can come to me. I see great things for your future and want to make sure you get it."

"I appreciate it. I hate to cut this short, but I need to get to the library or Headmaster Carlton will take it out on all of us."

"I won't hold you up. The four of you have done a good job keeping your teams focused."

I cocked an eyebrow. We still had some unruly players on both squads.

He chuckled. "Well, you've done what you can. You can't control *everyone*. I have the utmost confidence you'll do what you can to keep the wilder ones in check through the playoffs. It may not seem like it, but all the coaches are proud of you guys."

Coach moved aside so I could pass through. Having him and Mr. West care so much about me still took some getting used to. After reaching Shane and the girls, I looked over my shoulder to make sure no one was behind us before pressing my lips against Bri's luscious mouth. She gasped and deepened the kiss, making Shane and Mia groan.

I laughed while pulling away. "Get over yourselves. Neither of you are prudes."

"In case it slipped your mind, I already got more than an eyeful this morning. I don't need any images akin to it flashing through my head," Mia muttered, still mortified.

Shane burst out laughing. "Oh, this sounds like such a good story. Spill it!"

I pursed my lips together, pretending to zip them, and tossed the metaphorical key behind me. Bri did the same, giggling as she did. Shane feigned outrage at being out of the loop. Mia mumbled under her breath that it was for the better.

Just as we were about to walk inside the library, I planted my feet and Shane bumped into me. The girls skidded to an abrupt stop. We all stood in complete shock, gaping at the sight in front of us. Sebastian sat on a chair with his legs kicked up on a wooden table in the front row and his hands clasped behind his neck. His eyes were snake-like as he stared us down. I curled my fists and reminded myself I couldn't pummel his ass.

One would think serving detention with the librarian would make that impossible, but she barely makes time to ensure the four of us report before disappearing into her office and catching up on the shows she recorded for the week. I'm royally fucked!

"You've got to be kidding me," I muttered, exasperated.

Bri's face was set in a grim expression as she mumbled, "Well, it looks like my least favorite John Hughes movie just came to life right before my eyes. Kill me now."

"In this version, it's more like four jocks versus the jackass. I can't really classify Sebastian as an athlete. He's always been the weakest link on our football team and he's a dumbass in the classroom, so the brain is out," Shane replied, rubbing a hand down his frustrated face.

"'Don't You Forget About Me' was the only thing I enjoyed about that movie. What the fuck did he do to end up here? He never gets detention. The faculty has always been too afraid of his daddy to ever punish him," Mia sniped, her face as agitated as the rest of ours.

"You know it's rude to talk about someone right in front of them. We'll be spending the next four hours together. You should probably accept it now," Sebastian spoke up, his grin growing more superior.

"Shut up, Sebastian. You don't know the first thing about being a decent human being. Rude is your middle name. Actually, I'm pretty sure asshole is. If you know what's good for you, you'll keep your damn mouth shut," Shane snapped, his tone ominous.

"And if I don't?" Sebastian taunted, his eyes darkening.

"Your face and my fist will get really acquainted with one another," Shane seethed.

"Is West handling all your affairs now, Donovan? I know he's good at cleaning up your messes, but is he throwing punches for you now too?" Sebastian asked, eyeing me with disdain.

I walked to the very last row of tables and slammed my bag on it. The loud bang made the girls jump. I rubbed my temples to ease the headache that had set in. There was no way I'd last four hours in the same room as Sebastian and not kill him. Thank God there were a ton of shelves and tables on both floors of the library. Part of me considered going to the second floor, but that would only make flinging Sebastian off the side of it all the more easier.

"Ignore me all you want, Donovan. I'm not going anywhere. Eventually, you'll snap and it'll be glorious. There's nothing I'll enjoy more than watching your trailer trash ass get kicked back to where it belongs."

I gripped the table with all my might and took several calculated breaths to prevent myself from boiling over. You could probably cook an egg on me for as hot as my body was right now. Mia jumped up, ready to lunge at him, but Bri shoved her down. Shane secured her arm to ensure she remained in her seat.

"You might as well get used to it. He's going to do this the entire time. Don't let him get the best of you," Bri hissed, patting my leg.

"We haven't been here for fifteen minutes and I'm ready to punch him. If I make it through today without knocking out his teeth, I deserve a fucking gold medal," I bit back.

"You can do it. I'll make sure of it and reward you with more than a medal," Bri promised.

My dick twitched, but remained dormant. The situation at hand wiped away every fantasy I'd had of Bri during practice. She tried to look reassuring, but her reservations were written all over her face. Shane and Mia shared the same strained expression as her. I grabbed my backpack and pulled out my History book, along with a pen and notebook. Sebastian turned to face us with his arms resting on the back of his chair.

"It's barely ten and I already need a stiff drink," Mia grumbled.

"Back to movie trivia. One of Hughes' best is *Sixteen Candles*. That's one of your favorites, isn't it, Bri? Too bad it wasn't called *thirteen* candles. That's more up your alley," Sebastian snickered, drumming his fingers across his chin.

I glanced at her for an explanation. She glared daggers at him and snapped, "Shut up, Sebastian. You're just trying to goad me into sparring with you to set off Trey. I'm not playing into any of your bullshit mind games. Stop being such an asshat."

The librarian popped up out of nowhere, like she usually did, and narrowed her eyes on Bri. "That language will not be tolerated, Ms. McAndrews. I suggest you watch your mouth or you'll get another month's worth of detention. Do you understand?"

Bri faked a smile. "Yes, ma'am. It slipped out and I'm very sorry."

She walked around with a bowl to collect our cells. We grudgingly passed them over. I detested not having it on me, but I was even more reluctant to give it up now. With Sebastian here, he'd probably find some way to steal ours and that could be disastrous.

Mrs. Meyer clasped her hands together. "Good. You're not to leave this room. Trust me, I'll know if you do. That's nothing new for you four." Her eyes drifted to Sebastian. "Mr. Du Pont, your cocky attitude has been noted. If I were you, I'd try *a lot* harder to adhere to the rules today or you'll find yourself in a situation at home I doubt you want to be in."

He saluted her. "I promise to be the model inmate."

She strode out of the library and into her office off to the right of it. Sebastian stared at me, his face livid. "I'm glad you got some sort of punishment from our fight. It blew my mind when my parents didn't press charges, but I'm not stupid either. Clearly, you are, though. If you think I'm the only one who wants you gone, you're sorely mistaken. Something bigger is brewing, so I'll just keep playing my part to ensure you get the ending you deserve."

My body shook with the rage I couldn't hold in and I stormed off to the opposite end of the library. The oppressive way he looked at Bri while he taunted her made me want to strangle him. I heard a set of footsteps behind me and didn't need to turn around to know it was her.

"Trey, please calm down. If you don't, it's going to end badly for all of us," Bri pleaded.

The fear etched across her face was one I promised myself I'd never be responsible for again. I heaved in a breath to rein in the anger overtaking my body.

"What was he talking about, Bri? You may not think I've noticed it, but I see how he tries to provoke you and throw himself at you. I want you to tell me what that's all about."

Bri shook her head, her face paling. "Sebastian likes to go out of his way to piss everyone off. I'm not any different."

I banged my hand against the shelf next to us and a couple of books toppled to the carpeted floor. "Stop lying!"

She flinched and shot a vicious glare at me. "Are you out of your goddamn mind? You're already ready to murder him. I'm not getting into it with you here."

"If you don't want me to explode, you better give me something. I'm tired of the *'I'm not telling you here'* line. It's grown real old, real fast."

"He was in the same social circles as me while we grew up because of our parents, but I stopped hanging out with him a long time ago. I didn't have a choice back then. What do you want me to say? I can't apologize for having a past. You need to get a hold of yourself."

I jumped into her space and she took a cautious step back. My heart plummeted to my feet. I uncurled my fists, smoothed out my furious face, and inched closer to her. She didn't move, but her face remained wary. I gave her hands a gentle squeeze and the tension in her shoulders eased a little. I slid to the ground and brought her with me. She rested her head against my shoulder as I hooked my arm around her.

"I'm sorry, Bri. That guy just brings out my ugly side."

"I know, Trey. Why do you think I'm so freaked out right now? It's going to take an act from God to get through the day."

"I don't think I've hated anyone more than I hate him."

"Let's not talk about him. Maybe we can hide out here until two rolls around."

"I love your optimism, but I doubt we can avoid him the entire time."

"I was really looking forward to picking up where we left off this morning, but that's definitely not going to happen now," Bri muttered, annoyed.

"Still feeling a little sexually frustrated?"

"That's the understatement of the century. I'm glad you finally decided to move on to third. It's about time."

I rolled my eyes. "Since it's not happening while we're here, let's steer this conversation in a different direction. Does it bother you that we keep things private between us?"

Her face was genuinely shocked. "Not at all. I don't feel like we're sneaking around. It just works better for us. As much as it really sucks not kissing you during the day, I'm okay with it. The gossip mill has enough ammo around here. Even if people knew we were dating, which I'm sure plenty suspect that much, it wouldn't matter to me. What we have is ours and only ours."

"I agree. I wouldn't care if anyone found out either. I was just making sure."

"I can't make dinner tonight, but I was wondering if we could do it after our soccer team won our state title. It would be a fun way to celebrate for me. What do you think?"

"That's a couple weeks from now. When's the championship match?"

"Tuesday. We could plan on that Wednesday."

The inked skin on my right arm prickled and I absently traced my fingers over it. "After what your dad did to your jaw, I'm not sure that's the best day, Bri. Regardless of the circumstance, I'm no longer a fan of Wednesdays."

She giggled. "I would've never figured you to be superstitious. It's just a day, Trey."

"With certain things, I'm as superstitious as they come. If you're fine with it, then so am I. I'll let my mom know and see if my dad can make it."

"Perfect. I'm happy the invite wasn't revoked. I know you're not exactly thrilled with me."

I gave her wrist a peck. "I told you I wanted you to meet them. I wouldn't rescind the offer just because I got mad at you. How are things at home?"

Her head whipped back and forth. "There's no way I'm divulging anything on that front. You're already way too riled with Sebastian lurking around. I'm looking forward to meeting your family and honored you even asked me. I know it wasn't easy for you."

The desperation in her eyes was enough for me not to ask again. I didn't need my anger to grow even more. A maniacal laugh sounded down the row from us.

"Word to the wise, Donovan, she's nothing but a tease. Don't get your hopes up. She's probably slumming it with you to get it out of her system. I'll make damn sure you don't have a future with her. She's out of your league," Sebastian sneered.

I jumped to my feet, but Bri hopped up just as quickly. She shoved my chest, her eyes pleading for me to stand down. Holding up my hands, I took a few steps back so Sebastian's neck wasn't within reaching distance. Mia and Shane raced to our row, their eyes wide. Shane stepped forward, but Bri raised her hand for him to stay put.

Bri slapped Sebastian and snarled, "Go fuck yourself. I don't know how you ended up here today, but I'm betting the only reason was so you could try and coerce Trey into another fight. It's not going to work. Just give it up already."

He tried to touch her, but she stepped away. Her body recoiled and her skin turned strikingly white. As she stared him down, Bri shook nonstop. I trailed my hands down her arms to get her to calm down. An all-out panic attack was around the corner for her and I didn't want that to happen. Shane grabbed Sebastian by the collar of his white polo and dragged him away.

"If you want to know the truth, Coach Murray gave me detention. I'd love to tell you what I did to earn it, but you seem on the sensitive side, so I'll keep those details to myself," Sebastian boasted over his shoulder.

Shane clapped his hand over his mouth and shoved him toward the tables up front. I doubted Coach Murray giving Sebastian detention was a coincidence. This was the second time he'd set me up. It also appeared that he was upping his game when it came to putting me into hostile situations. I wanted to know even more who manipulated him to fuck up my future.

My head spun with the words and faces of people who made it clear they didn't want me at Chamberlain. What disturbed me even more than any of the shit spinning out of control in my world was Bri's reaction to Sebastian. I suspected he did something very bad to her. Once I knew, I wasn't sure I'd be able to let him live.

CHAPTER 21

BRI

My eyes drifted around our charter bus as we made our way upstate for our semifinal soccer match this frigid Saturday morning. Half the team made small talk while the rest of us listened to tunes and zoned out. Releasing a ragged breath, I watched the condensation spread across the tinted window before chipping away at my royal blue and white nail polish.

Mia poked my shoulder to get me to stop and arched an eyebrow. I shook my head and focused on the countless trees passing by in a blur. My leg jiggled nonstop and I wasn't sure if it was the enormity of the game or the fact Trey would be in the stands. This was the first time he'd see me play and I wanted to do good—not just for my team, but for him.

Who am I kidding? I'm not nervous about the game or Trey watching me play. My damn parents are going to be there. Trey and my dad in the same place at the same time isn't likely to end well.

After we made it through detention with Sebastian two weeks ago,

I was beyond grateful to my guardian angel and fairy godmother. I wished that was enough to get my anxiety in check, but it wasn't. I had this nagging feeling my luck was going to run out soon. Between my dad's threats and the petty shit Sebastian and his lackeys spewed at Trey, it was hard not to have my stomach eat away at itself.

I really wanted to know why Sebastian and most of the faculty targeted Trey. It didn't sit well with me that we had no answers on that front. I couldn't talk about it with Trey. Mia and Shane were just as worried as me, but avoided talking about it as well.

If I didn't have to deal with my dad's tongue-lashings and constant pressuring, I'd dig deeper into it, but he had a close eye on me. My heart hammered against my chest and I couldn't help but wonder why he hadn't brought Trey up in the past few weeks.

Not wanting my thoughts to go in that direction, I popped in my headphones and scrolled to the playlist Trey made for me. He boasted it would get my adrenaline pumping. The Bulls warm-up anthem filled my ears and my mouth curled into a small smile. We were having an early dinner after my match before heading over to the United Center.

Knowing I'd have the entire night with Trey brought on a wave of a calmness and I rested my head against the window. The song switched to "Sweet Caroline" and my mind drifted to our amazing day at Wrigley before I dozed off.

An hour later, Mia patted me on the leg. "Are you ready to kick some ass?"

I bumped her fist. "You know it. Let's destroy 'em!"

The hooting and hollering grew louder as we departed the bus and walked into the stadium. For nine in the morning, there was a good crowd. I figured more people would trickle in for the second half, but the stands were already pretty full. The grass was wet with dew. It was likely to be a muddier match—my favorite kind.

I looked around the arena for Trey, but it didn't take long to spot his smoking hot physique. He was with Micah and Shane toward midfield. Shane and Micah gave Mia and me the thumbs up while Trey flashed his dimples and mouthed good luck to me. Adrenaline pumped through my veins while I waved at them. Mia blew a kiss to Micah and set her duffle bag on the ground. I tugged my headphones out, put my iPod in my bag, and tossed it down on our sideline.

Once my jacket was unzipped, I ripped off my warm-up pants and did a few stretches. After my muscles were somewhat loose, I pulled up my long royal blue socks, laced up my cleats, and smoothed out my striped Nike jersey. My fingers ran along the number twelve on the front of it and I smiled, loving I shared that number with Trey.

We went through our pre-game drills before huddling up. Coach Nocky gave us a rather spirited pep talk and motioned for Mia and me to say something. Mia gave me a pointed look, making it clear she wanted me to do the talking. With all eyes on me, the energy from the crowd seeped into my pores.

"Ladies, we were perfect last season and we've maintained that perfection this season. I don't know about you, but I'm not ready to let go of that streak. It's all a mindset. If we believe we're going to win, we will. Are you all believers?" I shouted as we bounced around in a circle.

"Hell, yes!"

Coach Nocky flicked on the portable radio. "Welcome to the Jungle" blared from the speakers and we sang along with the lyrics while jumping up and down. Once the song came to an end, we sprinted onto the field. Kylie and Peyton did their traditional flips as they headed to their respective spots while the rest of the girls jogged to their places.

Mia and I ran to the center for the coin toss. I slid my hand along hers before grasping the tips of her fingers and bringing her in for a hug. The referee tossed the quarter in the air and we called heads. We won and selected the goal to our right.

The first half went by in a blur. Bodies collided everywhere on the field, each team determined to control the ball. For most of the half, the ball was kicked from one side of the field to the other with plenty of blocks and steals. A lot of shots were toward the net, but both goalies were on today.

With a minute left before halftime, Mia used her fancy footwork, stole the ball, and broke away from her defender. I raced down the center of the field with Peyton on the other side of me. Mia kicked the ball to me and I faked out the girl in front of me, dribbling the ball toward the goalie. Her eyes centered on me. Somehow over the roaring crowd, I heard Peyton scream we only had twenty seconds left.

I juked out the next defender and shifted my momentum to the right before sending a toe shot to the left side of the goal. Right after I kicked it, my legs were swept out from under me. Sharp pains shot up my back and through my left shoulder. The goalie followed my first movement but managed to dive to her left with her fingers outstretched. She tipped the ball, but couldn't stop it from going in. The whistle sounded to announce the goal just as the final seconds ticked down.

Mia and Peyton hauled me to my feet and wrapped me a huge hug, screaming as they did. During halftime, the trainer looked at my shoulder and told me I was damn lucky it wasn't dislocated or separated. Aside from the constant throbbing, which was more of nuisance than anything, it didn't bother me too much.

The second half went just as fast as the first one. The Cougars evened the score five minutes into the half. Mia scored two goals for us and they matched them. With the score tied at three apiece and the final minutes winding down, my legs were ready to fall off.

Their goalie made a foolish toss toward their sweeper and Kylie intercepted it. She sent the ball flying in the air. Adrenaline pumped through my body at its highest peak. I didn't feel or hear anything as I sprinted upfield with Mia and Peyton at my sides.

Peyton reached the ball, jumped up to nail it with her head and over to Mia, who cut in front of me. I redirected course to fall on the other side of her. Mia dribbled past her defender and lined up to pass it to me. I knew from the look in her eyes, she would put some air on it.

After she kicked it, I sprinted toward the goal with my defender right behind me. I got to the ball before her, jumped up, and sent it flying. My overhead kick had just enough force to sail past the goalie.

The stadium erupted in cheers. Our coaches and teammates on the sidelines hopped up and down, but I barely noticed it. The exertion I put into my kick, coupled with how high I jumped, didn't allow me to get me footing and I landed on my back. My eyes watered nonstop while I rested on my knees to catch my breath.

My back burned from the piercing pains running through it. I tried rotating my shoulder, but I couldn't manage it with the needles jabbing into every muscle and ligament. Mia ran over to me and the huge smile on her face dropped instantly.

I hissed in another breath and rasped, "I'm not coming out. Don't you dare call for the trainer. You play hurt all the time."

"Bri, you'll never be able to run for two minutes if you can't get a solid breath in now," Mia pointed out on our way to midfield for the kickoff.

I wiped away the mud on my cheek, forced air into my deprived lungs, and said through gritted teeth, "I'll be fine. Let's just focus on the win."

Mia held up her hands in defeat. By the time the final whistle blew, my chest was on fire. We shook hands with the Cougars and went to the sideline to grab some water. I walked away from everyone and heaved in as many breaths I could. Once I no longer panted like a dog on his last lap at the race track anymore, I joined my teammates. They engulfed me in hugs. People made their way down to the field, but I only had eyes for one person.

Trey was on his way toward me, his eyes full of pride and his face riddled with concern. After reaching me, he hooked his arm gently around my waist. "I'm so fucking proud of you, Bri, but are you okay? You took some nasty falls out there."

I nodded—not wanting to tell him that my back and shoulders felt like I'd been whipped by an angry mob. Shane gave Mia a high-five and came over to me. Trey stepped aside and Shane pulled me in for a bear hug. I gritted my teeth to fight through the sharp pain overtaking my upper body. After he set me down, reporters flocked around us and I saw stars from all the photographers snapping pictures.

"We'd love to get a photo of the captains of Chamberlain's undefeated teams. Will the four of you pose for a shot together?"

Mia stepped out of Micah's embrace and carefully placed her arm over my shoulder. Shane wrapped an arm around her waist and Trey did the same with me. My dad narrowed his eyes on me and the malevolent look on his face sent me into a tailspin.

I didn't stand a chance in hell at getting out of this stadium without my dad putting me through some sort of misery, but that wasn't what made my nerves prickle. The way he eyed Trey like he was fresh meat for the taking unraveled me. Noticing the shift in me, Trey caressed my side to help calm me down, but it was a futile effort. His gaze shifted to my parents and he went completely rigid.

The murderous glare my dad had pinned on us sent my nervous system into a frenzy. I knew he'd do something to goad Trey. I refused to be the reason Trey lost control of his temper and sucked in a few deep breaths. The second the photo was done, I stepped forward with Mia in tow so the reporter could interview us.

After a series of questions and congrats, I kept a tight grip on Mia's sweaty hand and dragged her over to my parents. Thankfully, Shane picked up on what I did and engaged in quick conversation with the reporter we abandoned. Now, Trey wouldn't be able to follow us.

Mia glanced behind us and muttered, "Trey looks like he's ready to blow."

"I know. That's why we need to keep him as far away from my parents as possible. There's no way he'll be able to control himself if my dad pulls something," I hissed.

Her face paled. "Maybe I should go back there to ensure he doesn't do anything stupid."

I balked. "Hell no! You're my buffer and a much-needed one."

Mia sighed. "Have I mentioned how much I really despise your parents lately?"

I snorted. "No, but I'll be sure to note the record. Just help me get through the next few minutes and then we can head to the bus."

She cursed under her breath, but nodded. I looked over my shoulder to confirm the guys were still with the reporter. Trey curled and uncurled his fists with his face a shade of maroon I hated seeing. The way he eyed my dad like he was ready to throttle him sent chills up my badgered back.

My dad was with a different group of reporters, but he paused long enough to fake a smile. Mia gazed between him and my mom, her lips in a thin line and panic in her eyes. Micah looked at us and stiffened when we reached my parents. The tension in the air was close to suffocating me and I forced air into my body.

The journalists motioned to my dad and me, wanting a shot of the two us, so Mia stepped off to the side. My dad gripped my injured shoulder tightly. He could've very well been stabbing me with shards of glass with the amount of pain coasting through my body. I almost fell to my knees, but somehow managed to stay upright. He tightened his hold and I bit the insides of my cheeks to fight through the agony attacking my muscles. Trey's eyes sprang open and he started to walk over to us, but Shane yanked him back by the hood of his sweatshirt.

My dad's security moved forward, a gleam in their eyes. They wanted Trey to come over. Mia glanced at them and didn't bother to hide her alarm. Micah shoved Trey in the opposite direction. There was at least thirty feet between us, but it was still way too close for comfort.

The photographers continued snapping shots of us. My eyes watered as the throbbing in my shoulder and back neared a point that would no longer be manageable to tolerate. Fortunately, Mom picked up on what he was doing and got him to loosen his grip, but my relief was short-lived. Before I could make a beeline for the sidelines, Dad grabbed me.

"You're damn lucky your mother and I are leaving for D.C. this afternoon. I know you've been seeing the Donovan boy when I told you not to, but now you've gone too far. You posed for a picture with him. You don't seem to care how much of an embarrassment that is to me. You'll pay for it when I return and so will he. Think about that while I'm away this next week," Dad sneered, digging his fingers into my arm.

His villainous threat almost leveled me, but I refused to let him get the best of me and gave him a sweet smile. "We couldn't turn down the photo op, especially since the press was begging for it. You should know a thing or two about that by now. And while we're talking about tact, I don't think threatening your daughter in public is good for your campaign. Wouldn't you agree?"

His eyes darkened as he stepped away. My mom gave me a stiff hug and joined him. He carried on about how "proud" he was of me and my stomach turned at the sound of it. I looked around for the guys and Mia, but I didn't see any of them.

Hopefully, Micah and Shane dragged Trey out to the parking lot and talked some sense into him. I didn't bother to look for them any longer. I couldn't be around them without tears falling and I wasn't about to let that happen in public. I walked back to the sidelines to get my bag and stormed to the bus.

After grabbing a couple of ice packs from the trainer's cooler, I went to my seat and propped them against my shoulder and back. Mia trotted down the aisle, sat next to me, and dropped her bag at her feet.

"Hey, are you okay?" Mia asked, gently resting her arm on mine.

I glanced at her. "As you like saying to me, nothing I'm not used to by now."

She frowned. "That's not what I meant. I saw what your dad did to you."

"I'll live. I'm more worried about Trey. He looked like he was ready to murder my dad," I replied, doing my best to breathe evenly.

Mia turned stark white. "Let's just be happy Micah and Shane were here. I'm pretty sure if they hadn't been, we would've had one hell of a situation on our hands. Thankfully, they got him back to Micah's car and talked him down."

"I wish that relieved me, but I have a feeling that plenty is brewing when it comes to my dad. It's a matter of when he's going to execute his plans."

"More threats from him, I take it?"

I nodded. "I don't care anymore. If he does something, then so be it. I'm done walking around on eggshells with him."

Her eyes grew wide. "Are you sure that's a good idea? Provoking him doesn't seem like a very good plan."

I narrowed mine. "It probably isn't, but I can't let him win any longer. I'll never be enough for him—no matter how hard I try. I don't even know why I do. He's a jackass. If I ruin his campaign, I don't give a shit. He doesn't deserve to win anyway. The world has no idea who he is behind closed doors. If they did, they sure as hell wouldn't vote for him."

"Bri, you try because you care."

"I'm not so sure about that anymore. Everyone has a limit of what they can take, Mia."

"I know that firsthand. You're not going to do something crazy, are you?"

"No, but he's not going to have a say in who I date. That's for damn sure. He's also not going on the growing list of people trying to screw up Trey's life."

She arched an eyebrow. "You're not saying it, but I'm assuming he's threatened to do something to Trey?"

I readjusted the ice packs and sucked in a sharp breath. "He enjoys threatening me every day, but the prospect of him going after Trey isn't good. Trey's got enough on his plate as it is."

Mia pinched the bridge of her nose. "I'd really like to know what the hell is going on. Sebastian's always at the center of shit going down, but seeing how the faculty continues to treat Trey is disturbing. I get the whole class warfare thing to a degree, but ruining a person's future is a little extreme."

"I wish I had a better idea of who was out for him. I'd go after them myself."

"God, you really are thinking of doing something crazy."

"If it keeps Trey's fists in check, I'll do whatever it takes. I told you that already, Mia."

"But not at the expense of your own future, Bri. That's not being reasonable. That makes you just as reckless as Trey. Knowing your dad, he'd probably lock you up if you landed yourself in serious trouble while snooping around to figure out who's plotting against Trey."

I banged the seat in front of us. "Ugh! I hate where things are at and that you're right. I wish we could fast-forward to graduation. We'd be free from our shitty households and the assholes at Chamberlain. Why does high school have to be such hell?"

Mia giggled. "I'm going to refer you to *Buffy the Vampire Slayer* on that one. At least ours isn't sitting on a hellmouth."

I glared. "That's *so* not funny, Mia."

She nudged my good shoulder, a playful smile on her face. "It's kind of funny, Bri."

I rearranged my ice packs, rested my head on her arm, and grumbled, "Do we get to off the principal? That seems like the appropriate retribution for our detention sentence."

Her face was thoughtful. "Unfortunately, no. That's only kosher in the cinema world. I think our senior year will go better, though."

"Why do you say that?" I asked, arching an eyebrow.

Mia bit her bottom lip and whispered, "I'm moving out next September."

My jaw dropped. "Are you serious? Can you even do that? Why didn't I think of that?"

She shrugged. "I'll be eighteen and an adult. Chase can't really stop me and neither can the state. I have plenty of money in savings from my folks passing away. You can't move out, even if you *are* eighteen and an adult. Your dad will never allow it. Since the penthouse has security crawling around it all the time now, I'm thinking of getting a place downtown. It won't be far for you to commute to when you need to get out of your house."

"Mia, that would be so awesome for you—for us!" I squealed.

She beamed. "I know. It's been on my mind a lot lately."

I giggled. "Well, yeah, now that you're having sex on a regular basis."

Mia rolled her eyes. "That's not the reason behind it." I scoffed. "Fine, it's a factor in it, but I think it'll make next year so much easier for us. We need that kind of change in our lives."

Before I could ask her more questions, "You and Me" played from my bag. I gave her a contrite smile, unzipped it, and retrieved my cell from the inside pocket. She waved it off, snatched her own phone, and texted Micah.

Trey: Are you okay? You were clearly in pain after the game and while you were standing next to your dad. If Micah hadn't dragged me away, I would've slugged the bastard.

Bri: I'm on the bus icing. It's nothing to worry about. The typical bumps and bruises that come with an aggressive game. It's not stopping me from going on our date.

Trey: I'll take your word for it, but I plan on inspecting you later to be sure.

My body was rather numb with all the ice on me, but the prospect of his hands roaming every inch of me warmed it right up.

Bri: I'm all for a good examination from you. Where are we eating at? You still haven't told me.

Trey: Park in the ramp at the United Center and call me once you arrive. I'll whisk you away from there.

Damn! His gift for keeping quiet rears its head at the most inopportune times.

Bri: I'm all for surprises, but you remember this was my gift to you, right? Shouldn't I get a say in it?

Trey: Not a chance, darling. I'm so proud of you! I had no idea my girl was a fucking rock star in the soccer world. I can't wait to watch you play on Tuesday.

Bri: Thanks, sweets. It's always a team effort. Mia kicked ass too. I'm glad we gave you a good game. Hopefully, we can win for you again.

Trey: STUBBORN GIRL TAKE A GODDAMN COMPLIMENT!!

I giggled so loud that Mia eyed me like I'd lost my mind. I shook my head while giving her a wide smile. She went back to texting Micah, a lovesick look on her face.

Bri: LMAO! Did you growl after you got done typing that?

Trey: Yes. I'm still growling. Grrrr!!!!

My stomach clenched tightly together, along with my thighs. I'd never get sick of hearing it or having it turn me on in an instant.

Bri: I think all the pain in my body just disappeared. You're definitely the best medicine. I can't wait to see what your lips will do later.

Trey: I have some ideas. Rest up on your way home. We have a big night. x T

Bri: Can't wait. x B

When the team trickled onto the bus, I stuffed my phone into my bag, put in my headphones, and selected a soothing playlist. My abused muscles found a sea of bliss in the coldness from the ice packs. After the driver started the bus, I closed my eyes. Images of Trey running his hands all over me was the last thing that flitted through my mind before I drifted off to sleep.

* * *

STEAM ENGULFED the bathroom as I hopped out of the shower and wiped my hand against the mirror so I could inspect my back. There were a few bruises on my shoulder that were on their way to becoming a dark shade of purple, but it wasn't anything new for me. At least the sharp pains between my back and shoulder were now a bearable ache. I wrapped a towel around me and headed back to my room. A pair of skinny jeans and my favorite red and pink Bulls T-shirt were at the end of my bed and I quickly changed into them.

After lacing up my Jordans, I sat down at my makeup table to curl my hair. It didn't take long for my long brown locks to fall exactly where I wanted them to. I switched gears and picked up several shades of red nail polish and redid my nails to support the home team tonight.

My heart fluttered in anticipation of my evening with Trey. After my nails dried, I put on my makeup, slipped Trey's charm bracelet on my wrist, and fastened a long, layered silver necklace, with various diamonds in the tiers, around my neck. My lips spread into a smile while I gazed at my bracelet.

Kelsey wasn't around when I headed out. On my drive to the United Center, I prayed Trey would be able to slip away for the entire night. It didn't take long to navigate through the increasing traffic downtown and park in the ramp. I got out, retrieved my cell, and hit speed dial for his number.

"You look absolutely breathtaking, Bri," Trey murmured.

I glanced around, my heart thrashing against my chest. When I pulled into this row, I didn't see his car. The fact he could see me was spooky. He chuckled and my rapid heart rate steadied with the sound of it.

"Where the hell are you, stalker boy?" I asked in a sing-song tone.

"You need to revisit your definition of stalker, darling," Trey replied, amused.

"You're lurking in the shadows. I'm positive that fits the description," I retorted, giggling.

Trey stepped out from behind a beam and marched toward me. The light blue jeans with holes in the knees hugged him in all the right areas. A multi-colored Jordan hooded sweatshirt peeked out from his open black bomber jacket. As he got closer, his hair was all over the place—just the way I liked it. He gently pulled me into a tight embrace and kissed my forehead. I released a content sigh while taking in his familiar musky scent. This was where I always wanted to be.

"You look hot. Where are we off to?" I asked, burying my head into his chest.

"I know it's a little chilly out, but we're walking there. Is that okay, babe?" Trey inquired, shoving his hands in his pockets.

"Is it cold? I hadn't noticed. Lead the way, handsome," I replied, falling in stride with him on our way over to the elevator.

Once it arrived, his lips slid into a sexy grin and he pressed his body into mine. He gently ran his hands up my arms, grasped my nape, and devoured my mouth. I twisted my tongue with his and relished the way every cell inside me pulsed from the electricity surrounding us. He rocked his body into mine, sending tingles throughout me. My heart rate tripled while he sucked along my neck. When he squeezed my ass, my lower half dampened and I grinded my hips into him. I met every swoop of his tongue with just as much eagerness as him.

The doors opened and he pulled away, breathless. My mouth chased after his, not quite ready to end what was sure to be one of our more memorable kisses. As we walked out to the street, Trey kept a protective hold around me. I doubted I'd ever grow tired of it either. The streets and sidewalks were packed with people. Most of them were down here to catch the game, but we strode past quite a few homeless people too and Trey always held me a little closer when we did.

By the time we reached Park Tavern, the sensual ache south of me was somewhat under control. Trey held the door open for me on our way inside and we snagged a round table near the windows. The leather black chairs matched the tablecloth. The décor was simple and that was why I loved this bar. Seeing the sports memorabilia on the wood walls brought out my Chicago pride. There were flat screens throughout it, making it impossible not to keep up with our favorite sports teams. My belly growled loudly while I scanned over the menu.

"Do you want to share something or is your ravenous stomach demanding a dish of its own?" Trey asked, chuckling.

I rolled my eyes. "Smartass, in case you forgot, I played in a soccer match this morning, so yes, I'm on the hungry side. I don't care if we share something. What did you have in mind?"

"How about a couple of appetizers? I thought we'd keep it light here. If you're starving, don't hesitate to order a full meal. It's important to me that you eat, especially after the brutal beating your body took," Trey replied, his eyes anxious.

I gave him a reassuring smile. "I'm really fine. When I'm this hungry, I get full fast. Keeping it light is perfect. The cheese curds here are to die for."

"Perfect. Let's get those, some spinach dip and chips, and some buffalo wings. We're sort of covering the food groups with that lot."

A blonde waitress strode up with a pitcher of water and glasses. While filling them up, she eye-fucked Trey. The emerald in my eyes probably matched the monster clawing its way up inside me. I really wanted to kick the chick. The sparkle in his eyes as he gazed at me made it clear he enjoyed my jealousy. I gave him a pointed look to give her our damn order so she'd disappear. He chuckled, told her what we wanted, and requested two sodas.

"You don't need to get jealous of other girls," Trey spoke up, still tickled.

"When a girl undresses you with her eyes right in front of me, how am I not supposed to be bothered by it? It's taking great restraint on my part not to slap some of them. Besides, you're always on the brink of losing your temper whenever a guy checks me out. You can't tell me not to get jealous," I replied in a punitive tone.

The blonde bimbo returned and nearly spilled our sodas as she placed them on the table. No shock there since she couldn't take her eyes off Trey. I cleared my throat and shot her a lethal glare. Her cheeks flushed and she scampered back to the bar. Trey gazed at me, his amusement all over his face.

I exhaled. "Let's table this conversation. It's just going to lead to a fight."

He pinched the bridge of his nose. "We've been tabling a lot lately. I think we'll end up having a pretty epic fight soon if we don't talk about some things."

"You know, it used to bother me when you didn't want to talk, but I'm beginning to think differently about it now. I know exactly what you want to discuss. We're in a public place and it's not a good idea," I rebutted, looking around to see who was here.

I didn't spot anyone I recognized, but that didn't do much to ease the pressure building in my chest. Trey's attention on me and the hard edge to his eyes wasn't a good sign. I sucked in a quick breath and kept my eyes on the table.

"That's the problem, Bri. You never do. You keep telling me I'm doing such a good job at controlling my temper, but I don't know if you're saying it because it's true or because you're trying to placate yourself. You keeping things from me is pushing my buttons more than anything else," Trey snapped.

"Considering Sebastian is still a factor every day, I doubt that's true, Trey. You've come a long way with controlling your anger, but I know it's a struggle yet. Why can't you trust my judgment with certain subjects?" I asked with a scowl.

"Why don't you let me be the judge of what I can or can't handle? Trust goes both ways. Tell me what happened with your dad at the game," Trey replied with a pointed look.

I took a sip of my soda and reminded myself I couldn't slam it down, but with the unfriendly fire brewing inside me, it was hard. His angry eyes remained on mine in demand for an answer.

"As you know, my dad is a jerk. He puts a lot of pressure on me. My mom is a borderline drunk, so she rarely steps in when he's laying into me about school or sports. He's been at a whole new level lately because he's trying to get reelected."

"What does that mean?"

"It means he threatens me a lot. Demeans me. He's a very controlling person. According to him, I've been stepping out of line and it could reflect badly on him, so his tongue-lashings have been more frequent."

"When you first talked about your parents, it sounded like they were just neglectful. You do realize what he's doing to you is verbal abuse. He's also hurt you twice. You could turn him in for it," Trey pointed out, gripping the table tightly.

I squeezed his hand so he'd calm down. His face was maroon, which is exactly what I expected to happen. My own anger fizzled as I focused on making sure he kept his cool. With my touch, his heated breaths evened out, but his eyes demanded more. I was flirting with trouble, but he wasn't anywhere close to backing down.

"I can't turn him in. He's a powerful guy. No one would believe me. My mom would never back it up. When he's not tearing into me, he's fighting with her. From the things I've heard over the years, they're only together for appearances and because they have a lot of dark secrets they can hold over each other."

Trey shook his head in disgust. "It's still not okay. He hurt your shoulder today more than it already was, didn't he? I saw how much pain you were in. If Micah and Shane hadn't gotten in my way, I would've given him the beatdown he deserves for laying his hands on you again."

"You're blowing the whole thing out of proportion," I responded as the color drained from my face.

He curled his fist together. "No, I'm not. I saw how he looked at us. It doesn't take a rocket scientist to know he hates me, but if he's physically hurting you because of it, I won't tolerate it."

My heart plummeted. "I got hurt during the game, not from him. He's not going to put his hands on me again. If he leaves physical marks on me, people will question it. He's never been like that anyway. He was drunk the night you came to my room."

Trey glared. "His threats have increased since we started dating, haven't they?"

I arched an eyebrow. "How'd you know?"

He tossed his free hand in the air. "I'd have to be an idiot not to know. You're not seeing me to piss him off, are you?"

I yanked my hand away from him, appalled he'd even think that—let alone verbalize it. He flinched and leaned forward to grasp my hand again, but I folded them over my chest.

"I can't believe you said that to me. I've told you how deeply I feel about you so many times. The fact you still question it sucks, Trey," I bit back, my eyes watering.

"I'm sorry, Bri. It just slipped out. I know how much you care for me. I hate how that man has hurt you. I hope I don't run into him alone. After today, I know I'll end up hitting him."

"That's exactly why I don't like talking about anything going on at home with you. I knew it'd upset you. Now, the anger is going to fester inside you. I know it. God only knows what will happen when it bubbles over."

"I promise I won't do anything stupid, but you need to talk to someone. It's not healthy to bottle that kind of stuff up," Trey pointed out, his forehead creased in frustration.

I wiped away a tear that escaped. "You let Mia do it all the time. Her homelife is a lot worse than mine. Why do I have to give a tell-all?"

He slid his chair next to me. "Her situation is different. When it's at its worst, she escapes to my house or Micah's and we take care of her. You don't have anyone looking out for you."

I sniffed and looked away. "That's not true. Kelsey takes care of me."

Trey tilted my chin toward him. "It's not the same. You're so damn strong, but dealing with what you just described can't be easy to do when you don't get out."

"I get out all the time," I argued.

"But at what risk, Bri? He's already threatened to send you away," Trey refuted.

"It's not going to lead to that. Having me around benefits him."

"I'm going to ask you something and I want you to be honest with me."

The seriousness in his gray eyes made me squirm. Before he could ask, the waitress returned with our food. Trey gripped the back of my neck and planted a deep kiss on me. Considering our heated conversation, it took me a few seconds to reciprocate. The softness of his lips as he caressed his tongue with mine made my toes curl and I cursed my treacherous body. I was beyond pissed with him, but that didn't mean shit to my hormones.

I gave way to the moment for a minute before sealing my lips. It was a first for me not to want to kiss him back, but my blood was still red-hot. I gave him a sharp look to not distract me with his lips again. Trey sighed and pulled away. Our brief kiss was enough of a show for Blondie to storm off.

Trey filled up a plate with cheese curds and buffalo wings and pushed it over to me. He dipped a boneless wing in some ranch, popped it into his mouth, and licked his lips. I knew the food here was some of the best bar food in Chicago and the invigorating aroma from the plate of burgers the waitress off to the left of me balanced on her side proved that much, but my appetite vanished with our fight.

I listened to the patrons around us talking about the spread for tonight's game and how the Bulls were favored to win. My eyes drifted over to the flat screens to catch the scores. Trey snapped his fingers to get my attention and pointed at my untouched plate. I scowled at him and didn't touch the food.

"So help me God, Bri, you need to eat something. I know you're hungry," Trey said, his jaw clenched tightly together.

"You insisted on bringing up my parents. It should be no shock that I'm no longer hungry. The prospect of putting food into my stomach is making it churn," I shot back, crossing my arms.

"Please eat," Trey requested, his eyes as soft as his tone.

My heart flip-flopped with his plea and I swiped some chips in the spinach dip to appease him. Trey stabbed his fork through a few curds, drowned them in the ranch, and gobbled them up. He wiped the corners of his mouth with his napkin and focused on me.

"Is seeing me going to cause you even more problems at home? I'll walk away before I let your dad hurt you again," Trey said, poker-faced.

Tears pricked my eyes. "I can handle whatever he throws at me. I have some leverage of my own. If he pushes me too far, I'll use it."

He shook his head. "That's not good enough. It's too risky."

It was like someone knocked the wind out of me all over again. I gasped to catch my breath and rasped, "Please believe me. You said yourself, I'm strong. I'll be the judge of what I can and can't handle at home—just as you are with your temper. If you walk away, it'll devastate me, and he'll win. He already controls every other aspect of my life. He can't have this one. *Nothing* is going to stop me from seeing you. Please have the kind of faith I do."

"I'm not going anywhere. I just wanted to be clear that I will if things get worse than they are now," Trey replied, his face as grim as his tone.

"How'd you manage sitting in the stands today with all those girls sending me to the ground?"

Trey blinked while shaking his head. He dove into what was left of the curds and wings on his plate. When it was all gone, he filled it up with more as a small grin spread across his face. Seeing it calmed the wicked thunderstorm going on inside me, I wolfed down some cheese curds before dunking a boneless buffalo wing into some ranch and popping it in my mouth. The two flavors mixed together was by far one of my favorites and I soaked another wing in the dressing.

"It wasn't easy. I jumped from my seat on more than one occasion. Shane shoved me down every time. When you fell before halftime, I held my breath until you got back up. I can go almost a minute without air."

"I like my guy being protective, but I really can take care of myself, especially on the field."

"I know my girl can hold her own, but that doesn't stop my need to protect you. I still plan on giving you a thorough inspection after the game," Trey promised with his naughty grin.

I wiggled my eyebrows. "I'm looking forward to it. Where is this examination taking place? Are you free for the whole night?"

Trey finished off his second round of appetizers. I pushed my plate away. My stomach was at full capacity. He motioned for the check. "I told my parents I'm staying at Shane's. The Waldorf is sort of our place, but I picked a different hotel. I think if we go back there, it'll be bad luck."

I snorted out a laugh. "You really are superstitious."

"You have no idea. Why do you think I haven't cut my hair? It's bad mojo if you screw with anything in your routine during a sports season," Trey deadpanned.

"I like your hair shaggy. It gives me something to tug on when we make out," I teased.

He smirked. "Enjoy it while you can. Once basketball starts, it's getting buzzed."

I winked. "I'm sure I can find something else to do with my hands."

Blonde Bimbo returned with the check, but Trey's gaze remained on me, his eyes undressing me. He signed the slip, passed it over, brushed by the waitress, and whisked me through the growing crowd in the tavern and out onto the busy street.

We strode hand in hand back to the United Center. As we walked, I glanced over my shoulder to ensure no one followed us. Since all bets were off with him, I wouldn't put it past my dad to have security tail me while he was out of town. Not seeing them brought a small sense of relief to my skittish nerves, but that was about it.

Trey arched an eyebrow every time he caught me fiddling with my bracelet or looking around, but he didn't question me. I was more than grateful for his silence on the matter, especially since he gazed through the thick crowd as well. I had a feeling he did it because he half-expected someone from school to spring up and start shit with him. I didn't want to think about all the things we didn't have control over. All I wanted to do was focus on my night with him.

My stomach fluttered while we stood in line to get into the arena. It didn't take long for our tickets to be scanned and to get to our seats. The energy around us was palpable. Soccer was my first love, but basketball was a close second. I loved playing the game just as much as watching it. Trey sensed my giddiness and gave me a loving smile.

The first half went by rather quickly. We slipped away before half-time to grab some sodas, pizza, and nachos. We took turns feeding each other while watching the guys on the court. As the game progressed, it became more difficult to focus on it. The sparks firing through my body got harder to ignore. Trey brushed his hands all over me while sneaking in kisses. I stole plenty of my own and trailed my fingers along his thighs and arms, enjoying the groans and growls that followed.

Out of nowhere, the crowd roared with applause, which was weird since it was a time-out. A couple of people in the row behind us patted our backs and pointed to the jumbotron. I looked up to see Trey and I on the kiss cam. I leaned over to give him a simple peck, but Trey tilted me over the side of my chair and devoured my mouth.

His tongue intertwined with mine and I lost all sense of reality. My lips greedily took his and the crowd went wild while we kissed one another without shame. I slid my tongue across the cool metal of his ring and moaned, making the people behind us holler even louder. Not caring we were in public, I threaded my fingers through his hair and explored every inch of his mouth until the fuzziness in my head reminded me that oxygen was necessary soon. Reluctantly, I pulled away. Trey brought me back to a sitting position and pressed a soft kiss to my forehead.

My heart pounded a mile a minute. Part of it was from the intense look on Trey's face, but a lot of it had to do with all the photographers who took pictures of us while we kissed. My dad would snap when he saw them. Knowing there wasn't a damn thing I could do about it now, I shoved away those thoughts, curled my hands into tight fists so I wouldn't fidget, and focused on the searing pool of desire between my thighs. Trey stared at me with such passion, I forgot about the basketball game, along with all our problems, and wondered if tonight would be *the night.*

CHAPTER 22

BRI

After the game was over, I practically shoved people out of the way to get outside. Trey's scorching kiss left an ache between my legs that demanded to be satisfied soon. He kept his hand clutched with mine as we strode into the bitter cold air. The loud crowd made it impossible to carry on a conversation. That was fine with me. There was only one thing I wanted to focus on and words weren't necessary for it.

We walked up a couple of blocks. With each step, my libido increased and I'd combust soon if Trey didn't finish what he started with that sensual kiss. Planting my feet, I rested a hand on my hip. "Where are we going? It's killing me not to have a clue."

Trey smirked while he hailed a cab. A yellow taxi pulled over moments later and we hopped inside. He pressed his lips to my temple and my irritation with being out of the loop faded. Trey focused on the driver. "Ritz-Carlton, please."

The guy merged into traffic. Trey's eyebrows creased together as he looked out the window, deep in thought. I nudged his shoulder to get his attention. He gazed at me, his face forlorn.

I gripped his chin. "What's on your mind?"

He chewed on his lower lip. "I shouldn't have kissed you like that at the game. It wasn't appropriate."

My eyebrows furrowed. "It was a kiss. We've shared plenty of them. Why are you so wigged out about that one?"

Trey gently caressed my cheek. "Because I did it in front of thousands of people and pictures were taken. I'm worried it'll cause you a lot of trouble at home."

My heart rate sped up and not in the way I preferred it did when we were in close quarters. Not wanting him to know I was a tad on the freaked out side, I placed my hand over his and gave it a gentle squeeze. His face remained strained, rattling my nerves even more.

"Please stop worrying about it. We've discussed how things work in my house. I'm sure the photos will come up at some point, but I don't care. You're going to have to trust me when it comes to dealing with my dad. Let's focus on us."

He gave me a crooked smile and ran his hands tenderly down my sides. "Ah yes, the examination part of the evening. I've been looking forward to that since this morning."

My mouth curled into a wily grin. "Believe me, so have I."

We remained lost in each other's intense stares, undressing one another with our eyes, and I cursed the slow-moving traffic. Trey brushed his hands down my thighs before his fingers journeyed to the place I was desperate for him to touch. He rubbed his hand over my clit and the onslaught of tingles that followed demanded for so much more. I bit the insides of my cheek to stop myself from moaning and gripped the windowsill to keep myself from squirming.

As he moved his fingers roughly around, it took every rational brain cell that wasn't scattered on the cab floor for me not to crawl into his lap and rock my body none too gently into him. His lips drifted to the crook of my shoulder and he sucked down on it very hard. My mouth traveled along his neck and up to the stubble on his jaw. I really wanted to stick my tongue in his mouth, but I'd lose complete control and end up jumping his bones in the back of this taxi.

Thankfully, we stopped at the Ritz moments later. Every nerve inside me vibrated in the best kind of way. I was in dire need of his very gifted hands and barely found the patience to let him pay for our cab ride. After he did, Trey hauled me through the doors and to the front desk.

"You deserve the best of everything, Bri. I hope this place measures up," Trey murmured, gesturing to the floor-to-ceiling glass windows, cream marble floor, and the huge golden fountain in the middle of the lobby.

I gaped at him. "You're not seriously trying to have a conversation about the décor in this place, are you?"

Trey gave me a panty-dropping grin—and Lord, did I want to do just that—and swept his lips across mine for a kiss that was far too brief. I glared at him before looking around and wondering why only one person was checking people in, especially on a game night for the Bulls. Trey angled my head to him and I faked a pout.

"You purposely wound me up just so you could watch me squirm."

He laughed and tickled my sides and I giggled along with him. The energy between us seeped into my pores and I loved how my body hummed from it. Trey released a content sigh as we stepped up to the counter. The redhead behind it licked her lips after seeing him. I gave her a vicious glare and slid my arm around his waist. She could look all she wanted, but he was *mine*.

"Two this evening?"

Trey nodded and passed over his debit card without looking at her. The carnal desire in his eyes made all the muscles south of my naval clench together. My impatience was back and I nearly stamped my foot while we waited for the chick to activate our keycards. Trey took them from the redhead, towed me toward the elevators, and hit the call button.

Once we were inside, a thought dawned on me and guilt consumed me for not realizing it earlier. His hands roamed all over my body, but I pulled them into mine. The shocked expression on his face was one I'd never forget and I couldn't help but giggle. It was a first for me to stop him. He arched an eyebrow, waiting for me to explain myself.

"I just realized you're always paying for us. I'm really sorry about not saying it sooner. It's the twenty-first century. I can pay too."

"Times may have changed, but I'm rather old-fashioned with some things. I'll be taking care of the check." I opened my mouth to debate about it some more, but he put his finger over it. "I know you have plenty of money, but it's not up for discussion. I earned a lot of spending money over the summer and I'll choose to spend it how I wish."

I bit on his finger until he removed it. His lips spread into his naughty smirk when the elevator came to a stop. "We've been staying in suites, but I don't really need that much space with what I have planned for you."

Somehow, my lower half got even wetter on our way down the hallway. He swiped the keycard, opened the door, and pressed me up against it. Our jackets quickly hit the floor as our mouths wildly connected. My hands slid underneath his shirt and I scratched down the creases in his abs before trailing my fingers to his V.

His lips became hungrier as he tugged off his sweatshirt and my T-shirt. My lacy red bra was the next thing to go before he glided his mouth along my collarbone and down my chest. I banged my head against the door after he cupped my breast and grazed his teeth along my nipple. My breaths escaped in pants. I tangled my tongue with his, relished his minty flavor, and rocked my body into his with force.

Trey stepped away and his eyes widened before he murmured, "Shit, I must've done that in the cab."

I blinked. "What are you talking about?"

He pointed to a dark spot on my shoulder. I glanced down to see a huge hickey. His face was apologetic as he said in a breathy pant, "I doubt that's from soccer. I'm really sorry, Bri."

"As long as they're not visible, I don't care," I replied, bringing his lips back to mine.

Trey picked me up and I wrapped my legs around his waist as he carried me into the bedroom. He set me on the king-size bed, unzipped his jeans, and kicked them to the side. I eagerly licked my lips and tossed mine aside. His black boxers hung off his hips and I couldn't wait to get rid of those too.

He hovered above me, gazing at me with such want. Blood rushed through my body and settled in all the right places. I squirmed in anticipation of having his fingers satisfy my unadulterated need for him. Trey pinned my hands to my sides and ran his lips down the center of my chest, pausing just long enough to suckle on my belly button ring on his journey further south.

Trey gave me a mischievous grin. "I like the matching panties. Very sexy, Bri."

I shoved his head between my legs. "Less talking, Trey. I've been waiting for this moment for months. Don't stop now."

He chuckled while sliding my underwear off. His lips drifted to my clit and he lazily licked his way around it. The tingling sensation his piercing brought with it nearly made me convulse on the spot and I arched off the mattress when his lips suckled with more urgency. He sucked and twirled his tongue up and down and his stud made my body throb for so much more. Erotic sensations traveled through me at warp speed and should be illegal. When Trey really started to move his tongue around, I clenched in preparation for a powerful climax.

"This feels so good. I had no idea it could be this amazing!"

I tugged on his hair and he licked me until I was about ready to burst at the seams. His hand drifted to my breasts and he twisted and tormented my nipples until they were both hard. He swiveled his tongue deeper and faster. Waves of euphoria washed over me as I ran my nails down his back and exploded around him.

"Oh. My. God," I groaned, trembling from the ecstasy overtaking my body.

Trey crashed his lips into mine for a kiss that left me even more breathless than I already was. I sucked in a few deep breaths, slid his boxers to his ankles, and pushed him on his back. He kicked them aside as my lips traveled down the center of his chest, pausing to graze my teeth over his nipples.

Once I reached his rock-hard erection, I lowered my mouth against his long length and circled my tongue around his tip before taking him deep into my throat.

"Holy shit, Bri. Your mouth *is* fucking gifted," Trey moaned.

I swirled my tongue along his shaft for several minutes. He bucked off the bed and gripped my shoulders tightly. My teeth grazed along him and came back to his tip before starting all over. I took all of him into my mouth and picked up my pace. My tongue drifted to his V and I sucked down hard against it before giving other areas just as much attention. Trey's breaths were intermittent as he tried to prevent himself from going over the edge.

When I got back to his cock, his tip was dripping. I took him in as deep as I could and he rocked into me as my mouth eagerly sucked up and down his shaft. I twirled my tongue even faster. He thrust into me and I felt his hot release trickle down my throat. His breaths came in pants as he tenderly caressed my sides in a way that expressed how much that moment meant to him. Knowing how deeply I affected him, not only physically, but emotionally, made my heart beat out of my chest.

He opened his eyes and I was on my back the next second. Resting on my elbows, I watched him become hard again. Most guys didn't have the capability of going more than once in a night, but clearly Trey was an exception to that group. I couldn't help but feel like I fell in that same category since my body was more than ready for his. Every part of me pulsated for him.

The slickness between my thighs begged for his dick. Pleasuring him more than turned me on. Trey nuzzled his head between my breasts and trailed his lips over them. I stroked his cock with as much vigor his mouth gave my breasts.

"I can't believe I didn't bring any condoms. I didn't think we'd go this far. I don't want to stop, but I know I should," Trey breathed, his teeth gently biting down on a nipple.

The scorching heat within my pores was sure to make me liquefy any moment. I grinded my body into his and pleaded, "Please don't stop, Trey. I want to feel you inside me. I've wanted that for so long. I'm on the pill. If that's what you're worried about, don't."

His conflicted eyes centered on me. Trey placed the hand I had around him on his hip and I gripped his other one tightly. "But you said you always want double the protection."

I shoved his body down so his cock was inches away from my wet core. The look in his eyes shifted to the hungry one he had earlier as he teased me with his tip. He slid his dick along my clit several more times, making me whimper, and I urged him to just take me already.

"Please, Trey. I don't think I can handle another minute without you inside me," I begged.

His mouth claimed mine as he roughly entered me. I cried out and he pulled back at a much slower pace. My body adjusted to his hard length and he thrust into me again. His tongue danced with mine while he gyrated his hips into me. My hands drifted to his ass, encouraging him to go faster.

Trey drove into me harder and faster. My hips matched his eager thrusts. Our breaths were ragged as our bodies became slick with sweat. I tugged his hair and he hit an even wilder pace. The fire inside me quickly approached its explosion and I clenched against him while he rocked into me with force.

Out of nowhere, he rolled us over and I found myself on top. My hips circled against him in swift motions to keep up with the fast pace he'd set for us. After several minutes of riding him hard and quick, he sat up, pressed his lips into my chest, and sucked on my nipple.

"You're so fucking amazing, Bri," Trey moaned.

I dug my nails into his shoulders. "I'm so close. Please let go with me, Trey."

His thrusts became unremitting and I matched his momentum as we approached the precipice of our climaxes. Trey gripped my ass and rocked even deeper into me. I clenched around him as the waves of ecstasy cascaded through my body. His lips urgently kissed along my neck as he found his release.

We remained locked in our passionate embrace with our noses touching while we worked to catch our breath. My heart beat at a rapid rate, but I wasn't sure if it was from the mind-blowing sex or our intense connection. Having nothing between us went far beyond any words I could describe. Pure bliss lingered within every facet of me and I hoped it'd be like this every time we were intimate.

All too quickly, Trey pressed several soft kisses along my neck and jaw, leaned back, and slid out of me. He maintained the same devoted look on his face that matched mine and crawled up the bed, lying on the pillows and bringing me with him. I rested my head on his chest as he sucked in spurts of air. His fingers trailed through my hair while I listened to his heartbeat. It raced as fast as mine and that familiar tune they created when we were together filled the room.

"I've never had sex without a condom. That's another first, Bri," Trey whispered.

My hand drifted to his cheek. "I can't even begin to explain how extraordinary it felt to have nothing between us, but once my brain starts working again, I'll be sure to tell you. I can tell you're stressing about that and I don't mind showing you my pills, Trey."

He placed his hand over mine. "That's not what I'm thinking about."

"What are you thinking?"

Trey kissed my nose. "I'm thinking that was mind-blowing and that being inside you without anything between us is a moment I'll never forget. Most of all, I'm thinking it was so incredible because it was with you."

"It was definitely the best sex I've ever had. I don't have the right words to describe how magnificent it was for me," I murmured, tracing my fingers along the Celtic moon tattoo on his chest.

"Me too, babe," Trey concurred, a satisfied smile on his face.

"I wish you would've been my first. I'll never forget this moment. It was perfect," I admitted in a soft whisper.

"Yes, it was indeed. Who was your first?" Trey inquired.

An icy wave shot straight through my gut. I damn near kicked myself for opening that door. "I don't think we really want to talk about something like that after our first time together. I shouldn't have said it. As usual, my filter drifted off to another dimension after your tongue started its magic work."

The intensity to his gaze while he stared at me made my insides quiver in a different way than they had been so far. After a minute, his expressionless face shifted to a playful grin. "I'm pleased to hear you enjoyed my tongue ring. You were a great guinea pig for it."

I slapped his chest. "You better not be planning on testing it out on anyone else."

"I'm not. You've gotten so violent since I've met you. I hope you aren't picking up my bad habits," Trey murmured, kissing my palm.

I rolled my eyes. "I only feel the urge to hit someone when they make a stupid comment."

Trey chuckled. "Duly noted, darling. Just so we're clear, I'm not worried about your pills. I know you'd never do that to me. I don't think you're ready to be a parent any more than I am."

"Ah, no, not even close. Maybe when I'm like thirty or something, but not anytime soon."

"So, you do want kids someday?"

I rolled my shoulders. "Yeah, I guess so. How about you?"

He smiled. "Absolutely. I love kids, but I kind of have to since my siblings are so much younger than me."

"How old are they?"

"Thomas is ten and Tory is eight. Tara and Tawney just turned seven."

My eyes grew wide. "That's quite the age difference. How come they're closer together?"

Trey shrugged. "I think they tried a lot after me, but couldn't conceive. Now, it seems like they can't stop having kids."

"Does your dad know that another one is on the way?"

"Yes, my mom told him last week. Hearing he was going to have another child brought out an elation in him I rarely see."

"Is he unhappy a lot?"

"No, he's just not around much. He loves being a dad and a husband more than anything else in this world."

A tear slipped down my cheek. Hearing Trey talk about his family filled my heart with so much love. He clearly enjoyed being a big brother as much as his folks loved being parents.

"Hey, don't cry. We don't have to talk about my family," Trey said, caressing my arms.

"No, I love hearing about them. I'm sorry. I'm being emotional for no reason," I replied, snuggling deeper into him.

Clear anger flashed through his eyes. "Don't apologize, Bri. There is a reason and you should cry when you need to."

"What was your childhood like?"

He snorted. "I'm guessing a lot different than yours."

I narrowed my eyes. "I know that much. Have you always struggled to control your temper? I know you're not a violent person. I guess I'm just curious when it all started."

Trey rested his chin on my head. "Sadly, yes, I've always had a very angry side. Over the years, my parents have done things to channel it. I did karate for the longest time and it helped for a while, but that was years ago."

"No wonder you're so good at fighting," I muttered under my breath.

"It's more of the competitive side to me that makes it hard to beat me. I don't like to lose and sometimes I forget that in the heat of the moment."

"Aside from Sebastian, have you seriously harmed someone?"

"Yes, and I regret that day just as much as the night with Sebastian."

"Who'd you hurt? It sounds like it was someone important to you."

"It was Mia."

A shocked gasp slipped out of me. "You didn't hit her, did you?"

He shook his head. "We were twelve and playing basketball with a bunch of kids. I was mad she tagged along with Micah and me. She was always around and sometimes it got annoying, especially when I wanted to just hang out with the boys."

I stared at him, enthralled in where this was going. His face scrunched up, like someone jabbed red-hot iron rods into his side and created an unbearable pain.

"The game got aggressive, which Mia was used to since we never went easy on her, but this time was different. The anger bubbling inside me boiled over. We went up for a rebound and I nailed her in the jaw with my elbow on purpose, nearly breaking it. Micah slugged me so hard, he broke my nose."

He paused to point to a very small crook in his nose I didn't notice before now. His eyes were distant before he said, "Mia and I were a bloody mess on our way back to my house. My mom cleaned us both up, sent Micah home and Mia upstairs to rest, and then proceeded to give me a hiding I'll never forget. She was so mad and it downright terrified me."

"You always seem so protective of Mia. It's hard to imagine you hurting her on purpose."

His chest quivered and his eyes misted over. "It was the first time my temper got the better of me. Having it unfold on her is something I'll never forgive myself for and neither will my mom. She yelled at me for hours after it happened, telling me I should never hurt a girl. Mostly, she made me promise I'd always protect Mia. She reiterated how much Mia needed Micah and me, along with our families. She carried on about how there will be plenty of things throughout our lives that will challenge us and push our relationship to the limits, but to always remember she was part of our family. It's one promise I won't break. I felt so badly about what I did. Mia forgave me right away, but I didn't deserve it."

"Mia has got a good heart. It's not surprising she shrugged it off," I pointed out with a small smile.

"Yeah, she's definitely way too forgiving at times. Considering how shitty Chase treats her, it's a miracle she's turned out the way she has," Trey replied, his tone acidic.

His face turned a dark shade of red I'd grown to fear. I squeezed his side and whispered, "I can tell he's a trigger for you. Let's not talk about him."

"He definitely brings out the angry beast inside me. Someday, I'll figure out why he hates Mia so much and make him pay for it. If I don't, Micah will. He's wanted to kill him for years."

"As I said, we probably shouldn't talk about him. What helps to stop your anger from getting to the point of no return? I want to know so I can help—just like you wanted to know my methods for coping with panic attacks."

"I'm still figuring out all the ways to stop it. Having you in my life definitely helps me keep it in check better than I have before. Knowing I'll always have Micah and Mia helps too."

"Have you, Micah, and Mia always been a package deal? You don't talk about hanging out with anyone else in your neighborhood."

"Since the day Mia arrived, we've stuck together. Micah is my best friend. Now that I've switched schools and he's shagging Mia on the regular, we don't see each other as much, but he's still my boy. Mia means a lot to me too. It may not seem like it, but I do love her like a sister. I have other friends around the neighborhood, but it's hard to keep in touch with our different schedules. I've always been in sports, but most of the other kids I hung out with weren't. They traveled down the same path as Micah."

I tapped his chest. "What path is that?"

He sighed. "The 'drop out of school and become a drug dealer or part of the mob' path."

"Is he dealing drugs now?"

"I think so, but I'm not sure. He's had a ton of money lately and it doesn't make sense. Granted, we made *a lot* over the summer, working construction jobs for my dad, but it just doesn't add up. Plus, he's very elusive at times with his whereabouts when he's not hanging out with Mia or me. His behavior whenever he sees the Fitzpatricks has also shifted. Throw in skipping school and it's hard not to think he's dealing or tied up with them in some way."

I bit my bottom lip. "Being involved with the Fitzpatricks in any way isn't a good thing. That can spiral out of control really fast. Does Mia know?"

His eyebrows furrowed together. "I think she suspects it, but doesn't want to dig deeper into it in fear of what she finds out. Things are going good between the two of them. Something that big will rock the honeymoon period they've been in. How do you know about the Fitzpatricks?"

"I'm not oblivious to their reign over Chicago's mob scene, but if you really want to know, I overheard something my mom said to my dad. I think he has ties to them, but haven't looked into it," I admitted, my chin quivering.

His eyes grew wide. "If I didn't hate your dad before, I sure as hell do now. It's no secret that a lot of Chicago's rich and privileged want to be on their good side and I'll never understand why. Being involved with them is really bad. If your dad pisses off Sean in any way, it's game over. Your dad may be powerful, but I doubt he's got what it takes to feign off anything Sean and his colleagues would send his way if things got ugly."

I shivered. "Let's not talk about him or whatever connection he has to Sean. What did you mean about Micah's behavior changing around the Fitzpatricks?"

Trey frowned. "He's no longer scared of them the way he used to be. It's always been a rule of thumb to have a healthy fear of them and he doesn't have that anymore."

"Do you think he's using drugs and that's why it's so easy for him to be around them now?"

"I'm not sure. I've been wanting to talk to him about it, but he hasn't been around a lot lately. I'm hoping our trip will allow us to hang out alone while you and Mia shop or something."

I beamed. "Oh, we can definitely get out of your hair. I love shopping, especially in New York. Mia doesn't care for it, but I'll drag her along anyway."

Trey laughed. "I didn't think I'd have to twist your arm there. I'm glad you're still planning on coming. I wasn't sure with how up and down things have been at home."

My smile vanished. "Of course, I'm planning on it. When are you going to get it through your thick skull that I'm not letting anyone come between us?"

The conflicted look I hated seeing on his gorgeous face returned. I pressed my lips against his chest, licking and sucking my way around it. He groaned, rolled me over, and hovered above me. A mischievous smirk fell from his lips as his fingers fiddled with my belly button ring.

"I think it's time I get back to inspecting your sexy body, Bri," Trey said, sucking a nipple into his mouth and roughly grabbing my other breast.

My back arched as his hand slid down my stomach and to the spot that was more than ready to have his magical fingers do their handiwork. "I'm all yours, babe."

CHAPTER 23

BRI

On my drive home from school, I pondered what to wear to dinner at Trey's tonight. I wasn't sure if I should go dressy or keep it simple. Since Mia had no fashion sense whatsoever, I didn't bother asking her. I was the only reason she had somewhat of a decent wardrobe. After parking my car and retrieving my bags, I made my way into the house.

"I hate to be the bearer of bad news as you walk in the door, but your dad called. He finally saw the photographs from Saturday. He inquired about your whereabouts and I had to remind him for the hundredth time that you were at school but coming straight home. If he calls while you're out, I'll cover for you, but please try to make it an early night," Kelsey said, her face tense.

I grimaced on my way upstairs with her right behind me. "He was going to see them eventually. I'm sure he'll put me through hell once he gets home. I'm not wasting any energy on thinking about what type of misery he has in store for me."

Kelsey sighed. "That's probably a good idea. How's your shoulder doing today? You took a lot of hits last night and didn't have very much time to let your previous bruises heal."

My lips curled into a slick smile and I was thankful Kelsey couldn't see me. She didn't need to know I was far sorer from getting naked with Trey whenever we had the chance over the past three days than I was from soccer. We had sex several times before parting ways Sunday and after the guys won their game Monday night.

I suspected she knew that much since we also went at it here last night after Mia and I played the game of our lives to bring home our third state title. We weren't exactly quiet while we got acquainted with each other's favorite positions and she more than likely heard us, but was kind enough not to say anything.

Kelsey snapped her fingers. "Earth to Bri. Did you even hear what I asked?"

I trotted up the last few steps and carried on to my room. "My shoulder is fine. Having the rest of the week off from basketball practice will help all the lingering aches fade. We didn't get to talk much after you met Trey. What do you think of him?"

My heart walloped against my chest. Her approval of Trey meant the world to me. Kelsey eyed the mess of papers and books on my desk before taking in the mess of clothes at the end of my bed.

"I really wish you'd let me tidy up your room."

"You know how I feel about you cleaning up after me. I'll get around to it before my parents return. I can tell by the worried look on your face that's what you're concerned about. I don't want to talk about them. I want to know what you think of Trey."

"I was only offering to help. I don't want your dad to have even the smallest of things to pick apart."

I held up my hands for her to stop and narrowed my eyes for the answer I wanted before heading into my closet. I tossed several outfits behind me and ignored her mutters of disapproval. The growing mess in my room was the least of my concerns. My stomach was in knots. I couldn't eat breakfast or lunch and wasn't sure I'd even get down supper tonight.

Kelsey giggled. "Well, this boy sure is something. I've never seen you so out of sorts and I don't think it has anything to do with my opinion of Trey. I have a strong suspicion you're freaking out about dinner and you need to stop. They're going to love you, Bri."

I strode out of my closet and held up a black skirt that wasn't too short, a low-cut multi-colored shirt, and a white cardigan. "This says I'm classy, but not stuffy, right? And you still haven't answered my question. I'm dying over here."

"That's a very respectable ensemble. As far as Trey, I think he's a wonderful young man. I haven't met very many teenage boys who are as polite and considerate as him. He clearly cares very deeply for you and that's all that matters to me," Kelsey replied, her face serene.

I ducked back into my closet and quickly changed clothes before sliding on a pair of black heels. After doing a once-over, I grabbed my nail polish, shoved a bunch of crap on my desk to the floor, then sat down to work on my makeup.

"I'm really glad it worked out for him to come over last night. We've slowly been sharing more with one another. I really wanted him to meet you so he understood our relationship better and that you take care of me."

"I'm happy to hear you've shared more about your life around here. Like I said, it's important he knows. From our conversations over the past few days, I know you haven't told him nearly enough and I hope you consider opening up more with him. That's so important when building a foundation with someone you're considering handing your heart over to."

I removed the different shades of purple from my fingers and painted them all bright red. It was odd to have them all the same color, but I didn't want my wilder side to be so prominent, especially since his mom would probably see right through me anyway.

Before walking out of my room, I fastened a diamond necklace that matched the studs in my ears around my neck and slid on Trey's charm bracelet. Kelsey couldn't help herself and picked up a bunch of clothes from the floor, tossed them in an empty laundry basket near my door, and followed me. I rolled my eyes but refrained from calling her out. With each step I took, my heart pounded even harder against my chest. The tan I acquired over the summer had faded some over the past few months, but my arms were practically stark white by the time we got downstairs.

Kelsey pulled me in for a brief hug. "You look stunning, Bri. I know you're really nervous, but don't be. Just be yourself."

I wrung my sweaty hands together. "It's never mattered to me if a guy's parents liked me or not, but it matters *a lot* to me now. I just hope I have enough control over the stupid things I tend to say when my nerves are this high-strung."

Kelsey opened the door. "You'll do fine. Mia will be there to help you through it. Don't be too late. I'll talk to you when you get home."

I fidgeted with the charms on my bracelet on the way to my car. Trey offered to pick me up, but I insisted it wasn't necessary. I cranked the ignition and punched his address into my GPS. After I pulled into his driveway and parked behind his Acura, my lips spread into a small smile while I took in the two-story cream house. As promised, Micah and Mia were there, cuddled together on the top step of the wide porch.

Trey jogged down the stairs, decking Micah upside the head as he did. He scowled at him and went back to kissing Mia with no shame. Once Trey reached my Lexus, he opened my door and helped me out. Clasping my hands around his neck, I gave him a quick kiss.

Apparently, it was too brief for him because he picked me up and devoured my mouth. I gasped for air after he set me down and willed my knees not to buckle on me. He gave me a crooked grin, grasped my hand, and led me up the stairs to the large oak door.

"You look gorgeous, Bri, but you always do. Are you ready to meet the family?"

My heart hammered so fast I was afraid it'd fail me soon. Our passionate kiss zapped a great deal of my brain cells and I struggled to find words, so I nodded.

"My mom will love you. Stop freaking out."

We walked inside and Trey dipped down to pick up some toys that had made their way to the foyer. As we strode down the hall, he grabbed more cars and dolls. Wanting to help any way I could, I did the same. His siblings clearly weren't afraid to use their vocal chords and the noise brought a wide smile to my face. The girls were singing "Umbrella" and the boys grumbled over what I assumed was a video game.

Once we reached the living room, Trey deposited the toys in a wooden chest by the entryway and I dropped what was in my hands in too. Silence descended over the room as his siblings stared at me like I was the villain in their favorite cartoon. Their mouths were agape and their eyes lasered through me. My hands were slick with sweat and I looked at Trey for guidance.

He sauntered over to the chair the girls were snuggled together on and picked them up. "Tara and Tawney, this is Bri. I told you she was coming for dinner. Stop being so shy. She loves Rhianna just as much as you two. Maybe you can sing together after we eat."

Trey winked at me and I nodded to back him up. They looked at him with wide baby blue eyes before returning their attention to me. I thought about going over and giving them a hug, but they were holding on to Trey for dear life. Trey set them on the chair and strode over to the boys sitting on the couch. He grabbed their handheld video games and set them on the coffee table.

Trey patted the older boy's head. "This is Thomas. If you know anything about *Super Mario Brothers* or *Lego Star Wars*, he's all ears. He can't beat those games and could use all the help he can get."

Thomas shoved at Trey's shoulder, folded his arms across his chest, and glared at everyone. He looked so much like Trey when he was mad. I bit my cheeks so I wouldn't laugh. Thomas clearly wanted to be treated older. I extended a hand to him. His face scrunched up and I glanced at my hand to make sure nothing was on it. He quickly shook it and focused on Trey.

"I can beat them, Trey. I don't need any help, especially from a *girl*."

Chuckling, Trey plopped the other boy in his lap. He clutched Trey's sides so hard his little hands were white. "This is Tory. If you can build Lego cars as good as him, you'll be his new best friend."

All four of them continued to eye me like I was the Loch Ness

Monster. You could hear a pin drop for as quiet as it was. Mia and Micah strolled in with their hands locked together. Mia looked between me and the kids. She wrinkled her eyebrows, making it clear their current behavior wasn't normal. Mia strode over to the girls and tickled them. Micah did the same with the boys. The room erupted with innocent giggles.

Trey grabbed my damp palm. We walked along the spotless hardwood floors and through the dining room, which already had all the plate and cup settings on it. There were pictures on the walls and shelves of the family over the years, along with plenty of Irish paintings and knickknacks. What I loved the most about his house was that it felt like a home. It had a lived-in vibe to it that I'd never really experienced before. You could see and feel all parts of his family throughout it.

"My dad is going to try and make it. With his new job in its beginning stages, he's been working even longer hours."

"Does your dad sleep?"

"Sometimes I wonder. Anyway, if you don't get to meet him tonight, you will next time."

"Let's just get through this time before we plan the next time."

My heart pounded against my chest. It was clearly me that stunned his siblings into silence. The noise behind us grew as the boys horsed around with Micah and the girls sang with Mia. Goosebumps coasted up my arms and I prayed meeting his mom went a lot better.

"Don't worry about the hellions. They like giving new people a hard time. You'll get to know them soon enough and then you'll wish you didn't. They can get really annoying."

On our way to the kitchen, Trey's ironclad grip on my hand somehow got stronger. I held my breath when he pushed open the swinging door. His mom glided between the island and stainless-steel stove while she prepared what appeared to be quite the Italian menu. The granite countertops were covered. I really couldn't pinpoint a time in my life where I saw this much food that wasn't for some sort of event.

His mom wiped her hands on her red apron before coming over to us. A shocked gasp fell from my lips when she kissed my cheeks. "So, this is the girl that has my son so smitten. I'm so happy to finally meet you, Bri."

"Mom, seriously, you did not just say smitten. I think that's a bit of an exaggeration."

She gave him an admonishing wave. My lips curled into a shy smile. "It's nice to meet you too, Mrs. Donovan. Is there anything Trey and I can help you with?"

Her lips slid into a pleased grin. "It's Lillian, dear. I would love a little help. Do you know a thing or two about pasta sauces? I tried a new recipe tonight, but I'm not sure I got the spices right. I could use a taste tester."

"Actually, Italian is one of my favorite cuisines to cook." I paused and winked at Trey. "Well, next to Mexican, that is."

Trey choked on his next breath. His mind clearly drifted to the naughtier part of that evening. Squeezing my side, he kissed my temple. "I'm going to see if I can unwind the kids before supper. From the sounds of it, I'll have my work cut out for me. Micah and Mia always get them riled up and then bail when it's time to put them to bed."

Lillian beamed. "Kids will be kids, Treahbar. Let them have their fun. They love it when the three of you are around to spend time with them. If they get a little hyper, then so be it."

Trey hung his head. "Yeah, I think it'll get better over the winter. I'll be around more to help with them."

His mom squeezed his cheek. "Stop. You do enough. Now wipe that sullen look off your face and go spend some time with your siblings and friends while I get to know the girl who's consumed my baby boy's life."

Trey rolled his eyes on the way out of the room and I gaped at him while watching him go. My heart leapt out of my chest as I faced his mom. I *so* didn't expect to handle the typical parental interrogation on my own.

Lillian moved between the counters, island, and stove. She gestured for me to take over stirring a sauce to her right. I noticed there were no signs of anything coming out of a can. She cooked everything from scratch. Seeing as she had five kids and one on the way, that was beyond impressive and I wondered how I'd ever measure up to her.

She brought a spoon to her mouth and tasted the alfredo sauce. Lillian pursed her lips together before adding some more spices to the mix. I picked up mine and licked off some spaghetti sauce. My taste buds danced with the flavor, but it was missing a little kick. I pointed toward the spices on the counter, silently asking for permission to add to the pot.

Lillian grinned. "Absolutely. You seem at home behind the stove. With your upbringing, I wouldn't have expected it, but I'm delighted to see I was wrong."

I gave her a feeble smile while adding some oregano, parsley, pepper, and salt to the sauce. "Our housekeeper taught me how to cook a long time ago. It's something I've always enjoyed doing."

"I'm sorry, Bri. I didn't mean to offend you," Lillian said in a rush.

"You didn't. It's okay," I lied.

She tilted my chin to her. "Clearly, it's not okay."

I sighed. "Trey gets very stuck on that difference in our lives. It gets difficult to handle. Don't get me wrong. He's gotten a lot better with it. I shouldn't even be saying this to you. He's going to kill me."

"Trust me, he won't. I'd castrate him if he ever laid a hand on you. I won't say anything about it. I love my son with all my heart, but he doesn't always see the bigger picture. Well, that is, until you came along. You've opened him up more than anyone. I couldn't have picked a better girl for him to date. You're perfect," Lillian replied, a delighted smile on her face.

My jaw dropped at her openness. I shook my head to catch my bearings. "I wouldn't say perfect. It took a long time for us to find our way. I know we have a long way to go."

"Of course you do, dear. You're in high school. There's a lot of major changes coming your way. You'll find your way easily enough. I don't doubt that for a second. You're very smart and exceptionally gifted in sports. You've been a joy to watch."

"You've been at my games?"

Lillian laughed. "Oh yes. A lot of them. It was a little harder this year with Treahbar's games falling on the same days, but we tried to make the ones we could. I enjoy seeing Mia play just as much as I love watching Treahbar. Since you're Mia's best friend, and she's like a daughter to me, I've paid close attention over the years."

"Wow, I had no idea. Trey never mentioned it."

"Treahbar is a typical teenage boy and blocks certain things from his mind, so it's not shocking he never said anything. Mia is an important part of this family. We support her in everything she does."

"She's like a sister to me. I can't picture my life without her in it. The same goes for Trey. I want you to know I care for him a lot and would never do anything to hurt him," I admitted, my face filling with color.

She rubbed her hand down my rosy cheek. "I'm glad to hear it. Treahbar doesn't say a lot, but as his mother, I can get his thoughts out of him without asking. He's been happier with you in his life. That's all I want for him and I'm so grateful for the changes you've brought out in him."

My brain scrambled to keep up as I stood there, speechless. Lillian grabbed the spoon I was holding and tasted my sauce before passing over hers for me to try. The savory flavors of the alfredo sauce made me smack my lips together. It was amazing. She turned all the dials on the stove off and I put the pasta in a bowl as Lillian pulled out the garlic bread from the oven. The aroma wafting through the kitchen made my stomach growl and she laughed.

Trey returned as we were about to carry the food to the table. He grabbed the large bowl of salad, creamy asparagus, and plate of garlic bread from the counter. I followed him with the noodles and sauces. Lillian trailed behind us with roasted potatoes, fried ravioli, and mozzarella sticks.

She set the plates on the table and brought her fingers to her mouth. The piercing sound that came out of her mouth wasn't something I'd ever heard and the stampede coming toward us was even crazier to witness. The younger four eagerly sat in their spots. Micah and Mia strode into the room at a much slower pace and sat across from Trey and me.

They bowed their heads down and I followed suit, a tad on the confused side. Religion wasn't really something I had grown up with.

Lillian looked at Trey. "It doesn't look like your dad is going to make it. Treahbar, will you please say grace?"

He smiled. "Sure, Mom. Lord, thank you for another fine meal. Please bless this table and all the people around it."

Once he was done, the younger ones dove into the food. We passed the bowls around and filled up our plates. His siblings stared at me like I was an alien from outer space. My leg bounced nonstop while I played with my food before taking a small bite.

Trey squeezed my thigh, but I brushed his hand away. That course of action would bring on an onset of feelings I didn't want to experience around a dinner table with his mother and siblings. He winked and mouthed, "Later." I hastily crossed my legs. Lillian smiled at us and I was more than grateful she couldn't read minds.

She focused her attention on Mia and Micah. "How's school going?"

Her pointed stare lingered on Micah, making it evident she was aware of his skittish attendance.

"It's going really good. We have some big tests coming up before Christmas break, but they shouldn't be too terrible. What's your plans for the holidays, Bri?" Mia asked, clearly trying to take the heat off Micah. Her eyes zeroed in on me, desperate for me to speak up right away.

I opened my mouth, but it was clear by the sharp look on Lillian's face she wanted an answer out of Micah. I snapped it shut and waited for him to say something.

His eyes remained on his plate. "It's going alright. I think we have some exams coming up too."

Lillian rested her elbows on the table. She knew he was lying, but refused to call him out on it in front of everyone. I truly felt for her in that moment. It had to be hard to have her son's best friend traveling down a slippery slope, especially when he seemed to be such a fixture to her household.

When we finished eating, Micah and Mia cleared the dishes from the table and took off. I knew Mia well enough to know she was pissed. Now, whether it was at Micah or Lillian was hard to tell. I suspected it was Micah. She kept her distance from him on their way out the door.

After all the dishes were done, Trey brought me up to his room. As promised, it was spotless. I still wasn't buying he didn't have a messy side to him, but enjoyed looking around nevertheless. All the sports and band posters really spoke to his bad boy personality. I sat on the edge of his bed while he helped tuck in the little ones.

I wasn't sure how long I was lost in my own head, but when Trey returned, I almost jumped out of my skin. My hands pounded against my chest to jumpstart my heart. He took a seat next to me, tucked my hair behind my ears, and pressed a soft kiss on my lips before strumming on his guitar.

My eyes widened when the chords shifted into "First Time." The way my heart fluttered as he softly sang would forever be imprinted in my brain. It shouldn't boggle me that he remembered our very first *real* conversation, but it did. Without knowing it, he stole another piece of my heart. Tears pricked my eyes as his low voice filled the room. Once Trey finished singing the last few lines, he set his guitar down and slinked an arm around me.

"That was absolutely incredible, Trey. I had no idea you played so beautifully or had such an amazing voice," I stammered, my cheeks flushing.

He trailed his fingers down them. "On occasion, I play slower songs, but it's usually more along the lines of Linkin Park. Don't think too much of it."

I rolled my eyes and didn't bother to spar with his quick dismissal of the incredibly sweet thing he did for me. "Your siblings think I'm from another planet."

"They'll get used to you soon enough, Bri. They were just being brats tonight," Trey explained against my mouth.

"They're not brats at all. I'm someone new so their reaction was normal. Your family is amazing, Trey," I replied, resting my hand on his thigh.

"What's wrong then? You look like you're ready to cry,"

"I didn't realize that this is what a home should feel like. There's so much love behind these walls. I knew it existed, but it's different to actually experience it."

"It'll always be a home to you, Bri. My mom mentioned that to me more than once tonight. I knew she'd fall in love with you right off the bat."

"Why do you say that?"

"Because while we were tucking the kids in, she told me I better not fuck this one up. That it's a once-in-a-lifetime thing."

I laughed. "I recall saying the same thing. You're doing great so far."

Trey brought me down with him to lay on his pillows. "Such kind words from you, Ms. McAndrews. Aren't I a lucky guy?"

"Yes, you are, Mr. Donovan. You're not going to get lucky in your bedroom, but I wouldn't mind making out a bit before I leave."

Trey eagerly claimed my mouth over and over again for the next hour. I couldn't imagine a more perfect ending to an interesting night. Dinner with his family was a success, but a dark cloud loomed in my horizon. I wasn't sure what would happen when my dad returned from D.C. For now, I savored the peaceful waves flowing through me that only Trey's arms brought me.

CHAPTER 24

TREY

I gazed out the window of the airplane in the dark, cloudless sky. The past month had flown by and it was hard to believe we were on our way to New York City to see Fall Out Boy. Bri stirred in her sleep and I glimpsed at her strained face. Lately, she always dreamed about something that took her to a place that left her restless—*her fucking asshole of a dad.* I readjusted my arm so her head fell into the crook of my shoulder. Her eyes fluttered and she released a content sigh. I wished it eased the pressure crushing my insides the way it used to, but it didn't.

We won the state championship a few weeks back. What should've been one of the best nights of my life actually haunted me. I'd grown accustomed to having cinder blocks sitting on my chest. Every day, it felt like another one got tossed on the pile and it was close to suffocating me. Part of me debated discussing it with Mr. West, but when we spoke, I couldn't find the words to tell him. I was an idiot for allowing the memory to enter my damn mind now because there wasn't a way to stop it from playing out.

* * *

THE LIGHTS of cameras flash across the stadium and practically blind me. After several interviews with local papers, I walk over to the sidelines, my eyes in search for Bri. Before I see her, two men twice the size as me in dark, black suits with earpieces grab me by the arm. I try to get them off me, but their grip becomes tighter. With the celebration around us, no one notices as they drag me behind the bleachers.

I fight the urge to swing at the two jerks. Soulless green eyes bore into me.

"If you think I've brought you over here to congratulate you, you're sorely mistaken," Mr. McAndrews sneers.

"If that's not the case, you'll have to excuse me so I can get back to celebrating with my team. After all, they wouldn't have won without me."

He shoves at my chest. "You may think you're hot shit, but you'll never amount to be anything more than a south side punk."

I see red all around me and curl my hands together. Blood trickles from my palms as I try to control the last strings holding my frayed temper together. "I know who you really are and would love to air it out to the world. The only reason I haven't is because of how much I care about Bri."

John grips my neck and pushes me against the steel bleachers. Even with the padding on, razor-sharp pains attack my back. "I don't know what she's told you, but Brianna likes to exaggerate. If you speak one word to anyone, I'll make sure not only you suffer, but your family does as well. I can bankrupt your parents in a heartbeat."

My eyes grow wide as I gasp for air. His hold loosens, but he doesn't remove his hand.

"Leave my family out of this. If you want to ruin my life, that's fine, but don't do anything to them. If you do, I'll go to all the local papers."

He squeezes my neck. "I'm here to warn you to stay away from my daughter. Brianna refuses to listen to me. As much as I want to send her overseas so I don't have to deal with her being such an utter disappointment,

I can't. She's useful for keeping the polls in my favor. She continues to defy me by seeing you. You better walk away from her or you will *pay for it."*

My chest burns for air and I shove him. John releases me and he runs his hands down his black suit before adjusting his maroon tie. His face remains bright red, a ruthless look in his eyes.

"You can't keep us apart. I'm used to threats from people just like you. It may seem like you can intimidate me because I'm from a different social class, but that's not the case. When I have something to fight for, I always will, and your daughter is at the top of that list. If you do anything to my family, I'll go to the press with pictures of what you did to Bri's jaw."

He steps back, genuine shock spreading across his face, before he moves forward again. "I see you're not going to make this easy. I'm not the only person who wants you out of my life. If you don't heed my warning, you might want to listen to the others. I'm being polite with you. The other people gunning for you have no problem with killing you and making it look like an accident. Believe me, all of them have the resources to do it."

* * *

THE WHEELS of the plane touched down, bringing me out of that horrid memory. The idea of anyone hurting Bri made my chest ache in an insufferable way. I rubbed my sweaty palms down my faded blue jeans. Knives twisted through my heart and dug even deeper. Every day I was with her, I jeopardized her safety, but I couldn't bear to walk away from her.

Knowing I should leave Bri alone created a distance between us that we were both starting to feel. We didn't have very many deep conversations anymore. Most of our time together, which wasn't a lot with school and our conflicting basketball schedules, was spent lost in our bodies. I loved having sex as much as she did, but it became more of a coping mechanism than anything.

She knew I was keeping something from her and I knew she still had more secrets to share. Bri was more tight-lipped than ever with things going on at home. It seemed like her dad wanted to instill the fear of God in her, but who knew when it came to him. What puzzled me the most was he never followed through on his threats with her, but I doubted I'd ever figure him out. The only thing I knew for sure was he was one heartless bastard.

Bri was adamant about not letting him win. Her strength was admirable, but seeing the spark in her beautiful green eyes fade as each day passed nearly gutted me. It didn't help that I was always looking over my shoulder to see if it was the day I'd meet my demise and it was beginning to get difficult to handle. On top of that, kids around the elementary school still gave Thomas and Tory a hard time. I was desperate to get to the bottom of that mess. I hadn't been able to connect any dots so far and their unwillingness to talk about it had my nerves even more on edge than they already were.

The angry monster inside me clawed for the surface, begging to be released on the world. Sebastian had stepped up his asshole antics. Whoever had it out for me made a wise choice in picking him to instigate. There wasn't a shred of morality in him and it got harder to overlook, especially when he went out of his way to provoke Bri.

Part of me was ready to let Sebastian win, beat the shit out of him at school, and be done with it. I'd get expelled and everyone would get what they wanted. Every time I had the urge to do it, Bri intervened and the beast remained locked in its steel cage, but he rattled it more now than ever before. When her hands ran across my body in any way, I calmed down and my rage slowly fizzled out. I just wasn't sure how much longer that would work.

I shook Bri's shoulder to wake her up. Her groggy eyes met mine. Seeing a large wet spot on the side of my gray sweatshirt made me chuckle. She wiped away the drool from her mouth and gave me a sheepish smile. Bri stood up, crisscrossed her arms, and glanced behind her at Micah and Mia, who rubbed their tired eyes. I got to my feet and stretched out the tense muscles in my back. Bri ran her hand down my spine, easing my nerves some, and I brought it around to rest on my stomach while we waited for the people in front of us to grab their bags.

"What hotel are we staying at?" I asked, looking at Micah for an answer.

He gave Mia a wary glance. "TRYP. It's in Times Square and near Madison Square Garden."

Mia shook her head, a frown on her face. "I told you not to book that one. It's way too expensive."

Micah crossed his arms. "And I said don't worry about the money."

Mia opened her mouth to dispute, but seeing the tension between them grow, I quickly said, "We're splitting the cost anyway. It's not that big of a deal."

She glared daggers at me. I glanced at Bri, but knew right away she wasn't in any position to jump in with a different subject. She was on her phone, angrily texting, and I wanted to know with who but didn't bother to ask.

With our luggage in hand, we made our way off the plane and through the airport terminal. Since it was a short trip, we managed to get everything in our carry-on bags. I kept a tight grip on Bri's hand and tried to ignore the amount of times she peered over her shoulder —no doubt looking for her dad's security. The vein in my forehead throbbed nonstop and the headache that typically followed when the pressure in my head rose this high was right around the corner.

"Where the hell were you yesterday, Micah?" Mia asked in a bitter tone.

He eyed me and Bri. Since he missed her basketball game when he promised to be there, we were just as curious as her. It was one of the many times he'd bailed on me in the past month.

Micah scowled. "I said I was sorry about a hundred times, but if you really want to get into it again, we can talk about it later. Let's focus on getting to the hotel without blowing up at one another."

She huffed and picked up her pace. Micah took a deep breath and chased after her.

"Looks like that situation has gotten a lot worse over the past few weeks."

"Yeah, I'm looking forward to talking to him about his sketchy behavior tomorrow while you girls shop. You've been here before. What do you recommend seeing while we're here?"

Bri drummed a couple fingers across her chin. "The Empire State

Building is a must. The view is incredible. Central Park is pretty cool, along with Rockefeller Center."

A genuine smile spread across her face and I flashed my dimples to widen it, loving when it did. We reached the doors leading outside and strode over to the area where taxis were lined up. The temperature was in the low thirties and the cold air blasted through me. I zipped up my bomber jacket before blowing into my freezing hands.

I kissed Bri's rosy nose and whispered, "I'm so happy to be here with you. Another first, Ms. McAndrews."

Bri winked. "I promise to make it a very memorable trip for you, Mr. Donovan."

The next available cab pulled up and we hopped inside. "Take us to the TRYP, please," Micah instructed, pulling Mia close to him.

I wasn't sure what he did, but her agitation with him wasn't as prominent and she snuggled into his side. As the driver wove through an insane amount of traffic, I gazed at Bri, who peered out the window, her lighthearted mood gone. Keeping up with her emotional mood swings, along with my own, was likely to give me whiplash soon.

"So, what misery did you have to go through to get out of your house for the weekend?"

Her head whipped in my direction before she snapped, "Now is *so* not the time for that conversation. I told you not to worry about it when we got on the plane and you promised to drop it."

I narrowed my eyes and muttered, "It'd be a lot easier for me to drop it if you'd stop glancing out your window and the back one every five seconds, like you expect your dad's security to pop up."

She slid away from me, her glare murderous. I released my hold around her waist and crossed my arms while taking in the scenery. The bright lights from the skyscrapers and billboards were very different from the ones around Chicago.

My heart raced with the enormity of it all. The entire city buzzed with energy and I welcomed that feeling over the bloody mess inside me now. I brushed my fingers down her cheek and pointed at the Chrysler Building. "Have you been there?"

A small grin fell from her lips as she nodded. Her tense shoulders made it clear she was still pissed. My eyes drifted back to the multitude of buildings, people, and lights passing by in a blur.

Our driver blasted his horn at a bunch of drunk idiots who zigzagged their way across the street to a different bar. The slew of profanities he shouted out the window made all of us laugh. Hearing Bri giggle sent warm waves through my body and I took her hand in mine.

When we passed by the large Christmas tree in front of Rockefeller Center, decorated with more lights and ornaments than I'd ever seen, I squeezed her hand. "We're both probably on the naughty list, but what would you want Santa to bring you if he happened to show up on Christmas morning?"

Her mouth curled into a wry grin. "I haven't really thought about it. Just for the record, I think you've been way naughtier than me."

I chuckled. "Yes, that's very true. I'm not sure I buy you not thinking about getting presents. It crosses everyone's mind at some point during this time of year."

Her forehead creased, the way it usually did when she geared up to spar with me, and I damn near threw my hands up in frustration. If we couldn't even make small talk, it would be a really long two days. After the taxi pulled up to TRYP, Micah passed over the fare, hopped out, and seized Mia's hand while I helped Bri out. We strode through the sliding doors and up to the front desk.

After the woman behind the desk confirmed our information, she slid over our keycards and we headed to the elevator. Bri strolled over to the opposite side of it and pulled Mia with her. Micah and I did nothing to hide our confusion while they carried on in one of their notorious silent chats. By the time we reached our floor, they were using words again, but kept their voices low on our way down a long hallway with funky wallpaper.

Micah stopped at their room, swiped the keycard, and disappeared without a word. Mia massaged her temples and followed him. I stared at their closed door, wondering what the hell was going on with them, before quickly reminding myself I had enough of my own problems.

Bri took our card out of my hand and entered our room, a scowl on her face. I had no fucking clue what I did to warrant it this time.

Holding up my hands, I gave her a pointed look. "What the hell is your problem, Bri? I really don't want to fight with you, but you're making it next to impossible right now."

She tossed her bag on the floor. "I'm pissed you brought up my dad with Micah and Mia in earshot. I don't want to fight either. Let's just agree not to talk about anything going on back home. It'll be a hell of a lot easier for us to get along if we avoid those topics."

I refused to agree to what she asked and strode into the bedroom. After seeing a perfect view to the hustle and bustle on the streets below, I released a low whistle. Bri stepped behind me, slid her hands under my jacket, and scratched her fingers along my abs. I turned around, cupped her face, and pressed my thumbs to the corners of her mouth until she gave me one of her breathtaking smiles.

Achieving my goal seconds later, I brushed my lips lightly across hers. She opened her mouth wider and sucked my tongue into hers, stroking it with eagerness. I met her aggressive licks until my lungs burned for oxygen. I took in a deep breath, grabbed her bag, and set it on the dresser with mine before sitting on the edge of the king-size bed and patting the space next to me. She sashayed over, a devious grin on her face, and straddled me.

My dick sprang to life and I put talking on a sidebar—*again*. Her luscious lips connected with mine while she removed my jacket and sweatshirt. My white tank top hit the floor, leaving me half-naked and reveling in the potent desire taking over my body.

"These need to go *right now*," I growled, pulling off her leather jacket, pink skin-tight T-shirt, and lacy bra.

I eagerly teased the freckles under her chin until she whimpered. Her vanilla scent surrounded me, and I cherished the way it made my heart beat a little faster.

Bri tugged off my belt and unzipped my jeans. She peeked at me, batting her long lashes, and murmured, "Commando, huh. That's new for you. What brought on that change?"

"Variety is the spice of life, babe."

I kissed her breasts and flicked at her nipples until they were hard. My lips drifted over to a spot below her collarbone and I sucked down hard, knowing she enjoyed getting hickeys on her chest and the ones I gave her last week had faded. As my lips really started to move, Bri rapidly stroked my cock. My head fell back as she set into an unrelenting rhythm. If she kept it up, I wouldn't last much longer.

Without warning, her hands disappeared and I gazed at her in disbelief. She thrust her body into mine while lightly scratching her nails down my back. My dick was rock-hard, desperate to be buried deep inside her. As she rocked into me, her eyes centered on mine and the passion behind them tapped into the insatiable cravings going through me. She slid to her knees, discarded my jeans, and trailed her mouth along my shaft before taking me in as far as she could. I moaned loudly when her lips really started to move. Bri paused every so often to stroke me. Every time she came back to take me whole, it was with more gusto.

When my body started to tremble, I hauled her up, unbuttoned her jeans, and shoved them to the floor, along with her lacy underwear, and stuck three fingers inside her hot core, swirling them around until her back arched off the bed.

"Fuck, it's like you took a course in this and graduated with the highest honors. Whatever you do, don't stop!"

The muscles in her flat stomach rippled as she clenched against my fingers. I dipped in and out of her at a merciless pace until she exploded around me. Watching her come made my tip even wetter. Seeing her satisfied smile was all I needed to not let go myself. I'd give anything to keep it on her face and all her worries at bay.

"Holy shit, Trey!" Bri screamed, her eyes rolling to the back of her head as her body shuddered in my hands.

I didn't give her a minute to catch her breath and rocked roughly into her. "I'm just getting started, Bri. I hope you're ready for a long night of this."

Her breaths came in spurts, but that didn't stop me from pounding into her. I penetrated deeper and much harder than I had in the past. If this was the only way we communicated with one another these days, then I'd make sure she damn well knew how badly I still wanted her. Despite every obstacle around us, I *needed* her.

When I picked up my pace, she dug her nails into my shoulders. The intensity in her eyes matched mine and I knew she was just as much in the moment as me. She sucked eagerly along my neck. I arched away from her, my eyes warning not to give me a hickey there. Bri quivered beneath me as I gripped her breast and slammed even harder into her.

I slowed down to give her more drawn-out thrusts and appreciate all the ways her body quaked with each roll of my hips. Her eyebrows furrowed together to display her confusion with the sudden switch. I claimed her mouth in a very different way than before, exploring every part of it and taking note of all her heady moans. With each one, my heart thumped against my chest. As wrong as it was, I enjoyed stringing out my release, just so we could carry on in the euphoria being wrapped up in each other's bodies brought us. My entire body pulsated with its need for her.

We devoured one another's mouths while I grinded into her at a sensual pace. She ran her nails down my back, signaling she was about to climax and wanted me to go with her. I sped up and tangled her tongue with mine. Our bodies reached that point of ecstasy at the same time and I shook nonstop while pouring into her.

Resting my head against her shoulder, I listened to her heave in deep breaths. Bri tilted my chin up as her lips curled into an adorable smile, but her eyes still carried a worry to them I'd grown tired of seeing. She placed a delicate kiss on my forehead and wrapped her arms around me before I slid out and returned her warm embrace.

"That was something else, Trey. Thank you," Bri whispered after a bit.

I scrunched my eyebrows together. "We've been having sex every chance we get for the past month and you're thanking me now. That's new."

Her face was thoughtful. "Yes, we have crazy bunny sex anywhere and everywhere, but this time was different. I could feel your need for me and it matched my own."

My fingers trailed across her tight stomach to fiddle with her belly button ring. "I'm glad you enjoyed it as much as me. It's right up there with having sex in the janitor's closet at Chamberlain. I'm still not sure how we pulled that off without getting caught."

She playfully smacked my arm. "That was a miracle in itself. I had no idea I could be that quiet, but then again, having your hand cover my mouth the entire time probably made all the difference there. It was some pretty hot sex. It's definitely at the top of my list."

I chuckled. "What else is on your list? I'm intrigued."

Bri giggled. "The night we went at it on the deck outside your room was pretty epic. When that set of headlights settled on us, I thought I was going to die. I'm so happy it ended up being Micah dropping off Mia and that she didn't see us."

"Yeah, I think she got an eyeful. Micah brought it up with me later that week. She had to have seen something."

"At this point, all of our friends have seen more than enough of our bodies. I'm still miffed at Shane for interrupting us after your state championship win."

My heart skipped a beat, not wanting to open the door to this particular topic, but tired of avoiding it too. "That entire night was my fault. I forgot I agreed to go out with him and a couple of the other guys. As I recall, you got over it pretty fast."

Bri shrugged. "Yes, I did. Tequila will do that to a girl."

"I've noticed. You could barely walk by the time we left the party and it's been that way at the end of all the parties we've gone to lately. I'm not a fan of you getting that drunk. If you're drinking away your frustrations, which I assume part of you is, that's not a good thing. It can become a serious problem."

She sat up in a rush, crossed her arms over her amazing rack, and glared at me. I sighed and pulled the covers over us.

"Don't lecture me, Trey. I only drink at parties. You've been in such a strange mood since your championship game. Drinking calms my nerves when we're at parties. Keeping an eye out for anyone who's going to put you in an even pissier mood than you have been lately isn't exactly easy, since it's pretty much anyone these days. What pisses me off the most is you have the audacity to criticize me for not saying what's on my mind when you hardly ever do either."

The fire brewing in my gut spread through my pores. I searched around for the remote to put something on T.V. Bri gripped my chin, her eyes searching for an actual answer on the matter. I gently removed her hands and focused on the sappy romantic comedy on the flat screen.

What could have turned into a fun conversation for once was no longer the case. Her growing agitation was evident by the annoyed look on her face. Taking measured breaths to rein in her temper, she rolled onto her side.

I trailed my fingers down her back before running over the same path with my lips. It was dirty on my part, but I wanted this weekend to be special and it was off to a very rocky start. Bri released a heavy sigh and faced me. Her striking green eyes were misty and I kissed away a straggling tear.

We would have to talk about things soon, but I couldn't do it tonight. I returned to my previous plan of making her understand just how much I needed her and lifted her on top of me. I'd rather spend the rest of the night communicating with her this way than deal with the heartbreaking look in her eyes. Bri rolled her hips into me, making it clear she was on the same page. Closing my eyes, I let her take us to a more blissful place.

* * *

I GAVE Bri a welcome call well before sunrise. She was on her back, gasping for air, but the sated smile on her face was what I loved seeing the most. I was determined to make today better than yesterday. Once she caught her breath, I pulled her up from the bed and dragged her into the shower for round two.

By the time we were done, her legs barely held her up, and we actually decided to get clean. Once all the suds were gone, I hopped out and wrapped a towel around her. With her back against my chest, the sweet raspberry scent from her shampoo filled my nostrils and my heart raced in response. I ran the towel all over her body and tried to halt all the blood surging to my dick.

I'd love to take her again, but we had places to be, so I finished drying her off and draped a fresh towel around myself. She sashayed over to the black granite-top vanity, still completely nude, picked up her toothbrush, covered it in toothpaste, and brushed her teeth.

Her self-confidence was such a turn-on. I swept aside her wet hair and pressed tender kisses to the back of her neck, making her shiver.

Bri spat out the toothpaste in her mouth and faced me. Her bright white teeth were on full display with her ear-to-ear smile. "I love waking up in your arms, but I'll never complain if you wake me up with sex. Care to see how many times we can have sex in a day while we're here?"

My dick was at full attention. I kissed her nose and growled, "Stop trying to distract me with your incredible body. I promise to appreciate it plenty of times before we head back to Chicago, but I'm really looking forward to seeing the city with you too."

She gave me a salacious grin. "If you want me to focus on sightseeing, I suggest you stop growling." I rolled my eyes. Bri giggled and patted my chest. "I need to finish getting ready before evaluating my suitcase to determine just how much I can buy today without having to check anything on our way home."

Bri disappeared into the bedroom. For as much as she liked shopping, I was curious where she would drag Mia off to while we were here. Shopping was definitely her kryptonite. I picked up my toothbrush and quickly brushed my teeth. After I shaved and slapped on some cologne, I sauntered into the bedroom to see Bri tossing clothes over her shoulder in frustration. I chuckled and her head snapped up, a tight smile on her face. I released a heavy sigh, wondering what the hell made her mood shift so drastically in a matter of minutes.

"Looking for something in particular there, babe?" I asked in a joking tone.

She ignored me and continued to dig. To say she was on a mission didn't really cover it. Whatever she was in search of had her more than panicked. Her face was pale and her breathing erratic. I wanted to massage her shoulders to calm her down, but her rigid posture made it clear she didn't want to be touched.

I slid on a pair of black boxers and worn jeans before pulling my favorite Fall Out Boy T-shirt over my head. When I glimpsed at Bri, her body visibly shook with relief. She retreated to the bathroom with an armful of clothes and makeup.

A knock sounded on the door moments later and I hopped up to open it. Mia and Micah strode through the entryway with their arms linked together, looking a lot more at ease with one another than last night. Mia gave him a quick kiss and disappeared into the bathroom.

"Where do you want to grab breakfast?" I asked, scrolling through my phone to see what Google Maps suggested.

Micah's cell rang and his eyes narrowed to slits. He snatched our keycard from the high-top table and stepped into the hall. Resting my head against the closed door, I was grateful for the thick walls last night while having vigorous sex with Bri, but cursed them right now. I couldn't hear a damn thing and I needed to know who Micah was on the phone with. We didn't have secrets from one another and I was over being blown off and lied to.

When Bri popped out of the bathroom moments later, she almost gave me a heart attack. She had on a pair of skinny jeans, a cashmere sweater that matched her eyes, and knee-high black boots, with a smidge of makeup on her gorgeous face. She tilted her head, a curious grin on her face. I ran a hand down mine and truly debated which one of us was moodier on any given day.

"Ah...what are you doing?" Bri asked, arching an eyebrow.

Mia strode out of the bathroom, her face just as inquisitive as Bri's. Micah opened the door and glanced at the three of us, his eyebrows furrowed. I grasped the back of my neck with my sweaty palm. "I'm fucking starving. How does Johny's sound for breakfast?"

Bri gave me a wary look as she handed my jacket over and slid on hers. I hastily put on mine and opened the door for everyone to file out. Mia and Micah strolled past me—not bothering to hide their confusion over my evasiveness. I locked hands with Bri and closed the door behind me.

We made our way downstairs and through the lobby in silence. The bellboy opened the doors for us and the blast of cold air that followed was an unwelcome shock to my system. Small snowflakes swirled around us as we walked the short distance to Johny's.

After reaching the diner, we sauntered over to the yellow countertop and managed to snag four open seats together. It was close quarters, but I actually liked it. The graffiti mural in a variety of colors behind us spoke to the energy everyone talks about when they refer to the Big Apple. For once, positive vibes flowed through me and I couldn't wait to get out there and explore the city. A waiter dressed in a black T-shirt and jeans approached us minutes later with a coffee pot and menus in hand. He passed them over and gestured the coffee toward us.

"I'll take a cup and please fill it to the brim," Mia spoke up, licking her lips.

I shook off the request, but rolled my eyes at Mia. That girl had a serious addiction to caffeine. I quickly scanned the menu and found what I wanted to order right away.

Bri shrugged off her jacket. "I'll have one as well."

I gaped at her, but she remained indifferent to me. I placed my hand over the spot she was reading. "Since when do you drink coffee? Isn't that bad for your anxiety?"

She rolled her shoulders. "With Mia as my best friend, it's not surprising I succumbed to it. Don't worry about my anxiety. I can handle it."

I really wanted to point out that coffee was probably one of the worst things for her to drink with her nerves being off the charts most days, but wasn't about to pick a fight with her. Micah was on the other side of her, angrily texting away on his phone.

I tapped his shoulder and asked, "Are you still up for going to the Statue of Liberty?"

He didn't bother looking up and murmured, "Yeah man, of course. We'll do that before walking down Wall Street. Maybe I'll learn a thing or two."

It took great restraint on my part not to laugh at him. He'd actually have to start going to school for that to happen. Our waiter returned with a pen and paper in hand and nodded at me.

"I'll have the Bigman Breakfast with a glass of orange juice."

"I'm having what he's having," Micah echoed, handing over his menu and Mia's.

"How very *When Harry Met Sally* of you. You should've at least waited until I faked an orgasm before you ordered," I quipped.

Mia almost spat out her coffee. Micah reached around Bri, decked me upside the head, and rebutted, "You're terrible at faking anything. I didn't want to embarrass you."

"I'll take a breakfast platter with two eggs and sausage," Bri spoke up, giggling.

"I'm having the same thing, except with bacon," Mia said, sliding over her cup for a refill.

I opened my mouth to poke at Mia, but she shook her head and said, "Don't even think about saying whatever smartass remark you're about to."

Our waiter replenished her coffee and was smart enough to leave the pot. I ran my fingers down Bri's back. "What stores are you ladies going to hit up?"

She flashed a wily grin. "Pretty much every single one we can squeeze in on Fifth Avenue."

I chuckled. "I guess I can see why the coffee is necessary then. You're going to have your work cut out for you."

Bri jabbed my side. "I'm drinking caffeine because *someone* kept me up late last night and woke me up really early this morning."

I wiggled my eyebrows. "Guilty as charged and I'd do it all over again to hear you scream my name as loud as you did in the shower."

Her cheeks turned a dark shade of red before she smacked my arm and hissed, "Say it a little louder, why don't you? I don't think the whole diner heard you."

Before I could tease Bri some more, our waiter slid our plates over to us. The only sound for the next ten minutes was the chatter from the customers by us, the tunes streaming from the radio, and clinking of utensils on our plates while we devoured our food. I practically inhaled my eggs, bacon, pancakes, home fries, and toast. There was nothing like a greasy diner breakfast. To my surprise, the girls ate just as fast as Micah and me.

"We're going to hit the ladies' room before we leave," Bri spoke up, grabbing Mia, who was on the perplexed side.

Micah wiped his mouth with his napkin, tossed it on his plate, and pulled his wallet out from his back pocket. My jaw dropped after seeing the huge wad of cash in it. All I saw was hundreds as he flipped through the bills until he reached a bunch of fifties and twenties. He tossed two twenties down on the counter.

"Did you rob a bank before we left?" I asked, half-joking, half-serious.

Micah rolled his eyes. "Yeah, in all that spare time of mine."

I retrieved my own wallet and threw down three tens. Bri and Mia were on their way back to us, so I didn't push him any further on it. Once they were close enough, we hopped off our stools with their coats and slid them over their shoulders before heading back into the falling snow.

I held my hand out to hail a cab for the girls. Micah picked Mia up in a passionate embrace while kissing the hell out of her. I rested my hands on Bri's shoulders and greedily claimed her mouth. By the time a cab pulled up, my heart was ready to leap out of my chest. Bri swayed back in a daze and sucked in a quick breath. I wiped away a few snowflakes from her flushed face and helped her in the taxi.

Before closing the door, I leaned in and kissed her pink nose. "Have fun, babe. We'll see you ladies at the hotel at noon so you can drop off your shopping bags before we head over to the Empire State Building."

She brushed some snowflakes off my cheek. "You boys have fun too. Stay out of trouble."

Micah and I waved goodbye as the cab veered into the multitude of cars trying to make their way through Times Square. The flashing lights in every direction weren't as cool as they were last night, but still pretty spectacular nevertheless.

I retrieved my Cubs stocking hat from my pocket and pulled it over my buzzed head. Whenever it snowed, I missed my shaggy hair. It absorbed the water a lot better than the prickly stubble I had now. I blew in my hands and glanced at Micah. "I need to do a little Christmas shopping while we're here. It shouldn't take too long."

Micah nearly tripped over a homeless person covered in rags and ran right into a man decked out in an Armani suit. The guy he bumped into muttered under his breath about stupid tourists and I couldn't help but laugh at the vicious glare Micah pinned on him.

"Don't get bent out of shape about it. You know we do the exact same thing to tourists that come to Chicago and get in our way," I murmured, still chuckling.

Micah frowned on our way into Penn Station. "That's different. At least in Chicago, there's room to walk on the sidewalks. Between the snow piling up and more people than I've ever seen in my life, there's no way to avoid running into someone."

We stopped to get tickets at a kiosk before heading over to the next available train. Five minutes later, we hopped on one to Staten Island. I clutched the metal pole next to me and eyed Micah. He scowled at a message on his cell before shoving it in his pocket.

"What was that all about? You've been having that reaction a lot lately," I pointed out, arching an eyebrow.

He crossed his arms and snapped, "It's nothing, man. Don't think twice about it."

I shoved at his shoulder and rebutted, "I'm getting real tired of that line. What the fuck is going on with you lately? Mia's been on an emotional roller coaster because of you. It doesn't help you're never around when you say you'll be. You're constantly showing up late or taking off unexpectedly. We're supposed to be best friends and you barely talk to me anymore."

He pushed my hands away, his face scrunched up and almost pained. "That's not my damn fault. You're all tied up in your new world at Chamberlain. You're the one who's always busy or rescheduling to run off with Bri at the last minute."

"That's bullshit and you know it! I *always* make time for you."

A few passengers peeked up from their newspapers and stared at us. Micah gestured for me to be quiet. I released a riled breath to control the hot blood pumping through my veins.

"I'll talk as loud as I want until you tell me what's going on with you."

His face hardened. "Fine, but you can't say a fucking word to Mia or Bri. Those two share *everything*. It's gotten real annoying, real fast."

I gave him a sharp look to get on with it. He twisted his hands together until his knuckles were white. "I've been delivering packages for the Fitzpatricks."

The blistering rage from deep within me traveled through every pore. "Are you out of your fucking mind? Getting tied up with them in any way is just plain stupid. You might as well have signed your own death warrant."

More people gazed at us—no doubt expecting a punch to be thrown soon. It took restraint not to strangle Micah for being so stupid.

"Keep your fucking voice down. I knew you wouldn't understand. You don't get what it's like for people like me," Micah defended.

I waved my hands in the air. "What's there to understand? You're working for the mob. And what do you mean, people like you? We're from the same goddamn neighborhood."

Micah jabbed a few fingers in my chest. "I mean people who aren't as smart and talented as you. Trey, you don't get to judge me for playing with the hand I was dealt."

I shoved his hands away. "You live three houses down from me, Micah. Up until this last year, we went to the same damn schools. You're just as smart as me. The only difference is you're always looking for the easy way out rather than working for it. Your future is as promising as mine, if you'd put a little effort into it."

He shook his head, his eyes narrowed. "You and Mia don't get it. I'll never be able to measure up to your kind of greatness in the classroom or on the field. I'm simply accepting the direction life has pointed me in. I'm not doing anything illegal and won't do anything to land myself in the clink."

"Let me reiterate. You're working for the Fitzpatricks. Anything and everything about them *is* illegal."

I strung out each word to ensure he understood how stupid he was being, but he remained as indifferent as ever. When some people departed the train, I eyed how many stops we had before we needed to jump out.

"I drop off and pick up things for them when they call. I'm not dealing drugs, stealing cars, or offing anyone. I think you know me better than that. It's not a crime to be a delivery boy."

"It's a stepping stone to the other things. They'll coerce you into doing those things at some point. What will you do then? And you bitched me out for putting Mia in danger. What you're doing now is likely to get you, and her, killed."

His fists curled together. With how red his face was, he struggled not to slug me, but I didn't give a shit. He needed to hear me and get out of this mess.

"I'm not discussing it any further. I heard what you had to say and I'll take it under advisement. If you even think about saying something to Mia, I'll kick your ass. She's got enough to deal with and doesn't need to worry about me for no reason. If I were you, I'd focus on your relationship with Bri. You can cut the fucking tension between you two with a knife."

"Mia's not an idiot. She's going to figure it out eventually. The longer you keep it from her, the more pissed she's going to be in the end. Why is that so hard for you to grasp? Why can't you see what you're doing is wrong?"

"Bold words coming from you, Trey. Have you told Bri about what her dad did to you or about all the little punks giving Tory and Thomas trouble? And let's not forget how bizarre it is to have a bunch of rich assholes plotting to ruin your life!"

I gave him a curt shake of the head. He pinned a lethal glare on me. "I didn't think so. Do yourself a favor. Focus on whoever is trying to ruin *your* future and stay out of *mine*."

His acidic tone signaled the finality of this topic. He was as stubborn as me when it came to certain things. I had no idea how I missed

Micah getting involved in something so dangerous. My chest spasmed for being such a shitty friend to him. When we got back to Chicago, I needed to work a lot harder to get through to him.

My mind drifted to Bri. I'd have to put in some more effort there as well. I couldn't keep walking away from all the important topics any longer. I wanted to trust her with my whole heart and that wouldn't happen with so much unsaid between us. Part of me realized I'd fallen for her and I wanted to tell her. I couldn't say it without knowing more about all the things she avoided sharing with me. I'd never make her heart mine if I didn't have her trust.

A familiar ache ran through my upper body and I shrugged off the resulting shivers from it. I couldn't say it, but I'd find a way to show her with my Christmas gifts. I wanted her to know I'd always be there for her. No matter how hard people tried to break us apart, I wasn't ready to give up on us.

CHAPTER 25

BRI

"Are you going to tell me where your mind was most of the morning while we shopped or just continue to play it off like nothing was wrong?" Mia asked in a low whisper.

Her eyes carried an edge to them, making it clear she was on the pissed side with me. My gaze drifted to Trey to ensure he was still asleep. His eyes were closed, but his shoulders were tense. I had a feeling he was just pretending to be asleep. I glanced at Micah to see if I could divert Mia's attention his way, but he was a few seats down and on his phone.

No wonder Mia is grilling me. She's fed up with him. I really want to tell her everything, but not this weekend. I don't want to ruin our trip and that's all it'll do if I open my mouth.

The pain in my heart spread through the rest of my body and heavy weights followed it. I hated keeping things from Mia and I'd found out something I wasn't ever going to be able to share with anyone—not anytime soon anyway. Before I could prevent it from happening, my mind drifted to a conversation I overheard a few weeks ago.

* * *

I WALK THROUGH THE DOOR, *slide off my heels, and tiptoe upstairs. My dad is screaming at a few of his staff members about his numbers dropping in the polls. I hold my breath as I go by his office. What sounds like a book flying across the room makes me jump and I almost lose my balance.*

Just as I'm about to make a beeline for my bedroom, the conversation turns to me and I stop to listen to what his latest threat will be. He's already cut off my weekly allowance. I'm sure my trust is next, but I don't give a fuck. I barely have access to my car anymore. Someone is usually watching my every move. It's made getting out very difficult, but I'm still managing it with the help of the staff.

I don't know how many more times I can hear how much of a disappointment I am. No one should ever be told they were a mistake to this world, but that's been his line of attack for a while. We'll see if he sticks with that one or switches it up.

I know I'm feeding into his rage by seeing Trey, but he's not going to take him away from me. He can keep trying to ground me and I'll just keep sneaking out. If I don't, everything inside me will shatter. Trey is the only one who's preventing that from happening. He's a painkiller and so much more for me. When I'm with him, I can silence the hateful echoes in my head—even if it's only for a couple of hours.

A glass slams against his desk and I can almost hear the people in there flinching. If he's drunk, he doesn't give a damn what damage he does.

"Why can't security contain my miscreant of a daughter? She's seventeen and not all that clever. How she keeps slipping out undetected is unbelievable. If you don't get a better handle on her soon, I'll be firing every single one of you!"

"We're doing our best, sir. She's craftier than you think. Unless you want us to put her on lockdown, I'm not sure it'll be possible. That's flirting with trouble. Jamie has advised to back off Brianna or she'll go to the press with everything she has on you."

My eyes widen in shock. She's probably coming to my defense to piss him off. That's got to be the only reason. I'll always be a weapon they use to get back at each other. My mind races to determine what she has on him. I know she took pictures of my jaw and so did I for my own insurance, but it sounds like a lot more.

"Don't get me started on my worthless wife. I'll remind her who runs this house and she'll get lost in her Merlot the way she always does. I should send Brianna to boarding school and be done with it. I have much more important things to do than deal with her continued defiance."

"You're going to need to accept the situation with Brianna as it is. Your polls jump every time you get a shot with her at one of her games. Sending her overseas isn't an option. She's probably not what you want to focus on right now. Your son is proving to be a challenge to control as well. We've reminded him he belongs on the south side, but he's been putting up a fight to see Brianna."

My heart beats right out of my chest, floating into the air above me. I have a half-brother. Who is he? How have they kept him a secret all these years? What are they doing to him to keep him away from me? Why are they keeping us apart? What kind of morally corrupt people does my dad have working for him? Tears pour down my cheeks.

"That piece of shit needs to stay put. He's the biggest mistake I ever made. We have enough problems with the Donovan boy. Do whatever it takes to put him back in his place. If you can't control the situation, I'll speak with Sean. His fists usually do the trick."

"We'll handle it. I think it's best you remove yourself from any interaction with Trey. The Du Ponts, Dudleys, and Livingstons have a precise plan and it's best you don't interfere any more than you already have. With Brianna being linked to him, and you making your disdain on the matter known, it's way too easy for everything to fall back on you when they execute their plans."

"What the hell are they waiting for? It can't be that hard to get the worthless punk kicked out of school. Set him up and be done with it."

"It doesn't sound like they're going down that route any longer. Coach Barry has thwarted any attempt to ruin him on the academic front. They want retribution for what he did to Sebastian. They're out for his blood. It's all going to be a matter of timing for that to happen."

I release a horrified gasp. Bodies shuffle around in his office. I sprint to my room, shut the door before anyone realizes I was in the hall, and slide to the floor. My body shakes nonstop as the pressure in my chest increases. I try to breathe steadily, but I can't get any air into my lungs. My vision blurs with the tears I can't stop. I lie down and let the darkness win.

* * *

MIA SNAPPED her fingers at me. The people across from me on the subway eyed me like I was about to lose my wits. My nerves prickled and breathing became a struggle. Trey gave me a gentle squeeze, his eyes assessing me. Plastering on a reassuring smile, I snuggled into him.

"Everything okay, Bri?" Trey inquired, concerned.

"Yeah, you totally checked out on me. What the hell was that about?" Mia asked, irritated.

"I'm fine. My mind wandered for a moment. Are we almost back to the hotel? With all this snow flying, it's totally wreaked havoc on my hair. I'll need to redo it, and yours, before the concert."

Trey looked away from me, his face pained. Mia got up in a huff and went over to Micah. I twisted my hands together, hating myself for pissing off Trey, but it wasn't like I could tell him about that horrible memory. My mind drifted to our fun afternoon and I prayed our evening was just as great. The last thing I wanted to do was fight with either of them.

After Mia and I hit up nearly every store on Fifth Avenue, we met up with the guys at the hotel before heading to lunch at Carmine's in Times Square and squeezing in an insane number of landmarks. We visited the Empire State Building, Chrysler Building, Radio City Music Hall, and Rockefeller Center before hitting up Central Park to walk around and skate for a bit.

Chills ran up my back and I glanced around the train to ensure no one followed us. Every time I did it this morning, Mia questioned me on it, but I shrugged it off. My dad's security hadn't sprung up yet, but I wasn't ruling it out.

He was in D.C. with my mom and that was the only reason I pulled off this trip. Shane, Peyton, and Kylie were covering for me back in Chicago, but that didn't mean much. After what I discovered in my luggage this morning, my dad would definitely make my life miserable when I got home. It was just a matter of *when*. He was quite fond of screwing with my head. It'd probably be when I was at my most vulnerable. My nerves rattled even more. Fidgeting with my charm bracelet, I forced my thoughts in a different direction.

"We're almost to Penn Station. You'll have plenty of time to get ready. Are you sure you're alright? You're back to looking around every few minutes and really pale."

"Trey, I'm really fine. We had a ton of Italian food before skipping all over the city. I'm just a little tired and I blanked out for a minute. I'll grab a Red Bull at the hotel and get my second wind."

He released a drawn-out breath and sealed his lips. The veins in his neck throbbed at a relentless rate. Avoiding eye contact with him, my eyes drifted around the train. We were due for a fight soon. That was all my life seemed to be lately—one big fight.

The subway finally hit our stop and we departed with a bunch of other people. With the concert a few hours away, it was like the sidewalk population had doubled. Trey kept a tight hold on me and Micah did the same with Mia. A few minutes later, we reached our hotel and I paused for a moment in the lobby to let the warmth settle into my frozen limbs. Once I could move my fingers again, I slid out of Trey's embrace and tugged Mia away from Micah.

Mia narrowed her eyes. "What's with the rush, Bri? The concert isn't for a few more hours, but you're walking at a pace like it's twenty minutes from now."

"Is it such a terrible thing for me to want to spend some time with my best friend? You're so busy having sex, I hardly see you outside of school and basketball," I teased, pounding the call button.

"Oh please, that's complete bullshit and you know it. If you're using me to avoid talking to Trey, that's fine, just don't lie about it," Mia replied, annoyed.

"Keep your voice down. They're right behind us. You've been avoiding hashing things out with Micah for weeks, so you better shut your mouth," I snapped, exasperated.

The elevator arrived and we stepped inside. There were a few other guests with us, but that didn't stop Mia from stewing. My own blood pumped through my pores. Micah ran a hand down his tense face and kept his distance from Trey. It made me wonder what those two discussed while we shopped. Trey rubbed his buzzed head and released a disgruntled sigh. The look in his eyes almost made me laugh. Not having the longer strands to tug on frustrated him.

He caught me staring and flashed his dimples. My mouth curled into a wily grin and I threw in a giggle. His smile grew even wider and he kissed my temple. Tranquil waves coasted through me and I preferred them a hell of a lot more than the angry ones.

Once the elevator hit our floor, Mia and I stepped out first. The guys stuck to a leisurely pace behind us. I glimpsed over my shoulder. "Why don't you guys check out ESPN in Micah's room? While we get ready, it's going to look like a cyclone went off in ours."

Micah stopped at their door and Trey followed him inside with his hands shoved in his pockets. His smile vanished. He clearly didn't want to spend the next hour alone with Micah. I swiped the keycard to our room and strode over to the mini fridge.

Mia leaned against the wall and chewed away at her nails. I grabbed two Red Bulls and tossed one over to her. She caught it, sauntered into the bathroom, and hopped up on the black vanity, a knowing look on her face.

"If you keep acting so spacey, Trey isn't going to let it go much longer. He's already about to blow with the number of things you're keeping to yourself," Mia spoke up, her voice laced with her own frustrations.

I turned on the curling iron and pulled makeup out of my bag. She folded her hands over her chest, her eyes demanding I talk. I swiped the pad full of foundation and smeared it on her face until it was nice and even.

"My dad hates him and doesn't want me with him. Trey knows it. What's there to discuss?"

Mia snatched the blush out of my hand, set it on the counter, and squeezed my shoulders. "There's more to it. I can feel it. I'm really worried about you, Bri. You space out more than you think. This morning you were a million miles away while getting ready. I know it all goes back to your dad. Is his security out here? Is that why you're flipping between moods faster than the Tasmanian devil?"

I looked away. "Mia, I don't want to get into it. All I really want to do is forget about everything going on at home and focus on having fun."

Mia scowled. "Too bad, I do. You can't keep trying to shoulder everything on your own. You're about two seconds away from a meltdown. If you really want to have fun, you need to stop acting so damn twitchy and share something with me. Even the blind can see how jumpy you are at this point."

I exhaled. "I can tell you're not going to back down. If you must know, I found a tiny microphone, along with another small gadget, in my suitcase this morning."

Her eyes bugged out. "*Oh. My. God.* Your dad tracked you out here. Bri, that's *really* bad. He's gone off the rails with trying to keep tabs on you. When he finds out Trey was on this trip with you, he's going to flip out. What if he hurts you again?"

I shuddered at that prospect, but held on to the very little strength I had left. "My mom doesn't do much for me, but she's made it clear if he lays a hand on me again, he won't live to see another day."

Mia rubbed her face before taking a long drink of her Red Bull. "That's not all that reassuring. He'll find a way to do something to you. He *always* does."

I sighed. "I know. I'm trying not to think about it."

"What did you do with the tracking devices? Is there any way he might not get any information from them?" Mia asked, her tone hopeful.

"I have no idea how all that crap works, but I'll have to learn fast. I'm assuming he got something from them. At least now I know he's stooped to that level and I can do a thorough sweep of my car and room when I get home."

"Did you say or do anything before you found them that would land you in serious hot water?"

I smirked. "I'm always in hot water. All he'll hear between last night and this morning was a lot of robust sex. I'm sure that'll make him see red too, but I don't care."

Her eyes appraised me, full of concern. "I know you're not telling me everything. I wish you would because I have a bad feeling that things are going to get worse for you at home. How can I be there for you when they do if I don't know what's really going on?"

"I swear you know more than anyone. I can't think about it anymore. If I do, I'll have an anxiety attack and that'll open the door for Trey to interrogate me. I don't want that to happen while we're here."

"I realize you're not going to share as much with me in fear I'll slip up and say something to Trey. It's different now that you two are seeing one another. It sucks, but I get it. The one thing I will reiterate is that if you want a future with him, you're going to have to find it in your heart to share at least one of your secrets. If you don't, he won't stick around much longer."

My eyes watered while I thought about all the things I *should* tell him. He deserved to know Sebastian, Miles, and Aubrey's families are running point to get him kicked out of school, but I couldn't bring myself to talk to him about it—not until I knew more about what their plans were.

I wanted to tell Mia about it too and so much more than my discovery this morning, but the words weren't coming and it was probably for the best. Her persistence to get more out of me faded as she gazed around the room. I picked up the blush and resumed my handiwork on her cheekbones.

"Have you gotten any closer to figuring out what's going on with Micah?" I asked, applying a few different shades of eyeshadow to compliment her dark brown eyes and her black Fall Out Boy T-shirt.

"He's involved with some sketchy people for sure and I'm betting whatever he's up to is illegal. He's going to school just enough for his erratic attendance to go unnoticed. I'm not sure how he's slipping in and out, but he's managed to pull it off without anyone saying a word to his parents. I really want to steal his phone and get to the bottom of it, but I haven't brought myself to do it. That's such an invasion of privacy and grounds for breaking up. I don't want to lose him," Mia admitted, her petrified face reflecting her true fear of that happening.

"I don't think you're going to lose him. He's in love with you," I replied, applying the finishing touches to her eyeliner.

She wrung her hands together. "I'm not sure I'd survive without him. It's my fear of losing him that inhibits my actions."

"I totally relate to that much. It's how I feel about Trey. He's got so much sitting on his shoulders as it is. Shedding light on my fucked-up world would make that worse. That's what keeps me quiet," I confessed, adding mascara to her long eyelashes.

"You know he understands the differences there. He wants to help you so badly. His damn temper just interferes whenever he tries to express it to you."

"Exactly. He's still not totally balanced on that front. I know him. He'll take it upon himself to fix matters, and there are just some things in this world you can't fix, no matter how hard you try. You can't change people as cold-blooded as my dad and mom. They have to want to change themselves, but they're too blind to see their own flaws, so they never will."

"I hate that you're right on that front. All we can do is give it our best and hope things become more bearable."

"Sometimes the only thing we can do is ride the wave until it comes to an end and pray we don't fall flat on our face. We're going to graduate in a year and a half. Ninety percent of what plagues my life will be over. I'd rather keep Trey focused on doing his best in school and sports so he can get a scholarship to Eckman."

I took a long lock of her blonde hair and curled it. She fidgeted with the silver bracelets on her wrists. After a few minutes, Mia's curled hair was in a frilly ponytail. She jumped off the counter and pulled me in for a tight hug. I held her close and whispered, "I promise to share more. I don't want Trey to come between us. You're my sister, Mia. I'd be lost without you."

She sniffed. "Ditto, Bri. I'll try harder too."

Wanting to lighten the mood, I swatted her ass. "Go put on some skinny jeans. Send Trey back over here and try not to have sex while you're getting ready. We need to leave soon."

Mia giggled. "I can't make any promises and could say the same to you. See you in a few."

I proceeded to do my own makeup and pulled my hair into a bun. After changing into my Fall Out Boy T-shirt, a fresh pair of jeans, and my black knee-high boots, I was ready to go. Trey was on the bed, his face deep in thought. I sat next to him and ran my hand through his buzz-cut, loving how it prickled across my sensitive skin. He leaned over to kiss me and I got lost in his lips until it was time for us to leave for the concert.

* * *

THE REMAINING BARS OF "DANCE, DANCE" sounded throughout the arena. Trey and I hopped up and down until the song came to a finish. My back rested against his chest. He kissed the top of my head and slowly swayed us. My nerves pulsated in a good way as I soaked in the energy coming from the crowd.

"Thank you, New York City. You guys have been awesome tonight! We're ending the night with a song that will surely get your blood pumping!"

I grinded against Trey as "Sugar We're Going Down" started and loved hearing him groan with each twist of my hips. He whirled me around and thrust his body into mine, a mischievous grin on his face. I laughed, grasped his neck, and shook my head. We weren't having sex here. This place was packed to the brim and I didn't want to lose Micah and Mia. They were off to the right of us, jumping with each beat of the drum and pumping their fists in the air.

Trey rocked his body into me. Heady desires flowed through me and I bit my lip to keep myself from moaning. He tugged on my long locks and I stumbled away from him, praying my mind wasn't really going in the direction it was. Trey gaped at me, shell-shocked, and for good reason. I never reacted that way when he gently pulled my hair, but for some reason, it triggered the one memory I tried to bury deep inside me. It was now unleashed and ready to play out. I closed my eyes and tried desperately to stop it, but it was too late.

* * *

My head feels fuzzy. *I shouldn't have had those shots after playing beer pong. My parents are going to kill me if I don't sober up before this stupid party is over. I blink my eyes and look around. It's really dark and I don't hear the rest of the kids in the guest house anymore.*

I try to sit up, but I'm shoved down. A set of hands keep a firm grip on my forearms. I try to wiggle free but their hold strengthens. Even with the alcohol in my system, the pain shoots down my arms. My heart beats fast against my chest. A knee slides between my legs and I attempt to move again. Wet lips meet mine in a sloppy kiss. I can smell the tequila on his breath and my stomach turns with it. I force my gaze into a solid picture and see Sebastian's face.

"You know you want this, doll. Stop fighting it. You were all over me before we came up here," Sebastian slurs.

"What are you talking about? How did I even get up here? The last thing I remember was doing shots with Poppy," I stammer.

He forces my mouth open with his tongue, his hands drifting to my jeans. He unzips and pushes them down to my thighs. My body tenses and my throat closes. I can't breathe.

"You're going to do this with me right now or I'll ruin your perfect reputation, doll. I'll turn all your friends against you. I'll make your life a living hell until we graduate."

Sebastian drops his body on mine and I can't move. I want to speak, but I can't find any words. I know he really will turn my very fragile world upside down. I'm paralyzed with the terror running rampant through me. This isn't how it's supposed to be. I don't know how to stop him. He's stronger and heavier than me. I try one last time to free my arms and his ironclad grip tightens.

Before I can try a different tactic, he pushes into me and I cry out from the pain. He clasps his hand over my mouth and drives into me harder. I lie there and pray for it to be over soon. Eventually, I don't see or hear him. My mind blanks and the darkness is better than my current misery.

* * *

When I was finally with it again, Trey was staring at me, a terrified look in his wide eyes. I barely could focus mine with the multitude of lights flashing around. I gasped to catch a solid breath. My chest was on fire. It felt like an entirety went by for as deprived as my lungs were right now.

Grabbing my hand, Trey pushed people out of the way on his way toward the exit. Micah and Mia peered at me with concern. Before we were out of the arena, I planted my feet, knowing I had to do something to prevent what was surely going to be a *really* big fight.

"I'm not ready to leave, Trey. Let's stay for the encore," I pleaded.

He whipped around. "It's not up for discussion, Bri. You look like you're ready to pass out. Your anxiety is off the charts. We're going back to the hotel and you're going to tell me what the hell happened for you to space out for almost five minutes."

Trey picked up his pace on our way outside. The sidewalks were covered in snow and I was having a hell of a time keeping up with him. He stormed along even faster. I glimpsed over my shoulder to make sure Micah and Mia were still with us. After seeing them in a heated conversation a good distance behind us, my heart dropped.

"Trey, please slow down. I'm going to break my neck trying to keep up with you."

He swooped down and picked me up. I opened my mouth to tell him to put me down, but he pinned a glare on me that actually frightened me a little. I rested my head against his chest as he weaved his way through the cluttered sidewalk and over to our hotel. I willed my body out of the panicked state it was in as he marched through the lobby.

Trey didn't bother waiting for Mia and Micah. He hit the call button and stepped into the elevator. Thankfully, there were a few people waiting to get on with us and I was more than happy for the buffer, but it was a short-lived reprieve. The elevator came to a stop a minute later and Trey had us down the hallway at a brisk pace.

Once he reached our room, he set me down, swiped the keycard, and held the door open for me. I walked into the bedroom, slid off my coat, and tossed it on the bed. My heart raced about as fast as my nerves tingled—neither of them in a way I preferred.

Trey ran a hand down his face, shrugged off his jacket, and paced around the room before focusing on me, a determined look in his eyes. "I've asked you this so many times and never get a straight answer. Where did your mind wander to, Bri?"

His voice was in that low octave that immediately sent chills down my spine. I sat down at the edge of the bed, rested my elbows on my thighs, and massaged my temples to ease the pressure in my head. "It's late, Trey. I don't want to talk about it now."

Trey banged his hand down on the dresser, nearly knocking the flat screen television on it to the floor. I flinched after seeing his angry face. He wasn't going to let it go. *Fuck!*

"I don't give a shit if you want to talk about it, doll. I can't handle this deafening silence between us any longer. I don't care if either of us sleep. We need to talk about whatever you're bottling up because your growing anxiety and evasiveness isn't good. You're going to have a nervous breakdown soon if you don't let go of some of your pent-up emotions."

I charged over to him and shoved a finger in his face. "I told you not to call me that. If you ever do again, I'll slap you and feel no remorse whatsoever."

He tossed his hands in the air. "Let's start right there. Why does that nickname make you so angry?"

I swallowed against the giant ball in the back of my throat and took a step back. My chest burned as I whispered, "You don't want to know. You'll never look at me the same way again. I don't want to lose what we have by telling you."

Trey gently gripped my hips, his face set in a firm expression. "Bri, I won't look at you any differently, but if you don't start sharing some of the things you're bottling up, you *will* lose me. It's been a twisted role reversal with us and I'm sick of it."

Tears sprang to my eyes. It was like someone had sliced my heart out with the dullest knife in the drawer. His resolute eyes remained fixated on me. He was serious about walking away from me.

I don't have a choice. I can't risk losing him—not when he has my heart. I won't survive the loss.

"Trey, you have to promise me you won't do anything irrational once I tell you. I haven't shared this part of me for a reason. I know you, and you're going to snap. I don't want you to lose control because of something in my past that can't ever be changed," I begged, resting my shaky hands on his rigid shoulders.

"I promise to *try* and not lose my temper. That's the best I can do," Trey replied, taking my hands in his.

"Well, since we're almost a thousand miles from him, it's probably the best place to tell you about my first time."

"I don't want to know what triggered you to think about your first time. I do want to know why it made you lose all sense of reality."

I tugged him over to the bed. He moved to the center of it and I crawled in across from him. My heartbeat was about as erratic as my breathing. "It didn't go the way it should and was with someone I wouldn't have wanted to be with for that milestone." He tilted my chin up, his eyes demanding more. "It was with Sebastian. He called me doll that night. That's why I hate that name so much. I didn't want to have sex, but I didn't say no either, so it was my fault in the end."

Trey's face was hard and his upper body trembled with the rage spilling through him. "Did that motherfucker rape you?"

I shook my head as tears fell down my face. "I was drunk, but I knew what was going on. I didn't say no. I didn't try hard enough to remove myself from the situation. I wasn't exactly with it. I drank too many beers and shots. Like I said, it was my fault."

Trey jumped up and paced around the room. His neck and arms turned as red as his face. He curled his fists together and raised them in the air before bringing them down to his sides. I gasped in spurts of air. Watching him slowly unfold closed off my airway and I prayed he reined in his temper. He focused on me, his beautiful gray eyes broke my heart. There was so much pain behind them I looked away.

"Goddammit, Bri, it wasn't your fault. How can you possibly think that? Did you tell anyone what happened? Any adult with basic common sense would know you were raped. Why do you believe otherwise?" Trey asked, his eyes misty.

I cut him off before he made another lap around the room. I wiped away the tears streaming down my cheeks, rested my hands on his chest, and squeezed until he took a solid breath. He placed his hands over mine. The sorrow on his face shot straight through me and settled in an unbearable ache in my heart. I didn't want him to look at me any differently and that was exactly what he was doing now.

"I told my mom. She said because I didn't say no, it wouldn't matter. And that's true. I never said no to him. The Du Ponts would've aired out what happened in the press. I'm sure part of her answer was to save face."

Trey wiggled his hands free, walked over to the wall, and arched his arm back, but I grabbed onto it. The muscles throughout his body rippled nonstop. I pressed my body against his, hoping it would help calm him, but his rapid heartbeat didn't slow down.

"I'm so sorry that happened to you, Bri. I want to kill Sebastian and your parents. I don't think I can ever be in the same room with any of them. It won't end well if I am."

"Trey, you can't think that way. You're going to see Sebastian all the time. I still hold myself partially responsible for what happened anyway. I shouldn't have gotten that drunk."

"But you tried to stop him. Anyone knows that's enough of a signal. Why don't you see it that way? Why didn't you tell someone else?"

"I don't know what you want me to say. It's over and done with. I can't change that night or the days that followed it. And I did eventually talk to Kelsey."

"Why didn't she do something?" Trey asked, his face furious.

"It wasn't until weeks later. I had been really withdrawn and she finally got it out of me after I had a severe panic attack. I was scared I was pregnant. She took me to the doctor and I wasn't, but that was when I went on birth control and got medication for the anxiety. I know she talked to my parents about all of it, but there was only so much she could do. I'm not her child," I explained, shaking nonstop while tears dripped down my face.

"That jackass could be out there doing the same thing to another girl. For fuck's sake, why didn't anyone even consider that in everything? How could your parents be so heartless?"

"Are you mad at me?"

"No, I'm angry at the whole fucking world right now. I need a minute to process all of this and I can't do that locked up in this room."

He retrieved his jacket from the floor. My heart refused to beat as I watched him lose the last bit of control over his temper. I blocked him from walking out the door, my face begging for him to stay. The muscles in his neck twitched faster than ever.

"I need some air. Please move," Trey requested through gritted teeth.

"Please don't leave me," I pleaded, gasping.

Trey gently picked me up and set me to the side, placed a soft kiss on the top of my head, and marched out the door. I dropped to my knees as the hysterical sobs poured from me. I gave way to them for a minute, hastily got up, and snatched the keycard from the table.

I pounded on Micah and Mia's door. My chest constricted so tightly I struggled for each breath. My heart was splayed wide open and I practically could feel the blood trickling through my body. Mia stepped into the hallway, her eyes wide with concern. Micah followed her out, his face just as worried as hers.

"Bri, what's wrong?"

"It's Trey. He's left the hotel. He's irate. I don't know what he'll do. I need your help. We have to find him before he does something he'll regret."

Micah shoved past me, not bothering to grab his jacket. Everything spun out of control around me. I couldn't catch my breath, sank to the floor, and hugged my knees. The volatile bomb buried deep inside me that had been waiting to go off exploded and ripped away every facet of me. Mia dropped down next to me. She appeared on the blurry side, but I saw the panic in her misty eyes.

"Mia, stay with Bri. See if you can get her to calm down. If she's this freaked out, Trey's going to be lethal with anyone who says the wrong thing to him. I need to find him before that happens!" Micah shouted, jogging down the hallway.

Mia wrapped her arms around me. "Calm down, Bri. Everything will be alright. Micah will find him."

She tucked her arm underneath mine and pulled me up with her. Mia took the keycard out of my trembling hands. I gasped for air and struggled to walk the few feet into my room. Mia guided me over to the bed. I fell into it and curled into a ball. She crawled in behind me and ran her hands up and down my back.

I sobbed into the mattress, hating myself for setting Trey off with something that he could never change or rectify. The pain and pressure subsided as the self-loathing took over. Mia lay down next to me, her eyes begging for an explanation. My breaths became fewer and farther between and the battle to keep my eyes open overpowered every other feeling coasting through my tormented body. The fleeting thought running through my mind before darkness overcame me was I prayed Micah found Trey before he did something terrible.

* * *

SEVERAL HOURS LATER, I sat straight up after feeling fingers trail down my tear-streaked face. Trey was across from me, a hint of a bruise forming around his right eye and his knuckles were scuffed up. The anguished look in his eyes matched my heavily-grated insides. It was like someone tossed me into a cement mixer and walked away for hours before coming back to pull me to the surface.

My hand drifted to his right cheek. "Where did you go? What happened to your hands and face?"

He placed his hand over mine. "I'm sorry for leaving you when I knew you weren't okay. That was really shitty of me. I'm *so* incredibly sorry, Bri. Please say you forgive me."

My eyes watered. "I forgive you for leaving, but don't ever do that to me again. I can't even begin to explain how it felt to have you walk out on me like that, especially with what I told you. I don't think I can handle a repeat of it, Trey."

A single tear trickled down his cheek. I wiped it away with my thumb and gave him a tender kiss as he slid his arm underneath my back. "I'm so sorry. I wasn't angry with you, but I had to walk away to get a hold of the rage bubbling over inside me."

I rested my head on his chest and whispered, "I know. I'm sorry for triggering it."

He cupped my chin, a firm look in his eyes. "Don't apologize. You keep apologizing for things that aren't your fault. Stop it. You've got to stop letting people off the hook when they're shitty to you."

"Please tell me what happened after you left."

"I left with every intention of taking a short walk. I knew the frigid temp would help cool me off. About a mile away from the hotel, I spotted a junkie in an alley pressing himself up against a drunk woman who clearly didn't want him to touch her. My rational side disappeared and I pounded on him until he released the lady. I didn't stop beating on him until Micah showed up minutes later. Micah pulled me out of the angry fog I was in while swinging at that guy."

"I guess it's a good thing the guy was on the wrong side of the law. I doubt he'll report the incident to the police," I forced out.

Trey tensed. "He won't be saying a word to anyone. I probably should've stopped after he released the woman, but all I could think about was how badly you were hurt, and that no one protected you. I want you to know I'll *always* protect you. I need you to tell me something now."

I peeked up at him. "I don't think sharing anything else this weekend is a good idea."

He narrowed his eyes. "I'm not asking you to share anything else. I want you to say it wasn't your fault."

When I remained quiet, he raised an expectant eyebrow. I bit my bottom lip and mumbled, "It wasn't my fault."

His forehead creased. "Now say it like you mean it. You totally said that to appease me. I need to believe you when I hear it."

"It wasn't my fault," I repeated in a firm tone.

"Because it wasn't and you need to remember that much," Trey replied, aggrieved.

The sun poked through the half-drawn curtains, and I gazed at the clock. *Nine*. We needed to get a move on if we were going to hit up the last few places we wanted to see before catching our flight home. I slid out from under him and headed for the bathroom. Before closing the door, I glanced at Trey. His arm was over his eyes and it looked like he was having a talk with himself.

"Trey, are you going to be able to handle yourself when we return home?"

"I'll do my best, but I can't make any promises. You're just going to have to trust me."

That wasn't the answer I was looking for. I doubted he'd ever approach my parents on the subject, but Sebastian was fair game. Trey had even more of a reason to kick the shit out of him. When he unleashed on him, it would be all my fault.

Even though he wanted me to believe that night wasn't my fault, I still did. Now, it was a catalyst for him. My heart quivered from the sharp pains traveling through it. I didn't want to be the reason he ended up ruining his life.

CHAPTER 26

TREY

It was only Tuesday and I was hanging on by a tenuous thread. Hearing Sebastian run his mouth a few rows ahead of me as Mr. White put this week's homework assignment up on the whiteboard wreaked havoc on my limited control. My agitation got the better of me and I snapped my pen in half. Bri passed a pencil over her shoulder, letting her hand linger in mine to help calm me down, and I savored her soft skin before pulling away. My mind drifted to how fast the past two months flew by.

Over our winter break, we didn't see a lot of each other, but I managed to steal her away long enough to give her my Christmas presents. I put together a relaxation package with a bunch of her favorite candies and cookies in jars, along with a variety of candles and aromas, but the custom-made bracelet was my favorite present to give her. It had a simple heart on one side and our names inscribed between infinity circles. The way her eyes lit up when she saw the bracelet was all it took for me to fall even more for her.

The new iPod she got me, along with some concert tickets to some of our favorite local bands, was way too much and I thanked her profusely for them. What shocked me the most was she bought stuff for my parents and the kids. Her kind heart never ceased to amaze me. Knowing what Sebastian did to her made it downright baffling she held on to her lively spirit. Not very many people survived something like that and still found a way to look at the world optimistically.

Her asshole parents took a lot of her time the past two months, making it hard for us to see each other, but we managed to spend New Year's Eve at the Pier. It was the first time since New York that we spent time together without tension in the air. The kiss we shared to ring in the new year was one of our most powerful ones yet.

The last bell of the day rang. I stuffed my book into my bag and waited for Bri to collect her things before walking with her to meet Mia in the hallway. She paced back and forth, her forehead creased, making it clear Micah was on her mind.

I'd been doing my best to get him back on the straight and narrow, but he wouldn't listen to me. Mia was still in the dark with everything, and that was probably for the best with what was on her plate. Valentine's Day was tomorrow and I hoped Micah planned on bringing a smile back to her face because she was miserable most days.

"Will I be seeing you after practice or do you have to head out right away?" I asked, pressing a kiss to her temple.

Bri grimaced. "I'm sorry, babe. I have to attend a rally for my dad. I'd much rather spend time with you, but I can't skip it. If I can get out early, I'll call you for sure."

My mouth quirked into a crooked grin. "I enjoy your late-night phone calls. And don't stress about not being able to get together. You should stick to whatever they want of you tonight. That way we can keep our plans tomorrow."

Her lips curled into a wry smile. "You mean *your* plans. You haven't told me what we're doing yet. I enjoy surprises, but at least help a girl out and tell me what I should wear."

I winked. "Clothing is optional, but if you must wear something, then surprise me. You always look beautiful."

Bri rolled her eyes. "That so wasn't helpful, but I'll make you pay for it tomorrow."

I playfully shoved her toward the girls' locker room. "Looking forward to it. Try not to look so hot on the court. It's distracting. I don't enjoy having people strip the ball from me."

She wiggled her eyebrows. "I can't make any promises. You'll just have to try and focus."

I laughed even harder on my way into my locker room. I quickly changed into my navy-blue mesh shorts and white practice jersey and headed for the courts. Once I reached the gym, I shot around the perimeter while our coaches discussed today's agenda.

After I hit five three-pointers in a row, Shane took the ball from me, a wide grin on his face. "Damn, Trey. You're on a roll. What's got your mojo going?"

I shrugged. "Just feeling it, man. I want to kill the Jaguars on Friday. We're undefeated. I want to keep it that way."

Coach DeSalle patted me on the back. "That's what I like to hear, Trey. We need that positive drive to bring home a championship. With you boys at the helm, I know we can do it."

He called over the team and we huddled up to see what plays we were going to run. I did my best to pay attention, but the girls were on the court next to ours. Bri laughed with the girls as she shot around the key. I loved seeing her so carefree and happy.

About an hour into practice, the hockey team strode through the gym on their way to the weight room. Sebastian stopped in between the courts, pointed at the girls, and made lewd gestures in Bri's direction. What he did to her flashed through my head and bursts of fury shot through my body.

Just as he turned around to keep walking, I threw the basketball at his head, nailing him perfectly. Our power forward was over there and helped him to his feet. Shane picked up the ball and stared at me, his eyes wide with worry. Blood poured from Sebastian's nose, but I didn't give a shit.

Narrowing his eyes, he charged toward me. Sebastian pummeled me to the ground and got in a few good swings, but having my hands cover my head minimized his blows. A couple of guys dragged him away. I got to my feet and wiped off the blood trickling from my nose. My eyes drifted over to the girls' court. Their entire team was gawking at me. Bri's face was full of fear. Mia grasped her trembling hand. Coach Barry was on their sideline, shaking his head in disappointment.

Coach DeSalle handed me a towel. "What the hell was that, Trey?"

I rolled my shoulders to ease the tension in my back. "Justin cut over to that side and I saw an opening to push the ball up court for a quick bucket. I misjudged my throw."

Coach gazed upward while pinching the bridge of his nose. "You have one of the most accurate arms in the state. I'm not buying it, but I didn't see what happened either. I also can't ignore it. You've got Saturday detention this weekend."

Sebastian curled his hands together. "That's fucking bullshit! He threw the ball at me on purpose. My nose is broken!"

His coach jogged over and pulled him away. "That's enough, Sebastian. That language won't be tolerated nor will fighting on school grounds. You've earned yourself Saturday detention as well."

Coach Barry's eyes widened in alarm and so did Shane's. The two of us in a room for four hours was a death sentence. Sebastian's eyes darkened as he mouthed this wasn't the end of it before his coach led him off the court.

I glanced at the girls. Their faces were as white as their practice jerseys. Mia's arm was around Bri, seemingly to keep her upright. Razor-sharp pains slashed through my upper body. The anguish mixed with the anger sweltering inside me and the weight of it all nearly made me collapse.

Coach DeSalle blew his whistle to resume practice. He turned to me, his face still peeved. "Go to the trainer's office to have your cuts taken care of and then get back up here."

The girls returned to their drills. Bri's hands shook and she missed the pass thrown to her. I followed the trainer to the locker room and into his office—not bothering with any small talk. He seemed just as pissed off as Coach DeSalle. My chest constricted as I hopped up on the table and let him examine my nose and jaw. The cuts weren't very deep, so stitches weren't necessary.

After all the blood was cleaned up, I headed out of the room. Instead of going back to the gym, I made my way over to my locker, pulled out a piece of paper, and grabbed a pen.

Bri,
I'm so sorry for screwing up again. I probably sound like a broken record, but I'm trying to be better. Even though I don't deserve it, I'm asking you not to give up on us. You're the best thing that has ever happened to me. The kindness in your soul and your huge heart inspire me more than you'll ever know. From the moment I met you, I just knew you were going to change my life. I had no idea how much until now. You're the shining light in my world that makes me want to be so much more than I am. Someday, I'll be the man you deserve. I promise!
x T

IT WASN'T EXACTLY POETIC, but I needed her to know how much she meant to me. I folded the piece of paper, jogged over to her hallway, and stuffed the note into her locker. I sprinted to the gym to get back to practice.

Once it was over, I showered and tossed on jeans and a T-shirt. With my duffle bag and backpack in hand, I hustled over to the girls' hallway. Mia was on the floor with her knees pulled up to her chest.

I dropped down next to her. "I'm sorry, Mia, but the asshole had it coming."

Mia released a drawn-out sigh. "You're lucky you only got detention out of it."

"Where's Bri?"

"She headed home right after practice."

"Was she still upset?"

Mia avoided eye contact with me. "She didn't say much, but I know she found your note."

I raised an eyebrow. "Did she read it?"

Mia shook her head. "She didn't have a lot of time between practice and the rally."

My upper body trembled as the prospect of truly losing her hit me at full force. By the wary tone of Mia's voice, it sounded like Bri was more than likely pissed at me for being so damn stupid *again*. I rested my heavy head on my knees.

Mia squeezed my shoulders. "She'll read it before the night is over. Don't stress on it."

I rose to my feet and hauled her up. "We should head home. Are you having dinner with us?"

"Yeah, you're going to need someone to run interference with your mom. How are you going to explain your face?" Mia asked on our way through the parking lot.

"The truth. I never threw a punch. Technically it wasn't a fight," I replied, opening my car door.

Her face reflected her skepticism as she hopped in on the passenger side. Even though Mia got her license at the beginning of the year, she still wasn't all that fond of driving. Micah and I pestered her to go car shopping all the time, but she kept pushing it off.

She turned the radio on and gazed out the window. Her rigid body made it clear she wasn't thrilled with what I did to Sebastian either. Part of me wanted to bang the dash, utterly angry with myself, while the other reasoned it wasn't even close to what he deserved for being such a worthless human being. After I pulled out of the parking lot, my cell rang.

"Hey, Mr. West, I was planning on giving you a call on Thursday."

"Shane informed me of what happened at practice. Would you like to share why you felt compelled to give Sebastian a nose job?"

I chewed on the insides of my cheeks to prevent myself from

laughing. The guy had a great sense of humor. My upcoming detention with Sebastian chased away my amusement. Mr. West released an agitated huff and my chest tightened with the sound of it.

"He was making crude gestures toward Bri and I snapped. I'm sorry. I know you expect more out of me. I didn't mean to let you down."

"I've warned you to steer clear of him. How do you plan on handling yourself when you're forced to sit with him for four hours on Saturday?"

I made our turn for the interstate. Mia acted like she wasn't eavesdropping, but her ears perked up on that question. I gripped my cell a little tighter and replied, "I'll keep my distance from him. I'll hang out with the librarian if I have to."

"You shouldn't keep pressing your luck. The faculty and board have a close eye on you. There are several sets of parents on a witch hunt for your expulsion. You know that much. You've been handling yourself so well since September. They don't have anything to make that happen, but this latest incident isn't going to look good. Don't give them the ammunition they need to ruin your life," Mr. West advised in a stern tone.

"I know. I'm very sorry again for pushing things to the limit."

"Do better, Trey. You have all the necessary techniques to control your anger. In the end, it's what you *choose* to do. Start making better choices. There are always going to be people like Sebastian in your life. If you don't figure out how to deal with them now without resorting to violence, you never will. Now, I've checked into what we discussed on our last phone call. I don't think you need to worry about *him*, but he's also someone you don't want to underestimate. Be mindful of that when you're with Brianna."

I glanced at Mia. She was staring at me while fidgeting with her watch, more than confused by the look on her face. I focused on the road and said, "I'll take that under advisement."

"I've got a meeting, so this will have to be one of our shorter chats. Call me Sunday morning and recap how detention goes."

"Will do. I'm sorry again. I'll talk to you in a few days."

Mia opened her mouth, but I pursed my lips together. We rode home in silence. Once we were there, Mia walked into the house ahead of me, and I followed her at a slower pace. She dropped her things near the door and headed to the kitchen to help my mom.

Once I was upstairs, I tossed my bags in my closet and set my phone on my nightstand, then flopped down on my bed and covered my face with a pillow. Hearing the clear concern in Mr. West's voice made my stomach roll. I wasn't so sure if not taking John's threat seriously was solid advice, but he hadn't steered me wrong thus far.

He refused to tell me who the parents were that attempted to get me expelled from Chamberlain. Without a doubt, he was one of the reasons why they weren't successful in making that happen. I just wished he'd tell me who these pricks were so I could confront them. I suspected Sebastian's parents were in the mix, as well as Miles and Aubrey's, but with his insistence to let it be, it felt like there were quite a few others. Regardless, I couldn't confront any of them without something tangible happening to back up my theory. Nothing really serious had happened yet, but I suspected that wasn't going to last much longer.

I massaged my temples in a vain attempt to ease the pressure there. My head was ready to fall off my shoulders with the number of things going through my mind. I closed my eyes and drifted off to sleep.

* * *

"Collide" brought me out of my slumber. I answered my cell in just enough time to catch Bri. My room was pitch-black. I rubbed my sleepy eyes and glanced at the clock. *Midnight.* I stumbled over to flick on the light and the bright rays nearly blinded me. My mom was in here at some point. There was a plate with a couple of ham and turkey sandwiches, a bag sour cream and onion chips, a soda, Neosporin, and some Band-Aids sitting on my desk.

"Hey, babe. How was your night?" I asked, my heart pounding against my chest.

"Oh no, we're not talking about me. Why did you do it?" Bri countered in a sharp tone.

I anxiously ran my hand through my buzz-cut. "He was demeaning you and I couldn't ignore it."

She released a drawn-out sigh. "Trey, how many times do I need to repeat myself? He's not going to stop until he gets rid of you. Why do you keep opening yourself up for that to happen?"

"I'm sorry, Bri. It won't happen again," I replied as icy waves ran through me.

After several minutes of painful silence, she whispered, "I read your note and will cherish your sweet words forever. I'm not going anywhere. I promise."

"I meant every word. I won't keep you up any longer. I have big plans for you tomorrow, so it's important you get some sleep. I'll see you first thing in the morning. Good night, darling."

"Dream of me, sweets," Bri replied softly.

I beamed. "*Always*. You're all I ever dream about, Bri. Now hang up and go to bed."

She giggled. "So demanding. Bye, Trey."

After she hung up, I set my alarms, scarfed down the food my mom left for me, and changed the bandages on my face. I gathered the various dirty clothes around my room and tossed them in a pile near the door. Once I had everything together for school, I crawled back into bed and grinned like a lovesick fool as images of Bri's beautiful body ran through my mind before closing my eyes.

* * *

BUTTERFLIES FLUTTERED IN MY STOMACH, bringing me out of my slumber well before my alarm went off. Bri was the only person who could bring out this kind of nervousness in me. I'd never cared about Valentine's Day in the past, but she deserved the best and I wanted today to be perfect for her. Since it would be a while before the rest of the house was up, I headed for the bathroom to shower and shave. My cuts no longer needed to be bandaged and would probably be healed by the end of the week.

After putting on some cologne and deodorant, I wrapped the towel around my waist and poked my head into the boys' and girls' rooms. Once their school outfits were set on their beds and all their dirty clothes were in the hamper, I returned to my room and got dressed in my uniform.

I snatched a couple of the smaller things I got for Bri, stuffed them into my bag, and trotted downstairs. The first floor wasn't too much of a mess. I cleaned up all of the toys, books, and games scattered between all the rooms. I got everything back in their respectful places before checking the kids' bags to make sure their homework was in them.

Once they were ready to go, I headed for the kitchen to get some tea brewing for my mom and a pot of coffee for my dad. It was one of the rare days he didn't take off before the crack of dawn. He always enjoyed spending a little extra time in the morning with my mom on Valentine's Day.

I popped my headphones in, cranked the first song on my playlist, and darted around the kitchen to grab my ingredients. It took a couple of trips between the fridge and pantry to gather eggs, a loaf of bread, a box of pancake mix, a bag of potatoes, packages of bacon and sausage, and a variety of fruit. I quickly diced up the apples, strawberries, and oranges before putting them in large bowls and setting them on the dining room table.

As I peeled the potatoes, my parents strolled into the kitchen with their hands clasped together. I stopped peeling and dicing, pulled out my earbuds, and poured their morning brews. They sat down on stools at the large island, sharing the same quizzical looks.

"I hope I didn't wake you up. Breakfast should be ready by the time the kids get up. They're all set for school between clothes and backpacks," I explained in a rush.

Dad gestured to the feast behind me. "Are you a little nervous for your first Valentine's Day with a girl?"

I rolled my eyes. "Not at all. I just thought I'd help out this morning since I won't be around tonight."

Mom stood up, rubbed a hand over her growing belly, and refilled her cup. She eyed me carefully, a mother's intuition lingering on her face. When her stare lingered on my cuts, I went back to dicing up food. She pulled out a skillet, put some oil in it, and deposited handfuls of potatoes into the oil.

"I know whatever you do for Bri, she'll love it. That's simply how it works when someone is head over heels in love with you," Mom murmured.

I released a nervous chuckle. "I'm not so sure about that, but I'm pretty sure she'll like what I have planned."

Mom shook her head, but couldn't help but smile. I took the spatula out of her hand. "Please sit down. You two hardly ever get to enjoy breakfast without chasing after whatever the little ones are shouting for as they eat. I've got this morning covered."

She squeezed my cheek. "This is very sweet of you. Thank you, dear."

I stirred the potatoes and got pans of sausage and bacon going. I began cracking eggs and mixing batter up. My folks snuck in kisses as they fed each other strawberries. By the time, I finished getting their plates ready and slid them over, the sun started to rise.

"I think we'll have another athlete on our hands, Terrence. This boy sure does have a swift kick. It reminds me of when I was carrying Treahbar." She gazed at me, a loving look in her eyes. "You kicked like crazy. I thought for sure you'd play soccer."

Dad's eyes had a twinkle to them as he rested his free hand on her stomach and gave her a bite of his food. My jaw was still on the floor. A playful grin curled up on Mom's face. "Did I forget to mention we're having a boy?"

I rounded the island and gave them a big hug. "Congrats, you guys. That's great news. Got any names picked out?"

"I like Trevor, but your mom is fond of Tighe. Whatever we don't use this time, we'll use on the next one," Dad murmured with a wink.

He finished off his scrambled eggs and put his empty plate in the dishwasher. I filled up a plate for myself and sat across from Mom. Dad strode back over to give her a tender kiss.

"Thanks for breakfast, Trey. Have fun with Bri tonight." He leaned into my ear. "I don't know what scuffle you got into yesterday, but I'm not oblivious either. Please be the young man we know you can be and stay out of trouble. You've been doing so good lately. Don't make us question our judgment. We meant what we said about doing whatever it takes to give you a good future."

He walked out the back door without another word. I rotated my shoulders to loosen the knots in my back. Mom gobbled up the rest of her plate and rested her elbows on the island while finishing off her tea. The ceiling shook and it sounded like a herd of elephants running around upstairs.

"I'm going to check on them. Thank you for doing all of this, my boy." She pressed a kiss to my cheek. "Please try harder for all of us. We need you around here. I love you very much, Treahbar."

I still had a decent amount of food in front of me, but I wasn't all that hungry. Guilt settled into a deep pit in my stomach. I forced a couple of more bites down, placed our dirty dishes in the dishwasher, and got another batch of food ready.

A half hour later, Mom ushered the kids downstairs. I helped her feed them before heading out the door. Going to Chamberlain without Mia was weird, but Micah insisted on taking her today. I'd grown so accustomed to her crankiness and sarcasm in the mornings that the Acura had a deafening silence to it until I flicked on the radio.

When I pulled into the parking lot, I checked for Bri's Lexus, but didn't see it. Hopefully, Mia was here and could help me with my first surprise. I grabbed my bags from the backseat and made my way toward the school. After seeing Sebastian and his lackeys at my usual entrance, I opted for a different set of doors.

The chill in the air coasted through my body. I blew on my hands and picked up my pace. After walking through the underclassman's side of the school, I finally hit the girls' hallway. Mia was at her locker, a dreamy look on her face. Micah obviously started the day off right with her. She spotted me, ran down the hall, and shoved her wrist at me so fast she almost hit my jaw.

"Look at what Micah gave me," Mia said, practically bouncing from her excitement.

I eyed the diamond bracelet and noted the matching earrings. The Fitzpatricks were definitely paying him well. "Very nice, Mia. It looks like he's pulling out all the stops today. You deserve it. And thanks for helping out last night."

She waved it off. "It's second nature, Trey. You don't have to thank me. Micah took me out for breakfast before school and promised it was just the beginning of his plans for the day. I'm excited to have him stick to a plan. It's been a while. He's been so evasive with his whereabouts when he shows up late."

My face remained impassive. It wasn't my place to tell her what Micah was actually up to these days. She'd figure it out eventually and I'd be there for her, but I wasn't going to be the one to reveal the truth and break her heart in the process.

I pointed at Bri's locker. "Can you help me? I know you have her combination."

Mia quickly fiddled with the dial and opened it. I sifted through my backpack to grab the jar of chocolate kisses, custom-made teddy bear, photo pendant, and a single red rose. After arranging them on her top shelf, I faced Mia.

"Looks like you didn't do too bad yourself. Bri's going to love everything."

"Thanks, Mia. I'm going to head out before she gets here."

She crinkled her eyebrows. "You're not going to wait for her?"

I winked. "Nope, I'd rather watch from a distance. I'll see you later."

I sauntered down to where the hallway intersected with another one and leaned against the wall. A few minutes later, Bri strode down the hall, looking as radiant as ever. She almost made me not hate the uniforms around here. No one pulled off the navy and light blue plaid skirt and white blouse combo like she did. Mia skipped over to her. Judging by how fast her lips moved, she was talking a mile a minute while showing off her new jewelry. Bri raised her eyebrows and said something that made Mia giggle before opening her locker.

Her eyes grew wide as she took in her presents. The serene look on her face while she smelled the flower and took out the teddy bear made my heart rate skyrocket. After picking up the necklace, her mouth curled into an adorable smile. I made my way in between the lovers and haters and over to her.

"Happy Valentine's Day, Bri," I said, kissing the top of her head.

She threw her hands around my neck and kissed my cheek. "Thanks, Trey. I can't even begin to tell you how much I love all of it, especially the photo pendant. That was one of my favorites of us at the Empire State Building. I have something for you, but was planning on giving it to you tonight. Are you still going to keep the details of the evening to yourself?"

I smirked. "My lips are sealed. I'm glad you like everything so far. As you know, I'm not an expert with this stuff. I'm happy it's up to par."

Bri lowered her hands to my back, her green eyes full of passion. "You're a lot better than you think. In fact, you've raised the bar in more than a few areas."

Her husky tone and flirtatious bat of the eye had my dick hard in an instant. "I know what you're trying to do. Your amazing mouth can do a lot of things, but it's not going to get those details out of me. As much as I'd love to start the day out with some hot and sweaty sex, I'd rather not risk it."

She faked a pout. "Fine, but that doesn't mean I won't wear you down. I'm pretty good at getting what I want."

I kissed her forehead. "Yes, you are. I'll let you ladies have your usual morning time and will see you in English Comp."

Bri squeezed my sides before giving me a playful shove. The trail of heat it left behind made it difficult for me to walk away. I strolled up the stairs to my hallway and over to my locker. The fresh coat of paint on it was all I needed to see to know Sebastian stopped by between last night and this morning to put up his *'gutter punk'* message.

I heaved in a deep breath to keep the friendly fire Bri created from swirling into an angry inferno. Coach Murray and Headmaster Carlton strode past me, a darkening look to their eyes. The pit in my stomach that grew by the day led me to believe that this social class warfare was about to escalate very soon. Everything so far was child's play. When they took it to the next level, I wasn't so sure I'd walk away on the winning end of that battle and that scared the shit out of me.

CHAPTER 27

TREY

School and basketball practice moved so fucking slow, I had a hard time maintaining my patience, especially after finding out Mia, Shane, and Bri got issued Saturday detention. They all mouthed off at some point, but I knew exactly why they did it. I appreciated them looking out for me, but I didn't want them to keep getting into trouble just to protect me from myself.

I pushed my heavy legs forward and out to the parking lot. Bri left right after practice to go home and get ready. The minute I spotted Mia standing stock-still, her face ashen, a sickening ache settled in my gut and I raced over to her.

When I neared my car, my body was ready to burst with the rage overtaking it. The driver's side window was smashed in and it had been keyed up pretty bad. I opened the door and picked up the brick wrapped in paper.

You brought this on yourself, trailer trash. Take a hint and go back to the double-wide before someone you care about gets hurt.

Heat poured from my exposed cheeks and hands. I looked around to see where the bastard was, but only saw a couple of terrified freshmen and sophomores. My grip on the brick intensified and I was close to tossing it at one of the many fancy cars around us. Mia took the paper from me, muttered several curse words under her breath while reading it, and got in on the passenger side. I brushed away the broken glass from the doorframe and my seat before getting in.

I banged the dashboard and revved the engine. A few kids slid across the icy lot and scurried for their cars. Mia's eyes grew wide as she watched the hand I had on the stick shift curl into a tight fist. She rested her hand over mine and squeezed it.

"I'm so sorry, Trey. I don't know what else to say. There aren't really words when something this shitty happens."

My face hardened. "It's taking everything inside me to drive straight home and not over to his house and return the brick in a similar fashion. I'm so tired of these rich pricks getting away with anything. I don't understand how we can live in a world where so many people can turn a blind eye to it."

Pressing the clutch, I threw the car into first gear before peeling out of the lot. My grip on the wheel grew tighter with each passing street. Snowflakes poured through the broken window and the frigid February air engulfed the car. With the rage sweltering inside me, it didn't faze me in the least, but Mia shivered, so I blasted the heat.

All I saw was red in front of me. I tried a few different breathing techniques to regain control over the fury blistering inside me, but it was a feeble attempt. A few snowflakes hit my face and left a cool trail down my cheeks. I willed it to go even deeper within me.

Mia flicked on the radio, blew on her hands, and pulled out her phone. Her fingers flew across the screen before she said, "Micah is going to meet us at your house and help you replace the window. You guys should be able to get it done without it throwing off your plans with Bri."

"I appreciate his help, but I don't want it to interfere with your night. A piece of cardboard and duct tape will work for a few days."

"It won't mess up our evening. It's still pretty cold out and you can't drive around without a window. I don't want you to end up getting sick. That wouldn't be good for you or your family."

A miniscule smile spread across my face. "I'm sure I can live through a case of the sniffles. You worry too much, Mia."

"I worry because I care, Trey. Micah does too. I think you should know that by now, but sometimes I wonder," Mia replied, trying to contain her scowl, but not doing a very good job.

"Can you do me a favor?"

Mia arched an eyebrow. "It depends."

I sucked in a quick breath. "Please don't mention any of this to Bri. I don't want her to obsess over it. We both know she's got enough to handle. If she hears about the threat, she's going to go off the walls trying to figure out who's pulling Sebastian's strings."

She twisted her hands together in her lap. "I don't like keeping things from Bri, but you're right. I'll keep it to myself, but I don't like being put in this position. I've explained this to her as well."

"I'm sorry to ask. I don't like putting you in an awkward position any more than I like keeping things from Bri. I'm just trying to do what's best for her. I don't want her getting tangled up in this social class warfare with Sebastian."

"Trey, she's dating you. She's already a part of it."

A piercing pain shot through my heart. "Well, I'm trying to keep her out of it as much as possible."

Mia nodded before looking out the window. We listened to sappy songs on the radio for the duration of the ride. When I pulled into my driveway, Micah was in the garage with a sheet of glass and all the necessary tools. He opened Mia's door and gave her a swift kiss. She walked across the icy path to our back door and disappeared through it.

Micah ran his fingers along the key marks, some dents I didn't see until now, and released a disgruntled huff. "Looks like we'll have our work cut out for us. It's going to take some serious wrench time to get it back to the way it was."

"Come spring, I'd rather work on the Camaro. We can touch up the Acura, but something tells me it'll just keep happening."

He rolled his shoulders, popped the hood, and unplugged the battery. I tossed my bags by the door before kneeling by my door with a screwdriver. Once all the bolts were off, I pulled off the trim cover, window controls, and brushed away the shattered glass.

"I'm guessing you're not going to tell your folks about this, right?" Micah asked, grabbing a wrench.

I kept my eyes from him and removed the door panel. "Nope. It's not like they can do anything about it. There's no point in worrying about them when they got enough going on."

Crouching down next to me, Micah removed the window regulator. We picked up the fragments of glass within it. Micah spotted the crumbled paper and brick on the passenger side. After he read the note, his face turned bright red.

"If you continue to keep this stuff to yourself, it's only going to get worse. This promises that much, Trey. I think you're in a little deeper than what you believe. It looks like this rich prick is going to take it to the next level soon. People like him won't hesitate to off you and make it seem like an accident."

I grabbed a rag from the workbench and wiped off my hands. "Micah, there are plenty of people, rich and poor, that could pull that off. I think you work for some of them."

"Don't start that shit. I don't want to fight with you about it anymore. You've said your piece and I've heard you out. Just let it go already," Micah snapped, his face furious.

I waved the white drop cloth around in the air. "Fine. Let's get this finished up so we can get ready for our dates. Where are you taking Mia?"

Micah eyed the track carefully before lowering the new window. Once it was properly in place, he secured the mounting plate. "We're going to the Signature Room. Even though she's been to the Observatory plenty of times, she's never been to that restaurant. The menu looks pretty good and the view is awesome. Afterwards, I'm taking her over to the Garfield Park Conservatory. It's not my thing, but I hear it's romantic. That's all that matters."

I let out a low whistle from behind the hood and reconnected the battery. "Sounds like a great evening. Are you planning on crashing down there?"

"I'd like to, but with it being the middle of the week, there's no way it'll fly. Your mom and mine have made it hard for us to spend a whole night alone together," Micah replied, securing the door trim and reattaching the window controls.

He hopped inside, cranked the ignition, and tested out the window. Seeing it move seamlessly up and down, Micah shut off the car a minute later, got out, and grabbed a rag. He rested his elbows on top of the Acura while wiping some grease from his hands.

I closed the hood. "Yeah, I hear you there. I think the last time I spent the whole night with Bri was when we were in New York. As much as my mom made me promise you and I were sharing a room together, she's not an idiot. She's put an end to sneaking out after curfew."

Micah chuckled. "You'd think they'd loosen up a little. If we haven't impregnated the girls by now, we're probably not going to, which means we were paying attention to the sex talk."

Mom popped up out of nowhere and decked Micah upside the head. He wheeled around, rubbing the spot she struck. His face turned beet-red. A loving yet irritated look entered her eyes and she shook her finger between the two of us.

"I'll be happy to revisit *the talk* with both of you. You're way too young to be running off till all hours of the night with Mia. You better have her back here before midnight," Mom said sternly to Micah. She narrowed her eyes on me. "The same goes for you. I don't want to find Bri in your bedroom past twelve ever again. It won't end well for either of you."

Micah backpedaled toward his Mustang parked on the street. "I'll drop Mia off before then. I need to head home and shower. Please let her know I'll be back within the hour to pick her up."

Her gaze flickered between me and the Acura, a worried look spread across her face. She rubbed her hands together and placed them on the bulge of her belly.

I picked up my bags. "I should get a move on. I promise to be home before curfew."

"You better be. The dynamic in this household is going to shift soon. I need you to be smart with the choices you make. You need to think about your little brothers. They look up to you and believe whatever you do is okay. Having sex in the house isn't setting a very good example."

"We weren't even doing anything the night Bri snuck in. She needed a break from her house and came here. We studied and that's it. Next time, I'll make sure she uses the front door."

Her face became more concerned before she said, "If there's something serious going on with her at home, you know you can come to me about it, right? She should know she can come to me too."

I helped her across a piece of ice and opened the back door for us. Before heading into the kitchen, I picked up the salt bag on the side of the house and dumped some on the slick path. Mom had a careful eye on me as I tugged off my Cubs stocking hat and unzipped my jacket. I pulled out a stool for her, grabbed the kettle, and poured her a cup of tea.

"I really need to get ready. I promise to be smarter around the kids. I love you, Mom," I said, handing her the warm mug and kissing her cheek.

"I love you too, Treahbar. I don't want you to be late. We'll revisit this conversation soon," Mom murmured, giving my hand a squeeze.

I took the stairs two at a time and went straight to the bathroom. Once the water was nice and hot, I slid off my sweatpants and stripped off my sweat soaked T-shirt. After taking one of my fastest showers yet, I wrapped a towel around my waist, slapped on some deodorant and cologne, and headed to my room.

My dark blue faded jeans and light blue button-down were on the back of my desk chair and I quickly changed into them. After fastening a black and royal blue tie around my neck, I brushed away the water droplets in my buzzed hair and shoved my cell and the jewelry box into my front pocket. My phone vibrated and I pulled it out while walking downstairs.

Bri: Alright, Romeo, you can't withhold the location any longer. I'm on the way. Tell me where I'm going.

Trey: Valet your car at Lincoln Park West Garage. I'll collect the ticket and you in about twenty minutes.

Bri: So stubborn!! Why won't you just tell me where we're having dinner?

Trey: Because I enjoy torturing you! ;)

Bri: Grr!!! Yes, you do! I shall be retaliating very soon.

Trey: Looking forward to whatever you want to do to me, darling! You never disappoint. See you in a few. x T

Bri: Drive careful, sexy! x B

I strolled through the kitchen to pick up my bomber jacket and headed through the chaos in the living room. Mom blew me a kiss and returned to helping the girls with their homework. I patted Thomas and Tory on the head and held up a finger to my mouth so they'd keep their bickering down. They rolled their eyes, but heeded the warning. I picked up a few toys before walking out the door.

It didn't take long to drive through the semi-snowy roads and over to the florist to pick up Bri's bouquet and an overly-expensive chocolate box. Thankfully, the line wasn't too bad and I was back onto the freeway in no time.

I pulled into the parking ramp and found a spot a row away from her. Judging by the grim expression on her face, she was on the peeved side as she texted on her cell. I grabbed her gifts and slowly made my way over to her Lexus. With flowers and chocolates behind my back in one hand, I tapped on her window with the other. Bri dropped her phone and clasped her hands over her chest. A drool-worthy smile fell from my lips and I opened her door with my free hand.

"It's way too easy to do that to you," I remarked, chuckling.

Bri rolled her eyes and shoved her cell in her large purse. "You enjoy doing it way too much."

"That I do. These are for you," I murmured, giving her the lilies and candy.

After she sniffed the flowers, her mouth spread into a sweet smile.

"This is so thoughtful, but way too much, Trey. You have to stop spending money on me."

"It's not nearly enough, Bri. It never is when it comes to you."

She pulled one of the pink and white lilies from the bouquet and put it behind her ear before setting the flowers and the chocolates in her backseat. Bri slid her arm around mine on our way onto the street. Snowflakes swirled above us and we leaned closer together while watching drivers navigate their way through the slick streets.

Five minutes later, we were in front of Geja's Café. Bri stared at me with her jaw ajar. I ran my fingers under it, kissed her cheek, and ushered her inside. We stopped at the hostess—*Megan*. Her face was a cross of managing the Valentine's Day frenzy in the restaurant or bolting through the door.

"Reservation for Donovan."

Megan scanned through her black book and paused once she reached my name. She tucked her unruly brown hair behind her ears, checked her watch, and picked up two menus. "You're right on time. That's appreciated. This way please."

We stopped long enough to check our coats and followed her to the corner of the restaurant. The ambiance was perfect for the day of love. The lighting was nice and low. After hearing the quartet playing, Bri gave me a shy smile. Grasping her hand a little tighter, I flashed my dimples. Small candles on top of maroon tablecloths brought out the twinkle in couples' eyes. I couldn't help but notice that everything around me was some shade of red or pink—right down to the flatware and dishes.

Bri looked absolutely stunning in a sleek-fitting red dress with large armholes and a deep V on both the front and back of it. Her curled hair fell over her shoulders and that familiar vanilla scent was hard to miss. My body pulsated in the best possible way and I took another whiff of it.

"You look gorgeous, Bri. I can't wait to take that dress off later," I whispered, pulling out her chair.

A deep blush settled between her neck and cheeks. I gave her a mischievous smirk and sat down across from her. Megan handed us our menus and briskly returned to the front to handle the growing crowd. Bri scanned over the menu for a minute before setting it at the edge of the table. She scrunched her eyebrows together while fidgeting with her charm bracelet and picking away at the different shades of pink on her fingernails. I arched an eyebrow for her to tell me what was on her mind.

"This place is amazing, Trey, but it's really expensive."

"Enough, Bri. You've made your thoughts known. It's my money and I'll use it how I wish," I declared, sliding my finger down the menu. "Do you want to get the beef and lobster or the beef and shrimp? The deluxe seafood platter looks pretty good too."

Her face hardened as she shot back, "I won't be silenced by you. I get enough of that at home. I don't like you spending this much on me when it should be going to other things."

My head snapped up and I set down the menu. "I'm sorry, Bri. I didn't mean for it to come across that way. I make plenty of cash over the summer working for my dad and at odd jobs around the neighborhood. The money I choose to spend now isn't even from my college savings."

"Apology accepted, Trey. I think I'd be more comfortable if we started splitting things going forward. I work during the summers too," Bri pointed out, a tiny grin teasing her succulent lips.

A waiter in black pants and a white shirt with Valentine's Day buttons came to our table. He filled up our water glasses and set down a bowl of cheese fondue and assorted breads and crackers. A few more people from the waitstaff showed up with gourmet dipping sauces and a variety of chips and breadsticks. When the head waiter's stare lingered a little too long on Bri, I kissed the top of her hand and shot him a fierce glare to look elsewhere.

His gaze shifted to the center of the table. "Sir, what will you be having today?"

I gestured for Bri to place our order. She handed over our menus. "We'll have the beef tenderloin and jumbo shrimp with the assorted veggies that come with it and two Cokes."

"We'll get your order in, miss. Enjoy your fondue and sauces."

I sliced off a piece from the multi-colored bread, dipped it in the cheese fondue, and offered a bite to Bri. She nibbled on the edge and licked her lips in appreciation once she was done. I took a larger portion than her and savored the delightful flavors dancing on my tongue. Bri cut up some more for us. I soaked it in some cheese and took half of it down.

"So, what do you do during the summer for work?"

"I lifeguard and teach swimming lessons for part of the time."

"And the other half of it?"

"Mia and I help out with the basketball and soccer camps hosted by a couple of different suburbs around Chamberlain. It sucks getting up early, but I love seeing the smiles on the kids' faces when they learn how to dribble a ball on the field and on the court. I also babysit for extra cash."

I dipped a chip in a spinach looking sauce and joked, "People trust you with their kids? You're always so skittish around my brothers and sisters when you're over."

She feigned outrage and rebutted, "Watch it, smartass. I'm actually pretty good with them. Your siblings have been the exception."

"They've grown quite fond of you in the past month," I remarked, picking up another chip and trying a reddish sauce this time.

Bri giggled. "Bribery will do that."

I chuckled and dabbed a piece of bread into the spinach sauce. My amusement faded when the hairs on the back of my neck stood up. I glanced around the restaurant to see if anyone was watching us because that was exactly what my body told me. Bri tapped on the top of my hand to grab my attention.

My fingers itched to rub my wraparound tattoo, but I refrained from doing so. "True. They stopped treating you like a pariah and playing pranks on you after getting their Christmas presents. What else keeps you busy during the summer?"

Her eyes flickered around to try and gauge what had gotten under my skin. I gave her a bite of my bread to distract her. The savory sauce brought a beautiful smile to her face, ceasing the chills running down my back.

My lips spread into my signature smirk and she blushed on cue. Bri shook her head a few times to get rid of what was sure to be a dirty thought. "Mia and I are attending two elite Nike camps. The one for soccer is in Tallahassee and the basketball one is in Baltimore. Both will be for a week and on college campuses. They're highly recommended. Hopefully we pick up some new tricks. I'd like to finish high school on a high note and win some more championships."

I raised an eyebrow. "Sounds pretty prestigious. How come Mia hasn't mentioned it?"

She swiped a chunk of bread into the fondue. "I think she's unsure about being away from Micah for two different weeks. I know she's going to go. Our coaches have already sent off the paperwork for us."

"That's not surprising. She's never spent that much time away from him."

"Exactly. The camps we attended in the past were local. Since they've become a couple, she hasn't been too keen on going on any vacations with me."

"I'm sure she would. Any trips planned for this summer?"

"I haven't thought that far ahead. Usually, I have something in mind, but I'm sure I'll be spending time on the campaign trail, which will suck. Hopefully, I can get away at some point."

Seeing the doubtful look on her face made my heart drop. My lips spread into a reassuring smile before I said, "I'm sure you will. You seem to have a knack for it."

Bri gave me a half-hearted grin. "A lifetime of doing it kind of has made me an expert. Well, it's that and having a staff around the house that adores me and despises my parents. What are your plans for the summer?"

The waiter returned with our sodas. Before heading back to the kitchen, he refilled our bread and chip baskets. I took a sip of my Coke. "We'll get to those in a minute. I have a much more important event that I wanted to talk to you about."

She crinkled her eyebrows and the adorable crease in her forehead that made an appearance when I confused her was prominent. "What's that exactly?"

"I figured you would already have this particular milestone on the brain. It's a tad shocking you're at a loss on it." Bri narrowed her eyes for me to get to the point. My grin grew even wider. "Prom is a couple of months away, but from what I've gathered from Mia, you girls need to start looking for dresses soon. So, Ms. McAndrews, I was wondering if you'd do me the great honor of being my date?"

Her mouth spread into a shy smile. "It'd be my pleasure, Mr. Donovan."

I reached into my pocket, pulled out the jewelry box, and slid it over to her. "Perfect. I was thinking you could wear this that night."

Bri opened it and gasped after seeing a necklace with tiny diamonds around it. Inside of the two circles in the center of it there were two hearts intertwined together. The top one had my name on it and the bottom one had hers.

I pointed to the two diamonds at the crease of the hearts. "Ironically, both our birth months allow for two different birthstones. I picked peridot for you. It symbolizes great strength and I've never met anyone as strong as you. The other one is opal. Seeing as you're always telling me I'm moody, I figured this one suited me. Every stone is one of a kind. It seemed fitting."

She wiped her misty eyes, moved the candle out of the way, and planted a deep kiss on me. When my head became fuzzy, I swayed away. She heaved in a breath, pulled out her purse, and removed a medium-sized box. I truly wondered how big that bag really was because it seemed bottomless most days.

Her eyes sparkled as she whispered, "That was so thoughtful of you, Trey. Thank you so much. Can I wear it before prom, though? It's already easily my favorite piece of jewelry." I nodded, a pleased smile on my face. She pushed the wrapped present my way. "This is for you. With all the things you've done for me today, it doesn't seem like nearly enough, but hopefully I can make it up to you in other ways."

A salacious grin curled from her mouth and made me chuckle while I unwrapped her gift. My favorite baked goodies were in different bags at the bottom. My eyes bugged out upon seeing the autographed Greg Maddux baseball. I gaped at Bri, utterly speechless.

She picked up an envelope and gestured for me to open it next. My heart stopped beating after I saw an original Frank Chance circa 1909 baseball card. A Certificate of Authenticity accompanied it."

"Bri, this is *way* too much. I can't keep it," I choked out, still baffled.

"I can't take it back. Besides, it'll be great for your Cubs baseball card collection."

She picked up the remaining box and placed it in my shaky hands. I was still processing the fact I was now the owner of a very rare card. I unclasped it and saw a sterling silver chain with the number twelve covered in diamonds at the bottom of it. My jaw dropped as I stared at her in disbelief.

"I know you don't wear any bling on the football field or on the basketball court, but I thought it'd be nice to wear your number in between seasons," Bri said softly.

Two waiters showed up with several plates. As they arranged them on the table, I put everything back in the box. My mouth watered from the different aromas coming from the plates. After replenishing our water glasses, the waiters turned to check on other guests. I grabbed a knife, cut through the tenderloin, and put a piece of it on Bri's plate. She clutched her fork and shoveled some vegetables and shrimp onto my plate before filling up her own.

I stabbed the beef. "Thank you for everything, Bri. I really wish you wouldn't have spent so much. I know your parents cut you off. That had to have been almost all your extra money. You should've saved that for yourself."

Bri finished chewing the buttered-up shrimp she popped into her mouth. "They may have, but my grandparents didn't. In fact, they've been more of a presence lately—and not just financially."

I cocked an eyebrow. "I thought your grandparents were dead. How come you haven't mentioned them before today?"

My sharp tone made her flinch. Bri swallowed her steak and grasped my hand. "On my dad's side, they are, but not on my mom's. You know I don't like talking about my family. It puts us both in a bad mood."

I scowled. "That's not a good enough reason anymore. It's a pretty big shift for you, so you should've told me."

"They've been around a lot more since the beginning of the year. They contribute to his campaign and like to see where their money is going. It drives my dad up the wall to have them involved, but he can't afford to cut them out either. He needs the status they bring to the table."

"So, your grandparents are giving you money? Are they stepping in anywhere else?"

Her face fell. "If you're asking if they've gotten my dad to back off, the answer is no. He always finds a way to corner me alone and get some sort of tongue-lashing in. It's just a little less frequent than it was this fall."

The tight grip I had on my fork made my knuckles turn white. I flexed my fingers to ensure I didn't bend the utensil.

Bri ran her hand along the inside of my arm. "Don't let my situation get the best of you. My dad hasn't really lost it on me in months. I thought for sure after New York, I was in for it, but he didn't even bring it up. If he hasn't by now, I doubt he will. He's far too busy with the campaign."

I forced a smile for her. She finished off the meat on her plate and moved it aside. I polished off what was left of mine and did the same. The waitstaff returned with chocolate fondue, tiny pretzels, marshmallows, biscotti, and a variety of fruit and bread. The lead waiter handed me the bill and I set it off to the side.

Part of me wanted to grill her for more details about things at home, but I didn't want to sour the evening any more than I already had with my growing nerves. An icy chill ran up my back and I couldn't ignore it. As discreetly as possible, I gazed around again, but didn't see anyone or anything out of the ordinary. My willpower to not trace my wraparound tattoo disappeared and I anxiously rubbed it until my unease was somewhat under control.

Thankfully, Bri didn't notice. I intended to keep her distracted and picked up a strawberry, dipped it in chocolate, and offered it to her. The corners of her mouth curled into a naughty smile and I didn't need to ask where her mind drifted to. It wasn't the first time I fed her fruit or covered her luscious lips in chocolate. Once we gave everything a try and our stomachs were more than stuffed, I tossed cash down on the table to settle the bill.

On our way up front, Bri's body stiffened and she picked up her pace. When we got to the coat check, there was a line of people ahead of us. She fidgeted nonstop while eyeing the door.

I held her hips and asked, "What's going on, Bri? I know how long it takes you to do your nails and you've scratched off nearly half the paint on them in the last minute."

The color in her rosy cheeks faded and she looked away. I gently brought her face back to me and narrowed my eyes for an answer. Her lower lip quivered before she mumbled, "I don't think it's a very good idea for me to say anything here."

I glanced around to see who shook Bri to the core. There really was a set of eyes on us this evening. After several scans around the restaurant, I didn't spot anyone I recognized. My face flamed and I curled my hands into tight fists. She ran her trembling fingers down my arms to calm me, but couldn't hide her own anxiety. I caressed the small of her back so she'd start breathing evenly.

"Please tell me what you saw. If you don't, you're going to end up having an attack," I requested through clenched teeth.

The line ahead of us moved and only a few more couples needed their jackets. Bri took several shaky breaths and said, "Sebastian's parents are here, along with a few other people I know. It's just a little unnerving to have them end up at the same restaurant as us. That's all."

All the food I consumed pressed upwards. I swallowed against the bile and asked in a heated whisper, "Who else is here that you know?"

"Miles and Aubrey's parents are with them. Don't put too much thought into it, Trey. They go out as a group all the time. Usually, my parents are in that mix, but they're at a gala in D.C. Let's just focus on the rest of our night and be grateful my dad's security isn't here to harass us," Bri replied, doing her best to appear calm, but failing miserably when she twisted her hands together.

"You never mentioned your parents still spent time with that lot of people. That information would've been good to know. I can't help but wonder what else you might be holding back," I snapped, handing over our tickets to collect our coats.

Bri gazed away while clutching herself tightly. My mind and heart raced together as I tried desperately to determine if it was a coincidence the people more than likely planning my demise happened to show up at the restaurant I chose or if there was more to it. I ran a hand through my buzz-cut, slid over a tip, and took our jackets from the attendant.

The weight in the center of my chest shifted to my heart. I suspected Bri had more to share when it came to that group of people, but I wasn't going to push her—not with the way her body still trembled. All I wanted to do was bring back her gorgeous smile. I pulled her off to the side of the door, tilted her chin up, and pressed my lips against hers for a deep kiss.

After she caught her breath, her eyes watered. "Trey, I'm sorry. You've done all these wonderful things..."

I clamped her mouth shut. "Don't you dare apologize, Bri. I'm sorry I let my temper rear its ugly head. Let's get out of here. Those rich pricks aren't ruining our evening. We can talk about them another day. Tonight is about us and nothing else."

She nodded, but the worry remained in her eyes. I cupped her face until her lips spread into a breathtaking smile, pressed a kiss to her forehead, and slid on her coat. After putting on my own, I held the door open for her. Snowflakes floated above us and had piled up on the sidewalk. A cab pulled up rather quickly and I helped Bri inside.

"Please take us over to Second City," I instructed.

The driver nodded and cautiously merged into traffic. Fortunately, it was only a short distance away, but with the snow and so many people in the city, it would probably take longer than usual. I wrapped my arm around Bri's shoulder and she snuggled into my side.

"I love all the acts there. How did you know?"

I shrugged. "I think they're pretty awesome myself and figured you'd like them. We tend to share the same sense of humor."

She giggled and my heart warmed with the sound of it. Bri rested her arm over my stomach. "Yes, our sarcasm is very similar. In case I haven't said it enough, thank you for everything. You're quite the Casanova when you want to be."

"You're very welcome. I like seeing you happy. I still don't verbalize myself very well, but I've improved a little on showing my thoughts."

"You're amazing, Trey. Every second I spend with you, I'm the happiest girl in the world."

I kissed the side of her head and savored the peaceful waves flowing through me only she could produce. I wanted nothing more for these feelings to stay with me for the rest of the night.

* * *

TWO HOURS and one heated romp in her car later, there wasn't anything that could take away the content grin on my face. As the echoes of Bri screaming my name ran through my head, my body somehow became even more sated. I opened my car door and checked to see if anyone was following me. Getting lost in Bri's body was a temporary fix and all the unanswered questions from earlier pressed to the forefront of my brain.

I did my best to shrug them off while weaving through the ramp, but it was a half-hearted attempt. My jittery nerves overpowered every other feeling in my body. Snowplows were on the streets to handle the heavy snow falling as I pulled into traffic. After peeking in my rearview and seeing a car following me a tad too close, my heart rate skyrocketed. I took my exit faster than I should've and my backend slid across the slick road. Seeing the vehicle behind me was still on my tail, a mixture of adrenaline and fear shot through my pores. I straightened out and hit the accelerator once I was on the freeway.

To distract myself, I fiddled with the radio dial, but stopped after the persistent BMW SUV with tinted windows behind me flashed their high beams. An uneasy breath slipped out of me and I swerved over to a different lane—just to see if the guy would follow me. After he did, my throat closed and I grappled to get a hold of my shaky nerves. My sweaty hands gripped the steering wheel tightly while I weaved between cars, trying to put some distance between us.

When the truck kept pace with me, icy waves of trepidation trickled down my spine. He was practically in my backseat. With the roads on the slick side, I wasn't sure about hitting the NOS. I glimpsed over my shoulder to see two more identical vehicles boxing me in.

There was no way for me to figure out who was in them either. The windows were practically black, but with who happened to be at the same restaurant as Bri and me earlier, I had a very good idea of who was behind what was on the verge of becoming an ugly chase.

My body bristled about as fast my mind raced. The two trucks on the sides of me swerved over the lanes and I punched the accelerator in just enough time to sneak past them. By sheer luck, I managed not to clip any of the cars on the road. Two of the SUVs veered over as the truck behind me sped up and hit my bumper. The impact jerked me forward and sent him over to the right lane.

After I cranked the wheel, I slammed on the brakes to slide behind the three of them. The stretch ahead of us was fully plowed and it would be my one and only shot to shake these assholes. Once my wheels were on plain asphalt, I weaved between them and punched the NOS. Everything blurred by me for the next thirty seconds and created enough of a distance from them. I took the exit, pulled into the first alley I saw, and killed the lights.

I tried not to think about what would happen if they spotted me. If they found me, I'd surely be a dead man and I wasn't ready to die. Air evaded me as my throat closed to a thin line. They blew past me minutes later. My hands shook as the reality of what happened hit me at full force.

I rested my forehead on the steering wheel and took deep breaths to regain control over my shaking body, but it was a futile attempt. Nothing could stop the food in my stomach from crawling upward and I hastily opened my door and proceeded to puke my guts out.

These rich assholes took this to the level I never wanted to see. With this bold effort to take me out, I doubted this was the last attempt to off me and the prospect of them hurting anyone else sucked the air right out of me. My heart splintered as the one thing in my world I refused to lose flashed through my mind. How in the hell could I continue seeing Bri with this looming over me?

CHAPTER 28

BRI

"What's the rush, Bri? Our fitting appointment isn't for another hour. We'll have plenty of time to shower and get downtown," Mia spoke up, trying to keep pace with me as I jogged off the softball field.

"I want to catch Trey before he goes home. Aside from school and the occasional weeknight I can slip away, we haven't seen a lot of each other lately and I need to talk to him. It's important, Mia. I promise we won't be late for our appointment."

She fell in stride with me. "I'm not worried about being late. I'll work on some of our assignments or call Micah."

Sweat trickled down my temples on our way to the locker room. For the second week of April, it was exceptionally warm. As I walked to the showers, I pulled my light blue Lions T-shirt off, snatched a towel from the rack, and headed over to my locker to finish undressing.

After I didn't smell like a sweat sock, I quickly dried off and threw on some deodorant with a few puffs of perfume before changing into a pair of indigo skinny jeans, a pink hippie tank top, and sliding on my sparkly sandals. Not particularly looking my best, but not like a homeless person either, I shoved my mascara into my makeup bag and strode back to my locker. With my bags slung over my shoulder, I headed toward the parking lot, praying Trey was still here.

Spotting Trey's car, I picked up my pace, hopped up on the hood, and waited for him to emerge from his locker room. A few minutes later, he appeared with Shane by his side. Judging by the hard expressions on their faces, they were in a heated conversation and I highly doubted it was about baseball practice. Once Trey saw me, his lips curled into a small smile and he gave Shane a fist bump before jogging over.

"Aren't you supposed to be on your way downtown with Mia?"

I jumped down and kissed his cheek. "I wanted to see you before I left. How was practice?"

Trey tossed his bags in the car and took mine on our way over to my Lexus. I planted my feet and arched an eyebrow for an answer. He glanced around, his eyes wide with alarm. "I doubt you stuck around to chat about baseball."

"Seriously, what are you looking for, Trey? You've been paranoid since Valentine's Day."

His sketchy behavior over the past month and a half had my brain working overtime to figure out what he was hiding from me. He looked over his shoulder all the time and was moodier than ever. I had my suspicions, but really wanted to hear it from him.

With a fierce glare in his eyes, Trey gestured to the street. "Now isn't really the time or the place, Bri. In case you didn't spot them, your dad's security detail is here and I'm sure it's a matter of minutes before they drag you away. So, if you want to keep your plans with Mia, I suggest you leave."

I groaned inwardly. "Son of a bitch. I'm so tired of them popping up."

Trey pinched the bridge of his nose. "Believe me, so am I. You should get going."

I rested a hand on my hip. "No, I want to finish a conversation with you for once."

"It's not my fault we hardly talk anymore. If you want to point blame anywhere, I suggest you speak to your dad about it," Trey bit back, tugging his shaggy brown hair.

Tears pricked my eyes. "I wasn't blaming you. I just hate this growing space between us. You're constantly on edge and I can't take it anymore. I feel like something really bad happened or is happening and you're not telling me to protect me, which is ridiculous."

With his hands on my cheeks, Trey lightly kissed my forehead. "We'll talk soon. Try to have a good time with Mia. I can't wait to see you in your dress on Saturday."

His definitive tone made it clear our brief talk was over. I fished out my keys from my purse and unlocked the car. Mia strode toward us, her eyes cautious as she got inside. A ragged breath passed through me, hating to leave things where they were, but knowing I really did need to go before security hauled me away.

Trey opened my door before putting my bags in the backseat. I cranked the ignition and rolled down the window. After he glanced over his shoulder a few times, his face turned white, making me want to know even more what was going through his head.

"We'll talk this weekend, Bri. Until then, don't worry about it," Trey said, his eyes pleading for me to agree.

My chest constricted, but I nodded to appease him. He headed back to his Acura. Mia's fingers circled her bracelet several times before she looked out the passenger side window. Lately, she was just as jumpy as Trey.

I nudged her arm. "Mia, it's been a month since you confronted Micah about working for the Fitzpatricks. He's not involved with them anymore. You need to stop worrying. If they haven't done anything to Micah or you yet, they're probably not going to."

She frowned. "No offense, Bri, but you don't understand how the Fitzpatricks work. There's no telling what they might do. I have a feeling we haven't seen the last of them."

I gave her a half-smile. "I know more about them than you may think." She arched an eyebrow. I waved it off and murmured, "Hopefully, he sticks to his word and stays away from them."

"The prospect of us breaking up if he didn't sever ties with them definitely scared him, but I'm not sure it'll be enough for him to stay out of trouble. He's back in school, but I think the damage has already been done. What scares me the most is I don't think he even cares if he graduates," Mia replied, wrapping her blonde hair around her finger.

"He's in love with you. He knows you won't stay with him if he keeps walking down the path he's on. That's a pretty good motivator for him to get his shit together."

"Micah crossed a line in our neighborhood. There's really no going back from it now. I want to believe he won't get tangled up with them again, but he's gotten a taste of the kind of money you can make when you work for the Fitzpatricks. I wish I had a crystal ball to see the future and how this whole situation with them plays out."

"You and me both. I'd really like to fast-forward to the end of next year. So many things will be behind us then."

"I take it you haven't found out much more on the whole Sebastian front?"

My palms dampened as I admitted, "No, it's been dead-ends. It seems like it might have more to do than just him being from the south side, but I haven't been able to piece together what that may be yet. You haven't said anything to Trey about it, have you?"

Mia sighed. "I promised you I wouldn't, but I really think you need to talk to him about it soon. It's obviously taken a huge toll on your relationship."

I scowled. "And that's precisely why I haven't. We haven't been all that in sync lately. Every time we even get close to having an actual conversation, something or someone pops up and we get diverted from it."

Mia gave me a sympathetic smile and turned on the radio. I glimpsed over my shoulder to check if security was behind us, but didn't see them. We rode the remainder of the way in silence. Since neither of our love lives were in a great place, it wasn't all that shocking.

I pulled up to Bella's, parked my car, and hopped out. We strode into the boutique and quickly changed into our prom dresses before joining the seamstresses.

"Do you think my knee will heal up before this weekend?" Mia asked, eyeing the nasty scrape on her leg.

We were only in our third week of softball, but she already sported more than a few abrasions. The seamstress, hemming the bottom of her black beaded, lace dress, looked between the slit and her cut—not bothering to hide her doubt.

I glared at her and almost took a needle to the leg from the lady altering my dress. Even if it didn't fully heal up, she'd still be gorgeous. With the large V neck and racer back, spectators at the grand march would see plenty of her exposed skin—not her latest softball injury.

My mouth slid into a wide smile. "Yeah, I think it will. I wouldn't recommend sliding anymore this week. Considering you just got the cast off your arm from our last basketball game, you might want to give your body a bit more of a break before you tack on any more wounds or broken bones."

Mia rolled her eyes. "We won the state championship, didn't we?"

I laughed. "Yes, but that's not the point. You're lucky you only walked away with a broken wrist. I'm pretty sure we would've won without you running full speed into a brick wall just to save the ball. That's what overtime is for."

"I wasn't willing to risk it. Now, we have back-to-back championships in soccer and basketball."

My gaze drifted to my multi-colored sleeveless prom dress. Various shades of dark purple and pink on the bottom transitioned into lighter greens and blues right before the very generous V-neck that would surely torture Trey or at least bring his dimples out of their slumber. My heart twitched and I shook off where my mind was headed.

"How many bones have you broken now?"

Mia yelped after getting pricked by the needle. The woman

working on her dress didn't bat an eye. An inadvertent snort slipped out of me after I saw Mia give her a murderous glare.

"I think my wrist was like my tenth one," Mia said through gritted teeth.

"With the way you play sports, I doubt it'll be your last. Just *try* and make it to this summer before having another emergency room visit," I replied, my face serious.

Mia smirked. "I'll do my best. I know how much hospitals freak you out."

"How you can stomach the things we've seen in the emergency room is beyond me. That guy who had a screwdriver in his head was by far one of the worst images I've ever seen. It still haunts my dreams."

"You survived. I can't believe prom is finally here. You're going to turn so many heads this weekend, Bri."

I grinned. "So will you, Mia. Micah won't know what hit him when he sees you. Are we still on for grabbing an early dinner before we have to head over to Chamberlain?"

Mia nodded. "The plan afterwards is to go to Kylie's pool party. It'll be nice to finally have a full night with Micah again. It's been forever."

My smile widened. "I know. I can't wait to spend a whole evening with Trey uninterrupted."

"Yeah, I think it'll be good for all of us. Are we tanning after this or do you need to get home?"

"We're definitely hitting the salon when we're done. It's already Wednesday and you only have two days left to get some bronze to your skin. You're not quite as pale as you were this winter, but you could use as many sessions as you can get before Saturday."

"Well, if I would've jetted off to the Cayman Islands for our spring break, I'd be as dark as you too," Mia joked.

"I didn't have a choice in the matter," I grumbled.

Her face softened. "Hey, I'm sorry. I was joking. I know your dad has really stepped up trying to keep you and Trey apart. I'm honestly baffled you're able to go to prom with him."

I forced a smile. "I told him I was going with Trey or I wasn't going at all. He needs the press to flock to the event so he can have his moment in the spotlight where he pretends to be a doting dad."

"Do you think it'll be better over the summer when he's on the campaign trail more?"

"No, he'll force me to go with them."

Sadness descended upon her face and I looked away. What had my body tied up in knots most days was the unknown with Trey. I wasn't even sure we'd survive a summer apart if things continued the way they were right now.

"Earth to Bri. Is everything alright?" Mia asked, eyeing me with concern.

I brushed my hair aside so the seamstress could make sure the top part of my dress fit perfectly. "Yeah, my mind just wandered. Do you want to grab dinner at Gino's after we're done tanning?"

Mia gasped and pointed at my exposed shoulder. "We'll get to supper in a second. When did you get those?"

She ran her fingers along the heart above the infinity circle and the inscription of *faith* below it before tracing the half-circle of arrows in between the caption of *hope*. Her hand shifted over to the multi-colored Celtic sun on my right shoulder and across the small script below it.

You're the shining light in my world.

My lips spread into a devious grin. "One of the stops in the Caribbean. What do you think?"

"I think it's a damn miracle you pulled it off. Your dad practically has you under lock and key. How did you manage to ink your body without him knowing?"

"He's tightened the reins, but I still have my ways of slipping away."

"They're beautiful. I'm guessing you got the idea from the bracelet Trey gave you. Does he know you have them?" Mia asked, arching an eyebrow. I shook my head. She gaped at me in disbelief. "How's that even possible? You guys screw whenever you have the chance. I mean, I can see why I haven't noticed them, but not him."

I rolled my eyes. "It's not like I was hiding them from you. It just never came up in conversation. You've had a lot going on with Micah, remember? As far as Trey, we haven't gotten fully naked while having sex in ages. He'll see them this weekend, though."

She crinkled her eyebrows. "He's not the only one who will see. Your dad is going to flip out on you after he spots them."

"My hair will cover them up. I'm not worried about him finding out about them anytime soon," I replied, waving off her concerns.

Our seamstresses gestured that we were done and we returned to the changing rooms. A couple of minutes later, Mia reemerged in her jeans and a floral print tank top. Her wide eyes expressed her doubts of me keeping my tattoos a secret from my dad as she followed me out of the boutique, but I didn't let it get to me.

I hopped in my car, fastened my seatbelt, and glanced in the rearview mirror to check if any of his security ended up following us downtown. When the hair on the back of my neck stood on end, I tightened my grip on the wheel and checked to see if the coast was clear. Not spotting anything out of the ordinary, I pulled into traffic.

The heavy weights on my shoulders shifted to my chest. Sadly, they were second nature for me. There were more than a few things I was hiding from my dad. Having a fight over a couple of tattoos was the least of my worries.

* * *

AFTER OUR TANNING session and grabbing a few slices of pizza at Gino's, I headed over to Chamberlain so Mia could get her car. Although, I still wasn't sure it was truly hers. I suspected Micah and Trey had more input on her decision to buy the silver and blue Nissan Skyline than she did. They had tricked it out with rims and racing stripes over the past few weeks.

Mia hopped out and rested her elbows on the edge of the window.

"Are you sure your parents will be gone before you get home? We should've skipped dinner so you could've made the event."

I narrowed my eyes. "I don't care if they are or aren't there. He makes me feel like shit no matter what. I might as well earn it."

She chewed on her lower lip. "If you say so. Please call me later."

"I promise. You better get going. I'm sure Micah is waiting for you so he can squeeze in a heated romp before the night is over," I replied with a playful grin.

Mia rolled her eyes as she got in her Nissan. Working on her car and his Camaro were the few things that brought a smile to Trey's face. His delectable dimples flashed through my mind and my heart fluttered the whole way home. My happiness was short-lived when I saw both my parents' cars were in the driveway.

As I parked my Lexus, chills ran down my back. Dad stomped around along the side of the house on his cell, causing my nerves to default to their supersonic mode. With my backpack and purse in hand, I made my way to the front door.

Before I reached for the knob, he grabbed my right arm with an ironclad grip. I whipped around to face him. His nostrils flared as he seethed, "It's about time you came home, Brianna. You were supposed to be here over an hour ago to accompany us to the gala."

"If it was so damn important for me to go to another pointless party just to pretend to be a family in front of the press, your lackeys could've dragged me away while I was still at school," I snapped, stepping forward.

He yanked me back. "Your grandparents aren't here to interfere this time. I'm putting an end to your defiance. Give me your car keys."

I glared at him and shoved my keys in his chest. "Take whatever you want from me. I don't give a flying fuck anymore."

Pinpricks ran rampant from my elbow to my wrist after he tightened his hold and dragged me inside, through the foyer, and into the kitchen. There were dishes cluttered on the counter and a sink full of water. I gazed around for Kelsey, but didn't see her. Knowing her absence wasn't a good sign, my heart plummeted. She'd never leave for the evening without making sure the house was spotless and everything was ready for tomorrow's meals.

Dad leaned into my ear and sneered, "She's not here and neither is your mother. It's just *you* and *me*."

I gulped down the rising acid in my throat and tried to think of a way to get away from him. He eyed my trembling hands and gave me a snakelike smile.

My eyes narrowed. "I dare you to try something. As I recall you saying on more than one occasion, having me around benefits you. Putting your hands on me isn't all that smart on your part."

His soulless eyes lasered into me. "Keep mouthing off and you're going to regret it."

"I think the only regret around here is my existence. Now, if you don't mind, I have homework to do," I bit back, doing my best to ignore the tightness in my chest.

"I'm not done with you yet," Dad sniggered, shuffling us closer to the sink.

Seeing the maniacal look on his face, coupled with his threatening tone, knocked the wind right out of me. I had no idea what he was about to do, but it wasn't headed in a good direction. I attempted to wiggle free, but he refused to loosen his grip.

My temper got the best of me as I shouted, "If you want to hash out how much of a disappointment I am, I think I'll pass. You might want to consider letting me go. I'm pretty sure Mom will ruin you once and for all if she sees another bruise on me."

Dad shoved an open envelope into my face. "If you think that's a threat, you're sorely mistaken. You'll need to work a lot harder to intimidate me. You better give me an explanation for this letter."

With every ounce of my strength, I jerked my arm away from him and was grateful my shoulder remained in its socket. A semi-shocked expression flitted across his face before he smoothed it out. I pulled out the piece of paper and read it over.

"I see you've been snooping around in my room again."

"It's my house. Every room is mine. Now, explain yourself."

"It's pretty obvious, isn't it?"

All the veins in his neck and forehead throbbed at a ruthless rate and I instantly regretted mouthing off. "Oh, if you had any idea, Brianna, you wouldn't dare cross me."

The villainous look in his eyes didn't promise good things for me and I took a cautious step back. My body was practically torn in two. One side of me boiled with rage while the other was ready to let my nerves take over, fall to the floor, and curl up into a ball.

"To answer what you already clearly know, the letter is my early acceptance to Eckman."

He clenched his fists together. "You're attending Yale and that's final!"

I smirked. "Actually, I'm going to Eckman. I'm bound to them now and there's nothing you can do to change it."

"Do you really think I can't reverse any decision you've made?"

"If you did, it'd probably look *very poorly* to the voters of Illinois. Who's going to want you in office if you can't even support your daughter's decision to attend an elite school in state rather than an uppity Ivy League one out east?"

Unable to contain his fury any longer, he grabbed the back of my head and dunked it in the dirty sink water. Floods of it entered my nostrils and I tried to push his hands away, but he locked them behind my back in a tight grip. Tears streamed down my face as water filled my ears.

Sounds faded out and I attempted to get my head to the surface, but he shoved it down even further. What sounded like a maniacal laugh came from him, but I wasn't sure with the copious amounts of water still pouring into me. I desperately wanted to take a breath, but bit the sides of my cheeks to keep myself from doing so.

When my vision waned, letting me know I didn't have much longer before I passed out from the lack of air, my fight or flight instinct kicked into high gear. I swung my legs toward him while struggling against his hold, but I couldn't get him to release me. The rapid beats of my heart slowed and with each attempt I made to free myself, my muscles became tighter, protesting any movement at all.

Please God, don't let this happen to me. Don't let me die this way. Not by his hands.

"You think you're really smart, don't you? Don't kid yourself. If you take anything away from this moment, it's that I always get what I want—no matter what the cost is," Dad said in disgust, bringing me out of the water and releasing me.

I fell to my knees, gasping for air. Tingling shards in the center of my chest spread through me as I struggled to breathe. I was close to shutting down completely and I wouldn't give him the satisfaction of seeing it happen.

With what was left of my miniscule strength, I fought off my tears and slowly got to my feet. "Someday, you'll get what's coming to you and I hope to see it. The world should know *exactly* who you are."

Dad grabbed both my arms and I braced myself for round two with the water. Before he lowered my head, the front door slammed shut and Mom strode into the kitchen. After seeing me half-drenched, her eyes narrowed to slits on my dad. He let go of me and I sprinted to my room, stopping just long enough to grab my purse.

I closed my watery eyes for a second and heaved in spurts of air to fight off having an attack. Once my breathing was relatively steady, I picked up my cell and scrolled to Mia's name.

Bri: Can you please come pick me up at my neighbors ASAP?

Mia: Of course! What did your asshole of a dad do to you now?

My hands shook nonstop as being trapped underwater ran through my head. Since he really didn't seem to care if he killed me, I didn't dare provoke him again. That realization sucked all the air out of my body and I nearly collapsed from the enormity of it.

Bri: I'll tell you later. Please hurry.

Mia: Oh, Bri, I'm so sorry. I'm on my way.

I went down to my messages with Kelsey.

Bri: Mia's going to come and get me. I can't stay here another second.

Kelsey: I knew something was off when he told me to leave early. Did he hurt you?

My blurry eyes drifted to my tender arm and I dropped my phone.

Seeing the dark shade of purple made me curl my fists together to get my hands to stop shaking. Once they were steady, I toweled off my wet hair, burst into my closet, and changed into the first T-shirt available I saw. My makeup was a mess, but I didn't have time to fix it. After tossing some clean clothes and uniforms into a bag, I returned to my abandoned cell.

Bri: I'm okay. Don't come back here. I just wanted you to know I won't be here in the morning.

Kelsey: That's not an answer. If I see he hurt you in any way, I'll go to the police. I don't care what he does to me or my family.

Bri: No! I won't allow you to keep putting yourself on the line for me. Mia's picking me up. I'll touch base with you later tonight.

Kelsey: You better! I want to know where you end up staying. We'll talk more about this tomorrow. Take care of yourself. Love you!

Bri: Love you!

I slung my bags over my shoulder, headed over to the window, and removed the screen. Sharp paints shot through my badgered arm, making it difficult for me to keep my grip on the ivory-covered fence, but I somehow managed to shimmy down it without falling. I jumped the last few feet and sprinted toward the lake. When I reached the road, my lungs burned and I fell to my knees to catch my breath, thanking God I was actually able to take another one.

I didn't have much time to regain my wits. Several black SUVs were on approach and I hid behind the stone ledge along my neighbor's property. My heart rate soared while I watched them speed past me. Knowing my dad figured out I left brought on a fresh wave of panic and I prayed Mia wasn't too far away.

Five minutes passed without another vehicle going by. I slid to the ground before resting my forehead on my knees. As the walls closed in, I had to really focus to steady my rapid breaths. Hearing tires squeal several seconds later brought me out of the darkness. I lifted my head to see Mia frantically looking around.

I forced myself up and hopped inside. She opened her mouth, but I shook my head. "Just get me out of here."

Mia sped down the road. Resting my elbow on the door, I propped my heavy head in my hand while taking deep breaths, praying it'd ease the weights still sitting on my chest. Piercing pains traveled from my throat and down my windpipe with each breath.

After several glances behind us to ensure we weren't being followed, Mia focused on me and whispered, "I know you don't want to talk about it, but you're *literally* a hot mess right now. Your hair wasn't wet when I left you and your arm is purple. He hurt you again. I need you to tell me what he did this time."

I turned toward her. "Don't start, Mia. We've had this conversation and as I recall, we're both in the same boat. Stop pushing me to do something when you never do."

Her chin quivered as she pulled over on the side of the road and crossed her arms. "I'm not going another mile until you tell me what happened."

All the muscles in my body were wound so tight that every move I made was excruciating. "He found out I took early acceptance to Eckman and lost his mind."

A tear fell down her cheek. "That's not what I asked. What did he do to you?"

My hands trembled as tears trickled down my face. "He held me under water to scare me. I'm fine. Please stop looking at me like I'm about to disappear."

Mia gasped, her face horrified. "You can't keep dismissing what he does as nothing."

"I need you to get me as far away from here as possible. *Please*, Mia," I begged.

Her face was torn as she drove away. I flicked on the radio and tried to find some sort of comfort from the song streaming, but the hollowness growing inside me was too strong.

I noticed we weren't heading toward downtown or the south side. "Where are you going?"

Her face paled. "I was at Trey's when you called. He wants to see you."

I narrowed my eyes. "If that's the case, why are you taking me in the opposite direction of his house?"

She took an exit heading toward Naperville. "I'm sure you'll end up at his place at some point."

"What did you say to him before you left? Where the hell are we going?"

"I didn't say anything to him, but he's not oblivious. He knows something is wrong. I don't know where we're going. Trey entered the information into my GPS and didn't say another word. I'm sorry."

I threw my hands up in exasperation. "That's just great. I'm going to have to tell him what happened and he's going to end up snapping because of me."

Her eyes widened. "Don't get mad at me for being worried about you. In case you haven't noticed, we've all been on the concerned side with anything involving your dad, but you keep shrugging it off like things are fine, when actually, they're anything but okay."

Hearing the unease spill over into her shaky voice made my heart drop. "I'm sorry, Mia. I didn't mean to snap at you, but you have to understand something." She glimpsed at me, her eyes watery. I pointed at my arm and wet hair. "Stuff like this doesn't happen very often. If he wants to get reelected, it can't."

A tear trickled down her face. "You're my best friend. I'll never stop worrying. On some level, I know he wouldn't seriously hurt you, but that doesn't stop my heart from breaking when I see and hear how much pain you're in. What happened to you tonight isn't something anyone should ever experience and you playing it off like it's no big deal is ripping me apart."

My own tears threatened to fall. My blood boiled over and I banged the dashboard. Mia stared at me like I'd lost my mind. I curled my hands into tight fists.

"I don't care what the universe is trying to tell me or how much agony I'm put through over the next year. I won't let my dad break me —just like you don't let Chase get the best of you. If we stick together, I know we can handle it. Promise me that no matter what is tossed our way, we'll deal with it together," I pleaded, my eyes desperate for her to believe me.

Mia wrapped her pinky with mine and whispered, "*Always*. That's what sisters do."

After this last go-round with my dad, I didn't know what would come my way next at home. My skin crawled as the reality of the situation hit me head-on. He didn't give a damn about me. All he cared about was his precious social status and climbing the political ladder. What sucked the most was, deep down, a part of me would always love him and my mom, when I really had no reason to at all.

I wanted to give in to the hysterical sobs beating for freedom, but focused on what was ahead of me. Short of lying to Trey, I wasn't sure how to go about explaining this evening. He'd surely snap once he knew the truth. My heart splintered with that thought and I leaned against the window, praying some sort of divine intervention was in my future. If it wasn't, this night was about to get a lot worse.

CHAPTER 29

BRI

After driving down a side road toward the Morton Arboretum, Mia turned into the parking lot and drove up to where Trey and Micah stood at the edge of it. The last time I was here was for my fourth-grade field trip. I forgot how many trees, shrubs, plants, and gardens spanned across the seventeen hundred acres. There were tons of trails and waterfronts throughout the place. A person could spend a full day here and never cover all of the terrain.

"Why did he pick this location?" I asked, wringing my hands together and eyeing Trey.

He remained in deep conversation with Micah. Their rigid postures didn't comfort me whatsoever. If Trey was wound up already, there was no way he'd control his temper once I told him what happened.

Her face was forlorn as she said, "I'm guessing it was so he could see you without your dad's security pulling you away."

"Where's his car?"

"I'm not sure. I left right after you called me."

My hands shook nonstop as I opened the door. Mia released a ragged breath and got out. I put on my jean jacket and took an unsteady step toward Trey.

"Were you followed by anyone?" Trey asked, his face firm.

My cheeks flushed before I admitted, "I wasn't paying attention."

Trey huffed. "With how our luck has been lately, I'm sure we can count on it."

"At least we have plenty of room to run if they do turn up," I replied, forcing a smile.

It was one of our warmer evenings, but that didn't halt the arctic waves coasting through me. Micah locked his hand with Mia's and walked over to her Nissan. He opened the passenger side door, his expression torn.

I swallowed against the growing lump in my throat and focused on Trey. "As much as I love your surprises, I've got a not-so-good feeling about this one. Do you want to tell me why they're heading out without a word? And let's not forget they left with my stuff."

Trey rolled his shoulders a few times. "Don't worry about your bag. We'll get it later."

He waved to them before his gaze drifted to the pavement. The residual anger still swarming through me overpowered all the doubts in my head and heart. I gripped his chin, forcing him to look at me.

After his eyes skimmed across every inch of my body, he twirled a lock of my hair around his finger. "I doubt your hair is still damp from your shower after practice and it's unlikely you took a shower before you called Mia, begging to be picked up. What happened, Bri?"

Releasing the strand, he trailed his fingers down my arms. A razor-sharp pain shot through my right one and I flinched. Trey pulled my jacket down and his eyes nearly fell out of their sockets after he saw the red and purple streaks that were close to the size of a silver dollar pancake.

Trey snatched his backpack from the pavement before clutching my hand. As he guided us along the edge of the brick parking lot, his jaw was clenched so tightly I wasn't sure how his teeth didn't crack under the exertion.

After several minutes of deafening silence, he angled us toward a trail that was off the beaten path. Trey's lips remained in a thin line. Between his refusal to speak and the sickening feeling in my gut that my dad wasn't finished with me for the night amplified every nerve ending in my body. I glanced around to confirm no one was following us.

I groaned after spotting several black SUVs turning into the lot. It had been a while since I went through all my things to see if any more tracking chips were in my room or car. Clearly there were because there was no way his security would be in this neighborhood.

"We need to get as far away from the parking lot as possible. In fact, if you know of a place in here that's really secluded, I suggest we go there *now*," I demanded, picking up my pace.

Trey glimpsed behind us and curled his hands into tight fists. "I'd much rather kick the shit out of those assholes."

I tugged on his arm and started jogging. "Fighting with them is going to get us nowhere. Let's just get out of sight."

This place was huge and I was more than grateful for it. Their footsteps grew louder, making my heart beat ferociously against my chest. We ended up in an all-out sprint as we darted in between the multitude of trees and hopped over the ledges of the bush mazes between us.

I looked over my shoulder to see they were falling farther behind us. Trey jumped over another grass ledge and I followed him. He dropped down to his knees and crawled over to the next row. I wasn't exactly sure what his game plan was, but I was happy to have a minute to catch my breath. My lungs had been through enough tonight and were close to quitting on me.

He stopped after a few rows. There was enough of a gap in the bushes for us to hide and remain covered up. We lay flat on our stomachs as they closed in on us. Trey squeezed my hand and I held my breath as they ran by. My heart beat out of my chest and Trey's pounded just as fast.

They continued poking the bushes and I almost yelped when one of them jabbed his gun right above the one we were under. Trey clamped his hand over my mouth and did his best to keep me from squirming. I shook so hard that the twigs started to tremble. The guy prodded around for several minutes. My breath caught in my throat and I didn't have much longer before I succumbed to the darkness looming over my eyelids.

"Sir, we lost them."

"How is that possible? You're tracking her every move with the best surveillance equipment on the market, and have been doing so for months, yet somehow, she manages to slip through your fingers more often than not. Get your asses back here. It looks like I'll have to deal with her myself."

Trey's face hardened, clearly not happy with that revelation. I held his hand tightly and sucked in a quick breath, doing my best to remain as silent as possible when all I wanted to do was scream at the top of my lungs. After what seemed like forever, their voices trailed off and Trey poked his head above the hedges.

"They're gone, for now, it seems. Care to elaborate on them tracking you?" Trey asked, his eyes enraged.

"I don't think now is really the time to chat about it. Let's just get out of here," I shot back, running in the opposite direction as security.

My lungs burned once again, but I didn't dare stop for air. Trey veered us toward one of the lakes within the arboretum. Once we reached a spot on the shore with really tall grass along it, he slowed down. Unless you were over seven feet tall, you couldn't see anyone in this area.

We walked around in circles while catching our breath. Color crept up from his neck to his face. Trey dropped his backpack on the sandy beach and pulled out a fleece Cubs blanket. Plopping down at the end of it, he rested his chin on his knees.

I sat next to him and stared at the rippling water. Purple and reddish colors from the sunset danced across the surface of the lake. I wished the beauty in front of me was enough to ease my unsteady heart rate, but it would take a miracle for that to happen.

I picked away at my pink and red nail polish before wringing my hands together and placing them on my knees. Every nerve in my body tingled while I waited for Trey to say something, but he remained deep in thought, clearly debating the words he wanted to use. Judging by the way his eyes darted around and the relentless way the muscles in his neck and arms twitched, whatever was on his mind was ripping him apart on the inside.

After a few more minutes of earsplitting silence, he turned toward me. "What happened with your dad?"

All the pain and fury within me mixed together, creating a sickening pit in my stomach. "I skipped out on an event and paid the price for it." He gestured to my wet hair. "Hearing the particulars will just tap into your temper and I'd rather not trigger it."

Grabbing a few of the larger pebbles next to him, he chucked them into the lake. They skimmed along the surface and the angry ripples traveling across the water spoke volumes, almost like he was showing me what was going on inside of him.

"That's not an answer. Tell me the whole damn story," Trey snapped.

I grimaced. "There was some mindless gala downtown he wanted me to attend. I chose having dinner with Mia over going to it. I was prepared for a go-round with him, but the bastard had more than one thing to bitch at me about when I got home."

Trey arched an eyebrow. "The last time I checked, you were keeping more than a few things from him. What exactly is it this time? And why's your hair wet?"

"He found out that I received early acceptance to Eckman. It ruined his Ivy League dreams for me so he was irate. I probably didn't help matters by being flippant about the whole matter. Things got physical. He pushed my head under water to scare me. I'm fine," I replied, running my clammy hands down my jeans.

Trey curled his fists together to prevent himself from blowing up, but seeing how quickly his face turned bright red, it was a losing battle. I went to touch him, but he swayed away. "That motherfucker tried to kill you and you're acting like it's no big deal. Are you out of your damn mind, Bri? You need to tell someone before something really bad happens."

"Trey, as I've said many times, it won't get to that point. It just can't and I don't want to talk about him anymore. I want to get to the bottom of all the things that have been unsaid between us," I rebutted, my face determined.

His shoulders sagged. "That's quite a bit. I'm not sure one night will be enough for it all to come out, but I agree we should try. I can't believe you got into Eckman. That's pretty incredible. I wish you would've told me sooner and under better circumstances."

I intertwined my hand with his. "I'm sorry. I wanted to tell you, but you've been so out of sorts for the past couple of months, I haven't known what to share and what to keep to myself. I haven't wanted to do anything to upset you any more than you already are on any given day. I *really* want us to get back to solid ground with one another. School will be over soon and I'll be gone a lot over the summer. I *need* to know we're going to be okay."

Trey rubbed his free hand down his face, seemingly to calm down, but it didn't remove the angry crease in his forehead that made an appearance when he hit his limit.

"Maybe space is exactly what we need for things to improve in our lives," Trey murmured, his voice hoarse.

Tears pricked my eyes and I crawled in front of him, straddling my legs around his and gripping his face. After seeing the panic in my eyes, he released a ragged breath. I fought against the cinder blocks sitting on my chest and forced out, "*Please*, don't give up on what we have. I can tell by the pain in your eyes that you don't want that any more than I do. Please work things out with me. I know it hasn't been easy, but it won't be like this forever. What goes down always swings back up. The past few months have been a low point for us, but I believe we have what it takes to get through anything."

He placed his hands over mine. "I don't want to walk away from you, but I can't help feeling like I should. I think it'd make things better for you at home if you weren't dating me. I can't handle seeing you hurt in any way. It brings out the fury within me in a way that's hard to get control over. After Mia left to get you, Micah had to pin me down so I didn't go to your house and give your dad the beating he deserves."

The deadpan look on his face made me cringe. "You can't think that way, Trey. I know you feel the need to protect me, but that won't help my situation at all—and neither will walking away from me. I *need* you. When things are at its worst with my dad, it's what I have with you that gives me the strength to handle it."

His eyes glistened. "You think you need me, but the truth is, you've always had the strength to deal with him. I've known that since the second I met you, so don't give credit where it isn't warranted."

I narrowed mine, ready to point out all the ways he made my life so much fuller, but he pinched my lips shut.

"I did something tonight and it's going to make you really mad at me."

"What did you do? Please don't tell me it has something to do with me."

He looked away. "Something I should've done a long time ago."

My nerve endings hit their electrocution setting as I rasped, "Spill it, Trey. I won't make it much longer without having an attack if you don't just tell me already."

Trey caressed circles at the small of my back until I took several solid breaths. He swallowed hard and admitted, "I told my mom about what's happening at your house with your dad."

I balked. "Why would you do that? She's going to confront him about it. You know she comes to my softball games and will see him there. If you really wanted my situation at home to improve, you wouldn't have said anything to her."

"I did the *right* thing, Bri. He's physically hurting you and that's not okay. I should've told my mom a long time ago, but didn't because I was afraid I'd lose you," Trey shot back.

Tears dripped down my face. "Is that why you said something now? Did you think I'd get so mad I'd walk away from you without a look back? Do you really think I'm that shallow?"

Trey thumbed away the tears in the corner of my eyes. "No, of course not. Knowing what you're going through at home breaks my heart. I said something because it's difficult for me not to make your dad pay for all the pain he puts you through. Even sitting here with you in my arms, reassuring me you can handle it, doesn't help the angry beast within me that's begging to put your old man in the hospital. With everything else I'm trying to handle, it's really hard for me not to just unleash it and let the chips fall where they may."

I chewed nervously on my lower lip. "No, I don't want that to happen. Promise me you'll keep yourself in check—just as you have since this fall. If you don't, you're not only letting my dad win, but everyone else who's been going after you outside of school." He cocked an eyebrow and I tilted my head to the side, a no-nonsense look on my face. "I'm not an idiot, Trey. I know things have been happening and that you've been hiding it from me. What exactly, I don't know, but I'd really like for you to tell me. All I have are some names of the families that are trying to destroy your future and hearing them won't shock you. In fact, you probably already know."

"Wow, I haven't heard you talk that fast in a real long time. What names do you have?"

"The Du Ponts, Dudleys, and Livingstons are the ones that are out for your blood, but I don't know why. It can't just be your problems with Sebastian, but every lead I've dug into has led to a dead-end."

"I think I'm starting to have a better idea as to why."

"What have you figured out that you're not telling me?"

He rested his hands on my knees. "It took awhile for me to see the bigger picture. I didn't really start putting much thought into it until after Valentine's Day."

I tossed my hands in the air. "Get to the punchline. I'd like to know what's going on. Who knows? Maybe there's something I can do to help. I know these people in a different way than you."

His eyes filled with sorrow as he said, "At first, I thought they were going after me and using Sebastian to do it, but that's actually not really the case."

My stomach churned. "What do you mean?"

"At the beginning of the school year, my younger brothers were having a hard time on the bus and at school. It improved for a while, but things started to get out of hand again after the first of the year. Thomas and Tory have come home several times with black eyes. My mom can never get a straight answer out of them when she asks why they're getting into fights. I felt like it was my fault for setting a bad example, but that's not the reason."

My mind raced at what was really at play here. "I recall seeing them roughed up at more than one dinner visit. Why wouldn't they tell your mom who's hurting them? What do they have to hide? Plus, I thought you said kids on the south side stuck together."

"Normally, they do, but as you already know, plenty of them turned on me. Logan, Jesse, Micah, and I have done a lot of digging over the past two months."

"I still don't understand why your little brothers would keep something like this from your parents. They're so small. Why would anyone hurt them?"

His face was stone-cold as he replied, "Why does anyone hurt a person, Bri? There's no justifiable reason for it. They kept quiet about it because they're a lot like me. Thomas said he didn't want to do anything to upset our folks. He made Tory keep quiet. After Tory ended up in the ER with a concussion and stitches because a bunch of kids pushed him around on the playground, Thomas finally broke down and told me what was happening. It took a while to get it out of him for how hard he was sobbing, but it helped me piece together the timeline better."

"And that would be?"

"It all goes back to over the summer. Remember when I told you about that big job my dad had a bid on this fall?" I nodded. Trey aimlessly sketched along the outline of his wraparound tattoo as he murmured, "When he landed the job, it was life-changing for all of us."

"Trey, I'm going to explode over here pretty soon if you don't get to the point," I butted in.

"He outbid all the major commercial construction companies to build the new F. F. & Sweeney building. It's a multibillion-dollar project that will be in the press a lot. Now, we know those owners are mob royalty, but they're richer than Croesus too. The Du Ponts, Dudleys, and Livingstons' expectation was the biggest construction company in Chicago, which they're all investors of, would get the job, and they could get their foot in the door with the mob."

I sighed. "Sadly, I get exactly why they want to have ties with them. They're the kind of people you want on your side if you need something on the shadier side handled and that happens with the rich and elite more than you think. What I don't understand is why those families are messing with you and your brothers and not just going after your dad."

Trey frowned. "It would be idiotic on their part if they went directly after him. They're trying to break one of us to send a message to my dad to drop the job, but they've underestimated me and my siblings."

I scratched my head, which was a jumbled mess and on information overload. "But why try and ruin your life? I don't understand how that is sending a message."

Trey caressed my sides. "If I got sent away or something seriously bad happened to Thomas, Tory, or me, my dad would never forgive himself. It'd rip apart our family."

"I can tell by the pained look in your eyes that there is more to the story. What else has been happening, aside from the fights?"

"There have been a few incidents at the house and at school that have made it difficult for me not to retaliate."

"What happened, Trey? Why wouldn't you tell me?"

"I haven't wanted you wrapped up in this mess, Bri. Your involvement has already posed more issues than expected."

"What's that supposed to mean?"

"They've escalated things in the past few months. Our house and garage have been damaged, along with my car. I think it's taking a turn for the worse because everyone in Chicago is aware we're seeing each other and that pisses off the socialites even more," Trey confessed.

A fresh wave of tears hit me and there wasn't anything I could do to keep them from falling. I rested my forehead against his and said, "We can't let them win. If we walk away from each other, it's not going to stop anything. We just need to find a way to catch them in the act and then blackmail them with it."

Trey wiped away my tears. "What did you have in mind? They have more money and resources than me. I've been going out of my mind to figure out the best way to beat these rich pricks at their own game. Micah and I have been doing as much damage control as we can around the neighborhood, but it only goes so far. We've put an end to anyone messing with my little brothers, but everything else has been fair game."

"Going forward, we need to talk about these things as they happen and not months after the fact. I'd rather get it all out in the open than have you become a moody mess," I grumbled.

Trey smirked. "I thought you liked my broodiness. Isn't that what makes me a bad boy?"

I rolled my eyes. "It is, but I prefer having your dimples make an appearance every once in a while and knowing what's going on in that brilliant mind of yours."

His face was serious as he whispered, "I'm sorry about the past two months. I've wanted to talk to you about it for so long, but I didn't want to add on to what you've already been dealing with at home. I'd never forgive myself if something bad happened to you because of all this shit surrounding me."

I cupped his face. "As far as anything happening to me, you need to give me a little more credit. I *refuse* to lose you."

He placed his hands along the back of my neck. "I'm not going anywhere. If it weren't for you, I'd be locked up in juvie. You're the shining light in my world. As the sun sets behind us, it's that healthy reminder of how much I *need* you. It's second nature for me to want to protect you from anything terrible, but I'm starting to get how important it is for me to be honest with you. We can figure out the next move to put an end to all the bullshit going on around us tomorrow. Right now, I'd like to appreciate every part of you."

"I like that plan a lot," I replied, leaning in for a kiss.

He caressed my arms and thighs, pausing between my legs and massaging centric patterns just long enough to spark an inferno between them. I was wet with desire and yearned to press him down on the blanket and ride him like I never had before, but it was clear by the way he was running his hands along my body, he wanted full control.

The smoldering look on his face was close to liquefying my insides and feeling his rock-hard erection only amplified the erotic sensations coursing through me. I wanted to connect with him so badly, just to show him how very much I *needed* him.

Trey brushed his lips along mine before slowly removing my jacket. I was less gentle as I yanked off his black fleece and pulled his white Nike T-shirt over his head. He chuckled before bringing his mouth back to mine, devouring it in one of our more sensual kisses. My fingers trailed down his chest and washboard abs before fumbling with the fly of his jeans.

He licked and nipped his way over to my ear and down to my shoulder before removing my tank top and bra, then gripped my breasts gently and sucked down hard on the spot below my collarbone he loved to discolor.

I moaned rather loudly, not caring if anyone was around to hear me. He ran his tongue between my breasts and kneaded his fingers along my nipples until they were hard. His mouth drifted over to my shoulder and he suckled along it.

My hands slipped between his jeans and boxers to stroke his straining erection and I hoped he got the unspoken message I was trying to send him. I needed those magical fingers of his to satisfy the rampant tingling south of me.

"I'll get there in a minute, Bri. I just want to explore every part of you before I do."

His teeth grazed my shoulder and I leaned into him. Out of nowhere, he stopped sucking and stared at me in disbelief. Before I knew it, I was on my stomach as his fingers circled my tattoos.

I bit down on my lip. "What do you think?"

"I think your pristine skin has always been beautiful, but seeing these makes it even more breathtaking. When did you get them?" Trey asked, kissing between my shoulder blades.

"While I was on spring break," I replied, loving how the scruff on his chin prickled along my skin.

"They're amazing and I'm going to love giving them attention when we're naked," Trey answered, his voice in that husky tone I couldn't get enough of.

He rolled me over and kissed down the center of my stomach, stopping to play with my belly button ring. Each flick of the tongue amplified the pulsating sensations going through me. Trey unbuttoned my jeans and pulled them off, along with my panties, and tossed them aside.

I sucked along his shoulder before licking the Celtic moon tattoo on his chest. He slid a few fingers deep inside me and swirled them around until I arched off the blanket and clenched tightly around him. Trey continued at a relentless pace until I felt my body begin to tremble. Every part of me sizzled as I fell hard over the edge.

"That's got to be some sort of record," I rasped, my body still quaking from the euphoria.

"One of my favorite sights in the world is your face after you come. Knowing I did it, makes it all the more satisfying for me," Trey declared, capturing my mouth.

As I shoved his indigo jeans and plaid boxers down his legs, my lips moved intensely with his, not getting enough of his musky scent and wintergreen taste. Everything about him not only surrounded me, but made every fiber within me desperate for more. I attempted to stroke him, but he locked my hands above my head. The flames still flickering within me burned even hotter. He pressed soft kisses to my forehead, cheeks, and along my neck before returning to my lips.

Trey kissed me with purpose before he thrust deep inside me. I wiggled my hands free, ran them through his semi-short hair, and tugged when he rocked roughly into me again.

He ran his nose down mine. "You've missed doing that, haven't you?"

I kissed along his neck. "Yes, but I've always found something to do with my hands when we're intimate."

I ran my nails across his back and he groaned loudly. Trey gyrated his hips as he pushed into me, taking on the fast and hard rhythm I loved. Our hearts reached that wonderful harmony they always did when we put reality on a sidebar.

Trey slowed down and I gasped at the sudden change. Our bodies became slick with sweat as we continued at an unhurried pace. My body clenched tightly in all the right places, but I wasn't thinking about my next orgasm. With each soft stroke of his hands as they glided across my body with reverence, I could feel his need to be connected to me and met every thrust of his with just as much zest to make it clear I needed him in the same way.

"Fuck, Bri. I wish there were words for how you make me feel," Trey groaned.

"I'm so ready, Trey. Please let go with me. It's been a while since we've done that together and I *really* need it to happen now," I whimpered.

He pumped into me until I was a quivering mess. My mind and body left this world, reaching that blissful place far above us that he seemed to have a direct line to. His hot release moments later nearly made me convulse all over again and I heaved in breaths to keep from passing out. Trey slid out and settled on the side of me as I rolled over, wiping away the sheen of sweat on his brow.

I rested a hand on his cheek and pressed a soft kiss to his lips. "I'm glad you insisted on seeing me tonight."

He chuckled. "I didn't plan on this happening. Not that I'm complaining it did, but it wasn't my motive for seeing you."

I scowled. "You better not be complaining."

Trey ran his fingers down my cheeks. "I'm not. After everything we discussed, this was just really unexpected."

I traced the Celtic moon on his chest. "Something had to change. I think, deep down, we both knew it. I know it was hard talking things out, but that's exactly what we needed so we could connect again—and boy did we ever."

Trey smirked. "We should probably get going. I told my mom I'd have you back to the house before eleven."

I groaned while slipping on my clothes. "She's going to make me talk about everything going on at home."

Trey pulled on his boxers, jeans, T-shirt, and fleece before putting the blanket in his backpack. "I know you don't like talking about it, but I think you need to." I gave him a sharp look and he waved his hands in the air. "Trust me, I get it. I deal with it all the time with Mia. For whatever reason, I can't change her situation, but I'll do everything in my power to change yours."

On our way back to the parking lot, I muttered, "I still don't understand why we can't change hers, but I'm too tired to wrap my head around it tonight. I get you're trying to do the right thing, but please talk to me first before you tell anyone else what's going on behind closed doors at my house."

Trey locked his hand in mine. "I promise to be more forthcoming going forward. I haven't been a fan of hiding things from you. I just want you to know I can't stand on the sidelines any longer when I know you're being hurt."

I squeezed his hand. "I know you're always looking out for me. I love that more than you'll ever understand. Just trust me to handle things on my end, though. As you said, the rich and elite do things a lot differently, and it's all about a matter of leverage to get things to work out the way you want them to on that front. I know how to deal with my dad."

The hard edge to his face made it clear he didn't really agree with me, but didn't dispute it either. We walked through the bush mazes in silence. Knowing the bigger picture surrounding what was going on with Trey made my stomach churn. Throwing the mob into the mix made matters even worse. I wasn't sure what lengths the DuPonts, Dudleys, and Livingstons would go to when it came to getting what they wanted.

I suspected something very big was about to happen very soon. Even though things were better for Trey and me, we were still only teenagers. Going up against the rich and powerful didn't really put the odds in our favor of coming out of the whole ordeal unscathed.

CHAPTER 30

TREY

"Where's your car?" Bri asked as we walked along the edge of the arboretum.

I glanced behind us to ensure we weren't being followed. Even though we heard her dad tell security to return to her house, it did very little to ease my jumpy nerves. I was more than grateful for the multitude of trees that kept us somewhat concealed.

Bri planted her feet and crossed her arms. "What's going on, Trey? Why isn't your car parked in the lot? You're a million miles away from here and we *just* promised to share what's on our minds."

I tenderly ran my hands down her rigid forearms. "I figured security would show up. I thought it was best to leave it elsewhere."

"Okay, I believe that much, but do you want to tell me the rest now because I highly doubt that's the only thing making you stop every few feet and gaze around. You've become as paranoid as me over the past couple of months." I frowned and proceeded to point out again why I behaved that way, but she shook her head. "I get why, but it seems like more. You're acting like you expect something terrible to happen. If that's the case, you need to tell me. You've got to stop trying to protect me from what you think *may* hurt me and allow us to approach these problems together."

"You're a very centric part of my world. It's only in my nature to worry. That's not going to change any time soon," I replied, trying my best to shake off the pit in my stomach.

"Sometimes I wonder if God put you on earth just to give me a reflection of my own stubbornness," Bri grumbled, looking around and taking a step forward.

I released a nervous chuckle. "I could say the same for you. Not to mention all the ways you torture me with your body."

A sinful grin fell from her amazing lips. "Wait until you see my dress this weekend."

Grasping the back of my neck, I groaned, "God, I can only imagine."

The street I parked on was a mere mile away. I continued to observe our surroundings, but did my best not to be so obvious about it. Bri continued to chip away at what was left of her nail polish like it was hazardous waste.

Aside from the sparkling moon and stars above us, there wasn't a soul in sight. I should take comfort in that much, but stumbled every time the breeze in the air shuffled around the leaves. My own shadow made my skin crawl.

Once we reached the intersection, I gazed in every direction to ensure there weren't any suspicious vehicles lurking on it. Not seeing any cars or people, we ran across the road and headed up the street to my Acura. When we passed by a house with a dog outside on a leash that barked nonstop at us, we nearly tripped over our feet. Outdoor lights flickered on and the owner collected the pup, glaring daggers at us as we jogged by.

"I'm trying really hard not to freak out, but having no streetlights is a bit disturbing. Throw in random animals and pissy homeowners and it's like a scene straight out of a horror movie," Bri muttered, her face pale.

I squeezed her hand. "It'll be alright, Bri. It's only a little bit further. I'd be really surprised if Sebastian and his lackeys drove all the way out to Naperville just to ruffle my feathers. Besides, you watch way too many scary movies. You need to stick to romantic comedies."

We made the final few feet to my car without anything else happening. After opening the passenger door for her, I slowly rounded my car and scanned over every inch of it to check if anyone messed with it while I was away.

Not seeing anything out of the ordinary, I got in and cranked the engine. The gauges shot back and forth, but that wasn't anything new. At this point, Micah and I fixed it every other week. I wished that eased the way my nerves were pulsating, but it didn't.

I glanced at Bri's ashen face before caressing her hand. As I did, her mouth curled into a shy smile. For as long as I lived, I doubted I'd ever grow tired of our touch being a calming talisman for one another.

After pulling out, I looked around to make sure we weren't being followed and my heart rate shot up when I saw a set of headlights coming at us. Seeing it turn into a driveway we passed on our way to my car did very little to slow down my frantic pulse. I sped along the dark road, wanting nothing more than to get to a better lit area.

Once I reached the interstate, I checked behind me again—just to be safe. Traffic on the freeway was light. The coast was clear so far, but that didn't stop me from kicking the Acura into fifth gear and weaving my way through lanes to get us home without anything else happening tonight. I cringed when the loud sounds from under the hood echoed around us.

Bri gave me a wary look. "We both know how very little I know about cars, but that doesn't sound so good. If it keeps up like this, will we make it back to your house?"

I forced a smile. "It'll be fine. This car has been on its last life for a while. It's a wonder it's lasted this long, but it'll get us home."

"Why don't you just start driving the Camaro? Aren't you close to finishing the restoration?" Bri asked, curious.

"It's getting there, but I don't plan on driving it until all this bullshit is over," I explained, merging between two cars and over to the middle lane.

Her face fell as she mumbled, "Yeah, that's understandable."

I sighed. "Let's not think about that crap right now."

Bri rested her head on my shoulder as I flipped on the radio. "Collide" filled the car. Listening to her sing the last few lines along with Howie Day warmed my heart.

"Your voice is as angelic as your laugh," I murmured, kissing the back of her hand.

"Really? Most of the time I don't even realize when I start signing out loud. Once I do, it makes me want to crawl under the table," Bri replied, blushing.

"Yes, really. I've always wondered why you weren't in choir or went out for the school musicals. You have a tremendous talent."

"Music has always brought me out of the darkness. I've kept it for myself. If I participated in musicals or choir, it'd just be something else my dad could leach off for attention and he already gets more than enough with sports."

"I get what you mean. You're the only person I've ever played for and wouldn't dream of playing for anyone else."

Her face was thoughtful as she whispered, "My personal rock star. You play so beautifully. I'm glad I'm the only one you share that side of yourself with."

"Don't get all dreamy. I plan on putting my ax down for a bit to see if I can pick up the drums. I've always wanted to learn. It'd probably be another productive way for me to get out my aggression," I joked.

Bri smirked. "I have my ways of making you play for me and I know you'll enjoy every one of them."

I gave her a playful glare. "Stop torturing me with those kinds of thoughts. You know it doesn't take much for me to give in to whatever mind-blowing ideas you want to try."

The corners of her mouth curled into a victorious smile. "I know and I quite enjoy having that control over you in all the same ways you love exerting your dominant nature over me."

I rolled my eyes while checking the mirrors. I didn't see any of the SUVs akin to the ones her dad's security drove, but I did spot three dark blue BMWs swerving their way through traffic.

"What's wrong, Trey? Your face went blank in a matter of seconds," Bri pointed out, her voice wobbly.

My cell rang to Micah's ringtone. I glanced behind us to see the cars getting closer. I put it on speaker and said, "Now's not a really good time. Can I call you back?"

"Something happened at your house. I don't have all the details yet. Mia and I were downtown walking around Millennium Park when we found out. We're hauling ass to get back home to find out. You need to go to the hospital," Micah replied in a rush.

My eyes widened about as fast as my heart sank. "Why? What's wrong?"

"Whatever happened made your mom go into labor. She left by ambulance. Your dad is on the way to meet her at the hospital. My mom has all the kids with her. They're fine. Don't worry about them. Mia and I will be there to help."

His edgy voice betrayed him in the worst way. Micah was downright freaked out. Bri's face fell as she grabbed her phone from her purse—no doubt to text Mia.

"If I find out Sebastian was anywhere near our neighborhood, I'll kill him. He's the only person that has been vandalizing our house lately," I snapped through gritted teeth.

"I know and I already have Logan and Jesse on it. As soon I get home, I'll talk to the neighbors and some of my other contacts to see if they know anything. With how dark it is, I doubt it, but it's worth a shot."

"Was my mom hurt? Is that why she went into labor?" I asked, fighting back the bursts of anger erupting through my body.

Micah sighed. "I don't know, Trey. My mom was in a hurry when she called and didn't say much, probably because the kids are with her and she doesn't want to scare them any more than they already are right now. I'll call when I have more answers, and you do the same once you know what's going on with your mom."

I eyed the NOS, debating whether to hit it so we could get to the hospital faster, but decided against it. My car wasn't in any condition to use it. Almost as though the Acura could hear me, it started acting up again.

"Fuck, not now."

"What's going on, Trey?"

I banged the dash in frustration. The gauges flipped back and forth again. "Something is wrong with my car. It's been acting twitchy ever since we left."

"Shit. That's not a good sign. We just fixed the last problem with it. Do you think you'll make it to the hospital?"

Bri stared at me, more than panicked by the tense look on her face. Her breathing dwindled and I didn't want to freak her out any more than she already was. I glanced in the mirror to see where the BMWs were and spotted them in a straight line in the left lane. Plastering on a smile, I caressed Bri's side to help calm her down.

"Trey, you didn't answer me. Will you make it to the hospital or should I meet you somewhere?"

Before I could answer, we were rear-ended by one of the BMWs. The force of it threw us forward and nearly made me lose control, but it was enough for some other cars on the road to get between us. Bri screamed and I fought against the heavy weights spreading from my shoulders to my chest before cranking the wheel and hitting the gas to get some more distance.

A burst of adrenaline shot through me as I glimpsed behind me. Whoever was after us was about to catch up soon. The fender on the one that hit us was close to falling off, making it hard for the driver to maintain control, and the other two BMWs flanked its sides.

My mind raced, debating my options. With Bri in the car, there weren't a lot of them. They were all far too dangerous and I wasn't willing to put her life at risk.

"Son of a bitch, not this fucking bullshit again!"

I gripped the wheel even tighter while checking the mirrors. Only a couple of cars separated us now. With nightfall upon us, it was hard to see, but the features of the person resembled Miles. If that was the case, Sebastian and Aubrey were in the other cars. I slammed my foot down on the accelerator and prayed we made it to the next exit without my car blowing up. The engine protested loudly with plenty of grinding and clunking.

"Yo, Trey, what the hell is happening?" Micah asked in a near shout.

I merged through a few more cars to keep our distance. The exit was still five miles away and with the smoke pouring from my hood, we'd be lucky if we made it that far. My heart pounded roughly against my chest. I glanced at my rearview mirror and saw the BMWs driving erratically to keep up with us.

"Someone is trying to run us off the road. For having unlimited resources, these rich pricks sure aren't quick to use them. After all this time, you'd think they'd try some new tactics," I snapped, my eyes flickering between the gauges and my mirrors.

"What do you mean *again*? This isn't the first time?" Bri shrieked. I shook my head. "What the hell? You should've told someone, Trey. That's vehicular assault!"

"Bri's right. I've been telling you for months that you need to report this shit, but you keep saying you can handle it. How you've managed to cover things up at your house is beyond me, but your fucking luck has run out. Just pull over and call the cops before something really bad happens," Micah yelled.

My brain kicked into overdrive, trying to come up with my next move since there was only a few feet between us. Calling the police wouldn't do us any good. Two of the cars pulled alongside me while the other one bolted up front.

The precision driving unfolding around us could only be done by experts. Sebastian and company were far from it. I dug down deep to grab hold of my remaining strength to beat back the terror coursing through my veins. The car to my left veered into my lane, nearly broadsiding my side, but I zipped past it with only the rear-end getting clipped.

Bri gripped my arm, her eyes full of fright. "I don't think you're going to make it much further with the smoke barreling from the hood."

"That doesn't sound good, Trey. You need to pull over!" Micah screamed.

My heart hammered roughly against my chest, knowing our time was about up, but I had to try to get Bri to safety and the exit was a mere half-mile away. If I pushed the Acura to the limit, we stood a chance of making it off the freeway and to the gas station on the service road.

I opened the console and eyed the NOS. It was a huge risk to use it now, but I didn't see any other way of getting past them. Just as I was about to flick the switch, we were nailed again and I barely maintained control over the car. I slammed on the brakes and veered from the middle lane over to the right one to pull over. If we were lucky, one of the vehicles in the other lanes would stop and help us.

The BMW leading the pack flipped around, zipped through oncoming traffic, and headed straight at us, smashing into the left front end and sending us into a tailspin toward the embankment. I tried to crank the wheel to prevent us from hitting it, but everything in the car failed. We hit the side of the concrete hard and our bodies bounced around like pinballs.

Glass poured into the car from the broken windshield, slicing our exposed arms and faces. It felt like an ax cut through my left shoulder as it was torn from its socket. My mind blanked for a minute. When I opened my eyes seconds later, I looked over at Bri.

Blood trickled from her head and mouth. She blinked a few times before going for the handle, but that side of the car was pinned to the embankment. I tried my door, but couldn't get it open.

As the smell of gas flooded into the car, I coughed profusely. Smoke pouring from under the hood brought on a whole different wave of panic and I fought with my handle even more. Bri gasped for air while looking around.

She focused her frantic eyes on me as tears poured down her face. "How are we going to get out of here? I don't want to die!"

All of the muscles and tendons in my left shoulder were close to fraying completely apart and I wanted to pop it back into place so the agony spreading from that spot would stop, but it was secondary to getting us out of here. I grabbed on to the small amount of adrenaline coursing through my pores, unbuckled my seat belt, and kicked at the shattered windshield. Sharp pains shot throughout me, but I kept at it until we had an opening.

"Stay calm, Bri. We *will* get out. No one is dying today," I replied, still kicking.

I wished the confidence of my tone would have helped her in some way, but she was as hysterical as ever as she struggled to free herself. My eyes centered on the bone protruding from her right arm and her face contorted from the pain as she tried to get the jammed seatbelt open. The blood pouring from the gash on her head was damn near a waterfall.

Smoke barreled from the hood and the potency of the gas smell became overwhelming. My vision blurred and I was having a hard time processing my surroundings. Every facet of my body became heavy from the growing pain overtaking it.

I heard Micah shouting from my cell, but it was a faint echo. My brain and eyes struggled to focus on anything, almost like someone scrambled my brains with the best taser on the market. I forced my shaking hands toward Bri's seatbelt to unfasten it and pull her out, but didn't get the chance. A guy in a black ski mask pulled me through the windshield and dragged me away. I tried to get up, but my knees buckled and I collapsed against the concrete.

"You fucking worthless punk, you were supposed to be alone. Now, we really have a problem on our hands and it's all your damn fault."

My disoriented brain tried to recall hearing that voice or his tall features, but it wasn't familiar at all. I rolled to my side, doing my best to fight the growing urge to pass out. Blood poured from my shoulder and face and I prayed to every higher power Bri made it out.

After what seemed like an eternity, a different guy in the same black ski mask emerged through the smoke with Bri in his arms. Her head was slumped over his arm and she was bleeding in a lot more places than I originally observed. Every ounce of pain I felt in the past several minutes was nothing compared to the sheer anguish attacking me now.

A loud explosion nearly burst my eardrums and my heart stopped as I took on the fire and smoke barreling toward me. Someone grabbed me from behind and pulled me from the fireball mere inches away.

Once I was safely away from the explosion, the guy disappeared into the smoke, along with the other two. Sirens echoed in the distance before the sound of screeching tires against the asphalt replaced it. I forced myself to my knees and tried to crawl to Bri, who was a few feet away from me, but the shards of glass in my hands and legs protested with every movement I made. After only making it a couple more feet, I collapsed against the pavement, screaming in agony with the vast amount of pain shooting through my body. I tried desperately to keep my eyes open, but the black hole I was fighting against finally won.

* * *

I BLINKED to get my blurry vision to focus. It took me a minute to figure out I was in a hospital bed. My left arm was taped to my torso. An IV drip pumped cool liquid into my veins and my foggy brain put together it was morphine. I noticed my right hand was cuffed to the side of the bed. Even with drugs, my body didn't have the ability to fight off the dread consuming it. There was no fucking way I was getting out of this mess and I didn't deserve to either.

Where's Bri? More important, how is Bri? I need to get to her. I pray she's okay. I'll never forgive myself if she isn't.

I struggled against my restraint until my wrist became raw and banged the rail in frustration. My eyes circled the room and saw nothing but white walls, making me wonder if this was the prison ward of the hospital. There were no decorations, colors, or signs of hope and healing you typically saw in a patient's room.

Before I tried sliding my hand out of the cuff again, the door opened and closed in a swift motion. John McAndrews strode over to me in a sleek navy suit.

"I warned you to stay away from my daughter and look where we are now. She's in the hospital and it's your fault," John sneered, gripping my neck.

His fingers squeezed around it until I gasped for air. He released my throat, but hovered above me with his hands curled into tight fists—no doubt wanting to take a swing at me or finish choking me to death. I tried to grab the remote on my bed to call for someone before he tried to kill me, but he moved it out of reach.

I really wanted to slug the heartless bastard. My face burnt to a crisp with the rage blistering through me. "Did you have something to do with this? I know you've wanted me out of the picture for a while now and have no doubt that you'd be fine if it was a permanent departure. For as shitty as you treat Bri, it wouldn't shock me at all to have you not give a damn if anything happened to her either."

His soulless irises pinned a lethal glare on me. "If you think I'd put my own child in the hospital, you're about as dumb as you look."

My blood boiled over. "You're one evil son of a bitch and tried to drown her. It's not outrageous to think you'd have someone fuck with my car and run us off the road. I know a lot more about you than you think."

His face slipped into a superior look before he shot back, "A worthless punk like you couldn't possibly know a thing about me."

"Really? Because I know why you hate me, along with anyone and everything to do with the south side," I said through gritted teeth.

He straightened up, a shocked expression wiped away his smugness. "You've got a brass set of balls for sticking your nose in my business. My disdain for the south side is well-deserved. The area and people in it are nothing but a drain on the city."

I scoffed. "I'll be sure to pass that much along to Sean Fitzpatrick and his sons. I know firsthand how enraged they'd be when they caught wind of anyone disrespecting our side of town. I don't think that's a very good political move for you. Word on the street is he's a pretty big component in your reelection campaign. Pity if those funds disappeared."

His eyes widened before he smoothed out his face. "You don't want to be on my bad side. I have ways of making people suffer you'd never be able to wrap your head around. Believe me when I say, I have no problem executing them on you."

My heart thrashed violently against my chest. "When it comes to the south side, even sworn enemies will come together to rip apart anyone who looks down upon us. You're an idiot if you think otherwise. As far as whatever you do to me, bring it on, you smug son of a bitch. My future is over anyway. Do your worst. I don't give a fuck."

"If I were you, I'd keep my mouth shut or I may just change my mind about the very generous offer I'm about to give you," John bit back, piercing his eyes on me.

"If it's coming from you, it's not legit. I'm not taking a damn thing from you," I snapped, spitting at his feet.

His nostrils flared before he leaned into my space. "If you want people to leave you and your family alone, you'll take everything I have to offer."

I glared daggers at him. "Your heart is black as coal. There's not a chance in hell you'd do anything to help me or my family."

"You have no idea how villainous I can be. The lengths I will go to in order to get what I want know no bounds. You're no exception. If you want a chance of amounting to anything, you'll shut your mouth and listen," John replied, clutching my throat again.

I gasped for air, but couldn't pull in a solid breath. My eyes watered from the lack of oxygen. His grip loosened and I coughed nonstop. The anger fueling me thus far puttered out as the reality of him hurting me or my family descended upon me.

Vivid images of the accident flashed through my mind and the shears slicing away at my tattered heart brought on a bone-crushing amount of pain. I didn't care what happened to me or my future any longer. With all the mistakes I made this year, I wasn't very deserving of a promising one anyway.

I was an idiot for thinking I'd end all of this shit without any real help. I should've relayed more to Mr. West or Coach Barry, but I didn't. How many times was I told to come forward when things got out of control? I ignored it and the person who mattered the most to me paid the price for it.

If I'd just walked away from Bri months ago, she wouldn't be lying in a hospital bed—broken and bruised. I hadn't shed very many tears in my short life, but my eyes watered nonstop now. Scraping the bottom of the barrel for my last shred of strength was all I could do to prevent them from cascading down my cheeks. There weren't enough words in the world to describe how much I hated myself as I nodded for John to continue with whatever he came here to say.

He crossed his arms. "I'm glad you came to your senses. All I want you to do is stay out of my daughter's life. If you do, I'll have the charges against you dropped and make sure the Du Ponts, Dudleys, and Livingstons steer clear of your family."

I gazed away. "How do I know you'll stick to your word? You lie to everyone. Give me one good reason why I should believe you."

John grabbed my chin. "I think you're aware of how much I've despised having you in Brianna's life. I couldn't get through to her, but you're in a position where you need my help if you stand a shot at staying alive for the foreseeable future."

I shook my head until he let go of me. "It's not as easy to take me out as you think. I still don't have any reason to believe you'll do anything to end everything."

"Let's just say a line was crossed in the worst way. You stay out of Brianna's life and get to live one of your own. It's that simple."

His take-it-or-leave it tone tapped into the angry beast within me, but he only popped up his head before ducking down below. We both realized there wasn't any other way to end this social class warfare. As much as accepting defeat crippled me, I was out of my league. I hated the whole fucking world for doing this to Bri and me. What was left of the frayed strings holding my heart together snapped and it shattered, along with the rest of me.

It felt as though I was strapped down and an endless amount of rubble and debris were being dumped over me. "I'll stay away from her under one condition."

He arched an eyebrow. "What's your condition?"

"I get to say goodbye to her. She'll need to hear what I have to say in order for her to accept we can't be together. Otherwise, she'll just end up finding a way to see me. Seeing as you've exhausted what I assume is a lot of time and money to keep her from doing so, it'd probably be in your best interest to let me say what I need to say."

"Once she's awake, you can have a moment with her, but then I better not see you around her again."

I glared. "I got the gist of the deal."

He walked over and opened the door. Moments later, two officers came into the room and uncuffed me. Passing them a USB drive, John advised, "I spoke with the Chief of Police and he confirmed through traffic cams that Mr. Donovan was in no way responsible for what happened this evening. I suggest you try finding the parties behind it and start with this."

The chubbier cop's cheeks flushed bright red as he mumbled, "Our apologies again, Senator McAndrews." He paused and looked at me. "The next time someone is chasing you on the road, do the right thing and contact the authorities. Do you understand, son?"

Biting my cheeks to prevent myself from mouthing off, I nodded. They disappeared out the door. With the machetes slashing away at my body, coupled with the steel rod running through my head, I lost the will to keep my eyes open. As I drifted toward the darkness, I welcomed the agony that would more than likely be my best friend for a *very* long time.

* * *

THE FOLLOWING few days went by in a blur. I found out from Micah and Mia that the incident at the house was a drive-by gone awry. I wasn't exactly sure I believed them, especially after Micah's latest involvement with the Fitzpatricks and everything I learned about the people going after me, but wasn't able to dispute it either. When it happened, my mom was outside with the kids and barely got them to safety. That put her into labor. She had my baby brother in the wee hours of the morning. After she delivered, Lyla informed my parents what happened to me.

My dad was in and out over the past few days to check on me, but I didn't want him here. It was actually that way with everyone who passed through to see how I was. There were a lot of kids from Chamberlain, including my coaches, along with plenty of people from the neighborhood, but I kept their visits brief, claiming I was still really tired from it all. The truth was, I'd let so many people down and the coward within me couldn't bear to look anyone in the eye and see the well-deserved disappointment.

On the day we were supposed to be heading to prom, I was cleared to go home. My dad, along with Micah and Mia, arrived at the hospital a few hours ago to pick me up. Aside from some broken ribs and an upcoming shoulder surgery, I'd make a full recovery. On the surface, I looked fine, but no one knew about the massive damage to my insides. Everything within me was a mangled mess and I wasn't even sure where to start to try and put myself back together.

Bri woke up this morning and had a slew of visitors. I wasn't at all eager to see her and let the countless amounts of people go in before me. I wasn't ready to be the person who destroyed Bri's beautiful spirit, but that was exactly what I was about to do. I grasped the back of my neck while pacing outside of her room. My heart faltered. The expectation was for it to keep beating, but it was having a hard time doing so.

Micah and Mia finally walked out with their hands intertwined. As soon as Mia saw me, the wide smile on her face vanished. I probably looked like a homeless person by now. Showering and shaving weren't a priority for me. I probably smelled a little fresh and looked close to how I felt.

"You're not leaving, are you?" I asked, fighting off a fresh bout of anguish.

Mia tilted her head to the side. "No, we were going to grab some

DVDs and food to have a movie night with you guys. We talked about this yesterday, remember? Are you okay, Trey?"

Between the weights sitting on my chest and what was left of my grated heart, it was hard to process a coherent thought. Both would cripple me soon if I let them in for too long. I rubbed a hand down my face. "The concussion hasn't fully passed yet. Some things slip my mind. I just wanted to make sure you weren't leaving for the night."

"Of course not. You two are way more important to us than going to prom," Mia replied, her eyes wide and a little hurt.

I peered at Micah. "Can you grab the movies and dinner for you two? I need a moment with Mia before heading in to see Bri."

Judging by the sad look in his eyes, Micah knew what I was about to do and pulled me in for a brief hug before striding down the hall.

"Trey, you're starting to freak me out," Mia spoke up, her chin trembling.

I rested my good hand on her shoulder. "I'm about to go in and see Bri. Please stay here. After I leave, she'll need you."

Mia's eyes watered. "Whatever you're about to do, *please* don't. She's the best thing that's ever happened to you."

If there was anything left of my heart, it would've shattered to fine pieces, but there was nothing left to break. Tears pricked my eyes as I whispered, "I know she is, but I'm the worst thing that's happened to her." Mia opened her mouth, but I shook my head. "I've already made up my mind. Please promise me you'll be right here when I get back."

She nodded while wiping away her tears. Forcing my lead-filled legs to move toward Bri's door took a herculean effort and I barely could raise my hand to turn the knob. As I walked into the room, my stomach left this dimension and I fought against the urge to throw up.

All the air in my body dissipated after I saw the cuts on her beautiful face, along with some more on her neck and collarbone. What seemed like a vice around my windpipe squeezed even harder after my eyes centered on her casted right wrist. My heart refused to beat as I gazed at her injuries—all because of me. A spark fired through her eyes and she crooked a finger for me to come closer.

"I'm very sorry, but I can't stay long. After you hear what I have to say, I'll doubt you'll want me to be here either," I forced out, keeping my distance.

Her monitor beeped louder. "I haven't seen you for days and you open with a line like that. What the hell is going on, Trey? Is something wrong with your mom?"

What was left of my minced heart went through the blender again and got shoved back into my body, barely beating. I heaved in a breath, hoping it would do something to help me focus, but all I could really think about was how every single part of me ached in an excruciating way I never wanted to experience again.

"No, my mom's fine. She had Trevor the night of the accident and they were released from the hospital yesterday."

Shoving herself up from her pillows, Bri winced after the pain in her casted wrist caught up with her. Everything inside me was desperate to comfort her, but I forced myself to stay put. Doing so destroyed the last few pieces of strength holding me together.

"My dad said they have the people who drove us off the road in custody and they've confessed to everything, including all the things the Du Ponts, Dudleys, and Livingstons have done to you and your family. Don't you see? It's over. You don't have to look over your shoulder anymore," Bri choked out, her green eyes misting up.

Hearing her growing anxiety and all the machines hooked up to her frantically beeping every few seconds finally won out. I couldn't handle being away from Bri any longer, slid a chair next to the bed, and took her left hand in mine.

"It's not over, Bri. I don't think it really ever is when social classes go toe-to-toe. Until I'm sure no one is lurking around the corner, waiting to take me out, I can't be around you anymore. Seeing you hurt in any way has always broken my heart, but knowing I was the reason for it is *unbearable*."

She gasped for air before tears poured down her cheeks. "Please don't give up on us. If you do, they've already won the war. We can't let them win. *Please* stay with me."

A single tear cascaded down my face. "I'm not ever giving up on you. I want you to know that I'll *never* give up. I told you that you're worth fighting for and you still are. I believe in us, but I just don't think this is our time."

The hysterical sobs coming from her broke my heart all over again. As the pieces of it fell to the floor, I gasped for my next breath. Before I collapsed from the weight of it all, I got up, rested my forehead on hers, and lightly brushed my lips across her mouth.

"Please don't cry. This isn't the end of the road for us. We're on a detour neither one of us could've anticipated. When things die down, I promise I'll *always* find a way to see you. It just has to be different going forward. Will you wait for our someday?"

I held my breath while wiping away her tears and ran my hands down her arms to try to calm her down. Her trembling stopped somewhat, but I kept caressing her sides, hoping she'd find some sort of solace. I didn't deserve any, but after everything Bri went through in the last few days, she sure as hell did.

Her eyes flitted around as she fought off another round of waterworks. She crashed her mouth into mine, pouring every ounce of her soul into that kiss with every swoop of her tongue, and I did the same for just a minute. With each gentle caress, I wanted her to remember how much I truly did care for her. As our lips parted for what I knew would be the last time in a while, I savored the softness to her lips and her soothing touch.

I wasn't sure how my heart would ever beat normally again. At the moment, it was ground hamburger with the expectation of keeping my body running and I wasn't all that confident it'd do it, especially since my heartbeats were fewer and farther between.

In between tears and sniffles, Bri whispered, "I believe that this isn't our end. So yes, I'll step into the shadows with you. When you walk out that door, you're leaving with my heart. Please don't break your promise. Do whatever it takes to find ways to see me."

There wasn't anything I could do to prevent my own tears. They flowed down my face freely as I nodded. Her sobs grew louder and I knew I couldn't be here much longer without losing my will to leave her.

I kissed the top of her head and forced my legs toward the door. She cried even harder while I walked away, making each step unbearable. Just as I was about to open the door, I turned to look at Bri one last time and nearly collapsed to the floor as I watched her entire body buckle, knowing I was the cause of her pain.

"Bri, you'll *always* be the shining light to my world. If it's the very last thing I do, I'll get us to our someday," I promised.

Without a look back, I shuffled into the hallway. Mia took one look at me and nearly burst into tears. I motioned for her to go and sit with Bri before I slid down the wall. My body no longer had the will to move and I didn't have a desire to go anywhere either. The only place I wanted to be was a mere few feet away and I willingly walked away from the one person in the world I couldn't live without and gave her a partial truth as to why I did it. I'd definitely come full circle with her. I was the same jackass she met last fall.

I clutched my knees as the tears began to fall at a relentless pace. I bit my fist to keep from screaming as waves of agony overtook my body. All the pain I'd experienced in my life up to this point was like a pinch to the arm. Taking in air became a struggle. It felt like I was caught in the undertow and didn't stand a chance at getting another solid breath and all I wanted was one more—if only to make things right with Bri.

I shoved myself upward, but didn't get very far. The insufferable ache sifting through me wouldn't allow for it and I collapsed on my first try. My tears hit the cool floor beneath me and I angrily wiped them away before taking a deep breath and pushing myself up again.

My sore muscles protested the exertion, but I managed to get to my knees. I heaved in a few breaths to get the tears to stop. Wiping my eyes with the sleeve of my shirt, I struggled to my feet and kept my hand on the wall while walking down the long, desolate hallway.

The only thing that kept me moving was knowing I'd find a way back to her. I'd get us to our someday. Bri was my reason to keep pushing back when life pushed too hard. To have her, I'd *always* fight back. This wasn't the end for us and that was all I needed to focus on to keep moving forward.

TO BE CONTINUED...

EPILOGUE

BRI
Four years later...

My mind wandered as my date sloppily explored the inside of my mouth. I willed myself to feel *anything* and was more than aggravated when nothing sparked. I knew the first time Trey kissed me he ruined me for other guys, but to actually have proof of it was downright frustrating. I'd hoped to have some sort of attraction to Spencer. None of that mattered to my dormant body and I didn't know who I was angrier with: Trey or myself.

I probably should've ended this make out session a half hour ago, but I didn't want to bruise his ego entirely. Spencer was pretty popular on campus with a reputation for knowing how to show a girl a real good time, but apparently that was nothing but hype. We definitely wouldn't be seeing one another again, and while I should feel somewhat bad about it, I didn't.

His tongue slid along the inside of my cheek and I refrained from shaking my head. It floored me that he didn't know how to properly kiss a girl. Then again, no one kissed a girl like Trey Donovan. His cocky smirk ran through my mind and my damn cheeks flushed on cue. I was so over my body betraying me when it came to him. I really didn't want to get into this make out session by thinking of kissing him rather than my date, but that happened more than I cared to admit.

My heart fluttered as Trey consumed my thoughts. Tantalizing tingles I wanted Spencer to actually produce ran wild throughout me. Knowing it was completely wrong on my part didn't stop my lips from getting hungrier. I really needed to get a grip on reality or else I'd end up doing something stupid—like sleeping with Spencer and imagining it was Trey.

I hate when this happens. Thinking of kissing or having sex with Trey while I'm with someone else makes me a supreme bitch and the sad part is there's nothing I can do about it once the ball starts rolling. I know it's wrong, but that never seems to matter to my body.

Since the day Trey left me in the hospital four years ago, I hadn't really felt whole. Sometimes weeks went by before we could find a moment alone. Being in his arms made everything around me richer and fuller, but not knowing how long it'd last or when we'd finally move forward again brought on waves of desolation I desperately tried to avoid.

In a year and a half, we'd be graduating. I didn't want to start the next chapter of my life with things the way they were with us now. Sharing the same social circles and going to the same college, yet pretending we didn't want a thing to do with one another, was downright exhausting. I wasn't about to start a career under these circumstances.

My frustrations with where things stood with Trey got the best of me and I bit down on Spencer's lower lip. He pulled away, a shocked look on his face. "What the hell was that all about, Bri?"

"I'm sorry," I muttered as my cheeks burnt to a crisp.

Spencer gripped my arm to the point of pain. "There's plenty of girls lining up to have a shot with me. Don't flatter yourself by thinking you're the only one."

"Get your goddamn hands off me, you jackass," I snapped, wiggling my arm free.

His hold on me tightened before he sneered, "I thought you liked it rough. At least that's what I've heard."

This went from a really awkward moment to a dangerous one. I ignored how badly my nerves stood on end and reminded myself I was no longer a scared, thirteen-year-old girl. A rush of adrenaline coasted through my body.

Narrowing my eyes to slits, I yanked my arm free. It had been a very long time since anyone grabbed me like that and I promised myself no one would ever inflict that kind of pain on me again. I hopped up from his couch, slid on my black leather jacket, and retrieved my purse.

Spencer stared at me in disgust before jumping into my space. My heart rate hit supersonic mode. I strode to the door, opened it, and snapped, "If you ever touch me again, I swear to God, you'll regret being born."

"If you think I'm scared of you or your daddy, think again. I guess the rumors about you are true then, huh?"

"What are you talking about?"

He crossed his arms. "That all you do is use guys to get back at Trey Donovan. Everyone on campus knows it. If you had half a brain, you'd see he's just using you when he sees fit. It's called a booty call, doll. That's all you'll ever be. You're kidding yourself if you think otherwise."

I gave him a murderous glare. "You're just trying to build up your own ego because I rejected you."

"You're hotter than most of the chicks on campus. I figured what the hell, especially since the word on the street is that you're also pretty easy. Truth be told, I only asked you out to piss him off. Seeing as you don't give a fuck when you use someone, I plan on playing a game of my own and *I'll* be the one deciding when it's over," Spencer replied in a chilling tone.

I swallowed against the bile creeping up my throat, stormed out of his apartment, and ran down the hall. He followed me, pounded on the side of the doorframe, and shouted, "You can run, but you can't hide."

My nerves were on high alert as I raced down the stairs. By the time I reached the bottom, my hands were shaking. The jackass behind me was definitely part of the reason my body spiraled out of control, but it was also my own damn fault. If I wasn't always trying to pretend I was with someone other than Trey, I wouldn't have put myself in such a horrible position.

Even though we were careful not to be seen in public, I suspected people knew we were still tied to one another. There were just certain things we couldn't avoid when we were around each other. I'd caught him in plenty of lusty, lingering stares, and was guilty of it myself. It'd take a complete moron not to know something was still going on between us.

Every time I brought it up with Trey, we fought about it. Since we hardly found time to get lost in one another's arms, I didn't bring up our fucked up situation very often. I hated wasting any precious second I got with him and put it on a sidebar. *No more.*

The anger rolling through my body was something I'd gotten used to in the past four years, but the heaviness spreading between my chest and my heart would cripple me any day now. I couldn't handle feeling like I was about to suffocate on a daily basis. Tears pricked my eyes on my way to my red Audi A8. Thunder rolled from the dark heavens above and the impending rainstorm was definitely a reflection of everything going on inside me.

As I got into my car, Spencer's parting words ran through my mind. Part of me knew it was an empty threat, but I couldn't help looking over my shoulder to make sure I wasn't being followed. The lot was clear. I cranked the ignition and pulled my jacket down to assess my throbbing arm, which was slightly red.

I rested my head on my steering wheel. As the pressure in my chest became harder to ignore, my tears pressed for release even more, but I refused to let it happen. Blistering bouts of anger coasted through my veins and chased away the panic. Banging the dashboard in frustration, I knew I couldn't keep doing this any longer, but it was up to me to make a change. Otherwise, I'd keep going in the same circle.

The reasons Trey listed off for us to remain apart from one another didn't apply anymore. All the pricks who tried to ruin his life were no longer a factor. None of that mattered to Trey. He still claimed it was best we kept our distance from one another in public and I had no fucking clue why.

My stomach twisted and turned as our accident flashed through my head. Something happened in the days after it that made Trey distance himself from me. Everything that went wrong with us was somehow tied to that day. I needed to get the bottom of it or I'd end up having a nervous breakdown. I couldn't handle pretending to lead two different lives any longer. My body was being ripped to pieces. Sitting on the sidelines waiting for something to change between us was no longer an option.

Love was a tricky and complicated thing. I couldn't keep letting the chips fall where they may when it came to Trey and me. I really wanted to believe love truly did conquer all, but the piercing pain in my heart made me question it. Standing in the shadows, waiting for our someday, wasn't something I could do anymore. Whether Trey liked it or not, he needed to make a choice to either be with me or let me go.

ACKNOWLEDGMENTS

A very special thank you to my critique partner, Kat. I honestly couldn't do this without you. I appreciate your help more than you will ever know. Your input has made this book so much better in the end and I can't thank you enough for it. Above all that, I'm so very blessed to call you one of my dearest friends. Thank you so much for always pushing me to be at my best, whether it's in writing or my life.

Thank you so much to Jamie, Kelsey, and Autumn for taking this book in its beginning stages and reading it. Your thoughts and suggestions mean the world to me. I truly hope you all know how much you mean to me. More importantly, I'm so very grateful our paths crossed and that I can call you my friends. You all mean so much to me!

I cannot thank my designer, L.J., enough. With each cover you design for me, you just blow my mind away with your talent. You always manage to capture the stories I tell so beautifully with your designs. I can't wait to see what you do with the next one!

I'll never be able to thank the blogging community enough for all the hard work you do. You are the rock stars of the reading world and I cannot express enough thanks for what you do for me and every other author out there. You're all seriously my heroes!

Finally, a very big thank you to all the readers. I will never be able to tell you how much it means that you took a chance on me as an author. Thank you so much for your continued support of me! It truly means more than any words will ever express!

ABOUT THE AUTHOR

Photo Credit: Amber Eckman

M. M. Koenig, a graduate from the University of Minnesota. She is a passionate person with many interests. The greatest of those is a good story accompanied by a killer soundtrack and her loving dog by her side.

Find M. M. Koenig online to stay up to date on news, teasers, deleted scenes, and upcoming projects at her website https://www.mmkoenig.com/ and her social links below.

EXCERPT OF WAITING FOR SOMEDAY

THE SOMEDAY SERIES #2

Thunder roared from the angry clouds above me. A few drops of rain fell from the bristling skies as I hustled out of the restaurant and over to my car. Even though my latest date ended up being another dud, it was better than the one I had with Spencer last week. Goosebumps prickled along my arms as his parting remark ran through my mind.

Seeing as you don't give a fuck when you use someone, I plan on playing a game of my own, and I'll be the one deciding when it's over. You can run, but you can't hide.

I glanced over my shoulder, noticing someone at the edge of the restaurant. Panic slithered through me until I realized it was only a waiter disposing of some trash. When Spencer spewed that nonsense, the pure hate behind his soulless brown eyes was undeniable. For someone who was the poster boy for Abercrombie, from his blond hair to his perfect physique, it boggled my mind he was so angry things between us didn't work out, especially since it was only *one* date.

He could be with any girl on campus, so his fascination with me was unsettling to say the least. I wasn't sure what his agenda was, nor did I really want to find out, but I couldn't help but wonder if my less than stellar dating record played into it. If things between Trey and I weren't such a mess, I wouldn't have entertained the idea of dating Spencer or anyone else.

Part of me was still angry with myself for even agreeing to go in the first place. Since he was in the same frat as Jackson, I had gotten to know a little about him over the years, but always wrote his flirting off as a simple crush, which was why I didn't think twice about a simple date. If it didn't work out, I figured he'd move on to the next girl. Never in a million years did I expect it to end in a threat I couldn't seem to shake. Utter frustration mixed with growing terror, creating a toxic sensation on its way to becoming all too familiar.

Wrapping my arms around myself, I picked up my pace. Knowing I just saw someone from the restaurant staff doing their job should've been enough to ease my nerves, but my hands still twitched and my heart pounded at a relentless rate.

I sucked in a deep breath and pushed Spencer's heinous words from my mind. He was like so many other spoiled rich kids. Letting him get under my skin was very weak on my part. Unlike him, and a lot of people with an elite upbringing, I refused to ride the coattails of my parents. For a second, I thought maybe that was why he was so pissed at me, but quickly dismissed it.

Being the daughter of a power-hungry senator who had no problem putting a security detail on me, I should have been used to unwanted people popping up out of nowhere and the occasional threat tossed my way, but I wasn't, and probably never would be.

As I reached my red Audi A8, the heavens opened and the rain came down in sheets. I unlocked my car and jammed my key in the ignition before blasting the heat and looking around one last time to make sure the coast was clear. Aside from a few patrons darting to their cars, there wasn't anything out of the ordinary. I gently rolled my neck a few times, praying it'd be enough to cease the chills coasting down my back.

Thankfully, the coping technique worked to a degree and my fingers stopped trembling. After checking the mirrors one last time, I pulled out of the parking lot and into traffic. On my way to the interstate, "Home" rang from my cell.

"What's up, Mia? I thought you were spending the night with Micah."

"Well, that was the plan, but he flaked on me *again*. Oh shit, I just remembered you had a date tonight. I'm not interrupting, am I?"

"No, you're not. It ended early—and on a sour note," I admitted, not hiding my frustration.

Mia released a heavy sigh. "The lethalness of your tone means Trey messed things up again. When are you going to stop letting him interfere with your love life? I don't understand this weird state you've been in for far too long. You guys either need to commit or move on."

"I'm not in the mood to pick apart all my issues with Trey," I shot back.

"I'm sorry. I didn't mean to come off like a bitch," Mia murmured, her tone apologetic.

"Why did Micah end up canceling on you this time?"

"Apparently, he got called into work, but I'm not sure if he's telling the truth. I can't tell anymore. He's barely been clean for six months. He promised me he was done dealing and using, but I can't help doubting him at times, especially when he still hangs out with his friends who deal."

Whenever Mia rambled that much, she was close to her breaking point. Completely aggravated with the men in our lives, I bit the inside of my cheek to prevent myself from releasing the cathartic scream begging for freedom. A frustrated huff slipped out in its place. The sad part was I didn't have any words of wisdom for her.

I weaved over to the right lane and took one of the exits for Eckman. "Since your night was shot to hell, I assume you're in the journalism building. I'm heading that way to pick you up."

"Somedays, I swear you know me better than I know myself," Mia mused.

I didn't need to be with her to know her smile matched the wide one spreading across my face. "That's just because you don't have enough faith in yourself as you should."

"I could say the same about you, sass. With how we grew up, it's a miracle we turned out somewhat normal," Mia muttered, her tone humorless.

All the tension in my body resurfaced in an instant. "Let's not take a trip down that *particular* avenue of memory lane."

"Good point. So, what do you have in mind for tonight?" Mia asked, trying to sound excited, but her situation with Micah was clearly still on the forefront of her mind.

I rotated my neck a few times to ease the stiffness. "Let's grab a drink at Shorty's and see where the night takes us. God knows I could use a break."

As I drove along the side streets, the rain came down even harder. Another loud clap of thunder sounded. I could've lived with the way it tweaked my nerves; it was the beep of an incoming text that sent shivers up my spine. The nagging feeling in my gut led me to believe once I hung up with Mia, I'd have another cryptic text to deal with.

Focusing on the one person who still calmed my nerves the best had become a bittersweet coping mechanism. Trey crept into my thoughts. The storm was a good reflection of the fucked-up state we'd been in for years. Piercing pain shot through me and settled in my chest. With each year that passed, the boulder sitting there grew, probably rivaling Ayers Rock. When Trey left me in the hospital after our accident, he walked away with my heart and never gave it back. I never had the courage to ask for it either.

Plenty of smoking hot guys attended Eckman, and I'd gone on a lot of dates, but not one guy made my heart flutter the way Trey did. Being wrapped up in his arms was still the closest thing to home I'd ever experienced. I tried *really* hard to give whoever asked me out a fair shot, but as much as I wished sparks flew, they never did.

Having Trey constantly interfere when I did have a date didn't help matters. But that was a separate issue in itself—especially since seeing other people was his damn idea, even though it went against his jealous nature. Every time I pointed that fact out, it led to an argument. The side of me that couldn't walk away from him always won and I'd back down.

I didn't like the way things were between us, but it was better than not having him in my life at all. Anything was better than the agony I experienced our entire senior year. His refusal to acknowledge my existence during that time was by far the worst pain I'd ever gone through, so I was willing to take what I could get with him now. It probably didn't make sense to a lot of people, but when you give your heart to someone else, reason and logic didn't always line up with the way things *should* be.

Over the last few years, we had dated other people to make it look like we weren't a couple, then would sneak off when we thought no one was paying attention. Our friends were aware we still spent time together behind closed doors, so other people probably did too. My grip on the steering wheel tightened, utterly frustrated with myself for not having the strength to force a much-needed change with Trey.

Ignoring him in public hurt like hell. He claimed it was necessary, but refused to explain why. Since we didn't see a lot of each other, I was too chicken-shit to call him on it. I never did get to the bottom of why we stepped into the shadows in the first place, but it was time I started putting a little more effort into it. Not tonight, though. Being a good best friend to Mia came first. This past year had been anything but easy for her. I had to be there for her in all the ways she was for me when I needed her the most.

If it weren't for her, I never would've survived our senior year of high school. She spent countless nights letting me rant and cry my eyes out. I barely had the strength to function most days. Mia was the one who kept me focused on my future and reminded me what went down always found its way back up. To say I was a bit of a handful to deal with was an understatement. Looking back on that time still made me cringe. On cue, my body recoiled as unpleasant memories and my abhorrent behavior drifted through my mind.

Knowing Mia would always be there for me brought a wave of comfort. She was the sister I never had, and I was so grateful our paths had crossed in junior high. A lot had happened over the years, but she'd always been the constant in my life.

Mia cleared her throat. "Bri, did you hear what I said?"

I pinched the bridge of my nose. "Sorry. My mind wandered for a minute."

"No worries. It happens to me all the time. Do you want me to see if Jackson and Shane are around?"

Most days, Jackson annoyed the hell out of me, but his carefree nature was infectious, and I was grateful for his friendship. His upbringing had been similar to my and Shane's, but he was a lot like us when it came to our parents' notoriety—he wanted nothing to do with it and was more than determined to make his own statement on the world without a lick of their input or help.

Mia met Jackson our freshman year, and he'd instantly fit right in with the rest of us. Well, with the exception of Micah, but that had more to do with his undeniably hot physique and charismatic personality. Micah saw him as a threat, which was understandable since Jackson and Mia had *a lot* in common.

"I'm surprised Jackson isn't with you. That boy follows you everywhere. You know that's half of your problem when it comes to Micah, right?"

"Jealousy is natural in any relationship, so there isn't much I can do to prevent it from happening with Micah. God knows I get jealous when girls throw themselves at him. Whenever you give your heart to someone, it's only human to be territorial when you feel threatened by someone else. Jackson is just a friend. He's a flirt and has taken more girls to bed than I can count. Nothing is *ever* going to happen with him. Micah needs to get that through his head."

"I hate when you have well-made points. Are you sure you don't want to consider taking some sociology courses with me next semester? They'd be a great minor or second degree and would certainly be helpful with the amazing journalist you're going to be someday," I said, hopeful.

I missed having classes with her. Our first two years at Eckman, we'd taken as many general courses as we could together, but now, we were more focused on our degrees. Mia spent most of her days on the opposite side of campus working on finishing her journalism degree while I split my time between the social science and business buildings to complete my sociology and management degrees.

"I'll stick to writing. We live in one messed up world, and I'm not sure I want to analyze it any further than I have to for my articles."

"You're missing out. Go ahead and give the guys a call. They're probably already tearing up the town, but maybe they'll swing our way." I turned onto Lockhart Drive and found a parking spot in front of the Hennessey Building.

"What are Peyton and Kylie up to tonight? They always make for an interesting evening," Mia mused.

I scoffed. "I'm not sure what they have going on, but putting Jackson and Peyton in the same vicinity isn't a good idea. If they run into each other, I doubt it'll end well."

"You're probably right. Jackson won't tell me what happened between them, and Peyton being just as tight-lipped makes me wonder how things ended up so sideways for them."

Heavy raindrops pelted my windshield as I parked my car. "I'm here. Finish up whatever you're editing and give the guys a call on your way down. Oh, and try to keep your hair covered. It's pouring out, and there's only so much I can do for your crazy blonde mane without my blow dryer and curling iron."

"I'll be there in a minute. I have no doubt you'll work your magic on me. Besides, I don't need to be dolled up to kick your ass in pool and darts," Mia teased as she hung up.

I shivered, and it wasn't from the strong winds rattling around. Hearing the word "doll" in any form still made my skin crawl. After a lot of pushing from Kelsey, I went to a shrink to try to deal with it. I hadn't exactly been easy to deal with after Trey distanced himself from me, so it was the least I could do for her.

But all the therapy in the world would never change what Sebastian did to me. Having the shrink poke at my relationship with my parents didn't help either, so eventually, I stopped going. That wasn't a topic I could ever talk about—not without severe repercussions. Mia and I leaned on each other for everything, and that was all I really needed to survive whatever life threw at me. With that reassurance, I opened the text, praying it was from Kylie or Peyton.

Unknown number.

Keep looking over your shoulder. I'm always watching. This is only the beginning. The real fun hasn't even started yet.

Heavy weights overtook my upper body, and I heaved in several deep breaths to keep the darkness at bay. The message was too similar to a couple others I'd received over the past week. I really didn't want to give any of them a second thought. It was a simple scare tactic. If I let them bother me, Spencer would win, and I wasn't about to let that happen. He was simply messing with me to build his ego back up.

That was all it could be. I dug deep to grasp onto the strength that had gotten me through *a lot* of horrific things. This situation wasn't even close to some, and remembering that helped steady my erratic breaths. He'd grow bored soon enough. There was no need to overanalyze it any more than I already had.

Once the pressure in my chest was manageable, I pulled down my visor and opened the mirror. Seeing my green eyes mist free made the corners of my mouth curl into a small smile. I rubbed away the goosebumps on my arms, set my cell in the console, and unzipped my large, black Marc Jacobs purse to grab my makeup and bottle of Chanel No. 4.

After applying various shades of eyeshadow that complimented the vibrant colors in my dark purple, low-cut blouse and black skirt, I retrieved my eyeliner and mascara. I ran a few fingers through my long brown hair a couple times to get it to frame my face.

My gaze drifted across the brick structure to see if the lights were off in the paper's office. The wind picked up even more, sending yellow, red, and orange leaves into the air before they fell on the trimmed hedges in front of the building.

A loud horn blasted from the street, and I dropped my perfume. My heart thrashed against my chest as I leaned over to grab it. I glanced around a few more times to check for any new cars in the lot. When I didn't see any, I released a riled huff, more than annoyed with myself for getting worked up *again*.

Sheesh. I really need to get a handle on my paranoia. If I keep thinking the worst-case in every situation thrown at me, I'm going to put myself in an early grave.

I shook off the lingering jitters and flipped the radio station from hard rock to pop. Just as I tossed my makeup and perfume back in my purse, "Never Say Never" echoed through the car. I picked up my phone and stared at Trey's damn cocky smirk. A strong surge of tingles spread between my legs and a small band of butterflies stirred to life inside me. Not particularly caring for the effect Trey still had on me after all this time, I cursed my traitorous body and cleared his call.

I peered through the rain crashing against my windshield to see if Mia was on her way. Watching her dart around large puddles with her messenger bag over her head brought a wide smile to my face. She hopped in before tossing her bag and purse behind her. Mia rubbed her hands together, but gave up just as fast and put them in front of the heater. I rolled my eyes and hit the gas once her seatbelt was in place. For the beginning of October, it was on the chilly side, but she acted like it was the dead of winter.

Mia gave me a playful glare. "I'm not overreacting. It's freaking freezing outside. The white shit is going to fly soon, and I'm already dreading it."

The Fray filled the car again, and I chipped away at my purple and black nail polish. You'd think Trey would take the hint. If I sent his call to voicemail once already, it was clear I didn't want to talk to him, but I wasn't all that surprised. He was still the most stubborn person I knew.

Mia's shoulders sagged. "You don't have to worry about him popping up tonight. Trevor and Tighe have chicken pox, so he went home to help his mom."

Their cute little faces ran through my head, making my heart twinge. Over the years, I never stopped caring for his family. To this day, Lillian still checked in with me, and it meant more than she would ever understand. She was very good about leaving Trey out of the conversation, but I knew she wanted us to find our way again.

After setting the windshield wipers on the highest setting, I made my way through the small streets on campus. My eyes flickered between her and the road. "Did you reach the guys?"

She fiddled with the bracelets on her wrists. "Yeah. They're heading to Shorty's. Apparently, Jackson is striking out left and right, so it didn't take long to convince them to join us."

I smirked. "No shock there. It's only a matter of time before he figures out he's slept with half the student body."

Mia rolled her eyes. "I swear you and Jackson get some sort of weird pleasure out of making fun of one another. Just try to be nice tonight. I think his ego is a little bruised."

"I'm not making any promises. He usually deserves my colorful comments. It's probably not a bad thing for him to figure out he's a womanizer."

"He's got such a great heart. I wish he'd share it with more people, but he's got it tucked away, and I can't help but wonder why," Mia replied, her face thoughtful.

I squinted while making my way through the tight side streets. The rain didn't look like it would let up anytime soon, and seeing anything in front of me was difficult. I was grateful it was only a five-minute drive.

"I don't think you're the only one who's curious about that one, but I also doubt you'll get an answer any time soon." Mia scowled at me. A sincere smile quirked from my lips. "You know I'm teasing. Jackson's a great friend. Aside from you and Shane, I've never met anyone as loyal. He's been a great addition to our tribe."

"Did you just refer to our circle of friends as a tribe?" Mia asked, amused.

My grin widened. "Yes, I did. It's from one of the paintings Peyton and Kylie picked up for our house. I have to give them credit. It's a pretty inspiring message."

Tilting her head to the side, she inquired, "I figured it was something you picked up in one of your sociology classes. I don't remember seeing that one. What does it say?"

"That's probably because it's been a few weeks since you stopped by and they just got it a few days ago."

She anxiously wrung her hands together, and her face fell, a guilty look overtaking it. I placed my hand over them, hoping she'd see the apology in my eyes. "Hey, I'm sorry. Please don't beat yourself up. You've had a lot going on. It was a crappy remark on my part."

Mia sniffed. "There's some truth in it. I've been so wrapped up in Micah, I haven't done a very good job at being there for everyone else. I'm really sorry."

Intertwining her pinky with mine, I declared, "We're making a promise right now. We're not going to discuss Micah or Trey for the rest of the night. We owe it to ourselves and our friendship to have a great night."

Mia tightened her hold on my finger. "Deal. So, back to the painting. I'm curious, especially since Peyton and Kylie bought it. They usually purchase posters about partying or abstract pieces of nude men."

I stopped at the intersection and waited for the light to turn green. My eyes centered on the road ahead of us to see if there was any parking available in front of the bar. Just as the light changed, a car vacated a spot not too far from Shorty's. I hit the gas and zipped over to it. Mia watched in awe as I maneuvered my Audi into the tight space with ease and killed the ignition.

Before we got out, I turned to her. "It's a pretty simple message. 'Find your tribe. Love them hard.' I stared at it for a half hour after the girls hung it on the wall. It made me realize how lucky I am to have you guys as friends. Even with all the ups and downs with Trey, I'm still grateful he's in my life. You all challenge me and inspire me to be a better person. A lot of people believe you won't hang on to very many friends from high school or college, but I know in my heart the four of you will always be a part of my life, and that's why you're my tribe."

Mia beamed. "You're totally stuck with me for the rest of our lives. Let's brave the rain and see if the crazier ones in our tribe are here."

We grabbed our purses and made a beeline for the bar. I glanced around the packed pub, hoping we'd find an open table. Aside from the entrance, there was hardly enough room to walk, but that was to be expected on a Friday night.

Neon green, blue, and purple lights circled above us, giving the bar a club vibe that made me feel right at home. Whenever I needed a break from life, I could always count on shaking my ass to the latest tunes on the radio. Framed pictures of monumental moments in Chicago's sports history covered the walls, along with other photographs and paintings from local artists.

Groups of people surrounded all the pool tables lining our left side. Almost all the high round tabletops in the middle and off to the right were full. I saw Shane at the back of the bar, motioning for us to join him and Jackson.

Mia and I waved at a few familiar faces lined up at the bar as we made our way over to the boys. With the long wait to get drinks, part of me considered stopping to grab our first round, but Shane held up full beers.

Seeing his teddy bear face and crooked smile chased away the lingering coldness in my limbs. Since high school, his burly physique had gotten more defined. More than a few girls licked their lips while undressing him with their eyes. He would never be more than a brother to me, but I saw why girls fawned over him.

Jackson slid over two bottles of Miller Lite. "It's about time you ladies got here. Now that the two hottest girls in the bar are at my table, my night won't be a total loss."

I tugged off my black leather jacket and placed it on the back of my chair before setting my purse on the table. Mia kept on her white fleece, slung her purse on the side of her seat, picked up her beer, and downed half of it. I arched an eyebrow at her, taking a smaller swig out of mine.

Mia focused on Jackson. "I'm sure plenty of hot girls will be throwing themselves at you soon enough. Bri and I are more of a cockblock than anything."

Jackson gave her a flirtatious bat of the eye, and I couldn't help but roll mine. How Mia was oblivious to his clear attraction to her really made me wonder, but I'd promised I would go easy on him, so I bit my tongue. Jackson ran a hand through his spiked, jet black hair as his dark blue eyes flickered between the two of us and then around the bar.

"The girls in this place are definitely hot, but they don't hold a candle to you ladies," Jackson professed, turning up the charm.

I snorted. "You're laying it on pretty thick. Flattery isn't going to get you anywhere. Judging by the hopeful look in your eyes, you have a favor to ask, so you might as well just spit it out because shit's starting to get really deep."

Shane burst out laughing before saying, "I told you not to bother with buttering them up. I knew Bri would see right through you. I love being right."

Jackson smacked his shoulder. Shane trailed his fingers under his chiseled chin before he released the top button of his navy blue dress shirt and cracked his knuckles. Jackson's hands shot up, clearly retreating, before he ran them down his red polo. Shane would never punch him, but he couldn't resist putting him in his place. Jackson was certainly built in his own right, but was definitely smaller than Shane. His tattoo sleeves of various gothic and tribal symbols definitely made a person think twice about taking a swing at him, but they didn't faze Shane.

After Mia finished off the last of her beer, she gazed around for a waitress. I doubted they'd get to us anytime soon, so I hopped up. "I'll go grab us another round. Try not to take this one down as fast as the last one."

Shane slid off his chair. "I'll come with you. We can grab some pitchers."

We made our way through the growing crowd and over to the long line of people waiting for drinks. Loud cheers erupted up front, and I turned to see several good-looking guys exchanging high fives and tossing pool sticks on the table before collecting cash from their opponents. "Your Love is My Drug" burst from the speakers throughout the bar, and a few girls started bumping and grinding with the guys next to them.

"Scoping out the competition is never a bad thing, but don't be so obvious about it," Shane murmured while running his fingers through his trimmed brown hair.

"Actually, I was seeing if there was anyone worth dancing with." I scanned around the establishment again. When my body remained dormant, I released a disgruntled sigh.

Shane's deep brown eyes centered on me. "Trey messed up another date of yours, didn't he?"

I chewed on my lower lip, not wanting to admit the truth. His clear disapproval was all over his face as he crossed his arms and grumbled, "I try my best to stay out of your business when it comes to him, but I can't tolerate it any longer. I'm going to tell him to leave you alone."

"I appreciate your concern, but that's really not necessary," I rebutted.

"Bri, it's been almost four years. You may talk on occasion and screw each other when you think no one is paying attention, but it's not right. That's not a relationship."

Forcing a smile, I said, "A relationship in this day and age can be defined in a variety of ways. Not all of them are cut and dry. Ours is simply on the unique side."

"Cut the crap. You're both playing the field but won't let each other go. That's not fair to the people you go on dates with or yourselves," Shane argued, his forehead creasing.

"I know. The next time I see him, I'm going to tell him things have to change or we're done. So, please, just stay out of it. I can handle this on my own," I mumbled, my gaze dropping to the floor as defeat consumed me.

Shane tilted my chin up, his eyes sympathetic. "I know you can. I just wanted to reiterate I can't sit on the sidelines any longer. If you're giving him an ultimatum, he'll either accept it or walk away. And if he doesn't, I'll make him."

Our line inched forward, and we moved with it. Needing a change of subject, I extended a thumb toward our table and asked, "What's Jackson up to? He rarely flatters me. I know full well he's only doing it because of Mia, but I can tell he wants something out of us."

Shane traced his fingers along his trimmed goatee as his mouth curled into a wily grin. I glared at him for an answer, and his smile widened. People in front of us shuffled away with their drinks, and Shane rested his hands on the bar as I leaned against it.

A frazzled bartender with long blonde hair approached us and yelled, "What can I get you?"

Shane flashed his dimples. "We'll take four pitchers of Miller Lite and some glasses."

After trailing a finger down the low V of her black T-shirt, a shrewd grin crept upon her face. "Coming right up, gorgeous."

"It looks like you're getting laid tonight. That's really going to ruffle Jackson's feathers," I remarked, tickled.

"I'm sure he'll end up going home with someone. I don't think he's ever spent a Friday or Saturday night alone. Lucky bastard," Shane muttered, annoyed.

"Are you sure about that?" I pointed at Jackson. His eyes were on Mia's ass as they slid our table over to an open pool table.

Shane shook his head. "I keep warning him to tone it down when it comes to her, but he doesn't seem to get it. He claims it's all in good fun and she'll never be more than a friend, but when I see him doing shit like that, it's hard to believe."

I crossed my arms. "He better start listening fast. Micah's going to beat his ass if he doesn't."

Blondie returned with our order, along with her number, not appearing anywhere near as wiped as she had when we stepped up to the bar. Shane stuffed the piece of paper into his pocket, placed two twenties on the bar, and waved away the change. Picking up two of the pitchers, he handed them to me before grabbing the rest.

Shane winked at the bartender. "You'll *definitely* be hearing from me."

As we turned to head back to our table, I spotted Kylie with one of the guys on Eckman's football team. Since it was rare for her to go anywhere without Peyton, I looked around for her. Shane bumped my shoulder, raising his eyebrow for an explanation.

I nodded toward the front. Shane found Kylie sucking face with her football hottie a step away from openly groping her and groaned inwardly. I stepped in front of him and weaved my way through the people dancing in the middle of the bar.

Before we reached Mia and Jackson, I paused. "Looks like the girls are doing the solo thing for now. When Kylie comes up for air, I'll go say hi and see if we should be on the lookout for Peyton. It's best to stay ahead of that situation or things will get ugly."

Shane grimaced. "I can't argue with you there. Let's just hope it's a drama-free evening. They seem to be a rarity these days."

We made it the final few feet back to the other two. After setting the pitchers on the table, I polished off my beer and poured a glass for Mia and myself. Shane filled up the other two, handed one over to Jackson, and sauntered over to the rack holding the pool sticks.

Out of nowhere, my stomach knotted, and I instantly surveyed my surroundings. The hairs on the back of my neck stood on end. Someone who looked like one of my dad's old security guards stood at the corner of the bar, watching my every move. Goosebumps coasted along my arms. The large, muscular frame and all black attire wasn't comforting in the least. They had always dressed down like that when tasked with following me around. And after what I put some of his security detail through my senior year, I *never* wanted to run into them again.

Blinking my eyes to get them to focus, I took a better look. The guy removed his black jacket and flipped his ball cap around before fist-bumping his friend. Clearly, it wasn't any of my dad's old security guards, but that didn't do much for my anxiety.

My body was practically screaming at me with all the warning signs that someone was lingering in the shadows, but it would take more than a few text messages and emails from random numbers to break me. Until I actually spotted someone watching me, I refused to believe it was nothing more than Spencer's childish game.